*Landscape: Memory*

# Landscape: Memory

## MATTHEW STADLER

Charles Scribner's Sons

New York

Collier Macmillan Canada

Toronto

Maxwell Macmillan International

New York, Oxford, Singapore, Sydney

"Safety" on page 63 from *Collected Poems of Rupert Brooke,*
Dodd, Mead and Co., 1915.

Translation of Aristotle's *De Memoria et Reminiscentia* by W. S. Hett on page
140 taken from the Loeb Edition.

Translation of Cicero's *Ad Herennium* by H. Caplan on pages 155–56 taken
from the Loeb Edition.

"Evolution" by Langdon Smith on pages 215–19 from *Evolution: A Poem,*
W. A. Wilde Co., 1911.

"The Sleepers" by Walt Whitman on pages 281–82 from *Leaves of Grass,*
David MacKay Publishing, 1900.

"Wynken, Blynken and Nod" by Eugene Field on pages 293–97 from
*The Children's Songbook.*

Charles Scribner's Sons
Macmillan Publishing Company
866 Third Avenue, New York, NY 10022

Collier Macmillan Canada, Inc.
1200 Eglinton Avenue East, Suite 200
Don Mills, Ontario M3C 3N1

This is a work of fiction. Names, characters, places, and incidents either
are the product of the author's imagination or are used fictitiously. Any
resemblance to actual events or persons, living or dead, is entirely
coincidental.

Library of Congress Cataloging-in-Publication Data
Stadler, Matthew.
    Landscape: memory/Matthew Stadler.
      p.   cm.
    ISBN 0-684-19185-7
    I. Title.
    PS3569.T149L35   1990
    813'.54—dc20      90-30144      CIP

Design by Ellen R. Sasahara

10  9  8  7  6  5  4  3  2  1

PRINTED IN THE UNITED STATES OF AMERICA

For  Patrick  Merla

# Contents

My heartfelt thanks to Frank and Rella Lossy and Bob and Sarah Pickus, for their generosity; Zoey (a.k.a. Fluffy) the dog; Sean Casey, MSW; Maureen Howard, for her support in both words and deeds; Gloria Loomis, for being so smart about so many things; and Robert Stewart, for his insightful reading and surgical editing.

*Landscape: Memory*

# A Memory Book

---

First imagine Lincoln Beachey, his smart leather cowl pulled on tight and warm, his thin little shell of an aeroplane rattling with noise and fury, climbing up into the bracing blue sky, just lifting off from the very ground.

The wind is salty and cold in his nostrils, ripping in off the gray-green sea. It drags up the face of Mount Tam carrying sea birds who glide on its lift and pull, and birdmen, like Beachey, daring enough to take the free ride up on treacherous winds. This whole place is spread out wide below him. The yellow-blue waters of the bay, lying flat up to the lip of the land, the hills rising green, then brown and burned golden across the high ridges rolling on east and forever.

Imagine him south now. He's come over the city, over the open green fields and thick woods of the Presidio, cannons blasting to mark the hour, down over Sunset and the dunes, south to the open hills running wild by the coast, thick fog pressing in on their western face. It's rolling over the ridges and

*1*

down into valleys, lying low and silent on the lakes. Imagine so high up over those hills.

Now look down below, along the rolling ridges. There's a man down there, a druggist from San Jose, wandering with no direction, nearly naked, and confused. He doesn't know who he is or was, having woken one night to a sound out there. The news report in *The Call* said he simply stirred and rose from bed, walking to the front steps to listen. His wife, who's been placed under a doctor's care, could not rouse him from the spell. He took his axe and stumbled out into the dead dark night.

That was days ago. He's scruff up to the ground now, sitting in the rough dry dirt, his pink fleshy face all cut and torn from stumbling. Not a moment past is present to his mind, all of it finally slipping away into nothing. *A shadow from high above passes over him.* Imagine when night falls. What is there, inside his mind, then?

Only a man in an aeroplane could find him, or would know, the rest of us too close to the ground to see so far and clearly.

I'll be both of them sometimes, to get a different view, and because I feel that way, like a man in an aeroplane or like I'm wandering the woods in a nightshirt with no memory. Some things happen there's no accounting for.

This is a book about memory.

A memory book is Mother's idea. It's for my sixteenth birthday. I'm to keep my memories in it.

"The mind is a template, pumpkin," she said to me, "a template made of gold—brilliant and malleable. The written word is fixed."

I see in *The Call* a man took a bullet in his nostril and was uninjured. It lodged there without so much as leaving a mark. Also, Mount Lassen volcano is blowing up for the first time in a hundred years, trailing tongues of lava and flames and boulders flung high into the sky, still red-hot and hissing horribly, turning lakes into steam in an instant. I certainly wouldn't want to forget that.

Father left another note, this tucked into the little rubber mouth of my hot water bottle. "Beware the Scouring Rush, cognomen 'Horse Tail.' Habitat: tender, moist ground around springs, creeks and ponds. Young Hickok was fed horsetail by the Yana, Ishi has claimed. The great chiefs said it was their finest delicacy and the boy ate of it prodigiously. He died beet-red, covered with bursting sores and his tongue bigger than a football, wagging about in frenzied spasms." Father knows I've been poking about down by the Fair.

What's got eighteen legs, no arms and is afraid of Tigers? The San Francisco Seals. Duncan made that one up.

## 9 AUGUST 1914

My most vivid memory is a moment at dusk in Bolinas four years ago with Duncan. It has several parts.

We took the ferry from the foot of Market and hitched rides across Marin, finally getting one long ride from San Rafael all the way to the foot of Bourne's Gulch on the east side of the lagoon. There we stood, the water stretching out west, shimmering in the noon sun, with Bolinas on the other shore. It was August and hot like it sometimes gets. I was dark as Duncan then (he's Persian, Duncan Peivand Taqdir, and brown like an Indian) because we'd spent so much time that summer tramping in the hills and birding with my father. The sun was on us and I could feel my stomach go giddy when a breeze would blow in off the water and across my bare skin.

Our project was to find a lost ruin from the quake, an asylum my father said was destroyed when the fault ripped through Bolinas on its way to San Francisco. It may not have been true (I've never known my father to make a clear distinction between fact and fancy) but this particular story appealed to me and Duncan, and we decided to go in overnight. Neither of us knew where it was exactly, so I made something up.

"It's on a promontory," I announced, "surrounded by oak trees."

I pulled some clover from the grassy meadow and chewed its stem, kneeling down now and looking up into the hills, looking for a direction. Doubts were creeping around but I paid them no mind. Duncan knelt down next to me and tugged at the wet grass. I knew the fault line tore right down the face of this canyon, ripping the black earth open and tossing trees in all directions. We could be torn in two. I felt that, and I felt the cool breeze blowing through me like I was empty, weightless and wide-open. This moment stretched on for what seemed like an eternity.

My father had said he'd been here after the quake. He never said why he'd ended up here or what exactly he'd done, but this is where he'd said he'd gone. To help in the relief effort.

"I was away at Bolinas, little fish. The Asylum. Help was needed." And once he said, "It was eight days before those that would return returned. Eight days of cleaning and clearing." That's all.

In my mind he has led a team of men up into the hills, bringing pickaxes and gauze bandages. He's pulled sobbing women and dead bodies from the rubble, silently separating them into bunches, ministering to the infirm, giving them soup, and pointing their attention to sea birds in the lagoon far below. He has buried the dead and is tilling them under in furrows for planting corn. He's brought birds to nest in the trees and built windmills. In eight days he has sewn white gowns and bandaged all wounds, settling his own silence over all to whom he ministers. In eight days the first harvest has come and the slow rhythm of the seasons has been set in motion, and he comes home.

Up through the ravine it was cool silence, our feet tamping the soft ground, the light filtered green through the upper branches and dark as in a cathedral. We followed a simple plan, always heading uphill so eventually we'd emerge into the open sun of the grasslands. I made straight and steady progress, my satchel slung up on one shoulder, feeling the even stretch of my strides. Duncan was scampering, going for cover behind the wide trunks and jumping high to see how far up he'd touch.

The building had taken shape in my mind. A simple two-story with thick stone walls, the main hall stretching north and south along the high ridge above the trees. One wing lay scattered in ruins running west down the face of the hill. Duncan was beside me now, having appeared from the shelter of a wide, empty stump, a circle of lush growth rising from the rot of some fallen giant. He'd taken off his shirt and wrapped it round his head like a burnoose. I did the same.

We came out of the woods and up over the first small ridge. The sun had swung to late afternoon, making the western slope of the hills warm and golden. The long yellow grass brushed against my calves and tickled me behind the knees as I came to the top of the ridge and headed down into the cool shadow of a gulch littered with tumbled-down rocks and pungent scrub. Scotch broom, coyote brush, Indian warrior. On the steep down-hill I held my pace steady, not scampering or stumbling, just feeling the blood fill the muscles around my knees and up the fronts of my thighs. Duncan was down low in the gulch poking and pulling at the scree. He had a small noose of string which he kept dipping into the rocks and then jerking back out again.

"Get oats," he shouted to me, still staring intently at the scree. "A handful," and he dipped his noose down.

I milked the long brown grass, both hands pulling blindly at bunches, while I moved forward toward Duncan carrying, now, small handfuls of flaxen grain.

From in amongst the rocks I could hear skittering and small squeaks. Duncan's shoe was jammed tight into one small exit and his big brown head hovered over the other. Inside was a fist-sized squirrel with a gray bushy tail pushing his black nose across each crack and crevice of the small room, dodging Duncan's noose indifferently.

"Squirrel," Duncan said without looking up. I imagined those cool stone walls around me, one shaft of light streaming in from above, then gone dark as an enormous head hovered close. Duncan dropped some grain into the hole and lay his noose low. I listened anxiously, leaning over Duncan's back, straining for a glimpse into the dark chamber.

"I think he's screaming," I said, a little sad at Duncan's conquest. He jerked up on the noose and the line pulled taut.

Jumping up quickly, the line held tight in his teeth, Duncan kicked his shoes away and pulled off his knickers to make a safe nest for the unfortunate animal. He stood barefoot and steady on the stones, his shoes ten feet away in scrub, and he tied off the bottoms of his pants before dropping the scampering squirrel down one warm leg. He tossed in a handful of oats and held the nest closed at the belt, looking up at me with his idiot grin. He was the desert warrior standing there in his pink-patterned boxers, the bright white burnoose trailing back off his head, an animal trapped on safari wriggling in his sack.

"What's he saying now?" I asked. I wanted to run up the next hill into the warm sun and see the ocean stretched out blue below us.

"Might be scared," Duncan allowed. He peered in, reaching down into the pant leg to feel the warm animal. "A free lunch is what he's got. And a safe little nest." I leaned close and looked in at the squirrel.

He was a muscular fur-ball, speckled gray and bristling from nose to tail. Damp nose, quivering tail. His eyes were black pools, bulging wet black pools, like licorice candies someone had licked. I pushed my face into the trousers and felt his whiskers brush across my cheek.

"Animal," I growled wickedly in the knickers. We both sniffed, our noses twitching. I heard his brief snort of breath and watched him close his eyes, settling calmly down into his dark nest, divinely sedated by the warmth and musty oats.

And then I licked him, secretly, and felt a bristling down my back.

The squirrel opened his eyes and sniffed again, but showed no instinct for retaliation. Duncan's head peered in next to mine. He looked in my eyes and I knew I had to tell.

"I licked him," I admitted, bashful but eager. We pushed our heads down into the dark nest.

"You licked him?" Duncan asked, fascinated and horrified, as though I'd offered him a delicious berry covered with hideous black insects. I inhaled the musty wool-and-oats smell of the knickers deep into my lungs and stared intently into the bulging black eyes. My head filled with blood and I was weak with hunger, my mouth madly watering and open. I wanted him. The very thought made me dizzy. I shook my body like a dog and growled to scare the thought away. Duncan had his tongue stuck out, timid and giddy, tense like a boy waiting for the water hose to come gushing to life against him on a hot summer day. The squirrel poked about contentedly at the bottom of his nest.

"On his fur," I prodded. "Come on then, lick him." Duncan stretched his neck but without the reckless abandon necessary to reach the patient squirrel.

"He's so far down there," he protested weakly. I wrapped my arm around him and smooshed him on the belly to give him courage. I made friendly noises and pushed my head close by way of example. Duncan was laughing now. We wavered a bit from side to side, our feet still pushing on the cool stones. Only a dim musty light leaked into our woolen nest. Only a dim light from that whole warm August afternoon, the sun dragging across the yellow-brown tops of those long hills. I could feel the wide sky stretching out above our backs. Light glistened on the squirrel's eyes. I imagined we'd find a dusty straw bed in the shelter of the old ruins that evening and pass the night curled in amongst the tumbled-down stones, protected from the wind.

Now came the magical part.

We found a ruin to the south and back down into the thick woods of Weeks Gulch. Small and overgrown, barely one square room of tumbled-down stones, but a ruin nonetheless. It stood on a small rise up the north side of the gulch, peeling madronas bent high over the rough, crumbling walls. The view west opened up through the tops of redwoods growing from deep in the ravine. The hot sun had burned down all day on their broad green branches so the air was sweet and dry. The lagoon stretched out flat for miles, its lip lying on a muddy strip of land down beyond the mouth of the gully.

I've made a map on which I've marked this spot "Asylum." Duncan says my father never went there but he's wrong. This was the same place of which he spoke. Lying quiet in those woods, our backs on the dusty ground, we stared up into the trees and the still blue sky listening to birds. Grosbeak, egrets, herons.

"My dad says they came on foot," I said to Duncan. "The roads were blocked and the trains weren't running."

"Uh-huh," Duncan said back, careful not to tread on my imagining.

"He didn't say much, but the buildings looked out on the ocean. It was in these woods."

"Why didn't he say much?" Duncan asked. The question was so simple and impossible. I really had no answer.

"He's just quiet," I tried. "You know that. He's just quiet about most things." Duncan rolled onto his side and looked at me. He just lay there watching.

"You could hear them from Bolinas," I continued. "Screaming and such from in the rubble. You could hear them, and when the men coming to help yelled back they went completely silent. Just absolutely still and quiet, like now. Not a sound."

The wind moved above us, us listening to the stillness.

In that last hour before nightfall we gathered wood and set up our small camp in the shelter of the ruins. We laid our blanket out and secured our little pet, its string leash tied to a thimble berry bush. (By morning he was gone.) We took stock of the few provisions I'd brought and sketched a crude map of our travels. Before night came we went down to the lagoon and swam. We splashed and screamed loudly, did dolphin dives and wrestled each other under for dunkings. We swam hard and fast out to an imagined marker and back again, Duncan being the fastest. We floated, slow and silent, to ambush birds who flew, and when they flew we burst from the water as if we could chase them through the air.

We did all that, of course, as *anyone* could have done. That is, it doesn't matter that we swam there and then. What I'm remembering isn't exactly that. It's a moment that concerns me, a picture around which my memory gathers.

Standing still in the cold salt water, our feet in mud, the thin surface of the bay slipping away flat and wide, cutting across us just below our bellies. Standing still and the air on our bodies, moving in the trees and soft through the hills. There was a moment in the evening sky then. I can feel precisely the position of my eyes, my head held still, looking west across the water and up into the last light of the sky going dark over the far horizon. Duncan stands still and silent close by me.

The wild, marauding birds have all taken flight, a line of dark simple shapes slipping farther and farther into the empty sky. Only the loons remain with us, still and perfect, floating in the absolute calm. Their small bodies bob in the strange dusk. They slip across the water. And their long, lowing song fills me, as full and enveloping as the sweet, cool evening.

That is my most vivid memory.


## 11 AUGUST 1914

All of Europe is at war. They've got pictures in *The Call* and maps with *x*'s and *o*'s. Father's brother Maury lives in Britain and he'll soon be fighting. Perhaps we should send in the Seals. This season already looks to be a bust. Two more months before the slaughter ends.

A ball club is being formed in Oakland for men with one or more artificial limbs. They've got an ex–minor leaguer and a bunch of big hitters with A. F. Ruff at the helm. I have a great interest in baseball and adversity.

Duncan doesn't share my enthusiasm. He is simply a *baseball* fan, without so much complexity as me. Mother says my fascination with oddities is a natural by-product of the sophisticated education they've planned for me. "Many athletes are tremendously susceptible to the effects of drink. So it is with the mind, pumpkin," she's told me. "The highly trained mind will naturally find intoxication in the strangeness of everyday life."

But I don't see it. It all seems so very separate. What has Ruskin to do with limbless ball players? Or Pliny with exploding aeroplanes? I'm happy with my studies, as Mother's planned them, but our little sessions are not nearly lurid nor seedy enough to match my everyday fascinations. Natural history, which Father teaches me, is far more titillating than the various cultural subjects (this year they include painting, art history and drama) for which Mother is in charge. The egret, I learned only yesterday, must vomit copiously into the nest as a means of feeding its young. And that is typical. I remain entirely thrilled by my subjects with Mother. Painting and drama, especially, are among my favorite things. But they occupy a world entirely separate from limbless ball players and vomiting egrets.

12 AUGUST 1914

This from *The Call:*

> Zelta Davis, seven months old, playing on the porch of her home, 428 Harrison Street, Oakland, today, nearly fell over the edge. Her mother, Mrs. Mary Davis, grabbed her and clutched so hard she paralyzed the child's left side. A cure may be possible.

I'm looking west down Pacific at fog lying low on the Presidio woods. Mother thinks I'm reading Ruskin, but it's *The Call* I'm more interested in. I save Ruskin for those cozy moments curled up by the fire, Mother and Father sitting close by to answer questions and tell me what words mean what, and how it is there's a Truth of Clouds and a Truth of the Sky and a Truth of Water. *The Call* is my private pleasure.

Father left this poem in my boot:
"Advice from the Elder," he'd entitled it.

> *As a cure for diseases of millet*
> *I must recommend, take a toad,*
>
> *Carried round the wide field on a fig leaf*
> *in the dusk of the night 'fore it's hoed.*
>
> *One buries the frog in the middle,*
> *with a pot for a coffin, and prayer,*
>
> *Thus preventing the damage of sparrows*
> *and worms in the black midnight there.*

> *Now dig up the damn frog with a hatchet,*
> *before the far fields are sown!*
>
> *Lest armies of insects, like Caesar,*
> *turn foul and enter your home.*

The poem, I suspect, is more for him than me, though it may pertain to my summer garden, which contains no millet, or frogs as of yet.


## 28 AUGUST 1914

Today I messed around with Duncan, mucking about the woods out west of the golf course and returning home around four o'clock for drawing. Mother and I've been working our way through *The Elements of Perspective* and will soon be on to Williams's *The Art of Landscape Painting*. Mother said I should choose a project to give focus to my studies and I've chosen to paint what I saw in Bolinas, that moment. The memory is still clear, it being just four years ago, and I want to capture it in a painting. I'm still no good at drawing but the Ruskin book is very specific and soon I'll be able to make the proper shapes. Right now my clouds are blobs and my land looks like fat serpents. I won't start with the paints until I get the shapes right.

Mother can't draw either, but she is working along with me, step by step, attempting a panorama of the fairgrounds. I can't imagine all those details, pillars and domes and thin minarets, each part tiny and perfect. But she seems content, measuring minute ornaments and touching her pinpoint pencil to paper, erasing more, it seems, than she puts down. My picture, being at dusk (crepuscular, Mother says), is not so demanding.

Running home, past Locust and Laurel, up near the top of our hill, I could hear her confident singing waft out the open window, mixing in with the various booms and bangs of construction from the fairgrounds. I saw her through the window, her thick brown hair pinned up in a messy bun, her jaw and mouth extended. It's that frog face she makes to help "open her throat," as the book instructs. Her voice quivers too.

I signaled my arrival home with a healthy banging about in the vestibule. She had the drawing kits out, flat wooden boxes with small metal hinges and button snaps to clasp them shut. Mine has charcoal smudges not just because I'm messy but also because I use soft charcoals. She's still sketching lines and will be forever. I'm trying to draw the very air so pinpoint lines won't do.

"You," she said, all motherly, turning away from the window. "You are a mess." I was. I was smudged and muddy and standing on our best carpet in the big front parlor. Mother stood shaking her head in silence. We both sighed, I with impatience.

"Up to your room with you now. We're late as it is."

"Won't we be drawing outside today?" I asked. It seemed silly to clean up for the outdoors.

"We'll be in the park. People do not enjoy filthy children in public parks."

"But *I* enjoy filth." This raised an eyebrow.

"You'll reserve that pleasure for more private settings. Don't be a pest."

"Father goes to the park looking like a dirty dog if he wants. No one pays him any mind." It was true. My father cares less about collars and clean shirts than even me.

"You're not your father, dumpling." She had her hand up to her temple. "Please don't make me tense." I knew it was time to be nice. I smiled and tried to look willing. "You may wear something colorful and light. No need to be fancy," she assured me.

"Will we picnic?"

"Of course, pumpkin. We'll feast."

———

I carried the feast: roast beef and French breads, peaches, soft cheese and cress (for minerals). A Nehi, of course, and sparkling water for Mother. With the sun disappearing and a low fog floating in, we forsook the park and took the steep steps down to Cow Hollow. I was bundled in my best white sweater, woolen socks pulled up to my knickers, the wicker basket held snug to my chest. Mother preceded me, the hem of her gingham dress sweeping the stone steps as she rushed along. The drawing kits and blanket were tucked up under her arm. I was hungry and that made even the air delicious, its salty moistness rolling in around us.

Cow Hollow marks the "Station Point" of Mother's panorama, the point from which the picture is seen. It's Lesson One in Ruskin: "Sight Point, Sight Line, Station Point, and Station Line." It's no surprise we end up there every third session or so, as her drawing relies on the visual and mine requires only memory. I'll draw anywhere. Her model can be seen only at the Cow Hollow "studio." "We're off to the studio," she'll say, and off we'll go, down the steps, a few hundred yards to the small grassy field. The blanket laid, we set up under our favorite tree, kits on laps, pencils in hand and soon the afternoon is gone.

Good enough for me. I love the panorama, the closeness and noise of the construction, the bare trace of swamp-smell creeping from out of the landfill when the wind blows in off the bay.

We spread the blanket out on our spot and placed Ruskin within easy reach (though Mother never consults the text, and I only intermittently). Our primary focus is on the play of charcoal and paper, *and* on the food.

"Do try the cress with a smudge of cheese, dearest," Mother implored me, balancing her sketch in one hand while she pushed the cheese about the plate with a knife. I was quaffing my Nehi and so could not reply. The cress and cheese, truth be told, was an innovation of mine from our last lesson, two days earlier.

I looked to the sky thoughtfully and tried again to imagine the shapes of the formless, insubstantial clouds that washed across that twilight memory from Bolinas. Inevitably I thought of fingers reaching, but when put to paper they proved as wrong as any other reconstruction. Mother's pencil was tick-tacking briskly across her panorama, marking each point with confidence.

"Do you suppose I could leave it all in darkness?" I asked, seeking instruction. Mother looked up with a bit of beef dangling from her bright smile.

"Your project must suit your ambitions, dumpling," she began, obviously as a preface. "But I understand your ambitions to be a good sight more than rendering the mere darkness. Don't be daunted so early on." And she gazed at my uncertain sketch with compassion. The fog moved in silence nearby the fairgrounds, tumbling now from the treetops high on the Presidio's hills.

"I want my rendering to be true, though, Mummy. What if it was truly darkness?"

"Well, was it? You're the best judge of that." She was no help at all. I put my soft charcoal back to the paper's face and made intuitive motions with my wrist, hoping the truth would emerge from some less conscious, perhaps muscular source. It was just no good at all.

"Perhaps you should pay closer attention to Ruskin. I believe this volume is meant to address just such problems as you might be having." She pushed the heavy book past some bits of bread and up against my tired bum.

Ruskin went on from the basic perpendiculars into ever more complex geometric puzzles, outlining in detail a matrix of simple forms which, if properly executed, would, he promised, guide one to a true rendering. Mother, it seemed, was right. I put aside my dirty sheet and began with Problem One, "To Fix the Position of a Given Point."

Our afternoon turned quickly into a cold, foggy dusk and we packed the picnic and returned up the steep stairs to the house and a warm fire (once I'd hauled the wood) in the fireplace. I kept reading Ruskin most of the evening, out of sheer enthusiasm for finally finding a guide who, it was promised, would lead me to fulfill my fine ambition. Father descended from his study to cook a hearty peasant soup and our evening ended with a chapter of *Melmoth* read by the fireside, mostly by me in my most dramatic voices, and then sleep.

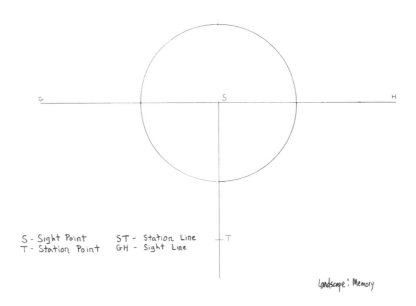

S - Sight Point        ST - Station Line
T - Station Point      GH - Sight Line

Landscape : Memory

A letter arrived today, to Father from his brother Maury. It said simply:

Dear Robert,
    I've joined up. Kitchener, and all that.
    Good God this boot stinks. Our captain's got us marching

six or eight hours each day. Rather nice countryside though, Sevenoaks or thereabouts. Could you possibly send me a piano? Oh, yes, the facts of the matter: Fifth Battalion, medical. I chop and sew. Two more weeks in Blighty, then to the front. I'm in for the duration, Christmas or thereabouts. I need (if not a piano) clean stockings. More American cigarettes, please (very valuable for trade). Jeffers, Tolland and Smithy here with me (and they smell worse than even I). Of birds here, many and cacophonous. I could not begin to name them.

Hymns sung to high heaven each evening at dusk. I'm taken by the wide green hills, though not so crazy in awe as those many east Londoners down with us. The likes of them haven't seen more than brick and coalbins since they came into this world. I'm reminded most of our boyhood summers near Cooperstown—waking with the noisy birds by dawn, the lush green trees waving in the slight winds, the world fresh and dew-covered. And oh, this regimen of marching and mock battles. I'm fit as a horse and dead asleep come every evening. A war at last. Thank God I came across the Atlantic to a civilized nation where they still fight wars. I pity you your neutrality and trust it will not last. More soon.

## 30 AUGUST 1914

Duncan and I slept with the windows wide open and woke to a pair of yellowthroats resting on the windowsill, which aside from being very storybook is rare enough that I got a tingle down my spine and tried quietly to sneak out and up the stairs to tell Father. But when we came back they were gone.

We used, it seems, to get many more and stranger birds around the house. Of course it might be like Christmas and birthdays in its just *seeming* to have been more glorious because I used to be little and when you're little everything else is so much *more* than you, so much bigger and grander and more mysterious. But Father tells me no, it isn't just that, there really *were* more and stranger birds then, and they've gone because the marshlands have gone.

Much of the flat stretching east from the Presidio was wetlands just three years ago, swamp and ponds and tidal marsh. Pickleweed, cordgrass. It smelled like a dying sea monster, like something from very deep and long ago slithering in amongst the muck. This was my father's favorite spot for birding, either up on the hill with his spyglasses or crawling about in the marsh. We built a low wooden shelter where we could stay and sometimes he'd be down there overnight to see or hear whatever was to be seen or heard.

The hut was a low lean-to facing east, covered with reeds and cordgrass for camouflage. It had a small cookstove near the open end. I saw it get buried under a river of mud from the dredging hose, in April two years ago, when they started filling in the wetlands to build the Fair. The dredging machine looked like an overgrown insect, with its metal-boxed body and that hideously long, belching hose jerking about as though with some strange life force. It buried our hut with one spastic blast and swung crazily away, spraying and spewing enough to bury the swamp in a matter of months.

Though that's forced the birds to nest in more distant parts of the bay, we have gotten, instead, something more and stranger than any exotic animal could ever hope to be. They're building the Jewel City on that foundation of muck pumped up from below the sea. The Panama Pacific International Exposition of 1915. P.P.I.E.! "The definitive event of our epoch," as the mayor has called it.

Already the central courts have the look of a unified city, planned in perfect symmetry and pleasing to the eye in all directions. Jules Guerin, the Color Master, has orchestrated the placement of each panel and ornament, the whole assemblage running the range from tawny earth tones to bright cerulean blue and bursts of orange, with every color chosen to accent the natural features of the bay and surrounding hills. Guerin, it is said, has even worked with the various tones of fog. Mother, who actually met this wizard, says Guerin has found his inspiration in the ancient cities of the Orient, with which he is familiar.

The grounds are open on Sundays now, despite the Fair's being still unfinished. Thousands come each weekend to see what there is to see and to measure the progress that's been made since the previous Sunday. Lincoln Beachey flies daredevil loops in his aeroplane above the bay. The throngs promenade down the broad avenues and amongst the beautiful gardens of the central courts. We saw Beachey's historic indoor aeroplane ride, the first and longest in history, from one end of the Palace of Machinery to the other. Duncan's dad got us in to see it, as he is an artisan in the Sculpture Factory.

Father hates the Fair.

1 SEPTEMBER 1914

Today the sky is clouds, pale and bruised on the underside, dropping low into the trees, wrapping round the headlands but not yet in on the bay. The salt air is in my nose and mouth, filling me in deep breaths. I fear the Seals are a lost cause, having dropped another series to Venice. Schaller is the only Seal not in a swoon and the pitching has never been capable of hindering even a flea. I've told Duncan that I won't go again until they put together at least a week at .500.

"Fat chance you won't," he says.

"If I do I'll stay mum in the stands. And no autographs or watching warm-ups." Really I intend to bring my Ruskin and do work while the hapless home-nine flails on field.

Mother will be Winged Victory, standing fifty-seven feet high where the Avenue of Progress bumps up against the Esplanade. Duncan's father will render her in false marble. He's invited us down to watch.

## 2 SEPTEMBER 1914

Duncan's mother is in Persia, leading an expedition to uncover the secrets of the Borj Rock tombs near Mehyd Salih in the Arabian desert. She's English and an archaeologist. She won't come over till next year, Duncan says. A letter arrived today, only seven months after it was sent.

"Having, as yet, little facility with the local tongue," she wrote, "I obliged myself to a Bedwin family for passage out of the low reaches and along Doughty's route to the rocks. In the stagnant mid-winter air only loathsome insects and the soft murmurings of Zeyd, my guide, and one of his wives were to be heard. Our desert peace was, most unfortunately, soon interrupted by gunfire ringing from the hills above us."

That's what Duncan showed me, to impress me with the danger of her adventure.

Duncan says he'd like to go out into the dry golden hills stretching east from the bay, just with me and a donkey and a small pack of provisions. We'd find mysteries greater even than the Borj Rock tombs or Bolinas, he says. Ancient places, older than the bristly-cone pines, hidden caves masked by volcanic steam and canyons dropping deep into the earth, peopled by mummies and exotic, sure-footed animals. We'd leave it all be and I'd sketch each detail in my drawing kit. We'd remember the stories the people tell and befriend all the animals, coming back with our little treasure, and never ever saying where.

At dinner Duncan's father came by unannounced. His English is odd and his bushy mustache kept getting filled with gobs of green caper gravy and little bits of lamb. Father asked about the various Middle Eastern plagues and Mr. Taqdir ignored him, chatting instead about his plans for Mother. Tomorrow Duncan and I go to watch them work.

Dear Robert,

Four a.m. and the trains are standing empty and impatient. We've been up and ready since three, no food in our bellies, but plenty of nerves and coffee to keep us jumping. Scores of rail cars have pulled in empty, hitching up in long trains, seven or eight abreast in the yards. We'll be loading up within the hour.

The sky is full and black above us. Tolland, Jake and Smithy and I've got a small fire in an old rubbish tin and there's plenty more with us crowding in close and singing. We'll sing our way east to Dover soon.

I should be at the fighting before the next dawn.

## 3 SEPTEMBER 1914

This drizzly gray morning we accompanied mother to her first day of work at the Fair. She will be modeling, first as Winged Victory, and later in a variety of more minor roles. What a strange and wondrous sight the grizzly workings of the Fair offered. It was like crawling inside some enormous mechanical body and seeing the bare iron wheels that grind secretly inside. It was like attending class in a doctor's surgical theater, watching him lift the unstrung muscle from off the armbone, the skin having been slit neatly from elbow to wrist and turned back like a bedsheet.

From a distance, you see (and *always* in the finished sections), the Fair gives the appearance of an ancient and glorious city, long-standing and whole. The heavy marble walls, the dense ornamentation, could only be the product of the centuries, marching ever forward, leaving their traces in accretions on the simple structures of the festival city. The fog-shrouded panorama, seen from the hill's crest on Fillmore, is breathtaking and utterly convincing. Mother compares it to the fabled cities of Khartoum and Damascus, which I have seen only on maps in the atlas.

But this dreary morning we crept closer, riding the trolley down Fillmore to the main gate, and passing through onto the unfinished grounds. It was all soft dirt and mud. The grounds were crisscrossed by a chaotic network of railway tracks bearing pump cars loaded down with wood and stone and steel. Men labored at the two-ended pumps, propelling their heavy cargo slowly along the makeshift rails and out into the low-lying fog. Rattling and bangs and the shouting of the workmen echoed from out of the fractured ruins.

It somehow seemed a grotesque reminder of the quake, this disassembled scene, a strange ghost hovering there amongst us. Everything was all split up into pieces.

Teams of men and mules tugged at the various parts, hoisting them on high pulleys to dangerous positions, spilling barrels of travertine plaster into wide, flat molds, fastening this to that and that to another. The low gray sky drifted in amongst the rising skeleton frames and scattered rubble. The steady calls of the workmen continued, muffled in the clouds. Before us, the muddy breadth of the Avenue of Progress opened up onto the bay. Its entire length lay cluttered with stacks of lumber and various carts and cars burdened with barrels and bricks and building parts—finials, capitals, pilasters and balustrades.

At the very heart of this busy scene, the source and center of all this earnest labor, was the Sculpture Factory. Filling fully three long warehouses, its interior ablaze with electrical lights, the Sculpture Factory was Mr. Taqdir's workplace and the focus of our morning's visit. It fed the furious construction of the Fair with an endless river of finished sculpture rolling out of its northern end. Twin tracks carried car after car of plaster casts: gods and horses, natives, nymphs, and winged women carrying torches, all enlarged to grotesque extremes. More sculpture than has ever been produced in any one place ever, or so *The Call* had said. We picked our way across the muddy boulevard and followed the railway tracks into the main building.

Mr. Taqdir was waiting. He kissed Mother's hand, and then he and Duncan kissed, which they do every time they see each other and Duncan says they always do it no matter how old you are, even if it's just family friends and not your father. As if to confirm it, Mr. Taqdir kissed me too. He smushed his thick bristly mustache into my face, talking between kisses, grabbing me with both hands and tousling my hair. He's a very big man.

The room stretched out forever, filled with strange fragments of bodies blown up to enormous proportions, some apparently made of marble, others covered with a porcupine layer of metal spikes, as if they'd broken out in some horrible iron rash. Dozens of horses with holes where their backs should be, each standing three-score hands high, leaned in long domino rows, stacked up and ready for placement. Mr. Taqdir even looked small here, stamping confidently through the littered remains, pointing and explaining the various stations in the warehouse, the destinations of the finished parts, and the competence or incompetence of his fellow sculptors.

"You see the smoothness," he said, and he took my mother's hand, passing it over an elephant's leg. "Soon it is gone on top of the Eastern World. The central courts?" He smiled with all his face as if that warm radiance could carry his complete meaning. He stood facing Mother now, apparently inspecting her for artistic detail, his glance passing from feature to feature of her fine face.

"You will be a beautiful giant soon. Smooth as the elephant," he said, by way of flattery.

Mother looked at him benignly. She had placed her foot on a tangled wad of gummy paper and was busily pawing at the ground, trying to rid herself of the garbage.

"Fascinating, Mr. Taqdir," she said breathily, drawing her datebook out from her mammoth handbag. "I'm in awe. We must, however, set a schedule." Mother put her pen to paper, awaiting word from her new employer. But he just smiled.

"The working begins now," he told her. "We will discuss timetables when it's time. Never hurry to go, I will be saying. One thing and then the next."

Mother pushed the datebook back deep into the folds of her ruglike purse, giving Mr. Taqdir a brisk smile.

Men in dirtied white coveralls worked in bunches around one or another mammoth construction, teams of seven or eight at each station, translating life-size clay models into giant sculpture by means of a three-dimensional pantograph. There must have been a dozen such machines all told, swinging this way and that, setting the surface dimensions of each piece, all working in the vast airy expanse of the open warehouse, white walls and plaster dust all around.

The pantograph has a stiff iron finger maybe three feet long extending out from a mechanical frame. By moving this finger over the surface of the model and touching it down at each important point of relief, the sculptor causes a corresponding part to define the same surface in immensely exaggerated proportions.

(Mother helped me with this part.)

At that other end, several men record these positions by pushing nails into a monstrous tangle of wood and steel pipes, railroad ties and chicken mesh, which has been welded, pushed and pounded into roughly the right shape prior to this finishing work. The whole thing is then covered in travertine plaster, the surface barely concealing each nail head. That way it has the same shape as the model.

It takes days for each piece, weeks for a whole sculpture. When they get it all set, the same machine is used to check the finished piece for accuracy. Actually molding the original model is the least of it.

That first day Mr. Taqdir finished the work in clay and got his assistants started on the lumber-and-steel monster with the afternoon not half done. Before we left we could see the posture and frame of my mother emerging from the chaos of railroad ties and bent pipes, wadded masses of chicken mesh stuffed in amongst beams to fill out her figure, her spine and limbs defined by the crude lines of thick timber and scrap iron left over from the construction of the buildings. Soon it will be "smooth as the elephant," as Mr. Taqdir says, the twists and ties of metal tucked in and hidden beneath its thin plaster shell. And then it will be ready, rolled out along the railway and positioned atop its pillar facing the bay. Winged Victory.

6 SEPTEMBER 1914

Dear Robert,

The weather is glorious here. Odd, isn't it? I'd been told a war was on. I've dug a fine ditch and may lie quite calm in the dusk watching the ocean of stars wash across this black night sky. I see in the paper the Queen's stepped down from the Palace to take a tour of a small handful of model trenches. Nothing so posh here, though we've the option of adding any rooms we care to dig out from the dirt. Which reminds me to ask, again, after that piano I requested not so many weeks ago. Where is it? I've built a music room in the second trench, carved from the mud and lit by a simple skylight (I pray it doesn't rain), and all I've been able to do is sing.

We're under some lovely strafing now. Probably I've given us away with my noisy pen scratches. That spit of orange fire from the machine gunners is a wondrous sight. It fairly jumps out into the black. Provided one's not hit, it's worth the poke of the head just to catch a glimpse.

Six hours at the cutting table today, a brutal sight. I don't fancy much more of that on the morrow.

On bright busy days, watching Mother work, say, at our late-afternoon drawing lesson, me sitting on our blanket in Cow Hollow, I will see her standing just so, staring toward the Fair, perhaps, the shroud of fog not yet hiding every detail. And I can't help but see the rough metal structure, the broken beams and welded rails there, in her posture, just below the surface. If I ripped her flesh away, there it would be, pounded, pushed and welded, the nails driven in to pinpoints by Mr. Taqdir and his team of sculptors. It's a horrible thought, but it's irresistible.

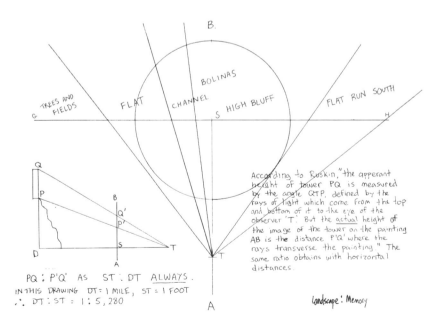

PQ : P'Q' AS ST : DT ALWAYS.
IN THIS DRAWING DT = 1 MILE, ST = 1 FOOT
∴ DT : ST = 1 : 5,280

According to Ruskin, "the apparant height of tower PQ is measured by the angle QTP, defined by the rays of light which come from the top and bottom of it to the eye of the observer 'T'. But the actual height of the image of the tower on the painting AB is the distance P'Q' where the rays transverse the painting." The same ratio obtains with horizontal distances.

Landscape : Memory

# *Watching Birds*

---

## 1 JANUARY 1915

Each year begins with an outing to the dunes, and this year Mother insisted we bring her golf clubs. It's a little fad Mr. Taqdir has introduced us to. Father says it's all very silly.

We five went together, Duncan and Father and Mother and Mr. Taqdir and I, wrapped and muffled against the thick chilly fog, burdened by the puzzling array of clubs and a bucket of balls. I had no concerns, really, save the giddy feeling of the New Year and the doggy smell of my woolen sweater, wet from sweat on the inside and the salty ocean mists on the outside. The trolley dropped us off along the western edge of Sunset and disappeared into the mist, clang-clanging its impatient bell.

This morning there was no wind, just the thick cold clouds settled down onto the sands turning the landscape gray and leaving the dunes silent and still and damp. We marched west into the long wet reach of sand, Father leading without a word. Duncan and I caddied the clubs. Mother and Mr. Taqdir followed close behind discussing war, which Mr. Taqdir held to be a beautiful, though tragic, achievement of the human spirit. Mother's pointy shoes kept digging uncomfortably deep into the mucky sand and she was soon panting like a poodle, prompting Mr. Taqdir's speculations with nothing more than an occasional grunt or nod of the head. Duncan looked at me with a determined grin. We were Swiss soldiers in the Alps now, or Eskimos on a pilgrimage across the barren tundra.

I watched Father's sturdy back advancing farther and farther ahead into the high-shouldered dunes. His spyglasses swung to and fro as he pushed on, easily mounting a steep ridge and disappearing down the other side. We were somewhere in the middle, Sunset gone from sight, gulls wheeling high above, calling into the thick clouds. Father appeared, small and steady, mounting a more distant dune, and disappeared again down its far face.

"Perhaps we should tee off," Mother panted. Mr. Taqdir was sniffing the listless air, gazing north or west or east into the indistinct mists, staring through the damp nothing, across that whole hopeless expanse of gray dunes, staring expectantly, as though the bright flagged pins of the real golf course might be out there, somewhere, beckoning.

He pulled a little square of turf from his canvas fishing creel and laid it neatly on the sand, puncturing its middle with a small wooden tee.

"Yes," he harrumphed. "It is time." Duncan handed him a hefty driver. Mother was fishing about the bottom of her ample carpet bag, digging for golf balls, while Mr. Taqdir took a few fierce swings at nothing, his bulky driver whistling neatly through the empty air.

"Pumpkin," Mother called. "We've only a half dozen balls."

"But I packed the little bucket, Mummy," I assured her. "There were several dozen, at least." Mother's golfing style required an ample supply, particularly out in the dunes, where a well-hit ball was almost invariably lost. Father was a black speck on the farthest horizon, a tiny black nothing standing still atop the final dune, his arms raised, apparently pressing his powerful spyglasses to his face. A little white spot seemed to dangle at his waist.

"Is that your bucket?" Duncan asked, pointing out there at the distant dot of white. Indeed it was.

Pelicans were diving out at sea, there beyond Father, wheeling through the sky and turning a sharp pivot down, straight down into the ice-cold waves. I was running strong and steady, running through the deep valleys, up and over the difficult hills, stumbling in the damp sand and running to get the bucket back. Father was, it seemed, a mile distant, stumbling down from off his dune, fixing, I imagined, on a better site from which to watch the marauding birds. I heard Mother's distant cry of "Fore!" and the soft thwack of her wooden driver.

That exquisite delirium came over me, that feeling when my blood is rushing so swiftly through the muscles of my legs, and my arms and body flexing with each stretching stride and pounding of my feet pushing into the sand, and my lungs stretched full force and aching, drawing the whole salty cold atmosphere through me, desperate for oxygen and hungry, hungry there at the very back of my throat. I ran and I ran like this so hard and long I finally stumbled and fell flat in the sand.

It all stopped, the quiet as sudden and complete as an earthquake. I lay flat on my back and stared, dizzy, into the sky. The clouds were opening up at sea, but staying thick with chilly fog in above the golfers. Mother's tiny sphere sailed silently off the lip of a far dune, a tiny little whiteness winging away into the drifting mist. And then, after, came the soft thwack.

I scooted backward up the dune, unching on my behind, to see farther and watch the full progress of the balls. The dunes sat in long rows of ridges, wrapped round in tangled turns and worked over every day by winds or rain. The sky opened up in patches, letting loose shafts of sunlight to shine down into the endless sand. And there was Father, two or three dunes distant, regarding me calmly through the spyglasses. I'd somehow run clear past him, making my way almost to the sea. Occasional wisps of fog would sweep between us, but his watch went uninterrupted. I lay there, staring east beyond him, staring after the silent white specks. They sailed through broad sweeps of blue sky where the clouds had blown suddenly clear. Father stood, caught in the bright sun, watching.

Amidst this crowded chaos of golf games and shifting weather his attention had fixed, as it always seemed to fix, trained and focused through the powerful glasses. His aspect was calm, his two feet firmly planted in the heavy sands. He stood steady in the slight wind, the dune rising under him like a lifting hump of whale.

Behind me the pelicans wheeled, tracing wide circles up into the disappearing mists and diving ferociously down into the cold ocean. Those idiot birds, driven through the sky on instincts and hunger, eyes wide open through air and icy salt water. They dove deep into the sea after fish they'd somehow spotted from high above. I wondered at this strange intelligence of theirs. Some queer dumb knowledge of each moment, felt in their tough muscled necks. Father was watching them, watching beyond me, this feston of birds.

I stretched my arms out and wheeled around the top of the dune, feeling for any intelligence that might emerge from my body, from the flex of muscles across my back. I dipped and danced, not thinking, or rather, thinking to not think, imagining perhaps Indians or mating quail. I tucked and bobbed and still nothing took me, no wave of feeling or intuition swept through me. I got dizzy and fell down.

## 10 JANUARY 1915

Mother went to a suffrage meeting this morning and left me at home with Father and the rain beating on the windows. It was as wet as it gets today, the clouds so full and low and dumping like a mammoth shower let loose. Our road's a river of mud. Lincoln Beachey had said he'd fly come hell or high water and I'd planned with Duncan to watch from Cow Hollow but they wouldn't allow Beachey up, or said that was the reason, and Duncan decided not to leave his house and probably not to leave his bed for that matter. I imagine he'll lie about in his nightshirt all day, bundled in his eiderdown and napping, listening to comical songs on the Victrola and emerging only for food or a toasty fire, if one is made. If I were a bird I'd fly there.

I'm not so sedentary as he and was up and about by ten, boiling water for breakfast mush and bringing dry wood up from the cellar.

Today I finished *Frankenstein*. I fancy the monster's a woman, as he seems to suffer all that women suffer. He's not allowed to speak. He's judged by his appearance only. He must stand by and wait for a rather infantile man to do the necessary work, allowed to help only through threats and cajoling. As it's written by a woman I imagine she intended it as a parable, but Mother tells me my reading is incorrect. It's about Prometheus, she says, and the horrible things that happen when man plays at being God. I don't mind that I'm wrong really, but I like imagining the monster in a dress.

I'm going to make a parlor play of *Frankenstein* with a woman as the monster. I'll use costumes from the attic and some from Duncan to give it an exotic flavor. We'll set it in the dining room with curtains hung across the archway so the audience can watch from the parlor. Mother can play the monster.

Father spent the day in his study, holed away in the very back of the upstairs. At lunchtime I took two bowls of bean soup and some hot bread on a tray up the steep, narrow stairs and down the dusty hallway to his study door. I knocked but he didn't answer so I opened up and went in. The room was bright and warm, its three walls of windows only half blocked by books and letting in all the light the day had to offer. Father was standing by the window, looking out at the wet green wall of trees that marks the edge of the Presidio, and he spoke up as I set the heavy tray down on a pile of papers.

"Isn't it remarkable," he said, still staring out at the sky. The clouds had lifted enough to see their movement east, the white-gray bottoms rolling like swells on the ocean. "You can fairly *see* the wind."

I sat nearby and looked out. I noticed the DeBardi kids mucking about in the muddy street, sliding full force down the hill, like the water ride at the Chutes. They were all colored a uniform yellow-brown with only the whites of their eyes and the black of their hair showing through the mud.

The sky *was* remarkable. I remembered watching the same patterns and movement from Mount Tam, watching from above what we now saw from below. I imagined the confusion of a man looping the loop in his aeroplane, racing through the two-faced clouds above the deep-blue bay.

"How can birds see in clouds?" I asked, wondering aloud. "What if it's dense fog from top to bottom and they can't find their way?" Really I wasn't worried about the birds. It was myself I was imagining floating lost in the fog.

"Birds don't get lost," Father said. "Some fly with their eyes closed, usually while in a flock. They're guided by the sounds of the other birds' motions." I felt an immediate kinship with these birds. "Some may best be described as sleeping." Sleeping birds. It seemed at once wonderful and terrifying.

"What if they all fall asleep?" I asked, pursuing my personal fears. Father seemed intrigued by the possibility.

"They must just continue forward. I'd be keen to chart their paths. Imagine, the patterns of sleeping birds. Fibonacci's works on the nautilus and pine cone might interest you," he continued, though it seemed obvious they wouldn't. I wanted to know about the birds.

"Wouldn't they starve? Or run into a hillside or drown or something terrible?"

"Oh, no, I don't imagine it like that at all. Guided by their own sounds and all of them sleeping? It all seems so beautifully mysterious." And I looked out at the sky and tried to imagine how he must see it. "Their path must be coded somewhere deep in their instincts, some ancestral, primitive knowledge of the winds and the land, blossoming only in their sleep. Don't you think?" And he rustled my hair as fathers do.

But I didn't think, and I didn't say, preferring to keep my fears silent and fill my mouth with bread and soup instead. I sat close by him and wondered at the terrible mysteries of navigation in fog, the possibility of disaster. I wondered how those birds could ever surrender to sleep, floating two thousand feet up in the insubstantial air.

Dear Robert,

Have I mentioned the aeroplanes? As a bird man you'd fancy them, I do believe, a good sight more than the rest of this war. They're announced by a thin distant buzzing and the wobbling speck on the horizon. Coming from the west they're quite welcome and I watch their crazy, weightless flight with pleasure and no small wonder. From the east is of course treachery and I retire to the music room post haste. I dream of giving up this horrible doctoring and taking to the air corps, though I fear I might jump, out of sheer curiosity, once airborne.

They're a wondrous sight, dipping and turning, buzzing down low to drop their small bombs. I've never managed to tell if it's the mail or a mortar that's coming. What a treacherous war! Something to do with surfaces, I believe. Surfaces dissolving. It was once clearly the land we fought on. What *is* that now? We've miners tunneling under to bomb us from below, and aeroplanes sailing over to bomb us from above. Mortar and shells come singing in from invisible artillery stationed somewhere beyond the curve of the earth. At sea there are U-boats, silent as sharks and deadly. It's no wonder I feel such affection for Jerry, dug into his trench just fifty yards distant. He and I are stuck here on our dirty bits of land, wedded to the same muddy field. And we sing with one another up and down the middle ground. It's all we can do to fill the empty air, to keep away the demons, the bombs, the shrapnel and gas.

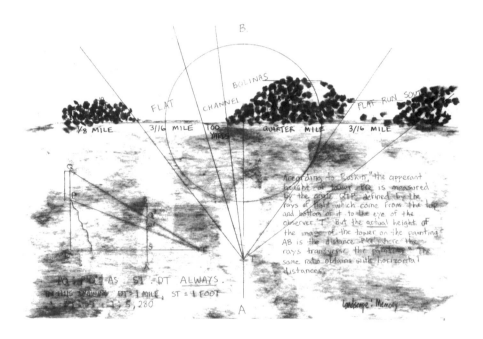

## 19 JANUARY 1915

I went to do homework with my friend Flora Profuso today. She's in her last year at Lowell, like me, but she's three years older, as she came back from the Philippines only last year after her father died. Her mother decided the Philippines was just too much for a woman and her little girl and they moved back to where her mother had grown up, into the same house actually.

Lowell said Flora would have to do the last year of high school again to demonstrate her competence and get a diploma. Flora drives a motorcar with a racing number on the side. She does all the engine work herself.

We're best friends ever since my "fight" with Jeffy Baird. Jeffy came up and slugged me in the face and I said, "You oughtn't have done that," meaning that hitting someone was wrong, but he took it as a threat and ran away. Flora, who was standing close by, was impressed that I was so principled and resolute in my pacifism, particularly in the face of an unprovoked attack.

"It's all so typically juvenile," she said of Jeffy, and she wiped my bloody nose with the grease rag from her motorcar. In actual fact Jeffy hit me because I'd been teasing him mercilessly all day long, but I kept mum on that detail and mentioned, instead, my ethical training.

"My mother's had me read summaries of all the Greeks, Mill, and most of the Germans. I'm required to speculate on their application to any number of dilemmas."

"How very wise," Flora allowed, truly intrigued. "I must meet your mother sometime. Is she involved in suffrage?"

I nodded yes. "And labor rights, though less so." Actually she had nothing to do with labor rights. I was certain, though, she would support the cause if given the opportunity.

"I've noticed you, in class." This drew my full attention, as all flattery did. "You're such a relief from all this," and she waved her hand about, stammering for a word to encompass the detestable entirety of things at Lowell, "all this *frivolity*. Young people are so flimsy these days."

"Yes." I had to agree. "Flimsy. Though my friend Duncan is quite principled," I added because I liked him so much and I was certain he wouldn't mind being principled.

"Your recitation of Whitman impressed me." She meant my report in Mr. Spengler's class. I'd memorized "Spontaneous Me," which I read aloud, save the three controversial love stanzas. It all seemed so breathtaking to me. I didn't say much after. I remember Flora asking Mr. Spengler about the missing stanzas and him insisting we should not condemn Whitman, for all great artists are blind to certain aspects of civilized life.

"Have you read the Uranians?" Flora asked.

"Ukrainians?" I had no idea what she was talking about.

"No, no. It was just a thought." And she brushed my shoulder, as though sweeping crumbs from the table. "I hope I don't bore you."

"No, certainly not. I like literature. I write my own little dramas and we play them in the parlor at home. You could come along to see the next one."

"Oh, could I? How sweet of you." She seemed to be distracted, though I understood her thanks to be genuine. I made nothing of it and smiled warmly into the silence. Then she squared up to me and looked into my eyes.

"Really I meant to ask a favor," she began. "My great ambition is choreography and I wonder if you would perform. In a dance of mine. So few boys are willing to participate in modern dance, I'm in a spot."

Really *I* was not inclined toward modern dance either, but I found I'd been charmed. "Is it ballet?" I asked, uncertain what difference that might make.

"Oh, no, no. Nothing old or stuffy. It's interpretive dance in the style of Miss Duncan. I'm looking for a Ganymede, and as he'll be bare-legged and bare-chested I must have a boy. He must, of course, be sensitive and modern in his sensibility, as you most certainly are."

Her dance involves five girls and me. It's all very artistic and "kinetic," as Flora says. I'm clothed in what most resembles a Hindoo diaper, a fine white cloth wrapped around my waist in bunches, the rest of me bare. The girls carry me above their heads, one assigned to each limb and one for the torso. I'm manipulated through a variety of motions. Incipient Spring carried on the cosmic winds. The season of growth begins as a helpless infant, Flora has explained to me, but becomes a locus of power and violent beauty. That's the tough part. I've not yet managed to whirl about with convincing power nor violent beauty. Too often I get dizzy and stumble, but we've another month and a half yet to practice.

Today we spent the morning preparing a report for Mr. Spengler. "Beauty and the Great War," we'd entitled it, intending to present poetry from the war.

"Dogey," Flora said, for that had become my nickname, "do you find Rupert Brooke handsome?" She held up a magazine that pictured the young poet bare-shouldered.

"Oh, yes, very much." And it was true, I did. "He looks so Greek. I imagine he's very strong and agile, not like some of those fat old Englishmen." I took the magazine and looked closely at the carefully posed photo. "I'm not so fond of this photo, though. He looks like a statue."

Flora took it back for close inspection. "But that's the style. They want to make clear his affinity to the Greeks."

I looked again at his smooth marble skin, the soft hollow at the base of his throat.

"Yes, I suppose. I'd rather see him shopping or falling in a lake somewhere. Maybe he'll read in San Francisco."

"He's at war, Dogey. Remember, 'Beauty and the Great War'? I imagine they'll all be over when it's over. All those Europeans. Maybe this summer, and we can take him out shopping or push him in a lake and you can take a picture."

I imagined shopping with Rupert Brooke. Would he wear a shirt? Would he stop to jot down poetic phrases with his quill pen and spill-proof inkpot? I lay there on Flora's bed, my head hung over the edge, looking at the photo there on the floor, and thought of this bare-shouldered man at war, dug into the trenches, the bullets singing through the air around him.

"Do you suppose war inspires great writing?" I asked.

"That's good, Dogey. That's good for the report. Our thesis

will take a position on that and we'll choose three or four poems to defend it with."

"I'm serious, though. I wonder about war a lot." It was true. I had a lurid interest, fed mostly by my uncle's letters. "Do you suppose war is sexually exciting?" I asked, confident I could broach even the most personal subjects with Flora. "In the trenches, I mean. Imagine Rupert Brooke with no shirt on, just his trousers, throwing down his gun and jumping up onto the parapet, baring himself to the stinging bullets. Don't you suppose—"

"That is hardly typical conduct for the war," Flora interrupted. "Throwing down his gun and taking off his clothes? Oh, Dogey, you should be in charge of the war. Of course *that* would be sexually exciting."

"But even without all that, isn't it like that anyway? Isn't the danger and sweat and all that sort of thrilling? Isn't it kind of sexy in a way?" And Flora closed her eyes to give my unlikely thesis a chance in her imagination.

"I can't imagine it, Dogey. All I see is mud and blood. I'm too disgusted even to think of it."

"I never said it wasn't disgusting," I protested. "Just that it was mixed up with other stuff. Of course the war's disgusting." This was something we'd long ago agreed upon, but which I got muddled about in private. "I'm only trying to make sense of its appeal."

Another note from Father, tucked in here on this page.

"Songs are remembered in the bones, and passed, like temperament, mysteriously through the generations. Wolves and wind and sandstorms. Wood warblers. The swift water in the rill, dropping down from glaciers. Your mother and Ludwig Theobold Kosegarten (I'm certain we're related). They all of them have their songs.

"Ludwig wandered the wide green meadows near Griefswald,

walking the rugged stony beach at Rügen. He wrote songs of that place, all there that sang. The root of memory is song.

"The song a cedar sings depends on its location, its girth, how deep in the soil it sits, the shape of its wood. How many years of winter storms have given it that particular voice, that long, low calling shaking down through the ground it's grown in? What songs do you sing, little fish?"

Dear Robert,

Does Belgium have its own primitive tongue? Something other than French or Flemish? God, we've made a mess of things here. A man in rags came dragging a sheep's head into the trench, weeping and bellowing some indecipherable syllables. Frisian? I suppose he once lived here.

Smithy's dead. I've no idea how. Out on patrol and never returned. His few books and tobacco are here beside me, drying out on the duckboards.

## 27 JANUARY 1915

We finished the *Frankenstein* script last evening and Duncan slept over as we had to be out before dawn to go birding with my father. Mother allowed us to camp out in the living room, our bedrolls stretched out by the dying embers of the evening fire. We left the windows open wide for fresh air and curled in close and warm.

At some silent, empty hour Father came banging in through the pitch dark, sounding reveille through buzzing lips and stepping, accidentally, he said, on both our bums, like stepping-stones in a pond, on his way to close the window.

"Mush," he said, calling us to breakfast. "Mush and coffee." And he disappeared as quickly as he'd come, turning the lights up as he went out.

I tucked the tails of my nightshirt into some warm woolen

pants I'd kept stuffed in at the foot of my bedroll and went to the kitchen where Father sat sipping coffee and giving a close inspection to a colorful hackle, plucked, I supposed, from the rough of some bird he hoped we'd encounter today. He had a magnifying glass and tweezers. I imagined the feather to be an organism of some sort, capable of sight and speech. My father was its doctor. Duncan walked past me in his undershorts, groggy and sniffling, headed, it seemed, for the mush.

"Are we after the owner of that hackle?" I asked Father, pulling up a chair beside him.

"We *are* the owner of this hackle," he corrected, raising his eyebrows at me. "I suspect we'll meet some relatives of its previous owner."

"Where?" I asked, leaning in for a close look.

"Lake Merced. We're driving."

Duncan looked up from his bowl of steaming oatmeal mush, his eyes bright with interest. "Can I drive?" he asked. "I'm very good and *very* safe."

"And very fast," I added.

"You'll have to wear pants and a shirt, of course," my father started.

"And goggles?" Duncan asked.

"And a helmet? And pads?" I added. "And can I drive?"

"You, little fish, may drive under a vow of strict secrecy. No one is to know. Not even me."

Nothing but an aeroplane could be more thrilling than our Model T. It *was* an aeroplane out Skyline Boulevard, us motoring through the clouds, lurching forward with every depression of the gas pedal, the wide road clear of all traffic in the dim gray light of dawn.

We sat three to the front seat, frozen to the teeth and wide-eyed from coffee, cold winds and the thrill of high speeds. Father drove first, to Golden Gate Park and west to the Great Highway. I took the wheel there. The least experienced, I'd be safe, Father figured, on the open straightaway that ran south along the shore.

It was pitch-black out to sea and various shades of gray to the east. I settled in, the motor idling, and took account of the numerous levers and pedals, the mysterious choke and the lively wheel. I had only the crudest understanding of the relationship of the various parts but felt too shy to ask any advice. The pedals, I was quite sure, operated on a principle similar to that of the pump organ, left down, right up, right down, left up and so forth. The fact that such essential mechanisms as the clutch and magneto in no way resembled any part of the pump organ was a source of some discomfort for me. But Father assured me the magneto was irrelevant and that I need merely pull out the clutch at his signal. Duncan would work the shift, also with my father's instruction.

"Comfy, little fish?" Father inquired, more mischievous than I wanted. "Clear of all pedals?" We bounced idly as the engine rumbled in its tin chamber.

"All clear," I assured him. Duncan wrapped his hand snug around the gear shift. He'd long ago memorized the various positions and their sequence.

"Clutch out," and I did, watching now as Duncan shoved the car into gear. "Engage the clutch now, slow, lots of gas, little fish, don't be timid." Father was almost screaming above the noise, bracing himself visibly and wisely as I complied and the car burst forward, spitting sand out from both back tires and veering left as I grappled with the wheel.

"Clutch out," Father screamed, feigning, I believe, hysteria. And I did and Duncan did and out it came again and more gas, all the way to third gear at which point Father settled into his seat and relaxed. Comfortably cruising south now, I began with the pump organ. Right in left out, left in right out. Once or twice was plenty for me to realize our car had little in common with the pump organ and I gave in to using just one pedal, the gas, and steering straight down the highway.

It was a glorious thrill, my head stuck out the side, face full into the salty sea wind, the powerful engine propelling us fast forward at the slightest touch of my foot. Duncan tugged at my sleeve to beckon me back and Father said I'd need to concentrate now as we reversed the whole start-up and came to a safe stop. Clutch out, engaged, and gas and brake and clutch some more, finally to a neutral idling and we'd made the three miles safe and speedy.

Duncan took the wheel with great confidence and sped off before my father could utter his first instruction. Our trip from the Great Highway to the southern flank of Lake Merced was fast, smooth and expert, Duncan controlling the auto like an extension of his own graceful body.

Along the southern reach of the lake Duncan pulled over and turned the motor off. As suddenly as that the machine went impossibly still and silent. The morning vapors rising off the lake drifted across the road waist-high. We three sat in silence, breathing soft clouds of breath and settling into the stillness. It was like being in church or dawn (which it was) or masturbation, which I may talk about if I wish and should not be ashamed. All of that fury and motion and then, after the climax, silent, empty breathing.

Father kept a canoe pulled up into the underbrush down along the southern shore. We loaded in, Duncan and I at either end and Father in the middle sporting his balaclava and muffler, a green woolen army blanket covering his lap. We paddled very little, mostly steering the boat and drifting, keeping close to shore and quiet. I had my sketch pad and spyglasses too.

Very little ever happened birding, but it was my favorite time. I felt my threshold completely lowered. Each rustle of the weeds or glimpse of color signaled something of interest. We three were wedded by our silence and our attentions, drifting through the open water in the same silent boat.

I resented my father's ability to leave, though, as he did more often now that I was older and he didn't have to worry about me. He'd nod his head upward, signaling us in to shore, and he'd climb out and walk off through the reeds without a word. If on foot, as we often were, I'd not even get the warning of a nod. I might hear a rustling and look up to see his back disappearing into the brush. When I was little I used to rush along after him, but he would whisper, "Don't follow just for my sake" and I knew quite clearly. Birding near to home, that might be the last I'd see of him. On longer trips it was assumed we'd meet up where we'd parted sometime in the late morning.

Having Duncan along was some help, as I could focus my good feeling on him, taking pleasure in his company and letting my father be. But I dreaded that nod of the head, even wishing, on trips like this one, that it would come sooner rather than later so I might be done with the waiting.

Despite all of that, the prospect of birding still thrills me, filling me with anticipation of silent time spent drifting. The calm, still moments stay in my mind, and even the dread takes on a precious quality, that moment of loneliness sitting in the wet reeds all mixed up in my joy in a way I couldn't possibly explain.

## 6 FEBRUARY 1915

The Fair will open in two weeks, and they've planned a celebration to alert the world. President Wilson will issue the official opening from Washington while the wires buzz with news of its beginning. Messenger pigeons will be released. Ships departing will carry word, and a round-the-world auto race will commence from the city, alerting all points along its forty-five-thousand-mile route. The Scintillator will play across the night sky as Beachey flies his daredevil loops illuminated by spotlight and bright trails of fireworks attached to his tail and wingtips.

If you flew by overhead, say in a Zeppelin, you'd see an impressive city of domes, gargantuan in aspect and harmonious in coloring. The festive avenues are lined with full-grown palm and eucalyptus. The Palace of Fine Arts is swathed in creeping vines and bordered by the finished lagoon, looking like it's been there a thousand years. You might land to the northeast, where the aeroplanes land, or come in by yacht, docking at the marina. Perhaps you'll just drop from the sky, piercing the thin plaster of the Dome of the Ages, breaking your limbs and revealing the flimsy wood lathing that supports these impostors. Father calls it a "glorious masquerade" and still refuses to go, sore, I suppose, about the filling of the swamps. But he's just being fussy and I rather feel as Flora feels that it is just the thing for a young city in these chaotic times.

Mother thinks she'll be done with her panorama soon and hopes to display it somewhere on the fairgrounds. But she had been hasty in her work, skimming Ruskin and blocking her sketches off by intuition rather than geometry. The result is appealing to the eye but hopelessly out of proportion. I've cautioned her time and again as our work has proceeded, but she pays me no mind.

"It *looks* right," she insists.

"But it *isn't* right," I tell her. "You've been fooled by the flat surface. It's all in the book."

"But if it looks right, pumpkin, it *is* right. We mustn't quibble over aesthetics." This was her accustomed retreat.

"This isn't 'quibble,' Mummy. This is fact. You're the one who said to use the book."

"Art cannot be explained in a single book, dearest. We mustn't become slaves to our teachers."

"*You* are getting lazy, that's all," I concluded. "A true picture is drawn through attention to detail. Geometry. Hidden structure. All else is just fancy, vapors of the mind." This was a phrase from my parlor play. It made her mad.

"The pot ought not call the kettle black, tenderness. A neutral judge would have no trouble selecting the 'true' picture if asked to choose between our two 'fanciful vapors.' You needn't throw stones."

I thought some about the comparative "truth" of our two pictures and fell into a long silence. Our discussion seemed to have shifted onto dangerous ground, though I wasn't at all certain Mother had even noticed. It was like tugging at a little thread and finding one's guts suddenly spilling forth from a swiftly unraveling wound, the garment and flesh having turned out to be one and the same. I couldn't continue for fear it would never be contained.

It's just that something troubles me about the Fair, what might count as a "true" picture of the Fair. Something about surfaces. It *all* seems so wrong. I can't help but feel queasy when I touch the bare wood lathing of an unfinished wall, or imagine the enormously thin shells of those gigantic domes. For all my glib agreement with Flora, the Fair always gives me the shivers.

I'll look down from the woods at the eastern edge of the Presidio, gazing down from the thick grove of eucalyptus through the scattering ocean mist, and take in that impossible panorama of golden domes and broad, palmed avenues peopled by milling throngs, dwarfed to the size of insects by distance and comparison.

And then my head feels empty and weightless, as though the wind is blowing through it, and my body becomes sensitive all over, like a shivering. Sometimes I just want to cry. What *is* it that's begun unraveling? It's all so elusive. To set the truth of my memory clearly down on canvas ... that thread seemed simple enough. But it's dug suddenly deeper into me, dropped down into my center. Something about the appearance of things unhinges me.

The only thing that's right is Maybeck's Palace, a hollow ruin built in a hundred days. He's asked that they plant cedars to mimic its broad sweep and that they leave it all be, the building to collapse and decay slowly over the generations that pass as the cedars grow tall among the ruins. I find that reassuring.

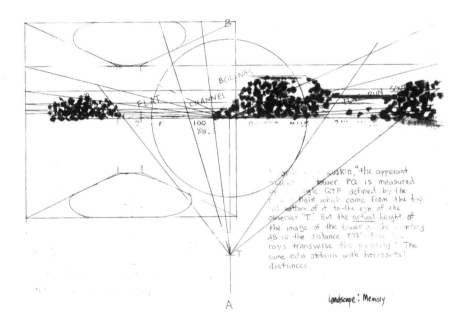

. . . uskin, "the apperant . . . tower PQ is measured . . . GTP defined by the . . . light which come from the top . . . bottom of it to the eye of the observer 'T.' But the actual height of the image of the tower . . . AB is the distance P'Q' . . . rays transverse the . . . The same ratio obtains with horizontal distances.

Landscape: Memory

# The
# Plunge

15 MARCH 1915

Lincoln Beachey's monoplane collapsed into itself two thousand feet up into the cloudless sky and plunged like a cannonball down into the bay. Beachey drowned and they haven't told his fiancée for fear she will suffer psychic damage. His mother has refused to believe that he died, waiting up late into the night for his return.

This is what the newspaper said:

> Lincoln Beachey, whose daring as an aviator has echoed round the world, was claimed by the elements he so long defied yesterday afternoon. The new German Taube, in which he had hoped to demonstrate his complete mastery of the air, folded its toylike wings and plunged from a great height into the waters of the bay.
>
> Before the horrified gaze of 50,000 people who had witnessed his flight from the marina, in front of the Palace of Mines, at the exposition, the peer of all aerial champions went to an end as spectacular as his remarkable career.

Beachey was on his second flight after having thrilled the spectators with a series of graceful loops and successfully had flown upside down across the blue expanse at a height of 2,000 feet, when the monoplane collapsed on the descent. Quivering for a fraction of an instant like a wounded bird, the machine, shrouded in flame and vapor, hurtled from aloft as a dead weight.

In that fraction of a moment it was apparent that Beachey, still exerting the nerve that made him famous, endeavored to direct his course for the bay. But the Taube was beyond human control.

The litter of the wreckage shot into the water between the transports *Logan* and *Crook* lying at the Fort Mason government piers. Strapped in the aluminum body of the car, Beachey disappeared beneath the waves. When the rescuers arrived a moment later there was hardly a ripple on the surface. Only a small piece of the wooden frame floated to mark the spot where the hero of the air had gone to his doom.

Just what caused the harrowing tragedy is a matter of supposition. Even experts and Beachey's mechanicians cannot definitely account for the disaster. The monoplane was faster than anything that the daring aviator had ever piloted and of a type with which he was not so familiar as with the biplane in which he had made over a thousand loops.

In looping the loop a few minutes before Beachey was evidently in complete control of the machine and also as he made the upside-down flight. It was as he straightened out for the perpendicular dive to the green that the new monoplane failed him. He had often dipped from as great a height in his biplane, but the double wings had withstood the tremendous pressure that was now exerted on the single fan of the Taube. The propeller's revolutions were reduced, for it could be plainly seen turning over.

THE PLUNGE · 49

Within 500 feet of the earth the wings could no longer hold. They wobbled and closed about the little car, from which trailed a wake of fire and smoke.

"Oh, God! Beachey is gone!" was the cry that came from thousands of blue trembling lips.

For a moment that vast ashen-faced throng stood frozen with terror.

Then hope and panic gripped them alike. Beachey, their hero, the youth who had convinced others of his often-expressed confidence that he would never be killed in his "game," they thought could not have been vanquished by the elements to which he was so closely attuned.

Mumbling hysterically, they moved in a great mass in the direction where the machine had disappeared behind the outer buildings.

"Maybe he'll land in the water! Beachey can't be killed!" were now the cries as the throng rushed toward the eastern fence. Even the guards, white-faced too, could not stem that sympathetic tide. Thousands poured through the work gates, tripping and stumbling, before the exposition police mastered the situation.

But the hope was in vain. Around the transport wharves the crowd swarmed, breathless, only to watch the grapplers and divers pry into the secret of that hideous sight concealed by the bright, placid waves.

Beachey, "the daredevil of the air," had paid the penalty for his valor.

A thrilling account, as one should expect from a first-class newspaper. And though I was actually there to witness this tragic plunge, I find my memory is pale in comparison. The actuality was so impossibly indistinct, filled with disjointed actions and bad smells. I was more aware then of the uncomfortable fit of my shoes than the "hope and panic" that gripped us.

They'll be showing films of the crash at the cinema starting tomorrow and *that* is what I want to see. It's so much easier to focus one's attention in a theater, and the view is better.

Mr. Taqdir, with whom Mother and Duncan and I saw the fatal crash, anticipated my incomprehension on the spot. As the crowd pushed and shoved us along through the gates, he gathered us all into his big arms and urged us to face the tragedy bravely.

"We cannot be passing it over with eyes closed," he announced resolutely. "Face this now, each of us." And we shuffled forward through the frozen throng to peer into the unchanged waters of the bay, looking, I supposed, for bubbles or blood, or the bobbing head of the dead birdman. There was nothing, the deep blue waters surging and lapping as on any other day.

I looked across the water to the steep green hills and up into the sky, empty and blue. I imagined how cold it must be high above the bay, how small and sad everything must seem from up there. A noisy flock of gulls hovered high above the esplanade, wheeling and squawking, waiting for more garbage to be dumped into the waters.

"Think now, boys. Fix in your minds what it is you will be feeling," Mr. Taqdir urged.

My mother, her chin up, stared out across the bay and nodded in solemn agreement. "Very wise, Mr. Taqdir, very wise. We mustn't bury our sadness. It's important, I think, pumpkin, to put pen to paper when we return home. I know how much this young aviator has meant to both of you." And she took Duncan's hand in her own, pulling me close with her other.

Dear Robert,

We're dug in deep near Le Touquet, doing what we can to keep the walls from tumbling in. Conditions have gotten a good sight worse as winter has come. Walls collapsing and cigarettes soaked, fires unthinkable and no prospect of exercise lest one's got a talent for dodging bullets and fancies a little stroll along the wire.

Do you recall Portsmouth? The week Father rented that bungalow with a rotted moss roof and dirt floor? It's been raining nearly that hard for two weeks now. If Mother had strafed us constantly with machine-gun fire you'd have had something a little like my current condition. God, how innocent we were.

Some terrible offensive is on, it seems. Tolland and I've been stretched to eleven- and twelve-hour shifts the last two days. Cut and sew, cut and sew. The work is disturbingly simple. The numbers are mind-boggling.

Do send books, I'm in need of distraction. How is the cinema? Do they show films of the war in America? I've seen crews set up here, but never in close. I've another "rest" in a few weeks but not back in Blighty. It'll be months before I'm off the Continent.

## 18 MARCH 1915

I got in a fight at school over the war. I said the way we fight war is stupid and we'd best take a lesson from the insects. They work in organized battalions, in direct confrontations. We used to but now we have sophisticated methods. Alphonse Bull wants to fly aeroplanes in the war and he punched me when I claimed aviators were cowards because they wouldn't fight face-to-face but resorted to tricks like flying over and dropping gas bombs.

## 26 MARCH 1915

We presented *Frankenstein* this evening to an audience of two, Father and Flora. Duncan ran the Victrola and lights, did all the sound effects, and played all the women in minor roles. I was the narrator, little William, an old blind man and the horrified Scotsman. Mr. Taqdir was Dr. Frankenstein and Mother played the monster.

We made Mother up beautifully, dainty and sweet like the

most proper Gibson Girl, sweeping about in her best floral party dress. She was instructed to speak sweetly, with no hint of gloom or growl, and to walk firm and erect. Dr. Frankenstein, however, was more ghoulish. We made his complexion pale and darkened big bags below his eyes. I wanted a bit of stage blood to drip from his teeth but Duncan convinced me not to.

Mother murdered me near the end of Act Two.

It was a difficult scene. I insisted that she not limp or stagger or steal about like a criminal, yet she needed to appear plausibly murderous. Judging from the audience, the effect was more comic than tragic, this upstanding Gibson Girl stepping briskly across the room and strangling a rosy-cheeked boy at play in the flower box. She smiled through the killing, which was unnecessary, and released my limp body to tumble to the floor. The lights went dark as she crept offstage. Dr. Frankenstein gave vent to his agony with doglike howling. All around him his family was being ravaged by the monster. An encounter was inevitable.

"There in the starry darkness of the moonless mountain night, in the shadows of the sharp tooth of Mount Blanc, the good doctor staggered across the rugged snows to a fate he knew not yet. And in the distance, moving with a staglike swiftness, the form of a woman, much larger and more agile than a normal woman, leaping across the deadly frozen crags toward him."

The rendezvous was played out in darkness.

"Why do you hunt me?" the doctor asked, lighting, inexplicably, a cigarette. The orange tip glowed, bobbing and floating there in the indistinct night. The cigarette passed, it appeared, to the monster.

"You are as the only parent of me," she began, drawing a deep breath of smoke, illuminating her soft face in the orange glow. "You have abandoned me. I am an orphan, helpless, friendless, a monster in this cold world." She flicked a bit of ash to the floor. "You will give in to my one request, as only human decency demands."

Duncan began a distant howling, the soft cry of the glacial winds sweeping across the broken ice floes, whistling beside the jagged peaks.

"You torment me," the doctor whispered. "All I value has fallen into your hands." He took the cigarette and held it, undrawn for a moment. "To be protecting what I love most, I will have no choice. What is your request?"

"I require a mate," my mother said. "One as ugly and un-wanted as I, one as ill-fit for this world." She rose and walked to the window, a sillhouette against the evening sky. "You must build me a wife."

The house was hushed as the doctor took a last drag and flicked the spent cigarette out the window.

"It is done, I have no choice," he said.

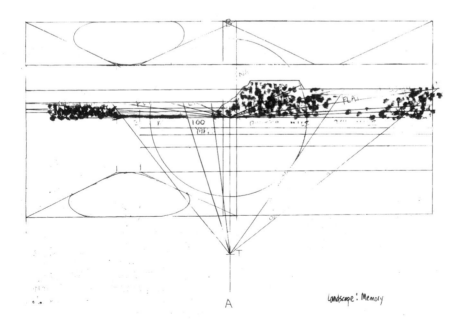

Landscape: Memory

## 3 APRIL 1915

Today I came home from school at lunchtime, which is a very special thing and which I was allowed to do only on account of my mother asking. Mother and Father were both at home and sitting there very stiff and formal with little sandwiches with no crusts and a fruit bowl and soup already served, just sitting there and not eating really except that my father had already finished his soup.

I could tell straightaway that someone had died or something. Mother swept across the room to me, cooing pumpkin this and pumpkin that and brushing her powdered hand across my cheek. She was all done up with lavender water.

"I'm moving to Bolinas, little fish," my father announced before I'd even sat down. "Your mother will be living with Mr. Taqdir." And I just stood there and breathed while they both watched in silence. The windows were wide open onto the spring day and birds cheeped and chirped, fluttering past to the feeders. Hummingbirds hummed, poking their long noses into the honeysuckle trailing up the corner of our house and wafting spring smells in all directions. There was even a soft wind to stir the branches and I sat down with no appetite and little distinct feeling, just a vague dread and curiosity.

"Why are you living with Mr. Taqdir?" I asked my mother stupidly.

She breathed a quick breath and looked to my father, who was busy with a little sandwich. "Certainly, pumpkin," she began, turning toward me, "certainly you're aware of my fondness for Mr. Taqdir." She paused for assistance, but I sat in dumb silence, unable and unwilling to help her.

"Yes?" I prompted.

"Your father and I, dearest," she began again. "Your father and I have agreed that it would be healthy for me to explore

my feelings for Mr. Taqdir, in a less encumbered atmosphere."
She smiled, as if this were a gift she'd given me.

I still didn't understand, but couldn't find the words to say
so. I looked at my father and he shrugged a little shrug, nodding
his head to the side and brushing the crumbs from off his hands.

"They're sleeping together, Max," he said. "They're lovers.
I'd rather not stick around for it." Mother crinkled her brow
at him. "Anyhow, it's a beautiful time of year to be in Bolinas.
I can get a lot done up there."

I realized I'd been squashing a little sandwich throughout the
conversation. Its smooth dry white-bread face had turned a pasty
gray in my sweaty soiled hands. It looked like my own dirty
face from when I was a fat little kid. All those afternoons, I'd
come running home from digging furiously in the sandy soil of
the Presidio woods, starting tunnels and smoothing the walls of
shallow little caves that passed for headquarters of whatever
secret club we'd started that week. I was so milky-skinned and
pale. Just a fat little kid with dirt on his face. I had a bunch of
sort-of friends, Rolph and Skinny and Paolo, and we played our
favorite games over and over, acting out the same adventures
over the same ground day after day. Soldiers, Forest Fire, Man
on the Moon, Tunnel to China or my favorite, Freight Train—
the six or seven of us in a snaking line, our hands resting warm
on the shoulders of the next boy up, running through the woods
on the winding, treacherous path, just making train sounds. We
could play for hours, running silly and breathless into the dusky
woods, the dark evening settling in and cold fog filtering through
the thick stands of cedar, mothers calling unheard into the night
and us running and running, taking turns at the glory of being
engine or caboose, running and laughing up Pikes Peak and over
the Suicide Leap, too fast through the Chutes, and down through
the wild empty woods.

———

I was pushing at the pasty lump in my hand. Outside the breeze kept on, soft and sweet with cedar and eucalyptus. My mouth was open but empty. I had no words. What I felt was stuck inside me, anchored, it seemed, to something in the very center, too heavy or awkward to emerge.

"We've made a choice, pumpkin," my mother assured me. "We thought it best to be honest with you."

"Will I have to get a job?" I asked, unable to think any closer to the center of the problem. I sat down at the table and put my little sandwich on my plate. Mother reached for it, to throw it away, I suppose, but I grabbed it back and stuffed it into my pocket. Father had moved on to Mother's soup, thoughtfully keeping quiet as he tipped the huge bowl up to his face. I mustered my voice.

"I'm sure it's all very adult and modern," I offered, trying to start on a positive note. "But I'm not certain what it means. Will I be living alone now?"

"I'll still be at home, pumpkin," Mother said, leaning forward as though the reassurance might die if forced to travel a longer distance. "I'll just be home less frequently. And Mr. Taqdir will be with me when I am."

"But I don't like Mr. Taqdir," I said without thinking.

"You needn't like Mr. Taqdir, sweetheart. You need only live with this change. Your affections are your own." My mother was a wall of good clear sense that I couldn't breach.

"You're abandoning me," I said to my father. But he didn't seem to notice.

"We wouldn't abandon you, pumpkin," Mother assured me, meaning her and whomever. "I'm certain you'll find the strength to be adult about all this."

I hardly felt my strengths moving in that direction. Our whole exchange seemed anything but adult. The requisite trappings of civility hung over it like heavily perfumed velvet curtains. I imagined a rabid, mangy hound, foaming through its blood-stained teeth, clipped clean with a poodle cut and decorated with a dainty bow. That was the gift I'd give at Christmas, if we had a Christmas.

"May I live in Bolinas?" I asked.

"If when school gets out you're so inclined I'll certainly make room for you," Father allowed. "But follow your own mind, Max. Don't come along just for my sake."

"Thanks," I said weakly. I fiddled with the pasty face in my pocket and pushed the spoon around my soup. Then I picked the heavy bowl up in one hand and flung it across the room, smashing it to soup-covered bits against the wall, and I ran away out the front door.

When I left the house I was in a blind fury, I suppose. I was insensitive to the bright spring day and the birds and all those smells that normally engage my attention. I could see only the few yards of ground stretched out before me and the details of our lunch playing back in my mind. Of course I thought of things I should've said or done. I should've grabbed my father and shaken him, for one. I should've screamed, "Don't call me pumpkin!" or "Mr. Taqdir is a boring creep!" Especially, I thought, I should've cried. But I didn't, and hadn't, and these were only thoughts.

I walked west through the dirty streets, moving as though in my sleep, and found my way onto the Presidio and back into the woods above the golf course. The hillside was steep and I scrambled up through a thick grove of eucalyptus, grabbing on to bushes and low scrub for handholds. There was a hidden clearing ahead through the trees and I was moving toward it. There, on the western slope of this high hill, the trees opened up around a small hollow tucked into the lip of the hillside. Nurselogs, grown thick with motherfern and saplings, bordered the little clearing. A carpet of moss covered the soft contours of the ground. The trees grew tall and thick around all sides, save a small opening to the north and west where I could look out over the rocky cliffs and into the gray-green sea. Sea birds were calling high in the branches above me and I lay back, my head propped on a pillow of moss, and watched the distant treetops swaying in the wind. It was a shelter, and a much-needed one.

I felt myself sinking back into the ground, drawn down by weariness and gravity. I felt wedded to the weight of the earth, turning on its inevitable course, its face stretching out from the tips of my fingers and toes. I drifted away, exhausted, and dreamed.

I am sick in bed with a fever. I'm just in my nightshirt and all wet from sweating. My throat is sweet and sore and I can barely breathe. My breath is shallow and slow because a lush, heavy orchid is growing in my lung. Mother puts me in an ambulance. She sits beside me and feels my heartbeat with her cool hand. She rubs me on the chest to keep me calm and stop me from breathing too deeply. I'm feeling so sweet and fragile. I can feel the flower growing, its stem pushing down deep into my belly.

The ambulance runs along the railroad tracks, over the muddy grounds of the Fair, and delivers me into the bright white operating room of the Sculpture Factory. A team of doctors or sculptors, it isn't clear which, is waiting, ready to remove the orchid from inside me. I'm placed upon a vertical rack and positioned by the workmen. I'm much bigger than before. The workmen manipulate several mechanical arms that play across me drawing lines and angles against my skin, as though measuring and marking me for the operation. They've undressed me and I'm feeling very sensitive all over. My skin feels sweet and tender and my head is going to burst from the flower pushing its petals up inside me.

The mechanical arms are peeling my skin away. They pinch at the points where the lines intersect on my body and then peel my skin back. I look down across my body at the loose skin hanging down off my abdomen like a skirt. Inside, beneath the skin, I see that I'm simply a tangled mass of metal parts, leftover beams and spikes, wire mesh, all pushed and shaped to form a body. The cool air rushes through me, fluttering the red petals of the orchid, there in my very center. It isn't painful but it makes me worry about what's inside my head. If the arm reached up and pulled the flap of my face away, would it simply uncover a mass of metal garbage? Would it just be empty air blowing through the bits and pieces, the petals of the orchid pushing up amongst them? If it was, would I see it?

The arms never reach for my face. The workmen stop and leave. I'm left aloft, still shackled to the machine.

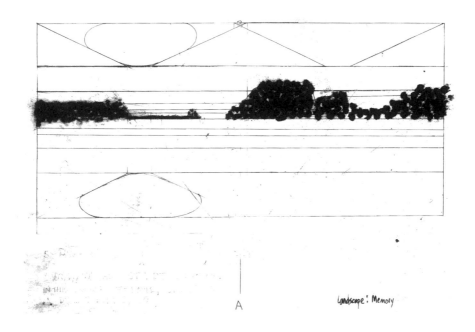

A                    Landscape: Memory

## 10 APRIL 1915

A well-to-do man called Weston Brown killed himself at the California Electric Crematorium by a shotgun blast to the head. He left a note.

Dear Sir: I wish to have my body cremated and I enclose thirty-two dollars to pay for the incineration. Thirty dollars is the regular fee and two dollars is for incidentals. I am quite sure you will have everything carried out faithfully.

I am a stranger here, single, childless and without property or friends in California. Keep my death from the public. Do not put my body in the morgue. There will be no claimants, as my relatives are far away. I have an acquaintance, a Mr. Carter, up the state, whom I have written concerning my case. Should he come, please tell him the particulars so he can inform my people, far, far away. There is no necessity for anyone else, especially the newspapers, to learn of my demise.

Yours truly, Weston Brown.

## 20 APRIL 1915

A woman asleep in her apartment dreamed an intruder scaled her back fence and came in through her open window. She awoke to find the man she'd dreamed of next to her bed cutting whole chunks of her long brown hair off her head. They say an infected bone buried inside her brain is the cause of her clairvoyance. She's in the hospital now and doctors hope to remove the bone surgically and end her suffering.

The British are holding the line in Belgium and France. They say a treaty may be signed on the exposition grounds, the two sides meeting here to affirm their belief in international growth and commerce.

## 24 APRIL 1915

I went shopping with Mother today. I want a European bathing costume where there's just undershorts. Mother was keen about the idea and thought we'd easily find some, San Francisco being so cosmopolitan and all. We didn't find any. I'm going to swim naked always just to make a point. Duncan almost does, being much bolder than me and quick. I don't like shopping. Saw Flora.

After all this with Mother and Father I've been quiet. I talked to Duncan I guess that evening. His father had told him too, but he didn't have so hard a time as I. I've not had so hard a time either, truth be told, as there's not that much to adjust to. Father is gone. Really, it means nothing. Mother is flitting about from one event to the next, trying to see each and every special lecture the Fair presents. I suppose it's only natural that she and Mr. Taqdir should be so preoccupied. The Fair is a once-in-a-lifetime thing. That leaves Duncan and me.

That first evening we tried to be practical.

"It's bad and all," Duncan began, "but there's a lot that's good in it." I felt insensitive to the good and bad alike. It was simply a physical presence for me, a thing too large to *have* qualities. Mostly I just listened to the reassuring tones of him speaking, unconcerned with content. I only wanted to hear a voice fill the empty night air, keeping these terrible thoughts present to mind and manageable, contained by his spoken words.

"We'll get to try out living by our wits," he continued cheerfully. "Breakfast and shopping and making it wherever on time."

"Mother and your dad will do all that," I answered. "I don't know that we'll get to do much new." I was loath to find cheer in any aspect of the day's events.

"Not if we don't want. There's two houses." Duncan's eyes got a wet sparkle with the very thought of it. Two houses. "We'll hole up wherever we want. No one says we've gotta tag along with those two."

It was a welcome thought. I had imagined he'd want to tag along with those two, or I'd want to. This new possibility became the simple obvious choice, just by him saying it.

"Won't we have to get jobs?" I asked, feeling very sad and sorry. "We'll need money for food and ice and house what-nots."

Duncan shook his head at me, smiling, and reached both his big arms around me. "You're gonna be sore no matter what, aren't you? Just don't think now. Don't think of them or any of it." And he rocked us over onto our sides. I closed my eyes and tried to rest my mind, sinking into him. And the night air was cold and moist and smelled of wood smoke, and we lay there and didn't say any more.

Dear Robert,

We've had heavy snow since Tuesday. It's buried this gray muddy sea and lent a queer grace to the burned remains of trees, all scattered across the pitted landscape. I felt like a boy whose school might be canceled, the signs of the war slowly obliterated by the feathery snow. Still I was wet and frozen, chattering in the small cave I'd carved out of the wall, looking, not through the lead-paned windows of King's, but through mist and smoke and the spark of snipers firing into the middle ground. May I tell you a story?

By dusk the snow had come over a foot thick and up and down the line we were engaging Jerry in a snowball battle that fell just short of bringing us up over the wall and out into no-man's-land. We'd lob long shots from the hole and listen to the laughing yells and feigned agony across the line if we hit, or the derision, spoken in fair English, if we didn't. Their big guns fired back, without the same accuracy they'd shown at Dunkirk but good enough to do what damage a snowball does.

With night come on we sent our team out to the wire and one boy too young to know better lobbed a quick shot in at the first line, just caught up in the winter play of it, like he was still a lad in public school.

The line lit up bright as day with a jet of flame shooting

near twenty yards out from Jerry's hole, like the mouth of hell had opened there and then. It wrapped round the dozen of them standing in that last moment before they disappeared into the blinding light of it. The jet kept up for a long minute or two until about fifty yards of the middle ground was melted back down to stinking mud and the bones of them could be seen, some movement there too, just in a pile and smoking by the wire.

I've been reading poetry by this young soldier Brooke. His more patriotic verses are quite popular among the men, but it is this one that stays with me. Herewith, Brooke:

### SAFETY

*Dear! of all happy in the hour, most blest*
  *He who has found our hid security,*
*Assured in the dark tides of the world that rest,*
  *And heard our word, "Who is so safe as we?"*
*We have found safety with all things undying,*
  *The winds, and morning, tears of men and mirth,*
*The deep night, and birds singing, and clouds flying,*
  *And sleep, and freedom, and the autumnal earth.*
*We have built a house that is not for Time's throwing.*
  *We have gained a peace unshaken by pain for ever.*
*War knows no power. Safe shall be my going,*
  *Secretly armed against all death's endeavour;*
*Safe though all safety's lost; safe where men fall;*
*And if these poor limbs die, safest of all.*

### 26 APRIL 1915

I cooked breakfast, as I do these days, and Duncan and I got off to school only a little late, as we do these days. Tomorrow Flora says she'll swing by and motor us there so we don't have to run for trolleys or hitch a jitney.

———

Duncan's kitchen is so full of elegant items, each meal masquerades as a fancy banquet, served up in ornate tureens and covered with fine metal tops. I play the sophisticated waiter at breakfast, bearing scrambled eggs or a well-cooked mush on platters fit for pheasant. I miss some things, like *Melmoth* by the fire and the particular view and smells of my own house. But life here is exotic. I'm on a Persian retreat in some distant land. I made tea with, I thought, sugar from the sugar jar. It was salt. I nearly threw up.

Mother and Mr. Taqdir are with us quite a bit, as it turns out. We sup together two or three times each week. It seems to be part of a larger design Mother has engineered. Groceries appear each week in our larder. Messes are miraculously cleaned and our lessons have continued apace.

Some evenings find the four of us, together with Flora, off to the Fair, viewing, once again, those horrible Futurist paintings Mother is so keen on. Duncan and I disappear to some distant corner of the grounds, wandering the Massachusetts shoe exhibit or the redwood Parthenon built by the state of Oregon. Flora, it seems, is everywhere, equally at home with the adulterous couple as with me and Duncan.

Tonight she came with us, leaving fine arts to the adults, and led us to the House of Hoo-Hoo which, she says, is a Maybeck. It's put up by the Lumbermen's Association and sits big as a giant's house made from thick, untrimmed redwood. It's all in scale, just two or three times normal size. I found it very appealing. It made my secret wish come true, and shrank me closer to invisibility.

"I like this," I said simply. "Can we be even smaller?"

"I think it's creepy," Duncan said. "I feel like the door's about to swing shut and, bang, we'll be trapped forever."

"And a giant ogre will bake you for his bread," Flora put in.

"Or maybe he'll just sit on us till we suffocate," Duncan

offered. I sat down, backed into a corner, and smiled benignly at their unpleasantries. I looked up at the faraway ceiling and tried willing myself smaller still.

"Dogey's gonna disappear now."

"I would if I could."

"Try closing your eyes," Duncan put in helpfully. "It always works for me."

I closed my eyes tight as could be and shrank smaller still, slipping into my empty black mind. Duncan started making fun, calling me "Disappearing Dogey." It made me suddenly very sad. I got up and walked to the far wall and sat very close facing it. Duncan and Flora were quiet then, and I stayed still through the heavy silence. It was just one of those moods that Mother says is from my being sensitive. I thought I might cry.

Flora knelt down beside me. "Let's just go back outside," she suggested.

I mumbled some meaningless words to her without turning. Duncan stood staring at me, wondering what to make of my sudden mood.

"Fresh air is a good idea, Max," he suggested, feeling my forehead with his clammy palm. "You're looking kind of green." They each took an arm and propped me up. But I didn't want to go back outside.

"Maybe I should be by myself," I offered, giving them a weak smile to appease.

"So what's up?"

"I don't know," I said honestly.

"Joy Zone?" Duncan offered.

"No. Thanks. Maybe I'll come later."

"No Joy Zone?" Flora asked unbelieving. "No Giant Babies? No Grand Canyon?"

"You go. I'll meet you."

They both squeezed my shoulders and left me there in the House of Hoo-Hoo. I heard the big door bang shut and closed my eyes again, feeling the enormous walls around me, their rough, sturdy timbers stretching up to the high ceiling, dwarfing all that was within, me shrinking ever smaller, slipping away into nothing.

I guess I fell asleep. They were closing and I was made to leave. I went out into the clear night and down the broad boulevard as all the lights went out. The drifting couples were quiet, their minds exhausted, I imagined, by the density of things demanding their attention. I walked under the archway in the Tower and out onto Scott Street, still busy with revelers and drunks. Fairgoers and delinquents roamed about in raucous throngs.

Their noises came disjointed, sharp and foreign and difficult to locate. The quick blasts of the car horns seemed so close, I jumped and started at each one, crossing Lombard as quickly as I could and headed uphill toward Pacific. I felt as though I'd not woken, but merely had been made to move on into the busy nighttime. There seemed to be dogs everywhere, standing watch on porches and roaming in packs up and down the wide street. A big sturdy shepherd stood up to the trolley, barking and growling, dashing clear of the clanging car just short of death. Empty bottles flew out into the night and broke in noisy shards at the feet of the running dog.

The heady smell of the cold night air preoccupied me. Sea salt and smoke and sweet cedar. My attention was fixed on the distant houses at the top of the hill, huge stone mansions, all dark save one where lights burned in every room. French windows opened wide, and women and men dressed to the nines drifted out into the evening, gazing at the panorama from their high perch. Their soft conversations and laughter carried on the wind down toward me, glasses clinking, it seemed, next to me, and then nothing as the wind shifted or the dogs let loose in howling, whole packs ranging down the pedestrian walk and disappearing into side streets as quick as they came. I wanted only to get back home.

Low fog rested on the lee side of Presidio Heights, pushing past the silent houses and up into the trees. I had no idea how late it might be, nor any concern. There was my house, straight ahead. Our lights were on, the living room dancing in the flicker of firelight. Only then did I remember I wasn't living there now. I stood in the wet bushes, looking in through the window at Mother and Mr. Taqdir sitting in armchairs both reading. I heard nothing, even as their silent figures would look up and their mouths move. Mr. Taqdir's hands and arms swept about in mute gestures, the two companions leaning forward in apparent laughter. A turn of the head. An exchange of books.

I felt I was watching my own past, like Scrooge, invisible and sad, looking in at events condemned to memory, seeing the dumb, unalterable play of things as they have been.

Was that my father once?

I am upstairs, asleep, their conversation and laughter, a warm murmur through the wooden floor. They're discussing me.

Are these movies?

I am drinking tea in the kitchen, looking at a picturebook. They're in the living room together.

I'm outside in the wide open night watching. They're a picture in a picturebook or a moving silent picture.

Dear Robert,
    Cigarettes and books, please.


27 APRIL 1915

I woke very late as I didn't get in till almost two o'clock a.m. and was so deep in sleep I thought Flora was Mother when she woke me, and I had little idea who I might be, though it all came back quite quickly. Flora said she'd honked and honked and finally just came in the kitchen window and found me there, dead to the world, out like a light.

"Up and out, lazybones," she called, shaking the headboard with her greasy gloved hand. "We're late late late." Indeed we were, almost two hours late, and Duncan was already gone, content to let me sleep the day away should I wish. "I've got ten minutes, Dogey, and then we're gone, dressed or no."

I lifted the curtain and looked out into bright sunshine.

"Where's Duncan?" I asked. "What time is it?"

"Duncan's at school where all good boys should be. It is ten-thirty and we've got good fun ahead, if we make it back in time."

"What good fun?" I asked, pulling on my pants and shirt from last night and rubbing the sleep from my eyes.

"Mr. Spengler's Philosophy Forum, dummy. Alphonse Bull will be defending chastity."

"Alphonse." It was all coming back to me. "Will someone attack chastity?" I ambled down the hallway without a reply and turned the faucet on full throttle. I fancied myself a primitive wildman, what with my hair all this way and that and my shirt not yet buttoned. I growled into the mirror and dunked my head in the brisk churning water.

Flora drove as she always did, fast and efficiently, zipping tight around the corners and revving along the straightaways. I braced myself on the safety bar and yelled to her over the noise.

"I'm not at all keen to enter into this discussion. I haven't any sense these days."

She looked at me as I talked so I kept it all short and to the point, staring straight ahead in order that I might inspire her to do the same.

"Just speak up as thoughts come, Dogey. You're perfectly coherent. Mr. Spengler would be crestfallen if you kept mum."

"*You* speak up, Flora. You'll say whatever I'd say and then I could sit peacefully. I'd make amends with Alphonse." His rather grim aspect and imposing physique swam through my dreamy mind. "We wouldn't want another brawl." And she laughed at this very serious worry of mine.

"No, no, Dogey. *You* speak. I'll punch it out with Alphonse after." We came flying over the crest on Buchanan, hurtling down the hill toward our date with philosophy, Flora's scarves flapping and my wet hair now wilder than any wild man's I could imagine.

"We'll have Duncan speak," I suggested brightly. "That'll throw old Alphonse."

Flora pulled at a piece of tattered rubbish that had flattened up against the windscreen. "Oh, Dogey, look there, sailors!" And there were, scores of them, spilling off the pedestrian walk, hooting and laughing like a pack of hyenas, looking, it seemed, for San Francisco. Flora sat up smartly and held her scarf aloft, giving them a crisp wave of the hand and a grim smile.

"Soon to be dead," she said matter-of-factly, leaning across the worn leather seat to plant that fact in my ear. We sped past them and out into the bright sunshine.

I looked back and imagined them torn and bloodied, their limbs useless or gone. I fancied their smart blue uniform. It had a nice close fit that showed the shapes of their bodies and the ornamentation was tasteful, topped off with a gay pompon. Watching their rough-and-tumble play, their mistaken sojourn through this dull residential district, no doubt in search of the Barbary Coast, I thought it would be keen to dress them as fish, a serviceable cloth costume with little fins and their own faces peering out through the fishy maw. The pilots could be dressed as birds and the army as landed mammals, antelope, leopards and buffalo. If that were policy, I'd join the armed forces straight-away.

Alphonse had brought charts. One showed "Spirituality Quotient" and its relation to chastity. He'd drawn colorful sketches of different sorts of persons, a priest, a college man, a flyer, a drunk, a harlot, Emma Goldman, and, begging certain questions that went unasked, a little boy. The bold, vertical bars of black that stood for "S.Q." descended sharply from left to right, excepting the little boy, whose dizzying "S.Q." was easily the equal of the priest's.

A second chart divided up the various races, both upper and lower, and assigned them each a Chastity Index. The Germans scored highest, followed by the rest of the northern races. The passionate Latins of the Mediterranean came in a good sight lower. Scraping the bottom were the Negroes, with the various Asian races receiving an N.A., not applicable.

"Most importantly," Alphonse was concluding, "the chaste man uses his passionate energies for the betterment of the human condition. Not like immoral men who can be seen doped up or asleep in doorways, all his energies gone to immoral degradation. That accounts for the first chart and the high S.Q. of chaste men and how horribly low the accomplishments of leches are." Alphonse nodded in agreement with himself, tugging at his ear, as he did whenever he presented work in class.

"Is Emma Goldman a lech?" Flora asked. Alphonse snorted a brief, breathy snort and rolled his eyes up.

"Miss Profuso has a point, Alphonse," Mr. Spengler put in. "How do you account for the tremendous energy of so immoral a woman?"

"And where would you rank our fighting men on the S.Q. chart?" Flora continued, fixing a scarf about her head in the manner of Miss Duncan.

Alphonse fidgeted briefly, tugging again at his puffy ear, and stepped back to his charts, tapping the tip of his long thin pointer on the face of the chart.

"Our fighting men, to begin there, Flora," he began. "Our fighting men are right up there at the top," he said, inching the pointer ever higher on his chart. "Right up with the priests, you gotta think. And Emma Goldman is something else again.

I couldn't pretend to account for her, Mr. Spengler. No, sir."
This was meant as something of a joke.

"If I may account for her, Mr. Spengler," Flora began again.
"Miss Goldman is above such distinctions as moral and immoral.
Her activity is spiritual in the best sense, urging an indulgence
of the human spirit that more 'chaste' individuals have kept
locked away from all of us. Alphonse seems to have confused
prudishness with virtue, and that may explain his inability to
understand Miss Goldman.

"As for the young child on Chart 'A,' it is the glory of children,
*and* Miss Goldman, I might add, that they remain ignorant of
the damning restrictions 'civilized' adults place on human be-
havior. They are blind, as we all should be, to Alphonse's precious
morality. They swim unclothed and hold and hug one another
on impulse. There's is a world rich in spiritual communion,
unfettered by petty civilities.

"By way of contrast, the fighting man's chastity is typical of
our tragic, if I may use so strong a word, tragic condition. Forced
to curb his natural desire for human contact and, if I may, Mr.
Spengler, sexual communion, forced, in a word, to be 'chaste,'
these men turn to barbarous murder, slaughter and, there is
evidence, dismemberment. Is this the high spiritual achievement
Alphonse is applauding?" Flora finished her strong speech, still
fixing her headdress and scratching at the back of her knee with
her bare foot. Alphonse looked meek and crestfallen. He had
tight hold of his ear now, milking it like a small, pasty udder.
He, like the rest of us, waited in silence for Mr. Spengler's
comment.

The wise Mr. Spengler said nothing.

"Alphonse," Duncan asked into the silence, polite as could be.
"Why are there Germans?"

Alphonse squinched his face and looked back at his charts,
trying to locate the meaning of this odd question. There it was,

jumping off the Chastity Index Chart on a bold black line. He slapped his pointer to the desktop and leaned forward with a menacing glare.

"If you'd been listening, Mr. Smartypants, you'd remember that chastity is a moral status, not just physical abstinence. Having babies within a legal marriage can hardly be condemned as unchaste."

"Oh," Duncan said. "I see."

"Soldiers aren't chaste," I said aloud, forgetting for a moment exactly where I was. "It's all of it so sexual." I looked to Flora, I imagine because I thought she was the only one there.

"Max?" Mr. Spengler interrupted my reverie. "What point is it you're making?" Mr. Spengler was always eager for my contributions, me being modern, as he liked to say, yet less confrontational than Flora.

"Excuse me?"

"Soldiers, Maxwell. You said something about soldiers."

Alphonse had a small spasm of snickering. I tried to focus my thoughts.

"Sir?"

"Soldiers, Max," Duncan put in. "Chastity."

"I see." And I began to remember. "I'm having some difficulty with my memory, sir." The windblown trees made wild shadows across the front of the room, dappling Alphonse and Mr. Spengler in a motley of bright and dark. I looked out the window. "Do you imagine memory can just disappear, Mr. Spengler? I mean, why couldn't it?"

The wind rattled the window casings. Mr. Spengler sighed a sigh and sat down on the front desk.

"It is odd, Maxwell. Odd and troubling. The mind is so elusive." He walked past the silent Alphonse and looked out into the wild spring day. "Everything shifts, I suppose. Sometimes so sharply we lose the thread. What connects one moment to the next."

I was watching the sky. A swarm of starlings dashed and

dove, buffeted by the winds, whipping and wobbling chaotically forward toward the western hills. I thought they'd be driven out of the sky, shot into space by an updraft, or buried deep in the black earth by a wild wind whomping down on them.

"I was in the Philippines, you're aware of that." He nodded at the class, and Flora in particular. "I was about to shoot a man, a sniper holed up in some thick woods. I'd flanked his position. I was within a few yards of him, and he turned and looked at me. We neither of us brought our guns up. Really we were too close. This pertains, I believe, to your question, Max. Stop me if I bore you.

"It was like greeting a man in the street. He offered me a cigarette, I suppose he didn't speak English, and we sat in those woods and smoked our cigarettes in silence. Just shaking our heads and laughing every now and again." He paused to remember.

"To get back, Maxwell, I could not connect those moments, before, stalking this sniper, and then enjoying this man's company. Somehow they're placed together, but in my head everything had slipped apart."

## 29 APRIL 1915

I met Mother for drawing in the afternoon. We met at home and took our picnic down to Cow Hollow like we've always done. April is rarely as stormy as it has been this month. All through it's been blustery and wet, weather whipping in every hour, a different season every day. I didn't know whether to wear my slicker or shorts, bring my sweater or go barefoot. Today I wore knickers, for old times' sake.

Really I wanted an actual lesson, with Mother teaching, and me maybe reading aloud, or following her clear directions. My mind was still adrift, blown through the crashing clouds and carried off above the ocean on a strong sea breeze. I needed a sturdy guide.

———

Mother spread our blanket and sat calmly, kit on lap, her little jelly treats within easy reach, no instructions forthcoming. She ignored my passivity, concentrating instead on her panorama. I opened Ruskin and began with Problem XI, "To Draw Any Curve in a Vertical or Horizontal Plane." Here was my anchor, my one stable mooring on this blustery afternoon. "Let AB be the curve. Enclose it in a rectangle CDEF. Fix the position of the point C or D." Of this I could be certain. It was older than the rich leather binding, old as the ocean winds. Mother smiled at my busy working hands, my careful lines. I sharpened my pencil every three inches or so, intent on keeping it razor-sharp, drawing the line as thin as could be. If I could locate each detail, isolate its form and place it in proper perspective, my landscape would, I was certain, come out right.

Mother got up to stretch, extending her arms up and back to improve her breathing, and twisted from side to side. She peered down at my crowded surface.

"That's a busy memory you have, pumpkin. So different from your earlier renderings."

"It's the structure, the forms and all. Before I was trying to make it up from the surface, eyeball stuff." This explanation sounded right enough. "This way it all comes out right." I looked up at her and forced a grin.

Mother smiled and looked away, strolling to the tree to lean there for a moment.

Maybe this is like my brain problem, I thought. Maybe memories have shapes like these and you lose the shapes or they shift and all your memories shift or disappear. If I found the proper set of forms, through which my memory would be accurately rendered. If I had the right steps, clear instructions from A to B. Maybe I have several sets pertaining to different things and they've gotten mixed. My weather forms all mixed up with my emotional memory. My family rendered as animals ought to be. Maybe there's an infected bone in my head. I thought of chastity and soldiers and Rupert Brooke buck-naked and spread-eagle in the mud of Ypres, ejaculating to the high heavens.

"What are you thinking, pumpkin?" Mother put in.

"Just how things are," I allowed, trying for honesty and tact. "I wonder about things."

She looked at me like mothers do, thinking, I supposed, that she was on my mind. And Father, and Mr. Taqdir, even though it wasn't that and I hoped against hope she wouldn't try to talk about that.

"Do you suppose my memory could collapse?" I started, before she got going about that. "You know, disappear somehow, or slip and shift till it seemed strange to me?"

She sat down, truly concerned, and brushed my dirty hair back with her hand. "Has something happened, Max?" I giggled from her hand tickling my ear, and it turned into a shiver down my spine. "Has something happened?" I thought. Has something happened? Has something happened? It wasn't that, exactly.

"Not exactly. I'm tired from staying up late." This truth surprised me. It was so simple. I hadn't thought I was about to tell her the truth. "Then sometimes I feel odd, like I'll never sleep again. Things can be so strange to me, like they're all the wrong size or they've moved somehow."

I became suddenly very frightened, as if these thoughts had been lurking and now came right around in front of me, freed by my saying them. Moments before I didn't know any of them, but now they all seemed so awful and real and true.

"Have you lost your appetite?" Mother asked, entertaining her own fears. It made me giggle again.

"No, no. I'm physically fine, except for not sleeping right. I just don't understand some things." But that sounded too much like *that,* and I could see the switches turning in her mind, adding what she was sure must be two and two. "It's not that," I said, by way of warning.

"Not what, pumpkin?"

"Nothing."

She paused and puzzled. "What do you mean about your memory, dearest? That troubles me."

I tried to think. I wanted to tell her exactly.

"I have trouble thinking sometimes. Not thinking really. I'm always thinking." But that wasn't it exactly. "It just feels strange, like I'm not thinking right, or I'm thinking *so* right and then I see things and my head is empty. I get shivers through my body." That much was true. I looked at her hoping she might see into my head and tell me what was happening. "Is that normal?"

She kissed my warm forehead. "You are not normal, dearest, thank the Lord. I fear you're upset by my actions."

"It's not *that*," I protested. "This isn't just that."

Now she'd done it.

"Pumpkin," she began, as if there were *any* words to undo what she'd done. I didn't bother listening.

"I am not just reacting to you or Father," I continued, not letting her speak. "I'm not just making up some false problem to puzzle over. This is *mine, my* problem."

"Let's not abandon reason, dearest. I was only suggesting."

"I don't care. About reason or you or Father or any of that. And I don't want your suggestions." How could she be so dumb? "I'm trying to understand something very strange to me, and you only want to talk about your stupid affair. Well, I don't want to talk about it." I wasn't sure if that was what I meant, but it seemed to shut her up. We sat uncomfortably silent, looking at various crumbs and goo-gobs on the faded tablecloth. It was getting dark now.

"What *can* I say, pumpkin? I want to help."

She had a knack for the wrong word. "I don't want *help*. I want a simple conversation. I was trying to share my thoughts with my mother, as all little boys should."

———

She began packing things back in the basket. The sky was black and clear to the east and deep blue over the hills west. I watched a yacht strung with colored lights chugging across the inky bay, puffs of white smoke trailing from its thin smokestack. I hated what I'd said but would not speak to undo it.

"I'm tired, pumpkin. I'm just very tired now," she said, and she took the basket and left me.

I walked around for quite a while, it might have been hours. My body was tired but my mind woke up as night came on. I thought maybe I'd walk to the Sutro baths and watch the people swimming but when I got there the baths were closed. It must've been almost midnight. I decided to go wake up Duncan.

"I want to show you somewhere," I whispered, lying down next to him and rocking his shoulder to wake him up.

He stretched and yawned, turning toward me and propping up on one elbow. "You're up still?" he asked. "I thought you'd been asleep all evening. Your door's closed."

"I've been with my mom."

"This late?"

"Earlier, for drawing. I've been walking around."

"Aren't you tired? You looked a mess today."

"I'll be tired, but I'm pretty awake now."

"You should've left a note on your door or something."

"Yeah? What would you've done if I left a note?"

He paused to think. "Nothing, I guess."

We lay there in silence, the nighttime breeze blowing in the opened window. I watched the blankets rise and fall with his soft breathing, and felt my own move in time with his.

"So come on. I gotta show you somewhere."

"No, Dogey, no. I'm so warm here." He started whimpering.

"Yes. I'm serious."

"Why? It's freezing out there." And he pulled the covers tight around him.

"It's not so bad once you're dressed and walking. You'll like it."

"You don't know that."

"I *know* that. You *will* like it, it's an adventure. It's a wilderness adventure."

"Ooohh, spooky." He made a horrible spooky sound. "Will there be bats and things?"

"Yes, yes. Horrible screaming."

"Mine?"

"Yours," and I pulled the covers off. "Come on then, before it's dawn."

We were soon out of the house, Duncan scoffing a biscuit and me leading.

I wanted to take him to the woods up in the Presidio, to that place in the woods, the hollow looking west. I hadn't been there in the dark yet but I felt certain I could find it. I remembered routes mostly by terrain and not so much by sight. Particularly in the thick of the woods, I followed the feel of my feet on the ground.

The bright half moon cast our shadows as we walked, the night full with cool ocean air. No one was awake, it seemed, anywhere. Silence stretched out around us. We scrambled up into the trees, the moonlight shut out now by thick branches. Duncan had hold of my shirttail and kept bumping up against me or pulling back. I felt his breath, warm and billowing, against my bare neck, and kept on, blindly, through the woods.

The rough ground rose and fell beneath us, the trees so thick we'd brush against them without seeing. The moon was gone. I knew the path and could follow it so long as I didn't try and think. Down a short drop, left and quickly right, up a steady rise, the ground harder underfoot, over a small ridge and onto soft moss. We were there, so suddenly I almost didn't stop. The trees opened up around us. The half moon came clear among the clouds again. We stood in silence, breathing, and listened to the ocean breaking against the rocks below. Buoy bells clanged their warnings to ships at sea. The water broke white against rocks caught in the dim moonlight.

"It's this," I said. "Right here."

Duncan sat down on the damp moss and looked into the soft rustling of the eucalyptus. He turned to me, his eyes bright white in the dark brown of his face. "Spooky," he said, quiet and quick, and he shivered.

"Yeah," I agreed. "Right here." And we both watched in all directions, the shadowy mess of treetops and down low into the thicket, around the soft stretch of moss and out across the wide-open water. I wanted to say how I felt here but that wasn't possible.

Hollow metal banging came crashing up from the rocks, scaring white birds out of the treetops. The waves kept up their rhythm, heavy and slow, drawing off the rough tumble of land and surging back again. The metal banged again with each wash of water hard into the rocks. Then there was a terrible sound, metal scraping metal, and men's voices yelling in some strange tongue.

We stretched and strained to look down onto the rocks. White foam splashed high and took the shapes of phantoms, ghostly blobs engorged against the black face of the rock, then gone back into the sea. In the waves we thought we'd spotted the prow of a boat, certain we'd seen its outline. Water washed over the gunwales. Its nose dipped dangerously and battered in close to land's end. It may have truly been a ship, but what I saw went under while what Duncan saw floated free and disappeared to the east.

The awful metal scraping started in again, gathering its pitch and wail to a pinnacle and a gunshot snap. The yelling was loud now, and angry. One water-washed phrase was garbled in the roaring waves, and a chorus of other voices yelled back, growing distant. And the metal banging was gone.

———

Duncan had leaned out over the edge, holding tight to the trunk of a heavy fir, and stretched as far as he could. We couldn't go down, for fear we'd never make it back up. The man's voice kept up a long time, more and more frantic, and then stopped.

"Anything?" I asked Duncan, hoping he'd seen what happened.

"Nothing. What we saw was waves, I think." We kept quiet and strained to hear, but the wind and water were as full of phantom sounds as the night was of ghosts. Each moan and call sounded like a dying man or a criminal, scrambling uphill all bloodied and ruthless.

"I can't tell if that's him," I said. It worried me, every sound was so ambiguous.

"That's water, or birds, I think."

Loud laughing came at us again, only now it sounded much more like wild water. Duncan looked at me and then peered out over the edge.

"That's water, too," he said.

"No. That's a man." And the sound came rushing up through the woods again, more watery still.

"That's water for certain."

I first thought he must be wrong, that everything I'd heard and seen meant this must be a man, crushed to death and bloody against the rocks. But that reality was too frightening and impossible to deal with. I huddled close to Duncan, seeking comfort in his explanation.

"It sounds so weird," I whispered to him. "It's like this here all the time."

"You heard it like this here before?"

"Yeah," I answered quietly, remembering my dream and the deep sleep of last time. "It's the shape of the hill, and the rocks down there. Every time it's weird. That's why I brought you here." It seemed possible.

Duncan smiled and looked up through the ghostly trees. "Jesus, Max, it's wild. It sounds so real." He rolled back across the moss and groaned hysterically up into the night, spreading his arms and pushing against the damp ground. I felt glad for his enthusiasm, and quickly buried my secret fear that what we'd seen and heard, however incomplete, could not have been simply rocks and water.

Duncan's laughter wobbled all around me. The tall trees, waving in the blackened sky, the water beating on the rocky shore, the empty night turning on its pivot toward dawn. I lay still in the hollow. The mystery of that broken man echoed inside my sleepless head, and slipped away to hide inside me.

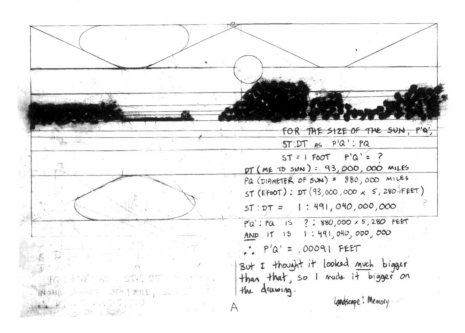

FOR THE SIZE OF THE SUN, P'Q',

ST:DT AS P'Q' : PQ

ST = 1 FOOT   P'Q' = ?

DT (ME TO SUN) = 93,000,000 MILES

PQ (DIAMETER OF SUN) = 880,000 MILES

ST (1 FOOT) : DT (93,000,000 × 5,280 FEET)

ST : DT =   1 : 491,040,000,000

P'Q' : PQ   IS   ? : 880,000 × 5,280 FEET

AND  IT  IS   1 : 491,040,000,000

∴ P'Q' = .00091 FEET

But I thought it looked much bigger than that, so I made it bigger on the drawing.

Landscape: Memory

A

## 2 MAY 1915

This from *The Call:*

> Joseph H. Hunt, wealthy fruit packer, and his wife are prostrated at their home in Oakland over the tragic death

of their thirteen-year-old son, Harold. Edith Akerly, the lad's girl chum, who made a heroic attempt to save him, is in the hospital.

The boy was thrown into the lake when his canoe was overturned by a gust of wind as he was paddling across to keep a tennis engagement with Miss Akerly. After swimming a short distance he suddenly sank, but came up again, calling calmly to his chum, "I am all right. I'll be fine." Miss Akerly told doctors that young Hunt swam about in small circles as though dazed. He looked around him, calling again, "I am all right, Edie. I'll be in soon" and then sank.

The brave girl was standing on the shore when she saw the boy sink, tore off her outer dress and plunged into the lake. She swam about waiting for him to come up. The body of the boy was recovered an hour and a half later but no spark of life remained.

Dear Robert,

There's a game we play with the four or five of us on watch when it's near to dawn and even the snipers have fallen into a dead sleep. Each man takes a card and slaps it face out up to his forehead so that everyone else can see and we proceed to bet good money on it. No one knows what card they hold. We're silent as church mice.

Could you send along a dictionary? We speak so seldom (silence being our best protection) that I fear I'm losing my English. Dirt flies off shrapnel bursts and my every thought is contained in action—sudden flight, a waving of arms, rapidly shifting facial expressions strung together like sentences. No words intercede.

I wonder about the night, its many secrets. Is that where wisdom lies?

———

## 4 MAY 1915

It must be three o'clock a.m. now. I've got a candle lit in a giant Persian lantern all filigreed and fancy, casting spooky shadows, dancing across the heavy carpets hanging on the walls, all shapes of women and animals and crouching men. Duncan's fast asleep and I will be soon, but this lantern's got me all dreamy and scared. I wanted to put it down *now,* not remembering.

The candle's burned an hour or so. It's bright inside the metal chamber, bright yellow brass. It's dripping wax out the bottom where the walls curve in and the shapes give way to a filigreed border. I can convince myself the flickering figures are alive. They jump and bob, knocking into one another, playing out some ancient play that's lived in this lamp forever, come to life with the flicker of flame, and composed of whatever they're cast upon. In this room it's wooden walls and carpets, books full of non-sense, and black windows they fall through.

I've blown it out now. The metal's going cold. There's enough light out there to see in the night, once you get used to it. I see shapes sharper than daytime and if I look off to the side I can make out the finest details, like the words I'm writing. I can see them only if I look sideways past them. But you've got to keep your eyes moving, otherwise things just disappear.

# The Fair
# at Night

---

24 MAY 1915

It was night again, and there was no moon out. I'd walked from the house through a neighborhood I rarely went to, just uphill from the Fair at its east end. It was still warm from the day and I sat on the stone steps of a large wooden house opposite a family's picnic, feeling the warmth of the stone through my thin cloth trousers. It was twilight then, and the evening stars were bright, other stars emerging, and the sky going black. I watched it all from the steps, just resting there, leaning back on my elbows, resting and feeling the breeze blow across my bare arms and face.

The family had two dogs with lace-lined party hats tied by bows to their doggy heads. The children were dressed up too, some as clowns and others nearly naked Indians. The mother came out the wide-open front door bearing bowls of punch and sporting a hatchet, its blade buried in her skull. It must have been a novelty. They had electric lights, as we did, but seemed also to have some uncommonly strong spotlights, perhaps stage lights and certainly bright enough to be.

I watched the night sky, the thick wash of the Milky Way now in view, and pretended to pay them little mind. It was a night much like all the other nights. The Tower of Jewels lit like a bloody saber, climbing crimson into the black sky, the promise of fog sometime before morning, and most of the city, it seemed, walking the broad avenues of the Fair or taking streetcars and strolling their way over there. I had dressed dapper, just because. Collar and tie, a pair of clean trousers, a soft snap-brim cap and my face well-scrubbed. I even wore a clean white shirt. I don't know why. It felt nice to dress neatly, I suppose, like camouflage.

There by this family I felt invisible, the night settling in and them awash in their own bright lights, playing some elaborate pantomime probably of their own devising. Its meager plot tumbled forward to a close, and then came the dousing of the lights. Everything went suddenly dark.

I felt bathed in the night then, it snapping shut around that big family, wrapping us all up together, and the Indians whooping their courage against the total darkness, whooping loud and long up into the cool, smoky air. Dogs howled and I howled too, on impulse and undetected, howling up to the stars, my neck stretched and chin way up till my head went dizzy, and I howled some more. I could see some now, not just the stars, but the ghostly glow of the pale-skinned Indians running and rolling in the big lawn, laughing and calling in some new game with the clowns.

"British bulldog, British bulldog," I heard one calling loud, and then all the rest rushed at him, all but one reaching the far end of the yard, and that one wrestled to the ground by the boy in the middle, an Indian shorter than me.

"British bulldog," he called again, and the pack rushed back, two now tackled by the two in the middle, so then there were four.

Neighbor kids were coming from out of the dark, running toward the call and joining the mob at one end of the soft, grassy lawn. They all pulled off their shoes and stockings, all familiar, I figured, with the rough-and-tumble of the game. I ran there too, tossing my shoes into the pile and pulling off my stockings as the throng went rushing into the fray, the middle now dense with Indians and clowns and neighbor kids all running and wrestling, wild and muddy.

I lined up for the charge, cocky and bold for no good reason, and I got in with an Indian, his bear hug well-timed and tight around my belly. I broke free when my top buttons burst and I twisted neatly out of my shirt and away to safety. There were eight of us left and nearly a score in the middle. I was tossed, my torn shirt, and I put it on again, always thinking.

"British bulldog" and we rushed in. I smartly lingered a moment, letting the hasty gangs engage themselves, each with a victim. Three of us made it through, I by guile and the other two by brute force.

I was down in an instant on the next rush, my shirt ripped away again and at least ten involved in my demise. The sweaty skin of several Indians smushed up against me and a clown puff fell within easy reach of my grabbing hand. We rolled and wrestled across the quickly muddied lawn, whole piles of dirty kids falling into the fray, no end to the game, and I uncontrollably laughing from excitement, dragging down whomever I could get my hands on.

The cold air was filled with hooting and howling, more kids than I'd ever grabbed before, rubbing each other senseless into the mud. It went on and on, of course, and ended as suddenly as that. Tired kids got up off the ground and poked around by the bushes, looking for shoes and shirts and this and that. They wandered back into the night, to houses whose windows were warm with firelight, up to their rooms or a bath and then bed.

I lay there and looked sideways across the muddy grass, my pale arms stretched out into the dark, and watched the bodies walking away. The ghost white of my shirt lay alone near the bushes,

one tear evident on the sleeve. My two black shoes were somewhere behind me. It was another moment like so many moments
these days. I watched the lights of the Scintillator playing its
curtains of color across the black sky above the bay and remembered that I'd meant to go to the Fair.

The Zone hooted and howled, its bare-bulb lighting shouting
up into the dark. Drunks reeled against the fence that ran down
Chestnut Street. I could see lines of revelers, their bowlers tipped
back, standing in wait for the Aerospace, watching its long iron-
boned arm lift the thin metal carriage up into space, an airborne
carton of gawkers leaning out against the fenced walls to see as
far across the fairgrounds as could be. Buddha gazed serenely
out into the night, from atop the center of Japan Beautiful, deep
in the Zone. Mother told me it was Buddha and that he always
looks sleepy like that.

I went in under the bright white lights at Fillmore, handing
my photo pass to a turnstile guard who looked at me with what
I took to be suspicion, though, given my appearance, it may
well have been concern.

"There's only an hour or so left," he warned me. "You'll not
be looking to stay in after closing now." He must have taken
me for a vagrant. A vagrant with a season's pass.

"No sir. I'll just be in for some rides. I'll go home to bed,"
I assured him.

I didn't go for rides straightaway, steering clear of the noisy
Zone and walking instead down the Avenue of Progress toward
the water. Bright banners hung high the whole length of the
avenue, beating about in the wind, casting shadows into stray
clouds of steam. They looked like lurid poppies floating in a black
pool, all poked and pushed by drunken fish, jumping around
there in the night. I got to feeling dizzy, what with the long
avenue leading off into infinity and the sky displaced by so many

colors. I turned into the shelter of the Court of Mines, its clean, manageable space marked off by high marble walls, sheltered from the wind and nonsense of the broad avenue.

I sat on a rough stone bench and took some deep breaths to relax. Really, the Fair was a bit much without a guidebook. Looking across through the central courts I felt buried by the avalanche of statuary and symbolic ornamentation, legions of nymphs and dryads and slumping Indians facing off against stout pioneers. And all the colors. The guidebook or Mother could set it all straight, accounting for each and every pairing and juxtaposition in the various courts. But now it was a dizzying muddle, what with the jumbled colors leaping off into the night and me feeling a bit piqued. I took some more breaths and looked down into the pretty pink gravel, just watching my two shoes set firmly on the ground.

I saw a pair of lady's boots come into view, a few feet from my shoes, their tips pointed toward mine.

"I see you're in distress," a lovely lady's voice announced. "You don't look well at all." She sat down beside me and put her warm hand to my forehead. "You'll forgive my impertinence, but I am a mother and will not stand on ceremony where a child's health is concerned."

"Do I really look as bad as all that?" I asked, soaking in her concern. "I know I'm a bit of a mess."

"More than a bit," she insisted, "and suffering chills to boot." She put a shawl about my shoulders and picked a clump of grass from my hair. "Your name, child. What's your name?"

"Maxwell."

"Maxwell," she repeated. "Listen to me, Maxwell. I am Mrs. Dunphy and Mr. Dunphy has gone home, as the Fair tires him. Are your parents with you?"

"I'm here by myself." I looked at her with sincerity. "I only need a little rest. I'm just dizzy from . . . all of this." We both looked out at the grotesque enormity of it all.

"It is a dizzying sight," Mrs. Dunphy agreed. She shifted

around on the bench, tilting her head toward me, beckoning some sort of response.

"I find the avenues leading out to the water especially difficult. It's so unclear whether they end, and the wind is too much for me."

"Yes, precisely." She nodded her head sagely. "The Fair *is* a difficult treasure, Maxwell. I'm afraid you've not been adequately prepared for its scope."

I took some very deep breaths and smiled a reassuring smile. Mrs. Dunphy kept her hand firmly on my shoulder, keeping me from getting up just yet. I felt bolstered by her strength and calm.

"We'll catch our breath for a few more minutes," she announced, "and then go on to the Court of Ages. It's important you not miss it. You'll need a guide, and it shall be me."

"Of course," I agreed. I was happy to oblige, glad to let myself into her care, rather than striking out into the mysterious Fair alone.

A tiny motorcar came chugging by, pulling a train of tourists in topless carriages, its many compartments hooked like railroad cars in a long snaking line. Off they chugged past the stone caldrons (bubbling thick with red liquid and steam), beside the tall walls of the Palace of Mining, and through the high arch leading to the Court of Ages.

"We'll soon follow them in," Mrs. Dunphy said, watching me stare in wonder at the disappearing lights of the caboose.

I ruffled my shoes across the gravel with vigor and smiled brightly at my kind guide, trying to cover my vague dread and nausea. Things still loomed too large and lurid. Grotesque figures stared down from parapets, tiny tourists ferried about below, like brittle little sticks in a raging river.

We walked from our sheltered spot past the grim stone murals, past the plantings and lovely green lattice, and through the Gothic archway into the Court of Ages. The black night sky opened up wide, let loose as the buildings drew back from their close arrangement in the side court. Here the plaza spread out in broad sweeps from the central fountain and throngs milled about the wide-open space, dwarfed by the architecture and towering statuary.

Mrs. Dunphy took my arm and led me toward the center.

"Mullgardt," she began, referring to the genius behind this design, "has succeeded in putting into architecture the spirit that inspired Langdon Smith's poem 'Evolution,' beginning 'When you were a tadpole and I was a fish.' The whole evolution of man is intimated here from the time when he lived among the seaweed and the turtles and the crab."

The whole evolution of man. It seemed an impossibly long time to have put into these massive walls. The presence of those ancient ugly fish swimming frozen in the stone was like a pressure on my eyes. I felt the walls might soon tumble forward, collapsing from the sheer momentum of the ages, let loose like some swollen river finally breaching the levees.

"Even the straight vertical lines used in the design suggest the dripping of water."

I watched clouds of steam roll out above the rough-blown water of the fountain. A light burned blood-red deep within the wide pool. Stone serpents twisted out of heavy caldrons along its perimeter, tangling their slithery forms around gas flames, their sharp eyes staring out in all directions.

"Did Mullgardt design the fountain as well?" I asked to be polite.

"That's Aitken, Maxwell."

"Is he also concerned with fish?" I lost sight of her as a cloud of steam blew in around us.

"Aitken has played with Mullgardt's elemental theme, drawing us back to our primeval origins, further back than even the fish, back, I believe, to the very origin of the planet."

I looked again at the fountain. A small child was playing on the lip, dipping her bare foot into the glowing pool, testing, it seemed, for depth and temperature.

"Specifically, the pagan conception of the sun, Maxwell. Aitken has used the notion that the sun threw off the earth in a molten mass to steam and cool down here and to bring forth those competitions between human beings that reveal the working of the elemental passions."

An older sibling sneaked up and gave the little girl a shove, neatly grabbing her wrist in the same motion. This set her to horrible screaming and an ill-advised tug away from her brother. Attentions turned toward them. Mrs. Dunphy drew me away.

We left the fountain and went west toward two enormous snowflake ornaments, lofted to midair on thin columns. The two flakes burned bright as suns on either side of us, obliterating all else by their light.

"They look like stars, don't they?" Mrs. Dunphy asked as we paused between them.

"From very far away, I suppose."

"Yes." And she paused, for just a moment, to entertain my thought. "And yet they have a history behind them." I closed my eyes to listen to all the sounds as Mrs. Dunphy picked up the thread of her lecture. "They are like the monstrance used in the Catholic Church to hold the Sacred Host, the wafer that is accepted by the faithful as the body and blood of Jesus Christ. These very ornaments contain the Sacred Host in a small glass bulb at their center."

I looked but could not see to their center. The light was too bright.

"They've got a bit of flesh?"

"As it were. Blessed wafer accepted as flesh." A brass band struck up from the Court of the Universe, their *oom-pahs* wavering in and out of sync with the strains of a string quartet close by the fountain. Voices were being raised again back by the lip and the little girl had taken to a constant wailing.

"Observe how the ideas in the structure of the walls of the

court are carried on in the ornamental details and the tower. The primitive man and woman repeated in a row along the upper edge, drawing the eye naturally to the religious figure in the apse of the tower. Some believe it to be Buddhistic in origin, but it belongs to no particular religion."

The string quartet kept on. All around us people seemed to be moving swiftly toward the central court.

"Will they really blow it all up this winter?" I asked, too dizzy and distracted to inquire about meanings.

"Perhaps not, Maxwell. Some say the city will set it all in stone, if funds can be raised." We looked around the full sweep of the court, I imagining it first blown to bits, then set in stone, a crumbling ruin fixed forever in gray, weathered granite.

Our costumes fluttered in the strong wind blowing in off the bay. Wild currents swirled over the high walls, raising rubbish up in dust devils around the broad court. The brass band and quartet had stopped, perhaps long ago.

"Are you quite all right?" Mrs. Dunphy asked again, looking in close to my eyes. "You seem rather dizzy."

I *was* quite dizzy, and suddenly very empty, feeling as though something in my center had been drawn out with my last breath. It rushed forward with the cold wind. The air seemed to have suddenly gotten much richer or thinner, a queer chill running across my skin. Mrs. Dunphy took my arm and led me on.

Men and women were gathered all around in silent bunches, clotted thicker as we came near the center of the court. Stone fish stared benignly into the night, and I wobbled a bit and lay down on the ground, staring up into the black sky. Mrs. Dunphy was silent now, mute and dumb, her mouth moving and her head drawing near, then away. She was rushing off in a flurry, away into the dark. I could hear nothing.

———

I lay still and stared upward. Past gabardine trousers and flannel overcoats, beyond the colored lights and brittle domes, up into the night, through the chilly thin air, beyond Beachey's altitude record, past the pinpoint stars, beyond the most primitive bird flying alone through the crystalline spheres. I focused as far away, as distant and dark as my eyes knew how. It seemed possible, just then, that I might see through to its farthest end.

The crowd paid me little mind as they shuffled to and fro. Mrs. Dunphy had disappeared into the night to search, I felt certain, for a doctor or a priest or my parents. The sandy ground was cool against my back. A soft thumping beat into my bones through the solid earth, a rhythm of bumps and rumbles that you had to lie down flat against the dirt to feel. I turned my head and laid my cheek against the ground. That little girl was lying by the lip of the fountain, all wet and tiny like a kitten who'd been drowned or just born. Two men held her body down. A third had drawn a thick wool stocking tight across her opened mouth.

"When you were a Tadpole and I was a Fish, in the Paleozoic time . . ." Bits and scraps of songs were floating inside my mind. I felt the little girl's convulsions beating into me through the ground. Her tiny body seemed so powerful just then. Her head swung wildly around and I saw her look into me with eyes so big and black I felt I might fall forever into them. The depth of them gave me a spasm of fright so sudden I rose from the ground with no breath left in me.

Mrs. Dunphy was gone.

I walked away through the pink gravel and down the bannered boulevard, now nearly empty. There, far ahead, by the sea, my mother stood atop a tall thin column. She stared out across the bay, her victory robes flowing, set in stone, a laurel wreath round her head. I saw her in the last illumination, just before closing. Her shadow was cast into the heavy fog. It was rolling in again, displacing the little wisps of steam produced by the Fair's elaborate machinery.

A buoy flying a small black flag floated offshore, lit by a single spot, marking the sight of Beachey's plunge. I dropped big white stones and watched them disappear into the black water. The last lights shut down.

An attendant in nursing whites pushed a limbless man in his wheelchair, rattling along the gravel of the Florentine Court, last and alone excepting me, rushing to the gates before they were finally locked. The little man bounced about like overstuffed luggage, tipping this way and that, righted on occasion by his attendant, talking a blue streak in a language I didn't understand. It made me cry, more for myself being last and alone, I suspect, than for the man's hardship.

I didn't think to stay.

25 MAY 1915

Dear Robert,

What was that song we sang as children? That song about egg nog plum? You and I made it up when I was just three or four and sang it incessantly. Mousie plum, you're in a scrum, egg nog plum and then I can't remember any more. I've been hearing it sung as I drift into sleep, but I'm certain it's just a trick of the mind. I've put in for a transfer off the medicals but it seems very unlikely.

There is something about the smell of things here, not just the blood and the sheer impossibility of ever burying the dead, but, also, our absolute failure. It's the stink of cordite and the mud and our own bodies too. I would ask you to send soap but soap is not what's needed. Lost Jeffers and Tolland both. Really I was quite lucky.

I can't sleep, it seems. I find my attention quickening as night comes on. And now that I'm up so long it seems a good idea to stay up even longer.

Duncan noticed today. He said, "You haven't slept, have you?" and I nodded no, I haven't. We were at home, him getting dressed and me sitting on his bed looking at the angle of the sunshine, it being very low and casting long shadows up against the fronts of houses. He sat down next to me and tilted my head back to look, I suppose, at my eyes or throat or something.

"Aren't you tired?" he asked, peering into my mouth.

"Not really. I feel kind of loose, like pudding."

He held me round the ribs and shook my loose body, testing.

"How long've you been up?"

"A day now. I slept pretty well before last night." I flopped back on his bed, stretching my arms up to the headboard, and looked for the battle lines of the Marne in the ceiling cracks. "I get all dreamy in my head, but not tired really. Do I make sense?"

He rolled up next to me and felt my forehead.

"You make sense. You just look a mess, like you're living in the woods. Take a shower. You'll think it's morning and you slept and everything." It seemed a good idea, so I did, and Duncan cooked breakfast and we went to school.

I noticed Flora's bosom today, how big it is and that I don't think she restrains it. My feet are too big for my shoes now. And Miss Gillian always closes her mouth when she's not speaking. I felt like prying it open by the end of class, it was so resolutely shut, as she listened with her bright eyes trained on the speaker.

Mostly I noticed the weather, it seeming so much larger and more important than all the talk. It really does move in over the whole face of things. You can smell it coming over the hills, foggy or clear, dry or damp or thunderstorm. It made me jumpy and frisky, just wanting to be out *in* it.

Flora and Duncan and I drove down the Great Highway and ran on the beach, letting all that air wash over me in waves and waves, air from far across the ocean blowing in steady over me, on my face, and I dove into the sand, and got up and dove again, and leaped as high into the air as I could, running far and fast through the wet salty air. I started to strip off my clothes, ready to run into the icy blue water, but Flora and Duncan bundled me off in bear hugs to the car, saving me from certain arrest and probably pneumonia. It was a wonderful day.

There is no more firewood here. I've burned all the wood wanting a good read by firelight. This room is beautiful in the flickering yellow light and shadows. It reminds me of the magic lamp, only these shadows and shapes are even older, unreadable, playing out in patterns you must unfocus your eyes on if you want to make sense of them.

I made it through one hundred and sixty pages of *Melmoth*. I read out loud to Duncan through almost sixty of those, until he fell asleep, curled in at my feet, next to the fire. That was very kind of him, as I know *Melmoth* is not what interests him. He's lying here still, drooling through his warm hand onto my sock, his head resting on my feet.

It's been foggy tonight, gray clouds hugging the ground, rolling close across the windows, close enough to take the flickering shadows of the fire on their faces, before they roll away again with the wind.

There is a light in a house across the way. It's the only light I see that keeps long hours like me. It's burned steady all night tonight, appearing and disappearing through the intermittent fog.

The house is tall and thin, with a stone path leading to its small porch. Inside, I'm sure, the stairs are steep and narrow, two flights of them leading up through the quiet, creaking night to the front room up under the eaves. That's where the light burns. Sometimes I see shadows moving across the curtains, and once or twice a face peering out, ever so briefly, through the neat gap between them.

I think it's a woman and I fancy she's writing a book, a romance adventure book, or thinly veiled autobiography detailing the horrible beatings she's suffered at the hands of her drunkard husband. He, no doubt, is buried in the basement, chopped to neat little bits and mixed with oatmeal, stuffed in canvas sacks and covered by six feet of dirt. She's got a dog, I'm certain, a St. Bernard, all full of fur and drool, who is her lover. Or she's Phoebe Hearst's secret lover, locked up on pain of death, showered with expensive gifts, and unable to leave her lonely prison. The dog, then, is merely her friend and confidant.

Her light has gone out. I wonder if she's seen me, and what she makes of me. There's just enough light left in the fire, I'm sure she can see that I'm still here, staying with her as late as she could possibly stay, last and alone. I'll go to get more wood.

26 MAY 1915

When I got up to go in search of wood Duncan woke and stretched and stirred, rolling his face toward the fire, and mumbled to me as if out of a dream, something about not leaving him just then.

"We need more wood," I explained. "I'm just going out to find some and bring it right back." He rolled back and wrapped around my leg.

"No, Dogey, no. You're staying here. It's warm and toasty. Be my friend."

"I am being your friend," I insisted, pulling my leg free. "I'm getting more wood to keep you warm." But he just lay there all pulled into a little ball.

"No, you keep me warm. Stay and read more, sleep here," and he turned his back again to me, scrunching up closer to the fire.

"I can't read in the dark."

He just shook like a shiver, pretending it was cold. I patted his shoulder and got up to go. I had set my mind on keeping this fire burning, just staying as we'd been, me reading through to the end and Duncan warm and sleepy by the fire.

"I'm going now," I said as nice as I could, pulling my boots on and buttoning a big sweater over my shirt. "I'll be right back."

"So wait for me," Duncan said, still sleepy but waking up just enough. "Dress me, get my pram."

"You *are* dressed, dummy."

"It's freezing out there," he complained, sitting up and yawning some more. "I'll need furs and a muffler."

"You're funny," I said, wrapping a throw rug around him.

"I'm cold."

I figured Lone Mountain was best for firewood, it being near and unlikely anyone would mind our clearing windfall from a graveyard. We walked down Divisadero to Turk and went west, the fog still hanging thick and silent. I felt we were walking out to sea, walking a long thin peninsula out into the dull gray waters, birds asleep or resting in the calm, the ocean surface like cold lead and silent, and all of it hidden by the heavy fog.

I called long and low, making the sound of a ship in distress, drifting with no compass. Dogs barked back. The clitter-clatter of their dog nails on concrete rattled up the walk, as loud as if they were prancing next to us.

"They need to install buoys," Duncan suggested, tugging his muffler down off his mouth.

The streets were empty as ghosts, nothing moving but us and the dogs. No motors ran, no children screamed or parents scolded, no trolley bells rang.

"Do you suppose we might get lost?" Duncan asked, bumping into me like a tugboat.

"If you like," I allowed. "We might get lost."

"I've never been lost in a graveyard."

"Have you been in a graveyard?"

"Yes." And he stopped bumping.

"I've only been for an uncle I never knew, and once just sneaking around," I said, remembering the odd formalities that attended my uncle's disposal. We all dropped black handkerchiefs into his grave.

"I went for a friend once. He died in the fire."

"The big fire?" I had just met Duncan then, on the boat to the lost-children's camp.

"Uh-huh. We buried him after I'd been in Oakland."

"After you'd been at the camp?" He hadn't said anything about his friend then.

"Yeah."

"Were you sad?"

"Yeah. We'd been best friends." He'd said something about a best friend before, but never that he'd died.

"You never told me he died."

"Nope. I don't think about it much."

"Why not?" If that had been my friend, I figured, that's all I would think about.

"It makes me sad, so I don't think about it." He looked at me now, to see if I understood.

"I guess I understand," I allowed. "But if it were me that's *all* I'd ever think about. I just can't help thinking about stuff like that."

We walked along Geary to the southern edge of Lone Mountain, looking through the mist up Greenwood, looking at the pale collapsing obelisk of James King of William. The Laurestina hedge was in need of a trim, all overgrown and tangled, reaching frantically up into the graying dawn like poisonous vapors. Duncan walked so silently. I kept looking to make certain he was there. He bumped up close and held on for a bit as we cut across the corner of Odd Fellows and on into Calvary.

This graveyard was not well kept. It was overgrown and thick with low twisted oak trees, all wind blown and shaggy, home to warblers and thrush. In its better days, my father told me, Calvary had an elaborate network of gas lines, feeding tiny guide flames, bordering all the paths at intervals of two or three feet. It was called then, he said, the Graveyard of the Eternal Flame, but the quake broke it to bits and now it's just Calvary again.

There was a row of Dunphys, laid out side by side, dead in a long succession of mothers and sons and babies who didn't have names yet when they died.

Dead flowers lay dry and crumbling on the flat gravestones. It looked so sad to me. I'd rather leave nothing than have it go so publicly bad. Duncan brushed them off into the overgrown yellowing lawn as we walked by. He was behind me, resting both hands on my shoulders as in Freight Train, only he didn't know about Freight Train.

I looked ahead, down the gentle slope of the hill. The rough grass covered its long face, disappearing down into the low-lying fog. We could see the black silhouettes of the oak trees gathered in a grove at the bottom. There seemed to be some broken limbs lying in the grass, fallen by their dead weight or blown off by the wind.

"D'you ever play Freight Train?" I asked Duncan. He was hopping now as we went.

"Nope," he said, sounding certain.

"It's just like we are now, except you need six or seven kids, all lined up, hands up on shoulders." Duncan started making train sounds.

"Does it have to be in a graveyard?" he asked, chugging right into me and taking the engine spot.

"No, but you've really gotta get a bunch of kids. Otherwise it's just engine and caboose and that's not right. You can't *always* be engine and caboose, it's just too much." But my caution went unheeded. Duncan tooted and chugged us down the hill without a second thought, and I just followed, attached by the game to his undisciplined engine.

We loaded armloads of mostly rotting wood and walked back up toward the crest of the hill. The sky had washed out gray in the east where the clouds had lifted up from off the land. At Masonic we tossed the wood over, hoping no one was up and about to be beaned by our treasure. The good wood bounced with a healthy bang, and the rest landed, we could hear, like crumbling sand or damp cardboard. The bad wood we left there, in the bushes.

Some assorted citizens were out, briskly taking their morning constitutionals, motoring past us on legs like pistons, grunting a hearty hello or making some comment about wood. It was good we lived near else our arms might have dropped off.

I walked behind Duncan and watched the lines of sweat drip out of his wet dark hair, down his bare neck, and disappear into his shirt. It was a night like so many other nights.

At home he slept and I stoked the dying embers with our damp wood, reading in the gray light of dawn while the oak smoldered and smoked, finally catching flame after a good half hour of slow kindling. It was an elixir to me, that plucky yellow flame, coming clean in the thick smoke, dancing up into the blackened bricks of the fireplace. I sat up close as could be, watching its wispy base licking the wood, uncertain what its connection must be and unable to locate its activity. When a flame is just catching, one can't really see the wood burn, only the bright, flickering light. I couldn't imagine those logs would eventually be consumed and I strained to watch as long as I could, waiting for the wood to turn to glowing coals, eaten hollow by the flame, waiting for the inevitable collapse of the whole thing, down into embers and ash.

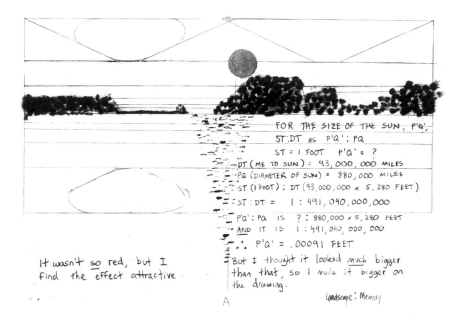

FOR THE SIZE OF THE SUN, P'Q',
ST:DT AS P'Q': PQ
ST = 1 FOOT   P'Q' = ?
DT (ME TO SUN) = 93,000,000 MILES
Pq (DIAMETER OF SUN) = 880,000 MILES
ST (1 FOOT) : DT (93,000,000 × 5,280 FEET)
ST : DT =   1 : 491,040,000,000
P'Q': Pq IS   ? : 880,000 × 5,280 FEET
AND IT IS   1 : 491,040,000,000
∴ P'Q' = .00091 FEET

It wasn't so red, but I find the effect attractive.

But I thought it looked much bigger than that, so I made it bigger on the drawing.

A

Landscape: Memory

## 27 MAY 1915

I'm not certain why or exactly when, but I went back to that small hollow in the Presidio woods last night. I was dirty and cut from the fog in thick so long it made mud of the woods. I was slipping and sliding and grabbing too late at handholds I couldn't see, it being night still. Birds were crazy in the trees this time. I listened for the laughing and the metal banging like before, convinced it really was the rocks and wind, but it wasn't. Not nearly like with Duncan. The wind blew stronger this time, and yet no sound came up, at least none so human as before. Something real is down there, I know that now.

First I thought of the man down there, and then the birds. I looked up to see them and the clouds got pushed away as if by a hand sweeping a black slate clean, leaving the pinpoints of white pocked forever into the empty slate. Those glorious stars, drenching the sky like milk, precious and liquid, a present to me. I was sunk down deep into the moss, my mouth open to the black, black sky and those thousands of inexhaustible stars. I couldn't sink down far enough, having nothing but air to press me down. If only I could be plunged into a volcano or swallowed by the ripping fault right then, the earth sucking me into its rich black dirt all wrapped around me and rumbling, shaking loose rocks and scree and trees knocked silly to the ground. I tried willing so many things there and then and none of them worked.

I looked down into the black water pounding white against the rocks. The wild shapes were rising again. I thought as clear as I could of that body that must have been battered, the rock cutting into its face and crushing the bones, and the fact of that man dead. I couldn't help feeling the hollowness of my own body.

Something inside me broke loose then. I felt it somewhere below my belly. This feeling broke loose and started a sort of wobbling, a sobbing rising up my throat like sickness. I hadn't known it was there inside me, but there it was now, filling me up entirely, making my body shake and filling my head with spit and snot, bursting in my head like a flower, all watery with tears and snuffling. It was all over me like warmth or a fragrance and I couldn't stop it. It broke out through my eyes and throat in tears and sounds I'd never heard from inside me before, scratchy awful sounds that rattled the bones in my head and stopped only to let me gasp my breath back in again. It was a sound beyond words, some terrible, primitive song inside me wailing in a roar through my body. I couldn't keep it in. I rolled up in a ball, letting it all run through me, like somewhere a river ran wrong and I was now its mouth.

My crying was a convulsion that ended by my body giving up.

Finally I could only lie still and stare down the long drop to the dead man silent and empty, wasted on the black rocks below.

———

It all got so soft then, the breeze calm and the sea gone to washing waves across the rocks, not crashing as before. My head had gone soft from all the noise and fury. And now it had all run dry, drawn out from the middle of me.

A memory came into my head then, like a dream. I'd known parts, but never all of it, and it came in like dreams do, running through my head from beginning to end.

I am seven. I sit up in my big bed, looking out the open window, a large oval of glass set on two pins so it pivots open. It is dark and very early, no *clip-clop* or *clanky-clank* from outside. No milkwagon or iceman or horses yet. I rest my arms on the wooden sill and stick my head out into the nighttime air. It smells exactly as it smells in the hollow, exactly. Mostly salt air and moist, but rich with dirt smell too, and sweet wood smoke.

The air is cool across my bare skin. I wrap my warm flannel sheet around my little body and walk sneaky slow like an Indian to the bad-boy stairs. My room is at the very tip-top and it's two long flights down, narrow and steep, but quietest on these stairs because they don't cry if you step right on their edges. I go slow, hiding very small in my sheet.

The parlor sits so quiet, the carpet and chairs and the heavy brocade curtains all sleepy and resting there in the dark. I drop my warm sheet and run frisky to Father's footstool and sit down with a shiver, the plush velvet bristling against my bottom, and me politely chatting with guests, very grown up and interesting, naked as a seal. There's skitter-scatter sounds all from the dark places. So I get my sheet and walk very bravely to the big front door.

Our frame house is wooden but the front steps are heavy stone. They stay warm even after dark but now they're cold. The top step feels cool and smooth on the bottoms of my bare feet. I'm looking west, over Josky's house and the Joyces' and then the high pale dunes, out into the black night sky, all clean and brisk and washed with all the stars. First are the play dunes and next are the big dunes. After that's the desert and it goes on forever. I can smell the sea. There's sand on our stone steps too and I push my palms against it.

Next door's Mattie's and then there's the big dog who doesn't like me. He's howling now, like wolves do but less brave, sort of whimpering. It's spooky but he has a fence. I walk across the wagon lane, along the Joyces' path and onto the sand, pushing my feet in deep to where it's still warm. It's lovely all over me. I doggy-walk on hands and knees up to the top and tumble down into the hollow. All the stars stretch out in the deep black lid above me. I scrunch and squirm, working my body back into the dune, staring up into the night.

There's a rumble like God's train is rolling right down the dunes at me, and it's getting impossibly deeper and deeper so it's not a sound anymore but a motion. Now the ground sets to bucking, bumping me up and down into the dunes like wild waves or a motorcar or Father bouncing knees on my bottom, gallop gallop gallop and him whinnying high and wild. An ugly sound comes over the dunes and into me like heat, a horrible sound, long and scraping like pulling metal spikes from concrete or raking giant nails down chalkboards. I feel it singing in my bones.

I remember it like this: my body going loose and the backs of my eyes feeling warm and full. Now I call it fear or terror.

The face of the sand kept dropping. There were crashing sounds from houses, snapping and tearing sounds, and that awful sound of things pulling apart.

The earthquake set all the church bells ringing. Fire bells rang. Mr. Crowley screamed "Judgment, judgment!" in a horrible cracking howl. I saw him in his undershorts carrying a broken chandelier. Our street was buckled and bent. It hissed and spat in places where pipes had broken through. I lay at the top of the dune and watched, silent and shivery. I couldn't speak and I couldn't move fast. Everything looked flat and far away like at the cinema.

Nothing was familiar anymore. All up and down the street the houses were broken, fences fallen. I could see through places where before I couldn't. Yards disappeared under rubble and the street did too, all tangled and blocked. Some places were big holes like one near me with metal pipes poking out into air and a horse's head I could see reaching up out from the rim, wild-eyed, baring its teeth and foaming. It was on its side, fallen against the dirty wall of the hole, not using its legs right.

I walked away back into the play dunes where everything still looked okay and it was quieter if I got far enough in. I stayed in there for a while. I couldn't think much about things.

A woman came later, after some time when I sat in the sand. Her nightie smelled of gas and lavender, brushing up across my nose when she picked me up and held me. She said her name was Mrs. Porfoy and she was big and flush-red in the face, like the fat lady in the theater show, but she didn't sing to me. I was still very quiet, just saying little songs I liked some, just to myself really.

Mrs. Porfoy led me back into the terrible street, walking me up some way to where a man stood stuffing four little bundles. This was Mr. Porfoy.

Mr. Porfoy gave me his pajama top, which was big as my nightshirt and smelled all of wood smoke and old stockings, and he went bare-chested, all big and pasty white and hairy up his front. He let me ride on his shoulders, my legs wrapped round his neck, bare feet bouncing into his fuzzy chest. Mrs. Porfoy walked beside, carrying two bundles, like Mr. Porfoy did, only smaller.

———

"Can I see Mother and Father now?" I finally asked. People hauled their burdens through what clearings there were, calm and steady, dressed and undressed.

"Soon enough, child," Mr. Porfoy said up to me. "Mrs. Porfoy will be leading us back presently, won't you, dear?" He wiped his sweaty cheek against my leg, all bristly-whiskered and scratching.

"Yes, yes. We're going back, there now. You live near the dunes where you were playing, am I right?" And she nodded her head all closed mouth and certain. "That'll be right to where we're going." The air was dirty and dusty, full of bad smells and noise. Small collapsings and many yells and bells kept on and on, as they did the whole day.

I watched out over Mr. Porfoy's shiny-skinned head. All of the insides of people's houses had tumbled out, spilling from half-torn floors, couches and beds and chairs hanging or caught halfway down. I looked in at a bright green bird in its big cage and then a dog wagging its tail and barking from a sagging third floor. A family came toward us through the dust, pushing a black grand piano past broken bodies and rubble. The father was roped up front like an oxen, with a handful of children pushing the heavy burden from behind.

"This isn't my street," I said. "I live on Kirkham Street."

"This is Kirkham Street, honey," Mrs. Porfoy said. "We're coming up on your place now." But she was wrong. Nothing was there.

"It's not my street," I said again. "I live in a blue house on Kirkham Street."

"Maybe the child lives farther on, sweetheart," Mr. Porfoy put in, patting me with his sweaty hand. "Don't be scaring him now. What are you thinking?" We stopped, Mrs. Porfoy all huffy and silent, just looking at us. Mr. Porfoy let me down off his shoulders.

"Stay right here, child," he said to me. "Right here now so

as Mrs. Porfoy and I can take a little look at our map." They walked off into the rubble a few feet away and had a fight. I stayed right there and watched a group of men lean their weight onto a broad wood beam, prying at a fallen wall that lay intact, fallen face flat forward into the street. A couple of kinds of crying came out from under it. A dog and a person and some baby cries all mixed in with the scream of heavy wood moving hard against itself.

I yelled hooray at them lifting and then at the buzz of an aeroplane high up in the blue sky. An aeroplane! Its engine roar so thin and distant, it wobbling its wings in the wild winds so high, high up in the cold cloudless sky. Oh, I marveled at it, flapping hard with my arms and running along the dirty path of people, roaring with all my voice.

"Hold there, honey," Mrs. Porfoy yelled long and strong, louder and clearer than anyone could yell, bringing me quickly back to the ground and turning me round from a good twenty yards away. It looked like a mile to me, far away as the aeroplane. I skipped briskly back, all breathless and happy to hear her yelling voice.

"Have you found them?" I asked, excited but tired now of playing. Mrs. Porfoy picked me up again and turned back toward the rubble.

"Mr. Porfoy's got some things to talk about, honey," she said, holding her warm hand to my cheek. "Some things he and you gotta talk about." She put me down in his little office, a neat arrangement of broken beams and barrel staves set around a bit of clear dirt. This was where they had fought. There was black smoke rising up over the hill now, and a steady flow of people north and east.

"What's your name, child?" Mr. Porfoy asked.

"Maxwell."

He nodded a lot, like he understood me.

"That's good, Maxwell. What are your folks called?"

"Mummy and Papa."

He nodded some more.

"I mean by other folks, what do other folks call your mummy and papa?"

"Mrs. Kosegarten and Mr. Kosegarten. Or sometimes Corny calls Mummy Mrs. K. and Papa calls her that too."

He nodded more so I stopped, even though there were more names they called each other and their first names which I hadn't said yet.

"Now listen good, Maxwell, what I'm telling you isn't simple. I've been on this here telephone and heard your papa's been gone to help out rescuing and such. Your mama, too," and he waved back behind him at the telephone or where they'd gone or something important because he kept on waving for a bit. "They went early, couldn't wait around for you."

"Where?" I only half-believed him.

"Oh, I don't know where, but they've gone now. Couldn't be waiting round what with all this disaster. Don't know when they'll be back." And he shook his head, all puzzled, I guessed, because he couldn't figure out why they'd gone so fast and without me.

"Maybe they're waiting," I said, trying to help Mr. Porfoy make sense of it all.

"Nope, not waiting. They've gone for sure," and he nodded some more. We sat there for a moment, puzzling.

"Can I talk on the telephone?" I asked, thinking it was almost as good an idea as my first one. "They'll probably want to meet me."

"Nope, no good. Phone's broke now, just after I heard about them two. It's a real shame, but what with the disaster and all." He waved his arms around at all that had gone wrong.

We sat there together, quiet and helpless. I got very sad and started crying and he held me and I cried and cried on him, wondering how come they left me and why I couldn't meet them at the house or somewhere.

Mrs. Porfoy sat down with us and stroked my hair which helped me cry more and I pushed my face in against Mr. Porfoy's chest, tasting my tears and his sweat, all snotty and snuffly and shaky in my limbs.

We joined the procession toward the city, me up again on Mr. Porfoy's shoulders and Mrs. Porfoy singing soft church songs and touching me with her warm wide hand.

She asked me questions about my school subjects. She asked, "And how do you spell 'torn.'"

And I answered, "T-O-R-N."

And she went on to more difficult words like "though" and "carry" and on to mathematics and geography. She kept looking about, right and left and right again. Looking always into the strange, shifting ruins that stretched away in all directions, all the time asking questions.

"What is the largest state in the Union?" she asked.

"Texas," I answered. "And California is second," I added because I knew that fact by heart. There were bodies laid out in rows all along the dirty street.

"And can you name three of the seven seas?" A wing of a great building up ahead shuddered and collapsed inward. At first there was no sound.

"The Pacific and the Atlantic," I began. The sound of collapsing reached us from up ahead. Dust rose in a heavy cloud, but there seemed to be no fire. "And the Indian Ocean," I finished, remembering a name I could only remember because I've seen Indians swimming in the ocean.

"And which is the only island continent?"

I didn't know the answer.

"It's Australia, honey," Mrs. Porfoy said. "Australia. Think of an ostrich," she suggested. "An ostrich buries its head to be alone. Australia is the only continent that is alone, an island. Ostrich. Australia."

———

We'd come in past the park and over the crest of a high hill. The bay spread out below, just visible through the thick black smoke drifting north across the city. Mr. Porfoy set me down to sit close by Mrs. Porfoy on a little plot of green grass. He went away to talk to soldiers.

"Where've Mother and Father gone?" I asked carefully, testing Mr. Porfoy's story.

Mrs. Porfoy smiled wide and sad and breathed out her nose like dogs do settling down.

"Don't know," she said simply. "I don't really know." And she rubbed my small shoulders and gazed out across the smoky vista. "I do believe Mr. Porfoy's asking those soldiers there right this very minute about your folks." I was glad. It seemed a good idea to ask soldiers.

"Are we going to a hotel?" I hoped we were. The time Mother took me to town we stayed in a hotel.

Mrs. Porfoy shook her head and chuckled, making me giggle too. "Oh, no sir, no sir. I don't know quite yet *where* we're going. Mr. Porfoy's got to find that out too." And she nodded her head up and down and up and down, yes, yes, yes, yes. I nodded too, giggling and silly now to make her laugh more, yes and yes and yes and yes, and she laughed out loud and pushed me and smushed me in a big hug there in the green grass.

Mr. Porfoy said the soldiers said to go to Golden Gate Park where there'd be food and tents and Mrs. Porfoy told him I wanted to go to a hotel.

"We'll do better than that for you," he said, picking me up in his big hands. "You'll get a boat ride to Oakland, over to a nice fancy camp."

"Why can't I go to your camp?" I didn't want to lose them just now.

Mr. Porfoy set me down and crouched as low as he could.

"These soldiers tell me your folks'll be looking for you in Oakland. It's a special camp, a camp for lost children."

I thought so many things at once I just puffed air out my nose and arranged my arms all impatient the way Father did. I started with the important stuff.

"Are they there now? Mummy and Papa?"

"Might be," Mr. Porfoy allowed. "Won't know till we get there."

"Are you going with me?"

"Well, now. I'm figuring Mrs. Porfoy to go over and I'll set us up here so we don't get left out in the cold. We'll get you over there safe, Maxwell."

I looked at Mrs. Porfoy to see if this was true. She raised her eyebrows some but didn't speak up. I figured that meant okay.

"Why do I have to go to the lost-children's camp if I'm not lost?"

"So your folks'll find you, sweety, like Mr. Porfoy said."

"Why couldn't the soldiers tell them to meet me at your tent?"

Mr. and Mrs. Porfoy looked at each other some and laughed a little but I stayed stern and steady, waiting for an answer.

"We don't know which tent's ours yet, honey," Mrs. Porfoy told me, wagging her head all fiddle-faddle like I was going to be a pest in a half second. "Otherwise we'd tell those soldier boys just that." I kept my lower lip out and arms tightly crossed trying to figure if there was anything I missed, but it all seemed unbreachable. I took Mrs. Porfoy's hand in mine as tight as I could.

We three stayed together into the city. The smoke was thick and Mr. Porfoy soaked handkerchiefs in water and we tied them over our faces like bandits do. A woman in a chair sat by a burned-up building with a rifle across her lap and clean white china stacked neatly beside. It was hot from the fire, and thunder rumbled long and loud from buildings blown up by dynamite. The army blew them up to keep the fire from spreading, Mr. Porfoy said. I don't like this part so well. Mr. Porfoy saw a man, we saw him too, in a window where soldiers were putting dynamite and he ran yelling because we thought maybe they didn't see the man. But they did see him because they yelled back at us. And when Mr. Porfoy went into the building, this man upstairs being so old and weak-looking we thought he must need help getting down and maybe the soldiers just didn't hear him, they blew up the building right then, when Mr. Porfoy was going in to help this man. They said it was martial law, which is what they said to Mrs. Porfoy to help her from being so hysterical and all, she couldn't speak through her crying. She was all tears and snot so it seemed she was choking and I thought for certain she was and couldn't breathe or hardly move. She just collapsed there onto the ground, with me leaning over her big back trying to hug her to keep from being so scared as I was by what was happening.

It was a long time there. There was nothing more she said to me. Finally, she was so tired she stopped shaking and was quiet and still. She looked at me and hugged me a long time so it would be better. I tried holding onto her, holding all I could reach while we walked away toward the water and the ferry dock. She wrote my name for me on white tags to put on my wrists and kissed me. She squeezed me, lifting my feet off the ground, and she left. I knew I shouldn't say anything so I didn't.

There were thousands of children from tiny to big and only a handful of mothers filling the wide flat ferries as fast as they came. I stood at the back of the boat and watched the water churning white behind us. The land and city and busted buildings were burning. Mrs. Porfoy and all of it were drawing swiftly away. The ocean air washed the smoke smell from out of my hair and blew salty strong and clean across my bare skin, puffing up my pajama top in gusts and filling my open mouth. A boy in too-small shorts, their top button bursting, stood next to me and looked at me tentatively, all red-eyed from smoke or crying and smudged with black ash all over. He said, "I'm not really lost," and I said, "Me neither," and this was Duncan. We said some things and jostled some and turned to watch the black smoke rolling up into the dusky sky. The late sun had turned blood-red and orange over the buildings still collapsing into flames. We stood there as close as we could, shoulder by shoulder, and watched the city burning.

It wasn't *so* red, but I find the effect attractive.

FOR THE SIZE OF THE SUN, P'Q',
ST:DT as P'Q': PQ
ST = 1 FOOT    P'Q' = ?
DT (ME TO SUN): 93,000,000 MILES
PQ (DIAMETER OF SUN) = 880,000 MILES
ST (1 FOOT): DT (93,000,000 x 5,280 FEET)
ST:DT =    1 : 491,040,000,000
? : 880,000 x 5,280 FEET
1 : 491,040,000,000
00091 FEET
- it looked much bigger
o I saw it bigger on

Landscape: Memory

## 31 MAY 1915

This part is very odd for me to write. So much of it is strange and new to me. The first part is two nights ago.

I fell asleep in my bed near dawn and slept almost till ten at night. I just slept like a rock must sleep, impenetrable numb, dumb sleep. Only when I woke up did I realize how dirty and hungry I was. I had mud and cuts on me and my whole body felt empty and eager for food.

I took a long soak in the tub and Duncan heard me filling the bath. This was the first I'd seen him since the previous dawn when he went off to sleep and I was gone God knows where before he woke. I hadn't been back here and awake till now. I felt like I'd gone overseas to the war and come back now. I felt so happy at seeing him, as if it had been in doubt whether I'd ever see him and there he was.

He'd been in bed not sleeping, wondering if I'd ever wake.

"I thought you'd decided to sleep three days now to make up," he yelled from his dark room, not wanting to leave the warm covers.

"Well, I didn't," I yelled back. "Get up. I'm hungry."

"Fuck you." He'd started saying fuck because, word was, soldiers at the front always said fuck.

"Do you remember us meeting after the earthquake?" I yelled because I wanted to talk about it.

"What?"

"The earthquake," I repeated.

"What about it?"

"Do you remember it?" I got out of the tub and shook my hair. I dried off on a towel Mother had brought over, and put on some shorts that were probably Duncan's.

"Come here so I can hear," Duncan yelled and I did, tossing the towel at his sleepy face and sitting on the bedside. "What about the earthquake? Was there another one?"

"Yeah, dummy, just on the hillside where the dead man is."

"What do you mean, 'the dead man'?"

I paused a long moment and then shrugged, not really wanting to talk about that.

"I meant *the* earthquake," I explained, "from when the city burned."

"Yeah? I remember that, clearer even than almost anything."

He looked up into the dark and just remembered for a while. "I met you then," he said and laughed a little.

"Yeah, after everything else terrible happened." I shivered some from thinking again and reached over to close the window.

Duncan lifted up the cover. "Just get in, you'll catch cold all wet-haired like that." I climbed in close and warm.

"I didn't think it was all so terrible," he said. "All those bells and bangs and fires everywhere. It was the best, better than the circus."

I tried imagining it that way but couldn't. Mrs. Porfoy's crying had soaked into my bones.

Duncan looked back at me, propped up on an elbow. "It's like the Fair's the only thing to match it since, all that fire and light and wild colors. God, I can't wait till they blow that thing up." He seemed thrilled by the prospect.

"Yeah," I agreed softly and a little low. Just like him, I could hardly wait for that inevitable end, that terrible, glorious dynamite boom. It seemed so perfect. But it always got me feeling so tender and sad.

"I met you then, after all of that," I said again.

"Yeah," and he lay still and remembered with me. I felt like it feels being so very hungry, all empty and cool inside my mouth and throat.

"*Hhhmmmnn,*" I began quiet and a little rough, like the sounds were drifting from deep inside me. I opened my mouth to speak and tried to think exactly but couldn't find words, like there was no thought there, just my blood and muscles feeling. Duncan leaned in closer to make sense of my odd sound.

"Max?" he said so quietly, sounding a lot like I sounded. I opened my mouth to answer but came up with nothing. He brushed his warm hand up across my belly and let it rest up where my heart beat. This got my blood to rushing all through me and made a shiver right down to the bottom of my spine.

I was breathing very deeply. I stared at the two small pocks on his forehead, just soft little marks resting there above where his brow knit together, like that was as close as I could get to his eyes. And then I slid my body over in closer so we touched all up and down our fronts. We lay still and close like that for what seemed to be forever. Then he kissed me on my throat and I giggled from the touch and drew back, and I kissed him on his and he laughed more and shook from the shivers and I reached around and put my hand on his butt and really felt it and down onto his leg and he was quiet and put his hand on the nape of my neck and pulled me to him and didn't kiss but felt me all over my body and me all over him all bound up tight together in each other's legs and arms tangled up in his bed and then drawing back some to feel our fronts soft with his hand just touching down across my ribs and on my belly. All the thousand things I thought then. It makes me blush remembering. It was all warm and muscular, just holding each other and touching and sort of kissing, our mouths close and us breathing each other's breath and we slept like that, as close together as we could.

I woke up when Mother and Mr. Taqdir honked their horn, as was their blessed custom, and roused us rolling out of bed, giddy from the fright of it and the queer feeling of having done what we'd done. We neither of us said anything thoughtful but grinned enough to make it all feel fine and Duncan did knock me down and kiss me full on the mouth, which made all the difference for the whole day for me, not from it feeling nice but because of what it meant.

Today was our special day on the town with Mother and Mr. Taqdir.

Mother was sweeping crumbs off the kitchen floor within moments of arriving. I came out from my room, rumpled and wild-haired but actually dressed, which was more than I sometimes did, and was given a kiss.

"Oh, you *do* smell like a boy, pumpkin," she began with a squinch of her nose. "You will wash before we go, won't you, dear?" I wanted to wash right there and then, as Duncan was showering and I could think of little else. But I compromised.

"When Duncan's done, Mother. I'll just smell till then," and I poked about the bread box, drumming thoughtfully on its wooden top.

Mr. Taqdir was arranging colorful ribbons on the tops of two small boxes, gift boxes, I could tell, about the size of satchels. He was humming a most unmelodic tune, something Persian I'd heard Duncan play many times on the Victrola, all quivery and off-key, notes sliding recklessly all over the face of it like pig's eyes being chased around the plate. I'd only eaten pig's eyes once, and each time I'd press the edge of my fork down onto their ugly green, they'd squirt out from under, sliding clear across the plate and back again. It was disgusting.

It said in *The Call* they had typhus in New York City now and also that Dunkirk was being bombed from guns they couldn't find, not anywhere near, they said. The guns are at least thirty miles away and still they bomb Dunkirk. Imagine them sailing in through the stars, whistling like impatient tea kettles, invisible and unerring. Just *boom!* and you're blown to bits from out of nowhere. I put the paper in the trash.

Duncan came into the kitchen, clothed and cleaned and wet behind his ears. He pecked Mother on the cheek, got hugged by his dad and bumped me down the counter with a hip. Mother looked at me from under a lowered brow and gestured toward the bath with a flick of her eyes.

"Yes?" I asked to be a pest.

"Yes?" Duncan asked me, unaware of Mother's signals.

"Mother's making faces," I explained. He looked to see, but she huffed and turned her attention to the little boxes Mr. Taqdir had set there on the tabletop, and I rushed off to wash.

———

The boxes had matching sets: a collar, plaid bow tie and lovely gray cap, a soft fuzzy felt snap-brim cap. We modeled them to oohs and ahs and polite clapping. They looked quite smart, that perky tie and sophisticated cap, so we wore them both and dark knickers to boot. Today we'd be motoring, and this would be our motoring costume.

"Can I drive?" Duncan called predictably from the backseat, as we settled in. "I'm very safe."

"And can I drive?" I echoed. "I'm much safer."

"Now pumpkin, you know you don't drive," Mother scolded.

"I do too," I answered, forgetting my vow to secrecy. We rattled a bit there in the carriage as Mr. Taqdir cranked it to life, Mother manipulating the controls to keep its spark burning.

"You do, do you?" she tooted. "With whom?" Duncan hit me on the leg and scowled a reminder.

"No one," I answered cautiously. "I meant I'd like to and that I *would* be much safer, if I *did* drive." Mr. Taqdir climbed into the driver's seat.

"Is it Flora?" Mother persisted. "Has she been letting you drive that horrible motorcar of hers?" I smirked at Duncan and pulled the motoring rug up on our laps.

"No, Mother," I answered truthfully. "I've *not* been motoring with Flora. You're so untrusting." I huffed a little, trying to be indignant. Mother turned around in her seat and engaged me as best she could with a firm direct stare.

"To be clear with you now, pumpkin. *If* you ever *are* out driving. *If.* I must insist you maintain a safe speed and never, ever drive in darkness. And never on busy roads or near horses. Am I clear?"

"Oh, yes, very clear," I agreed, nodding impatiently.

"Need I speak to Miss Profuso?" she continued.

"No, Mummy," I answered. "I really see no need."

Mother turned back to the front as the rear tires dug into the dirt and we sped away to our breakfast engagement. Duncan and I bounced and bundled in the back, the wind whipping past our smartly shaped caps and fluttering our little bow ties. I felt Duncan's hand come in under the rug and onto my leg, just reaching around on the inside of my thigh, making my stomach rise inside me and a big push in my pants. I smirked and squinted into the wind, doing the same to him. Mother and Mr. Taqdir yelled polite conversation in the front seat as Mother held her hat firmly down, the adulterous couple out motoring with their offspring.

Breakfast was to be had at the Cliff House. We ascended into a thick fog coming out of the park and up the last steep climb to Sutro Heights and the overlook. Nothing could be seen of the famous Seal Rocks. Some assorted grotesque noises came bellowing out from the impenetrable mists. Awful, flatulent honks and long rasping barks, that and the wild splashing of the surf against Land's End, a short plunge down.

I was a bit concerned about my appearance as we all climbed down out of the car and Mr. Taqdir handed the keys over to an attendant who motored away into the fog. But I watched Duncan who, as I'd hoped, had an easy solution, removing his cap and holding it in folded hands neatly below his belt. I did the same, no doubt impressing Mother with my politeness.

Our table looked out into the dense fog. All manner of sea birds swooped close by, calling into the cold morning. Outside the mist was full with ocean brine and gray salty seaweed smell, roaring up with the winds, off the rocks where the waves came pounding in. But where we sat was warm and toasty. A simple little gas flame flickered in its glass chimney, screwed tight to the wall, looking vaguely nautical.

The tables were set with white linen and heavy silver of many shapes and sizes, all fit for some mysterious use. The teacup I understood, and the sugar jar. I offered sugar all around, to be polite, before taking a lump of my own. I sat and sucked happily, careful not to slurp or let slip the dissolving cube out through my sticky lips. A sweet little drip dribbled out my mouth, but I caught it smartly on the cuff of my sleeve, wiping my chin clean on the follow-through.

A lovely murmur of conversation rose from the busy room full of breakfasters. Our table said "Reserved" and that was nice. "Reserved." I imagined it *pre*served in formaldehyde, like the wrinkled black frogs dangling head down in Miss Gillian's many glass jars. "Preserved," the little cardboard sign would say, the horrible squat table, shriveled and limp, stinking of sharp vinegar, peeling chairs collapsing under us like squishy piles of frog flesh.

"Your mother has many friends here," Mr. Taqdir informed me, speaking more to Mother than to me. "Reservations are given only for the very few."

I looked quickly round the bright, noisy room, noting the smart clothes and patient service. One waiter had been standing set to scoot a chair a good half minute now, waiting with a grave smile for his ancient patron to lower herself carefully down to rest on the stuffed brocade seat. She was slow as an oak tree, but still he stood.

"What's that?" Duncan asked, disgusted, as a plateful of pig's eyes floated past.

"Pig's eyes," I said because it was true.

"Maxwell," Mother sighed, "what sort of nonsense is this?" She drew back and stared at me. "Don't be disgusting."

I didn't understand. Father told me all about pig's eyes. "You never had pig's eyes?" I asked, plainly curious.

"Maxwell," she objected simply. "Enough."

"I don't understand," Duncan put in. Mr. Taqdir was talking to our waiter.

"Do we get whatever we want?" I asked Mother, eager to think of something more appetizing.

"We've ordered ahead, pumpkin. Everything's taken care of today."

"Do we get pig's eyes?" Duncan asked, thinking it was still funny. Mother covered her eyes and shook her head.

"The Cliff House doesn't serve 'pig's eyes,' dearest. The Cliff House serves Brussels sprouts which Maxwell thinks it would be amusing to call 'pig's eyes.' "

"I thought it was *disgusting*," I objected. "*Father* said those were pig's eyes." Another illusion had been swept aside. Really they didn't look at all like pig's eyes when you knew, but if you didn't there'd be nothing to give you a clue. It all seemed so plausible and horrifying, of course I'd believed him.

"Oh, please," Duncan whimpered, begging Mother. "Please let's do have them. Sprouts are so very good for you." Mr. Taqdir caught this tail end of our little scene and tapped the waiter's sleeve to indicate yes, bring the sprouts for the young man.

The sprouts arrived along with the rest of it, sweaty pink rounds of ham and a white china platter shingled neatly with broiled turkey breast, sliced paper thin and piping hot. There were light brown crumble biscuits shaped like dung which mother called scones. That and many jams and jellies, red jam and purple jam and even some green jelly which turned out to be mint. Duncan was busy carving and arranging, crowding over his plate like a blind seamstress. Mother poured the pitcher of pulpy orange juice, filling my glass to the tip-top.

"The yellow jelly is lemon curd," Mother said brightly. "It's British. You're to have it with your scone," and she showed us how, slicing neatly across the flat of the scone and splitting it open so it looked like one of Father's rocks, but fresh and steaming. And she lathered its face with gobs of yellow curd. I followed her lead, but found my scone was filled with horrible black bugs, steaming black fly flesh speckling its lovely white freshness. I flipped my little muffin closed before anyone could see, not wanting to raise a fuss.

"Soon," Mr. Taqdir announced, raising his juice glass up,

"you will be going on to other things." Mother patted my shoulder and smiled. I thought he meant breakfast was ending.

"Where are we going next?" I asked, scoffing my ham as quick as I could before we rushed away.

"Exactly, Max," Mr. Taqdir nodded, bobbing his glass up and down in time with his chin, "exactly. Where will we be going next? I hope you'll both be thinking of this." Duncan remained transfixed by his food, pushing it about his plate and tilting his head this way and that to get a better view.

"I thought everything was planned out," I objected, turning to Mother, who had assured me that indeed it was. A dirty sea gull flew in through a window some wag had opened, scattering a few feathers in panic and skittering in under a table somewhere behind me.

"Whatever do you mean, pumpkin?" Mother seemed puzzled, as though suffering from amnesia or purposefully trying to make me crazy.

A big fat man bursting the buttons of his vest stood and stomped madly about the floor in the vicinity of the gull, yelling out orders to the poor bird. It ducked in under a chair and took flight out the other side of his table. A waiter followed after it holding a tray in one hand and a round glass top in the other.

Duncan looked up smiling, unaware, I believe, of the bird. He carefully pushed his plate to me with his elbow, sneaking it over, unobserved by our distracted companions. Two slimy green sprouts sat on either side of a little round ham of pig's nose, set amidst a carefully rendered lemon pig's face. The ugly leering animal had a big broad potato grin and two little toast ears. A furious beating of wings rushed up from behind and the panicked sea gull sailed across the tabletop to perch safely on a wall sconce.

"Please pay it no attention," an older woman called out in a loud but calming voice. I turned to look and saw she was standing on her chair, her arms up like a conductor's.

"It is a bird," she assured us. "Allow it time and it shall leave of its own accord." Everyone in the room listened in silence. "Thank you," she concluded and stepped down. The waiters continued on their mission despite her wise words. I popped a pig's eye off Duncan's plate and into my mouth, pushing the other into his.

"We were speaking of your graduation, dearies," Mother began again, though I could recall no such conversation. She ruffled her bustle and settled back into her seat. "Your father," and she nodded smartly at Mr. Taqdir, "has asked after your plans. What do you intend for next year?"

Duncan looked at me, chewing on the tough little sprout.

"I intend," he began, musing. "I intend, good things. Good fun, lots of adventure. That sort of thing."

"Let's go to college," I suggested. "We'll be college boys."

"Let's be soldiers," Duncan said. "We can live in a tent and go on marches and maneuvers."

"Let's *not* be soldiers," I answered.

"Of course you're going to college," Mother put in. "There's no question, pumpkin. You mustn't waste your intelligence on anything else. Soldiering, business, any of that." I looked at Duncan. He'd slid the little pig nose onto his stuck-out tongue. It lay there like the blessed wafer, him flopping his tongue about as though to flip it like a pancake.

"Wonderful," I put in. "We're off to college then. Will we need gowns and flat hats, or letter sweaters?" Things still seemed a bit unresolved. "I'll sharpen the pencils," I offered brightly. Duncan washed his pig nose down with a gulp of juice, and wiped his mouth clean on his sleeve.

"Don't we have to apply?" he asked. "What if they don't want us?"

Mother started in but I cut her short.

"We'll go to Berkeley. Anyone from Lowell can go to Berkeley." I didn't want to have this conversation. "We'll plan it all out on Sunday. Don't you think?" I looked around, fishing for agreement. "I'll make calls. We'll explore options."

Everyone kept quiet, pushing at their various foods.
"Well, then," I concluded. "It's settled."

I grew distracted by a mix of inexplicable melancholy and nervous wondering. All the things I thought to say became unrea-
sonably complicated in my head and I gave in to sitting silently
near Duncan, who was dozing, and just looking out over the
open ocean, just looking across the bright rippling water to its
edge and feeling how big it is.

I felt a mood coming on. Not a bad mood really. A quiet,
deep-thinking sort of mood. Each and every separate thing was
coming to seem so simple and perfect, as though the entirety
was shifting into its proper place and order. The curve of Duncan's neck, for instance, where he'd curled his sleepy head into
his hands, started a feeling in my heart and stomach that was
as intensely joyful as it was sad. And it wasn't just that I wanted
to touch him. I got the same heady feeling from the shape and
weight of the pewter sugar bowl. It was so simple and sturdy
and it held sugar. The windows framed the perfect sky, each
degree of gray suffusing into the next with a kind of grace that
I could feel but not describe. The breaking waves marked the
rhythm and I was content to remain silent and breathing.

That river came to mind, the one I'd thought must have gone
wrong somewhere and entered into me so that I was its mouth.
I felt now as if I'd finally accommodated it, as if the barriers
that made for its violence, the bits and pieces in me that had
resisted the flow, were now washed away, eroded by the flood,
and I was an empty vessel, a surrounding through which the
river flowed freely. It felt like that, like I'd given up completely.

Mother, I'm sure, could have explained it all away and I'm happy
she didn't get the chance. I had a simple smile for her anytime
she turned her attentions my way. That and the satisfied calm
that seemed to emanate from my very bones were enough to

assure her my relative silence was not a sign of distress. She was, truth be told, so enthralled by her own brilliant plans that she noticed little else. Her perky narrative filled all the empty silences, glossing the day's events with historical information and provocative anecdotes: the train south along the Ocean Shore Pleasure Route; lunch and a swim at Half Moon Bay; a visit to the artichoke fields; Nob Hill; drinks at sunset on the terrace; a long stroll through the Latin Quarter.

By ten our feet were tired from the evening's stroll and my belly was beginning to grumble again. I had no doubts whatsoever that Mother had some miracle preplanned to deliver us into bliss at the close of the day. Indeed, she'd managed somehow to have a table saved at Sanguinetti's, which beyond being simply miraculous required both tact and guile.

We were squished up into a corner near the banjo player, all crowded around a table the size of my lap. Mr. Taqdir filled wineglasses all the way around.

The room was wild with laughter and the occasional chorus rang out to help the music along. "Hot Time in the Old Town Tonight" brought the house down, Mr. Taqdir singing, I'm certain, "Hog Time," rather than the conventional line. Mother had ordered ahead, all her favorite foods. Our table was filled with big bowls of pasta, hot garlic butter bread and a stewed veal shank that was collapsing off its bone under the juicy weight of its sheer deliciousness. It sat drenched in garlic-soaked juices, simmering in amongst onions and thin juliennes of zucchini, and more garlic, whole cloves roasted. There was salad and more wine. Already that delicious red warmth was running a soft, yawning tickle up the nape of my neck and helping me to lean lovingly into Mother or Duncan without remorse or ill will or second thoughts of any kind.

———

We walked back to the auto, over the hill, bundling along through the cold night air. My goodwill felt boundless. I thought it must be Duncan and how giddy and unknown it all made me feel, or it was the wine, running through my blood all warm and sloppy, washing at the backs of my eyes so I felt like weeping. Or it was how incredibly wide and cold the night sky was above us, stretching out to eternity, blowing a bracing breeze down around us from the chilly black nothing, the ice-cold stars twinkling there, right where they'd always been.

We motored west, clattering across the uncrowded city. Duncan and I bounced in the backseat, our caps pulled down tight on our heads, us bundled up in the blanket and taking the brisk night air cool across our flushed faces. I loved the way our lantern light dented the night, rushing along the open boulevards before us, barely staying ahead of our roaring engine, swinging wildly right, then left, sweeping across phantom shapes, making shadows of people and trees. We rattled over the high hills, past Lone Mountain, then along the low, curving paths of the park, under the windmills and down onto the Great Highway.

Mr. Taqdir turned off the lanterns and engine and we rolled quietly toward the dark edge of the highway.

Far off in the blackness I saw the ghostly white glow of the surf running a long line out across the sand. With the engine off you could hear it too, the roar and rolling of the waves coming in again and again. We sat quiet and exhausted, damp from the wet air rolling in off the sea, all salt and seaweed smell. It settled like dew over everything.

"I want to walk," I said, wanting to get closer to the water. Mother and Mr. Taqdir nodded their blessings but did nothing to get up and out.

"We'll stay, pumpkin," Mother explained. "Be careful of the water."

"I'll go," Duncan put in, pulling the blanket up around his shoulders. "I'll drag him out when he drowns," and we climbed out over the back with a jump off the sideboard and onto the beach. I fell over and lay happily in the sand, a few feet from the car. Looking out under its carriage I could see the sea, oddly disconnected from the black sky above. Duncan stood me up and wrapped the blanket around us both. He rested his chin on my shoulder and we stood for a bit.

"Let's go down the beach," I whispered into his warm ear. And we did, the blanket wrapped around our shoulders, bumped up close and getting silly.

I tried listening for the separate waves, trying to discern their beginnings and ends, but it was all so unclear, each wave rolling into the next. I steered us east with a push, getting us back onto a soft dune, back over a small rise and into a hollow.

Then Duncan stuck his hand down my pants, which is something we still hadn't done. It really was too much for me and I got all wild up my back and we fell over, pressed up close as we could there in the sand, his hand working around in my pants and me kissing him all over his face, hoping where we were was as dark as it seemed. I could hardly think to see, and just kissed and kissed. My tongue was all over his salty sweet skin wherever I could reach, and I tore his shirt buttons open to kiss down there. He'd pulled the snaps of my pants open at the top and tugged my boxers down so I poked out and up against him, rubbing all hard and furious onto his pants and up on his belly. Then he put his warm hand on me there and just held me soft and strong in his hand. We stopped flexing around all frenzied like we'd been and he just held me like I said, and pushed me soft into the blanket with his other hand warm against my chest. I lay there on my back, my shirt torn open down the front, feeling my body bare in the salty air and his spit all over me, me hard and warm in his hand. I kept thinking his name over and over like a sound in my mind, just like hypnosis or breathing. He undid the belt of his pants and pulled them down so I saw him, his I'm not sure what word to use, but it was so beautiful and warm and alive, pushing out from his waistband, over his soft black hair and curving up against his belly. He lay down on top of me, reaching his arms up across my sides and in behind my neck, our whole fronts bare and warm, all muscular and flexing against each other so slow and lovely. I tried breathing the whole of everything in through my mouth and throat, the air and the stars and all of him and the night, breathing it down into me as deep as deep could be, but there was always more, the cold empty air stretching out and away forever, and Duncan.

Landscape: Memory

# *Bolinas*

20 JUNE 1915

Today we packed our satchels and put the house in order, as we'd promised Mother we'd do. School is out, at last at last, and we are graduated. Flora and Duncan and I and Alphonse too. Father came and sat with Mother and Mr. Taqdir, the three quite chummy and chatting all through. I don't understand sometimes. We flung our caps and went for lunch (not Alphonse) at Coppa's.

Today we go to Bolinas, all three of us. I made Father agree over lunch that Duncan and I would be welcome and then he asked if Flora would come, them hitting it off so well as they do, and I hadn't thought to ask, which was rude, but imagined it would be wonderful and she surprised the adults by saying yes right on the spot and doing it. So we're off to Bolinas by stage. Father says Flora's motorcar would be unwelcome.

I've got a book about memory Mr. Spengler gave me at graduation. All spring I'd kept asking him questions about memory, hoping to find some reassurance in his answers. But my uncertainties had become so mixed up in everything else that really I'd succeeded in sorting out nothing. The summer seemed like a promising time to put my mind to the task and I told him so, which is why he gave me this lovely gift and instructions to be rigorous in my work, which is what I fully intend to do.

The book is lovely brown leather, all sweet with decay and that musty old book smell like the big library has in its crowded closed-off rooms. All those ancient volumes turning grandly to dust, stacked high into the dark rafters. It's a translation of the *Ad Herennium,* by Cicero, and has a whole long introduction filled with quotes and comments and excerpts from other classical works on the subject.

I've read Cicero for public speaking, as we all did at Grant, and he was dull as dishwater. But it was very kind of Mr. Spengler so I promised yes, I'd read it. Really, I rather fancy trying out some of what he says, as it appears to be a practical guide, like Ruskin for painting, a way to set things in a neat structure so they all stay just as they really were.

I've packed that and my drawing kit and paints because I should be getting on to colors soon. Mother was prostrate with fear, afraid I'd somehow ruin my hard work by impetuous application of the paints. She believes, I believe, that without her nearby I can't possibly move forward. But I think the paints will be the best part yet.

Both Duncan and I've decided to travel light: twill shorts, two thin cotton shirts, one pair of long pants and a sweater. Socks and boots and boxers too, of course, and our caps and bow ties to be fancy. All stuffed up in a satchel, plus my various books and what not. Father says he's got bundles of old things up there as well, in case we're cold or bored or feel like wearing beekeeper's bonnets.

We took the ferry to Sausalito and then rode a white steamer stage across the yellow brown hills to Bolinas and the sea. Flora was full of plans, explaining the situation of the town and its location on the fault line.

"Max and I found a ruin there once," Duncan said. "A cabin that got busted up by the quake." He pulled his lips in and raised his eyebrows, just nodding his head remembering.

"An insane asylum," I corrected. "It was an insane asylum."

"No it wasn't," he answered.

"Yes it was."

"No."

"It was, I'm certain. I marked it on a map." That seemed proof enough. Flora watched from the forward seat, watching back and forth as at a tennis match.

"What map?" Duncan asked.

"The map I made, when we were up there."

"And you marked that it was an asylum?" .

"Right," I said, glad he'd finally gotten it. "An asylum." I smiled at Flora.

"So you marked it wrong." Duncan could be very stubborn.

"It's on the map," I insisted. "Ask Father, he knows." I remembered him talking about the asylum, but still I felt uncertain about the prospect of asking him again.

"Fine," Duncan agreed. "We'll ask him." The stage dipped down into a cool redwood canyon, the high golden hills disappearing as we rattled through the thick grove of trees.

"Was your father with you then?" Flora asked brightly.

"What do you mean?" I said back, partly puzzled. "You mean was he on the hike?"

"Right," she agreed. "Was he with you on the hike."

Duncan bounced his leg impatiently against mine, fiddling with the door latch.

"It was just us, just me and Duncan." It made me warm all over just thinking. "But Father was the one who'd told us, me, about the asylum. He's why we went up, to find the asylum."

"Cabin," Duncan put in simply, leaning out to smell the morning air. Dust and the smoke of the noisy engine came rolling in with the heavy sweet scent of the woods. Flora pushed her face forward into the breeze so it washed across her, eyes closed and her thick hair all bustling about in the eddies. We both joined in, us three crowded together, sniffing in deep dog breaths the morning through our noses.

Father met us in Bolinas. We shook hands and he hugged Flora, getting a peck on his bristly-whiskered cheek. I watched and then I hugged him and kissed him too, just on impulse and to his surprise. We all laughed it away, except Flora. It was a fine, warm walk to Father's wooded acre, down along the dusty road with our little luggage, then up a hill and into the trees at the head of the lagoon.

There were vegetables in a clearing, and fat-faced sunflowers reaching high on their tough sturdy stalks. The woods were mostly fir and pine, the ground clear of brush, all soft dirt and needles, tamped and toe-worn along the well-traveled paths: one to the garden, one downhill toward the water and one leading back away from the wooden house, up through a little meadow and into another stand of trees. Father slept up there in a small gazebo with a bed and desk.

We were to sleep on the sleeping porch. Father led us through the one-room house out onto the wide screened porch. It faced the water, its two ends opened out onto woods. The screen door had little springs to swing shut and it did with a bang. There were two beds, one low little bed looking clean and comfy to the right and an enormous fluff-and-rumple bed, wide as the ocean and piled high with comforters. An obscenely baroque headboard leapt out of its upper end, all manner of buttresses and cupids and gargoyles carved into the dark wood.

"That's the boys' bed," Flora said smartly, pointing to the mammoth thing. "I'd prefer something a little more manageable."

She pulled her carpet bag along the worn wooden floor, and

sat down pertly on the little mattress. It lay nicely on its humble frame. "Perfect," she pronounced, tweeking the taut blanket with a flick of her finger. "When I'm here, here I'll be."

I asked Father if the big bed could stand bouncing and he said we could paddle it out to sea for all it mattered to him. He doesn't much like big beds or stuffed chairs or heirlooms like Mother has. He doesn't much like furniture at all.

"It was there on the porch when I got here," he explained. "It's nailed down and solid, otherwise I'd've busted it down into firewood straightaway." I bounced in butt first and it squeaked and whinnied and bounced me back up some. I rolled over into the middle and sunk in amongst the downy covers.

We three swept the cabin clean and sat around the one big table making plans. Father went foraging, gathering berries and garden vegetables for lunch.

"I'll build a boat," Duncan began. "From driftwood and willow branches." He wrote "Build Boat" in flowing script on the little plan sheets Flora suggested we use. "We'll sail home and dock at the Fair."

"I'll give you an hour's help each day," I volunteered, skeptical about the boat's prospects, but eager to spend all my time with him. "You can help me on my projects. We'll barter our labor." I wrote "Be with Duncan" in tiny letters near the middle of the page.

"*Work* with Duncan," Duncan corrected.

"That's what I mean," I agreed happily. "What else? Flora?"

Flora was staring off into space with a mischievous grin, clearly excited by some new thought.

"Miss Profuso," I sang as Miss Gillian did to get her wandering attention. "Young lady."

Birds sang back, a warble and twitters. All their lovely sounds cascaded through the branches and tumbled in around us.

"Oh, Dogey, I've the best project," Flora said, tapping pencil points nervously onto her paper. "Photography! Mother got a Rochester just last month and she *never* uses it. I'm certain she'd love for me to have it here."

"Is it big?" Duncan asked excitedly.

"Oh, it's enormous, a big box on a tripod. She's got a bag full of accessories too, lenses and French shutters and developing whatnot."

She began scripting "I. Photography" and filling in an outline below, "A., B., C.," all as yet blank, but evidence of some enormous ambition, just now kindled.

"It's an ancient old thing, at least twenty years old," she explained. "Mother was willed it by some horrible uncle in Colma. I don't think it's even been taken out of its box."

"You should try all the various styles," I suggested, thrilled by the thought of this enormous box. "Landscape and portraits and wildlife photographs."

"Oh, slow down, Dogey, slow down," and she scribbled in "Landscape" next to "A" and "Portraits" for "B."

"And photos of boats," Duncan added, "crude willow boats."

"And little scenes," I carried on. "You can cast little fantasy scenes with nymphs or satyrs and we'll act them out for pictures. You can put captions on them."

Father banged in through the sprung screen door, loaded down with a bowl of berries and lovely yellow squash, flat wax beans and deep crimson peppers.

I added "Photos" to my brief list.

I'd put nothing of my own down yet, save "Be with Duncan," so I stayed quiet at my place and thought. Duncan scooted up next to me and put his arm across my shoulders. He had his pencil to paper too.

I made a list of my regular things: "Drawing, memory book, Mr. Spengler's book." Duncan brought his pencil over to my paper. "Exploring, swimming, sleeping," he added. I wrote "together" after the last entry and then erased it as quick as could be, breathless just from writing it. "Mischief," Duncan added. "Food," I put down.

The list looked fairly complete. We sat and considered it for some time. Father and Flora gabbed a blue streak in the kitchen (mostly Flora). Father listened and laughed and put in an occasional phrase that kept her going. He chop-chopped the vegetables, the heavy knife cutting through the peppers and squash, cutting into the solid oak block. A big black pan sizzled with butter on the stovetop and the aroma made my mouth water. Father tossed on several cloves of garlic, finely minced.

Duncan began a timetable. "8:00 o'clock a.m.: Wake up. Swim. 8:30 o'clock a.m.: Breakfast." "9:30 o'clock a.m.," I continued, "Mr. Spengler's book." After breakfast was my best reading time. "Boat," Duncan added for that time. We paused. He wrote "11:00 o'clock a.m." We fiddled with our pencils and looked around the room thinking. "Exploring," I put in, not wanting to be too long by myself, then "1:00 o'clock p.m."

"Lunch," we both said out loud and laughed. "Lunch," I wrote down. Duncan sneaked his pencil onto the next line down. "2:00 o'clock p.m.: Swim." I erased it quick as could be. "Nap, then swim," I penciled in instead. Duncan shook his head in agreement. "3:30 o'clock p.m."

We looked around the room again. Father grated a brick of white cheese over the steaming pan. Flora stacked four plates on the stovetop and put a stew pot upside down over them, gesturing with her free hand and going on about emulsion fluids.

"Drawing," I wrote down, as that was the time I always did my drawing with Mother. Duncan stuck his lip out, tapping his pencil repeatedly on the paper. "Running," he wrote down.

"Running?" I asked out loud. He looked at me and shrugged.

"Like soldiers do for training," he explained. "I want to be as fit as I can by the end of summer." I thought he was quite fit already.

"You're fit as can be," I said, and stopped just short of kissing him there and then. He just looked at me and blushed, nodding his head and saying "You," and then nothing more.

"I still want to run," he added after a pause. "I can't just do drawing, anyway." I nodded along with his thinking. "And I don't want to be lashing boats all day long."

"Would you help me on my drawing just sometimes, when I need help?" I asked. I thought maybe I'd need to see him standing where we'd been standing, just to get it exactly right.

"Sure I'd help," he agreed. "I just don't want to be doing stuff I'm no good at." The food was being piled onto plates. I looked him in the eyes for a long moment.

"Let's finish quick," he said, "before lunch."

"5:30 o'clock p.m.: Swim," I wrote. "6:00 o'clock p.m.: Dinner," Duncan put in below. "7:30 o'clock p.m." We looked up at our list of activities, looking for what we'd left out. "Mischief," Duncan penciled in, grinning with it.

Flora put the steaming plates, piled high with garlic-buttered vegetables and gooey strings of melting cheese, at our places as we pulled the list into my lap and finished.

"9:30 o'clock p.m.: Memory Book." "Read," Duncan added, as that was the time he liked best for reading. "10:00 o'clock p.m. Sleep."

Our plan's in effect. Already it's almost ten and Duncan's reading and I'm writing, just as we'd said we'd do. Flora's all bundled up in bed wheezing into her pillow, asleep for an hour already. When we get into bed will be the most lovely because the cotton sheet will be soft and cool against our skin and I'll roll over on top of him all bare skin and tender and we'll kiss and kiss there in the big bundling bed, so very quiet lying in the cold night air.

———

## 21 JUNE 1915

When we woke it was still just seven and Flora was gone, her bed neatly made. We lay around and rolled around a good hour together and both came, rubbing up against each other's bellies. I put his whole penis in my mouth like I'd tried a couple times before, but the sounds he made were so odd I wasn't sure it was what he wanted. We don't talk about details like that. This time though he swung around and put his mouth over mine at the same time and from how it felt I could hardly think and must have made sounds stranger even than what he made. We held each other all warm and slobbery in each other's mouths like that for a long while, hardly moving except for our heads and mouths and throats and tongues and reaching round behind to wrap my arms round his butt and pull him in close to me. Sure it was dumb and reckless, what with the bright morning shining down into the trees and no idea who might come wandering in. But we were under covers, a bit unusual still, but at least under covers, and I'm sure we'll do it again tomorrow and every day this summer if we're given half a chance.

Our swim was brisk, chilly cold and wonderful. We plunged in directly and leapt and dove as much as we could, though the rocky lagoon ran quite shallow. Flora spotted us from a distance and marched right down despite our nakedness, asking politely if we minded and of course we didn't, being so desperately modern, as we were. She stripped off her clothes and dove right in, fast as a kingfisher, bobbing her head back up and smiling brightly. She was always one to set the tone, directly and unmistakably, and so she did.

We were back to breakfast (right on schedule), all wet-haired and noisy. Father joined us, alerted, no doubt, by the salty sweet smell of bacon and the hot black coffee. Duncan and I showed him our Day Plans, as we'd shown Flora last evening, and he clucked his approval of our busy schedule, promising to join us at mealtimes and advise us on exploration and mischief.

I did dishes with Flora, and Duncan went out in search of suitable planks for his boat, deciding to draw up plans after he'd found what materials were at hand.

"I think it's wonderful about you and Duncan," Flora said through steam clouds billowing out from the boiling water. She was pouring it over the piled-up dishes.

"Us being such good friends?" I asked.

"Oh, yes, that certainly," she answered in a leading voice. "That and everything else."

I looked out the foggy window and thought about "everything else": Mother and Father and Mr. Taqdir and the two houses; all the trouble I'd had thinking through it all. It *was* wonderful being so close to Duncan through all of that. Just *how* wonderful, I thought, she certainly didn't know. Still, to think everything else was wonderful too, just because it brought me closer to Duncan, seemed wrongheaded.

"It is wonderful, *despite* everything else," I said. "I wish some things had never happened. Though he makes things better for me."

Flora put a firm hand on my shoulder and leaned in close. "Not *despite,* Dogey, not despite everything. You shouldn't feel ashamed."

I felt a bit confused. I didn't feel ashamed.

"All that 'else' is *also* wonderful," she insisted. "As it should be and completely natural, no matter what society says." Though my selfish thoughts were just the opposite, I'd come to accept Mother's action enough to agree with Flora.

"I know it's natural," I said, still a bit reluctant. "And of course my friendship with Duncan is all bound up in it. It just still makes me cry and get mad and hate that it happens sometimes."

She pulled me close to her and cooed, "Oh, Dogey, Dogey,

you mustn't bring the judgments of society inside you. Just let it go. Feel what you feel without shame. Friendship, loving, all of it."

She was right and I knew that. Part of being here was to help me feel better about Father and Mother as things were now, not just feel a need for them to change back again.

"I know," I said simply.

Flora stayed in to read with me, us feeling very close because of our little chat, and she snuggled up on the rug with Ruskin while I started in to Mr. Spengler's book.

This part I read over and over because I thought it must somehow make sense: "Some men in the presence of considerable stimulus have no memory owing to disease or age, just as if a stimulus or a seal were impressed on flowing water. With them the design makes no impression because they are worn down like old walls in buildings, or because of the hardness of that which is to receive the impression. For this reason the very young and the very old have poor memories; they are in a state of flux, the young because of their growth, the old because of their decay."

First I thought of water, dreaming I was adrift at sea, and the problem of memories stamped into water. So often I'd felt as if my mind was washing away. It made me think also of that river I'd imagined running through me and how I finally felt satisfied and complete really, only once it had washed a part of me away. It wasn't erosion so much as the making of something, like rivers make their riverbeds. It wasn't loss so much as gain. That's what I thought about first.

Then I thought of old buildings, the walls all tumbled down and worn, like the ruins and like Maybeck's Palace at the Fair. This guy was wrong about the buildings, I figured. Old buildings hold so *many* memories. All the story and past of them crumbling is held and revealed right in the pattern of the dusty ruins. Old buildings hold so many more "impressions" because each event that happens to them leaves a mark. Their whole past is visible in the pattern of their decay. It's these new buildings that are unreadable, I think. Like the Fair. That must be what he meant by hardness. Those walls can't hold any "impressions." They're just rock-smooth and finished, and fake to boot. They're just frozen fake monuments. And then they'll just be gone and disappeared, blown up by dynamite before they've even had time to accumulate a real past.

But it was the last part that bugged me most: ". . . the very young and the very old have poor memories; they are in a state of flux, the young because of their growth, the old because of their decay." It was just like his mistake with buildings. In fact "the very old" have the best memories, the most cluttered and colorful and interesting memories. Just like old ruins holding more of the past. They *are* in a state of flux and will, I've found, often change their account of some past event, but always for the best. That is, the story gets closer to the truth, it's refined by their changes. That seemed to be the nub of it: this stuff from the book implied that any *change* in a person's memory would make that memory somehow worse, that memory should be a frozen, fixed thing, like a photograph.

I thought of nurselogs. It was hard not to, what with "decay" and "growth" written right there next to each other on the page. It seemed fitting, the thought of those big trees, felled by age and their own weight, blown over and rotting. Their decay is what gives rise to new growth. All the sturdiest saplings, the healthiest of the young trees rise from those fallen, rotten giants. And I think memory could be like that. What seems to us to be decay could be growth. Maybe good memory isn't simply like a camera. Aren't photographs as smooth and frozen and finished as those thin plaster walls of the Fair? Aren't they just as flimsy?

Duncan came back all dirty and breathless, dragging a bleached gray plank and sporting a willow wreath.

"I've found treasures," he called across the clearing, beaching the wooden whale with a solid boom on the ground. "This isn't even the biggest." I came out, my bare feet tickled by the decaying pine needles carpeting the cool ground, and took a closer look.

"Why'd you drag it all the way up here?" Our little yard seemed the wrong place to build a boat.

"To show off," he explained, flexing his sweaty arm. "I wanted one for here. I'm going to carve a prow and take it down to the boat when I'm done." We stood above the prone prow, admiring its fine solid curve.

"What else did you find?"

"Lots. Flat planks, two-by-fours, all bleached out and worn. I found half a wreck too," he added, shaking my shoulder. "Most of the front's busted up but the back end's intact."

"A trawler?" I asked, imagining something I'd never seen.

"Nope. A rowboat," he corrected. "But a real big one, five feet from port to starboard, at least," and he stretched his arms as far as that.

We went to the wreck first thing for exploring. It was up the east side of the lagoon, not far from where we swam, and partly sunk in mud. The dry stuff was great, shipshape and ghost-gray from the sun and salt. Where it got wet it crumbled rotten and soggy.

Duncan and I started kicking it loose, breaking the wet wood off and tugging the rest out from its resting place, dragging it up onto the dry dirty slope that rose up along the lagoon. There was a good third of a boat there. Its rudder was strong and operable, screaming loudly from its rusty hinges as we tried it right and left.

Scattered all along this same stretch were scraps of boards and huge twisted gnarls of trees washed in on storms. It must be from the logging, I thought. They take the trees down off the hills and float them off to sea. If storms wreck the barges, you get trees, whole and in parts, riding through the waves and washing up all along the coast, even dragging in on the lagoon. I nestled into the lap of a big mess of roots, sitting back into a hollow where the wood reached out in a tangle, now washed clean and smooth by the battering waves.

"Tree house," Duncan punned.

"Root cellar," I replied. "Only a buck fifty." Duncan squeezed in by me. "This could be the captain's bridge."

"Or the crow's nest," Duncan suggested. "I'll put it up top, on the mast." I imagined us hoisting the grotesque tangled roots by ropes and pulleys, dragging the ugly bulk up a tall thin mast.

"Your rowboat's got a mast?" I asked, teasing him.

He shook his head no. "I thought I'd try to make a sail. Something very simple, but one where we wouldn't have to row." He looked out across the water, its face all rippled by the strong breeze. "Your dad's got tools, and I've got plenty of time."

We explored along the east side, past the gullies of our earlier summers, and on to the mouth of the lagoon. The current drew strong out to sea through the narrow channel there, with Bolinas just a stone's throw away. We didn't try to cross, knowing we'd probably end up somewhere out in the freezing waves. We raced back for lunch, getting hungry and sweaty and tired and found Father and Flora setting out big bowls of cold potato soup.

After, we swam first and *then* we napped.

I took my drawing kit with me south along the shore, watching Duncan running off ahead, disappearing around a bend, off to Stinson Beach or Half Moon Bay or Mexico or however far his legs could take him in two hours. I walked as far as Weeks Gulch and turned to look out at the actual setting of the memory I'd been trying to paint, afraid of what I might see. There were, it appeared, some problems. The painting I'd made was markedly different from what lay before me. The beautiful hills I'd drawn were much higher and their descent to the water much sharper than what was there now. The lagoon itself—that is, the lagoon in front of me—spread out farther and into more mysterious nooks than I could find in the lagoon I had drawn. The position of the sun was impossible.

All in all I found my painting a good sight more satisfying than the actual landscape. I had several choices and I faced them boldly. I chose to make excuses and go with my aesthetic impulse. My impulse was to leave my work as it was and forge ahead. My excuse was that my memory was more like a nurselog than a camera. I was remembering the trouble I'd had with Cicero. If he was right, if my memory ought to be an accurate replica of the original experience, if that was so, my painting was hopelessly inaccurate. It was a bad painting of a fuzzy memory. But I preferred to think that memory is never frozen, nor should it be. My painting was a successful rendering of the dynamic memory that had simply *begun* with the original event. It accurately captured the decaying grotesque of memory that lay rotting in my head, that fallen nurselog out of which so much of value must be growing. My painting, I figured, was so very accurate in its depiction of this memory that it would inevitably look wrong when compared to the original model.

I packed my little kit and walked back toward home feeling glad I'd come to look. Several loose ends had now been tied up neatly, thanks to this dilemma, and I was confident my picture might eventually turn out right. I had trouble keeping my complicated conclusions straight, so I kept repeating them, like an incantation, as I walked, and jotted them down straightaway in the front flap of Mr. Spengler's book. I sat out in the soft cool dirt and looked into the trees, trying to put my thoughts straight, scratching and scribbling and reworking till they were clear. And that's how you see them here.

We all four swam in a beautiful small pond Father led us to up the road going north from the lagoon, up closer to Dogtown. It was a watering hole for cattle and horses dug by some ambitious farmer who hoped to save himself running the cows off to the neighbor's hole. All pristine clean and blue from the sky, thick green grass snuffling up to its edges and big broad oaks gathered in a shady group on its southern side. We wore costumes, I'm glad, as I'm not too keen to swim naked with Father and Flora both. Flora alone is something new for me and a bit of a shock. The water was a good sight warmer than the lagoon, and clear and fresh, leaving no salty traces on the skin.

Tonight we're going during mischief time to ask if we may tie a rope swing up into one of the trees. Father says there's rope and I fancy making this our morning, afternoon and evening spot, rather than tromping down to the salty brine each time.

Dinner was exquisite. Father roasted beef and I drowned it in a horseradish–soured-cream sauce. Mr. Squashtoe said yes, we may tie a rope swing but we weren't to tell any other kids, or otherwise attract gangs, and we spent the rest of the evening digging out ropes from this or that hidey-hole where Father had stashed them and tying them into a suitable length. I am sleepy and it's just past ten. I see Duncan out there in the dark dropping his ghost-white shirt and climbing into bed.

## 22 JUNE 1915

We swam at Squashtoe's pond today, morning, noon and night. It was the same as yesterday, Flora, Duncan and me naked in the morning, Duncan and me after lunch, and then all four of us in costumes before dinner. The rope swing is a great success, reaching back to a big high branch in an oak, and swinging out a good twenty feet over the pond and ten or fifteen feet high (if you give it a good swizz of the hips). Father even tried it, though he dropped in with his nose plugged, which gave the whole feat a comic effect. Plop and bubble, dropped like a rock into the water.

Yesterday I thought I'd come to a good position, giving up a bit on my hope to remember right. Not exactly that, more giving up on the idea that a "photographic" memory *is* a right memory. I'd decided my memory was like a nurselog in glorious decay, full with mysterious small saplings of unquestionable value. It was a seductive thought, given my love of the woods and the neat way it allowed me to justify my painting. It was so enormous and fragile, that thought. I carried it back home in my head like an overgrown exotic flower, some incredibly lush thing on the verge of falling apart. It held together, so long as I didn't touch it.

But the closer I get to it, the more carefully I inspect it, the more it makes my head spin. If all memories decay, what of them will really ever be left? What *is* it that's growing from out of the rotting material of old memories? Is every moment of the past simply done and gone forever? Why *can't* they be held intact somehow? It made me light-headed and nervous, like I'd peered in too close and the flower had engulfed me. I had nightmares of heavy lumber shifting, and walls collapsing down into ruins.

So today I read more Cicero, to try and find some solid ground. Cicero says that I'm simply suffering from a disorganized intellect. My distaste for his rigorous model is just a form of laziness. His diagnosis is reassuring. A competent doctor was just what I needed. He even prescribed a cure.

The *Ad Herennium* offers a demanding system to help train the untrained mind (like mine). It involves a regimen of memorization and the placement of "loci" and "images" on a sort of matrix formed out of a building or a plot of land, a landscape. As I understand it (with Flora's help), the student is to choose a familiar place to memorize, a house or building or landscape that is small enough to be thoroughly remembered, yet large enough to hold many distinct "loci." Loci are the separate locations *in* the place that's been memorized. For example, if I used the cabin as a matrix, our bed and Flora's bed and the door and the table and the funny stool could all be loci. To remember accurately, then, I must associate all of the "images" of the topic to be memorized with all of the loci.

"Images" are the details of whatever it is you want to memorize. To memorize "today" maybe I'd assign each hour to its own locus. The image of eight o'clock a.m. would be lumped onto our bed. Why not? And nine o'clock, say, on Flora's bed. And on and on. To recover the whole day, I simply "walk through" the cabin in my head and pick up each image as I pass its locus, missing no detail whatsoever because I've so thoroughly memorized the matrix, that is, the cabin.

It's sort of like Ruskin, but for memory.

I find the possibility attractive. If I put my mind in order, each part will take its proper place and the stuff I now let myself lose and forget would instead stay present to mind, set in its proper place where I can find it. If I follow the steps, working hard and getting them right, I'll not have to worry about everything slipping away like water and vapors. I'll not have to make excuses.

Duncan's drawn his grand plan, a twelve-foot dinghy with a flat sloping front and no point in the prow, save the decorative extension he's carving out front. The mast will stand six feet up and there'll be no jib.

The afternoon was wicked warm, no breeze blowing and the sun burning down hot as dust, making the woods smell sweet. We stayed at the pond right through from lunch to dinner, me sketching there and Duncan swimming laps in lieu of running. Also we fooled around, back among the trees, and this time I made Duncan lie down still all naked and glistening with water droplets and I knelt over him and ran my two hands slowly over his body, up across his soft brown chest and shoulders, my fingers across his lips, and down over his taut smooth tummy and along his thighs and on their insides and I took his penis all warm and bursting deep down into my mouth and more and again, making him stay lying still and working my hand up under his butt and back and I sucked and sucked so hard and lovely until he came all hot and liquid in my mouth and him in ecstasy groaning loud and long and flexing his body all strong and muscular and breathing so hard and deep and then reaching his arms way up over his head, him all stretched out and his back arched high so he was just pushed deep into my mouth and he came, like I said. He lay there all limp and dead to the world, but squeezing my hand so hard it hurt, and I just lay in the grass beside him for the longest time. And then we swam some more.

For mischief we walked along the road to town and peeked in the windows of the local bar. It was past dark by the time we came over the hill and down onto the small peninsula where Bolinas is. We had no trouble sneaking about the bushes outside and hoisting up into a strong hedge. Inside the men were just sitting around with drinks, talking. It was nothing at all.

## 23 JUNE 1915

Beautiful this morning, with low clouds slipping in across the water, turned orange and golden by the early light. Wispy and more like a sunset than most sunsets here. We had apple pancakes, nearly drowned in butter and syrup, and coffee that could kill a horse. I made the coffee.

Flora took the stage back to the city to get her camera. Her mother dropped a line saying okay and off she went the first chance she got. She's going to begin with landscapes and portraits, and if she likes that, Father says later on he'll help her try taking pictures of animals and birds.

I'm making pictures and she'll be taking pictures. What does that mean? Who does she take hers from? What do I make mine of? Can I take a painting? Can she make a photograph? We make up the oddest ways for saying things, or we take them up.

How am I *in* my landscape, if I'm the one looking?

I worked on Duncan's boat today. We floated boards in the bay, testing them for buoyancy. We've got one board almost a foot across and four inches thick. We had hold of it, standing waist-deep in the brisk salty water, when two great herons landed on its far end and stood poking their beaks about into air, looking back at us all crazy in their eyes like idiots, their fleshy pouches flapping in the breeze, jerking their necks around like a pair of spastics trying to yawn.

   We thought we'd be smart and push them out to sea and we did, giving the board a good sturdy shove and grinning with mischief as they floated out into deeper water. Of course we'd forgotten that birds fly and after a pleasant cruise they flapped their heavy wings and drifted off across the open waters. Our best lumber lay floating out toward the middle of the lagoon until finally Duncan dunked in and swam to its rescue.

Father left this note today, folded and set like a bookmark in Cicero. "Watching ships at sea one marvels at the simplicity of their design. A boat need simply hold air. It is just a shell placed in water. Containment, separation. The boat is an indentation riding across the ocean's top. Words cross my mind, ships passing, pressing their particular indentations into my soft surface, containment, separation. What cargo do they carry, what path to take? I'm swimming toward the shore, a shell placed in water, simply holding air."

## 24 JUNE 1915

All our explorations, it has developed, take us, just before lunch, through town where we watch the arrival of the stage from Sausalito and see if anyone's sent us mail that day. Today, of course, Flora was aboard, burdened with boxes and bags full of fragile camera parts and bearing notes for all of us from Mother and Mr. Taqdir. Flora was effusive, as always, hugging and kissing and parceling out bundles to whoever might take them as she climbed down from the coach. We'd brought Father's little wooden cart on wheels for her things and for milk and butter from Mr. Macken.

"I simply must have a swim" was what she said first. "I'm filthy from head to toe," and then she kissed us again.

After dinner Duncan took me to a field of rye up past the canyons at the far end of the lagoon. There was fog floating in and the sun had gone down, sunk below the hills, so I imagined we were in Belgium, lost behind the lines. The rye stretched out into the mists all dull and dirty green, obscured by the luminous fog and waving ever so slightly. Sounds carried in close to our ears, coming from mysterious sources, invisible and directionless. A cow came running through the field, passing by us four feet away and disappearing into the clouds. We rustled through the tall grass slowly, going in no particular direction, listening to the cow's woeful mooing. The dusk was settling in and a boat motor chugged low and steady, within reach of our hands it seemed from the sound. But no boat could be seen, nor the water nor the flapping sail that sounded, moving across from our right to our left and disappeared into the eerie calm. We wandered, I felt, forever, until the moon came clear and the field opened up in pale silver light and we walked out, only a few dozen yards from the water, and went down the dirt road home.

## 25 JUNE 1915

It was gray today, morning, noon and night. Low fog at either end and thick stormy clouds all through the middle. Duncan went down to work on his boat despite the cold, all bundled in his sweater and a floppy felt hat Father gave him. I read.

Flora's spread out in the big room, camera parts arranged in neat rows, the glorious box itself sitting high upon its tripod, gazing out over its dominion. Flora spent the day reading each and every instruction through, making certain she knew the full range of problems she might encounter and their various solutions. She'll take our portraits tomorrow, if the sun comes out.

I know it's wrong, but it looks right enough (as I remember it.)

Landscape: Memory

## 26 JUNE 1915

The sun burned through so glorious and bright. The branches of the trees steamed, letting off wisps of vapor in the early morning when the first sun washed over them, drying off the mists of the last two days. Our morning swim was a frisky frolic through dewy grass and then a wild leap off the rope swing and into the brisk clean water. We were told the intimate details of portrait-picture taking over breakfast. As Flora wanted to do Father first, Duncan and I went back to the pond for another swim.

This was the best yet, all naked and lovely among the flowers and trees by the south side of the pond. Duncan did me as I'd done to him, me lying there in his arms all stretched out as far as could be reaching back over my head to grab handfuls of grass as he pushed his warm mouth down over me and I came just bursting out my middle. I'd been unsure about his wanting to but he did, without my asking or even hinting the way you can do by how you move your body. He just took me there and then, while Flora took Father's picture.

When it was done I did a funny thing which, now that I think, perhaps I've often done. My muscles were all collapsed in sweet exhaustion. My head was resting on his ribs and I rolled my face over, like I do into my pillow sleeping. Then I began growling and humming, making sounds into his ribs, my mouth pushed up against him. It was a noise like a sleeping dog might make exhaling, a sort of humming, buzzing throaty sound. An odd song exhaled into him through the ribs and into his bones. It has a tune, but one I can never remember. Only when I'm dead-tired and spent does my body give in and let this little song emerge.

I've chosen the setting that I'll use as the matrix for my memory system. The landscape of the gullies east from the lagoon. Cicero suggests using houses or buildings but allows that one may use a familiar landscape, if one is so inclined.

I get lost in big buildings so I thought a landscape would be better. It has more places and could go on and on forever, and getting around it is easier for me. I know the way it goes. With buildings, though, I'm always being surprised. I turn a corner or go up a stair and it looks just like the last place I was.

The landscape I'm memorizing is in my favorite woods, up the east side of the lagoon. It's the same woods where Duncan and I went to find the ruins. Bourne's Gulch, and Weeks Gulch. I know them both well enough to get a good start, and I'll have three more in place by the end of summer, if I work hard. Five gullies, like a hand, you see. Once that's accomplished, Cicero says, my mind will have a reliable, structured organization. The organization of the landscape brought inside my mind will then allow an organization of my memories, giving a place for each one.

Flora took my portrait in the evening light just after supper. She set up across the road from our path where the low golden sun was still shining, casting long shadows of trees south and east, but bright and full on my face and body. She had me stand holding a wooden staff like a native's spear, my hand around its shank, leaning my weight against it. First she took one and fretted about this and that, complaining that her shadow was visible toward the bottom of the frame. So she made me stand for a second one before the sun sank too low, and said she'd develop both and we could choose our favorite.

Last night I dreamed I had a boyfriend who was the King of France. We sat in a field of flowers nuzzling and necking and a biplane flew in, bouncing about importantly on its landing. A man in goggles rushed over and told my friend he had to meet presently with the Prime Minister, and I said, "Oh, yeah, that's right. You're the King of France." We necked and nuzzled more, falling back into the flowers, and he told the man in goggles the Prime Minister would have to wait.

———

## 26 JUNE 1915

We watched a schooner get stuck on the sandbar. I thought it was a wreck for certain, but the waves kept coming, lifting it up in dolphin kicks from prow to stern and finally it wiggled free. I got bitten on the toe by a crab, ouch.

The sun is *so* hot when there's no wind and you're inland off the water. I lay down in a dusty hollow imagining I'd been captured and forced to lie exposed to the sun and die of thirst. I just lay motionless, and still sweat beaded up on my chest and rolled down my tummy in trickles.

Oh Pshaw tonight, three hours long. It's the longest we four've spent together at a stretch since getting here. Father won and claims we'll never beat him.

## 27 JUNE 1915

Duncan's made a pitch from pine and says he'll seal his boat by it. I did my reading by the shore so I could watch him all lovely and brown in his rough twill shorts, barefoot and shirtless and sweating. He made mincemeat of Cicero.

After, we swam.

Another note from Father, this in the pocket of my shorts. "It is possible the wisdom of cows goes far beyond ours. Sit quietly in the field by them and listen. Watch them watching through their big brown eyes."

## 28 JUNE 1915

A fire must be burning in the brown hills to the east. The air's been sharp and hot with smoke smell all day long and the sun set so gloriously blood-red I'm sure something's drastically wrong. Father says we can volunteer if a call goes out for firefighters.

The skeleton frame of Duncan's boat looks like fish bones. A big fat central beam, feathered down its whole length with even, sturdy ribs. He's dug up some tools, various hand saws and awls and clamps and buckets full of nails. I watched him hoisting the whole heft of it up on a pair of sawhorses. He eyed it down its length and planed away at bumps and bulges, and he pounded the hammer hard against the rib ends just to see if they'd bust, and they didn't.

Flora posed a photo with Father, Duncan and me. Father sat in the old swing that hangs in the big oak by the road. Flora made him wear his hat all floppy and pulled low so he looked like Walt Whitman. Duncan and I sat high up in a tree limb, our arms around each other and our legs dangling down. She took the picture so you could see the whole enormous oak tree all filling the big square frame of her photo plate.

## 29 JUNE 1915

There was an explosion in the night, an enormous boom that came rolling across the water, shaking our bed and raising us all up with a start. That was all. No one knew what happened, though everyone was abuzz with possibilities this afternoon at the mail drop. Mrs. Bladt says that German U-boats are blasting tunnels in under the Continent by shooting torpedoes into land. They aimed high, she says, and the thing blew up in air, leaving no trace.

We went back to sleep.

It says in Cicero that the simple and ordinary slips easily away from the mind, leaving our memories crowded with images of the grotesque and uncommon. "We ought, then," he concludes, "to set up images of a kind that can adhere longest in memory. And we shall do so if we establish similitudes as striking as possible; if we set up images that are not many or vague but

active; if we assign to them exceptional beauty or singular ug-
liness; if we ornament some of them, as with crowns or purple
cloaks, so that the similitude may be more distinct to us; or if
we somehow disfigure them, as by introducing one stained with
blood or soiled with mud or smeared with red paint, so that its
form is more striking, or by assigning certain comic effects to
our images, for that, too, will ensure our remembering them
more readily."

It confuses me some. What is it I'm remembering if the image
I place on the locus is grotesque and comic and exaggerated? I
guess I need to use the uncommon image as a marker, one that
triggers the actual recollection. That still leaves the problem of
*remembering* the actual recollection, but I suppose it will just trail
along, following the grotesque image to which it's wedded.

The mind is left in layers, real memories lying under odd
creations, odd creations populating memorized landscapes.
Something present becomes hidden, like the weight the undersides of painted clouds sometimes have, hanging heavy with
what's not seen, what's been painted over, in the sky of a
landscape painting. (Ruskin would hate *my* little painting. I don't
seem capable of rendering things as they actually are, present
to the eye.)

The architects of the Fair must have been reading this Cicero
stuff. They too seem intent on populating their elaborate "matrix" with grotesque images, clownish tableaus meant to stand
for some more prosaic thought or thing. Mother, for instance:
a monstrous winged angel meaning "Victory." Though at the
Fair I see no layers, only a thin plaster surface. Beneath the
plaster is nothing but junk. Wood lathing, spare metal parts,
the garbage of the Fair's construction.

We four met at the pond at the usual time, Father sporting a
sunbonnet and his reading glasses. Duncan and I dove in straightaway and paddled about all wet and breathless. Flora stood by

the shore and as we pulled ourselves out onto the grass she announced brightly that we ought all go unclothed. Father was, at the time, sitting calmly on the grass reading. I said, "No, thank you very much" quiet and to myself, jumping back in as quick as could be. Father just chuckled and said he'd blister and peel from embarrassment alone and thank you, he'd rather indulge his modesty. No discussion, thank God, ensued.

## 30 JUNE 1915

It was a day like all the other days—woke and wrestled and kissed and loved fooling around with him and us both just wrestling to exhaustion. We pulled our shorts on and ran to the pond to go swimming in the clear cool water.

We ate breakfast in the meadow up by Father's. The sun shone down through the broad green branches and dappled across the thick damp grass.

———

Fish filled the lagoon very suddenly today and birds came swooping in from all quarters, a thick carpet of them collapsing down onto the water, diving in furious flashes a good long hour till they were fed or the fish were all eaten or they'd swum away.

I did a flip off the rope swing.

This from Maury:

Dear Robert,

The spring has been unthinkable, lost on this dead landscape of trenches, mud fields and artillery craters. There is no land over which to maneuver.

Yesterday I was allowed light duty, told to scavenge a fresh battle sight for useful salvage. From a distance it looked plain enough, a sea of mud pocked by craters. Four of us set out to search haphazardly through the waste, dimly aware, though not saying so, of what must be buried there.

There are no trees here, any longer, no shrubs or ground cover, no grass or wheat or rye, nothing. Good land is solid and the rest is mud, sometimes waist-deep and impossible to tell until you're right in it. We'd been issued rakes and ropes for our operation. You can imagine the first find, my rake dragging into something heavy but manageable, the boot end coming up first and then it popping clean from the sucking mud just above the knee where it had been severed. One can be so willingly blind until slapped in the face, and then be blind again.

1 JULY 1915

This morning I slipped out of sleeping and felt Duncan's warm breathing across my neck. He was still asleep, his body all splayed and spread across me, our middles mushed together and our fingers tangled out at the ends of our arms. I was on my back and he was on my front and the covers were kicked down around our feet. We were just lying all bare and lovely in our boxers. So half-sleepy as I was, I found my throat growling its queer song. My mouth was pushed in against his throat, and when I exhaled I groaned and hummed, making my head bones buzz a little bit, and stirring up some unplaceable pleasure inside me.

I opened my eyes and there was Flora. We neither of us said a thing, though I felt myself blushing all flush and hot in the cheeks and I smiled as if an irresistible giggle was growing in me, but I kept quiet. She reached over and pulled the covers up on us and patted my shoulder and went in.

I walked up in the woods today, working to memorize the landscape, taking close account of the topography, the jibs and jabs of land, the clefts and crevices and sheltered places. I'll need to divide up each canyon into simple parts and know their order and interrelation.

I spent most of the afternoon in Morse's Gulch. Like the others, it's a steep-sided gully which rolls out onto broad shoulders, once you climb out of the woods and up into grasslands. (I remembered catching the squirrel up in the scree back of Weeks Gulch. The ruins still remain. They're so small and unremarkable. I cannot connect them to that memory.)

I watched a heavy barge out at sea, out past the high hill behind Bolinas. It was a long black speck on the wavering sea, sailing beneath its high white sails. The wide blue water quivered through the heat shivers rising up from the dry land between here and there. The ship crept along steady and slow, carrying some heavy black cargo south.

## 2 JULY 1915

Father sat by the open fire in our house today and read his little book while I sat near him and read too. I haven't done that in a long time. It was misty and gray out, that wonderful sad weather that just soaks into your bones, damp dank ocean clouds rolling low to the ground.

After lunch Father went back up to his gazebo. I felt housebound, so Duncan and I went for a swim despite the gray. It rained a real rain while we were out there, heavy drops splashing on the dusty road and raising that special summer smell. We ran to the pond and stripped in the grass and dove in, the cool water all over our skin and the heavy rain pelting into the pond.

Our clothes were all muddy so we dropped them in the pond for a cleaning, but that did no good. We put our shorts back on, all wet and clinging, and walked back through the rain singing comical songs. We gathered our clothes in a pile and put on some water to boil, giving them a good soak and a scrub in the washtub, and we sat the rest of the wet afternoon, bundled naked in our comforter, sitting by the fire reading books.

## 3 JULY 1915

Gray rain beating down from the clouds like it was winter in Seattle. There's a leak (happily, above the sink). We've almost run out of wood.

## 4 JULY 1915

The clouds've kept on, shutting out the sun, but the rain has let up. I told Duncan that soldiers chop wood for fitness. Flora is attempting a self-portrait. She wants to be captured flying off the rope swing into thin air. The ground will not be in the frame, nor will the rope. I'm to snap the shutter.

———

I went to the woods again, looking once more at Bourne's Gulch. Father was walking far ahead and I decided I'd follow along at a distance. The clouds rumbled in off the sea, butting up against the high ridges east of us, slinking in amongst the hills. Father had his spyglasses and a worn wood staff, that floppy felt hat all pulled down tight.

He walked past the head of the lagoon, cutting inland around another bend, walking up through a long grass meadow, stopping to run his hands over the blades now and again, sniffing it seemed, and generally looking for a direction. I stood quiet and hidden by trees, nearer to the shore and above him on the first shoulder of the northern ridge of this gully. He raised his glasses and watched, looking up and down the thick trunk of a fir, and then he walked forward through the grass, up into the first trees.

I felt curiously at home and comfortable, a bit tingly from the challenge of going unseen, but generally as though I was engaged in something very familiar, something with its own certain rewards. It was as if I'd been doing this all my life.

Father had disappeared into a thicket. I hurried along, up the gulch, running swift and silent over clear ground among the firs. I dropped down low coming up to a little ledge and peered over, across a broad bowl, cut through its middle by the creek bed. Father was down by the creek, bent over, sipping water, crouched like a little boy.

I lay low on the ledge and caught my breath, watching his progress east through a stand of redwood. The heavy trunks grew tall and straight, gathered together in small circles, family circles, the many offspring of a single giant all emerging from the crumbling stump. It was frightening to see how big the old trees must have been, their girth mimicked in the arrangement of the new trees. They were cut and hauled out on boats to build the city. Most of that lumber burned in the big fire, after the quake.

I'd lost him again, certain he'd headed up the other rise, going to higher ground on the south side of the gulch. I'd have a difficult time getting around where I could watch him now. The approach from below was too open and the path around the top of the gulch would take too long. I waited and listened. The clouds had come in low and heavy, their bottoms dragging down into the dark green tops of the trees. There was just the wind and some chattering up in the higher branches. No twigs snapped or spyglass straps squeaked. I scooted down off the ledge and scrambled across the bowl, jumping the creek in a smooth leap and running on up the opposite side. I kept checking right and left and straight ahead, but saw no sign of him.

It was raining now, high up in the trees. I flopped down in a hollow and looked up into rain, all of it washing down onto the canopy, leaving the forest floor dry. I wanted to strip my clothes off and run naked through the woods, up onto the grass ridges, and let the rain run muddy streaks across my skin. I wanted to run and grab my father and throw him into the sea. I lay still and listened for the rumble of the quake, the terrible roar. Nothing.

I ran up the hillside, going for higher ground, and kept an eye on the gully. But maybe he was ahead of me, at a vantage point above the trees, where he could look down and see if there was any nesting here. Coming over a rise, I stopped and looked up through the trees and brush, looking for a glimpse of his dark green sweater, his dirty brown hat. There he was, looking back at me from above, looking through his spyglasses. My eyes locked into those impenetrable lenses. He dropped them from his face and continued over the ridge, disappearing from view.

Something terrible happened inside me then. Something very tiny and awful there in the very middle of me, making my breathing deep and difficult and my heart race. I ran away up the hill after him, making little whimpering sounds and getting all snotty in my nose and teary-eyed. I tried a yell to him but my throat croaked and I stumbled, falling with my face in the dirt, and I clambered back up and off again, gulping the wet salty air and making those awful sounds.

He was nowhere. I came all the way up out of the woods and into the long yellow grass, the whole sky opening up gray and terrible, stretching out to every border and dumping rain over the land and in the sea. It was washing down over everything. I cried again there like I'd cried in the city, only now I was exposed out on this ridge, high up with the ground falling away in every direction. Down and down into the dark woods and down the falling face to that dirty path and the lagoon, and there was Duncan, running off alone in the muddy rain, running away, south through the storm, going as far as he could go in what time he had.

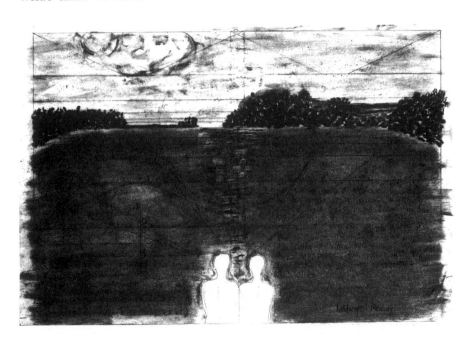

## 5 JULY 1915

I must've caught a chill in the rain yesterday. I slept the night so fitfully and shaking, burning a fever and trembling there in bed all night, curled up as close to Duncan as I could just for comfort.

Duncan and Flora were both very sweet, bringing me hot soup in bed and reading out loud from Cicero. I napped in the late morning and by lunch I felt strong and able enough to get up and out.

Father visited me at my sickbed, holding his hand to my forehead and clucking his concern.

"Did you see me there?" I asked him simply.

"Oh, yes," he said. "Quite exciting, really. You're so very quick with this memorization." He patted my hand by way of congratulations. "I hadn't expected you'd be up that far so soon. I prefer working in isolation, you see."

"I know," I assured him. "I'm sorry."

"Oh, don't be silly, Max. What's to be sorry for?"

I thought quite carefully. I *did* feel sorry, very sorry about something, and I wanted to tell him as clearly as I could.

"I'm not sure," I began. "I'm sorry I was there disturbing you. I'm sorry I went running like a pig all through your woods and chasing about when you had your watching to do."

He smiled through his bristles and ruffled my hair some. I waited for him to answer, to help me figure more closely what I felt sorry for. He gave me a kiss on the forehead.

"Apology accepted, little fish. If we're more careful with our planning, things should be just fine," and he scooted his chair out, getting up to go. "Lunch?" he said.

I nodded yes and put my clothes on and joined them for lunch.

———

I put the first color on my landscape today, a deep reddish orange in the upper right corner. It's like the real sun has finally begun to set in my drawing, its light cast into the little corner, a spreading, effusive glow, so soon the whole neat structure, all of my carefully drawn lines will be taken over, inhabited by the presence of this real, gooey, wet, glowing thing.

6 JULY 1915

I'm well again. Slept and slept, nuzzled in so deep into bed I thought I might never emerge. But morning kept getting to be more and more, more bright sun dappling down and birds keeping up their crazy calling and then a fresh breeze through the screens and we were up and out to the pond in a flash.

A dog adopted us today by the boat. A big brown dog, all shaggy and with his mouth full of slobber. His tongue wobbled in the wind. He swam after sticks and jumped up, front paws all muddy,

166 · MATTHEW STADLER

to dance whatever dance dogs do. We went home to lunch and
he went trotting south, off to Stinson Beach I imagine.

## 7 JULY 1915

Hot again, if you found the right shelter spot, up away from
the water and free from any wind. Up Bourne's Gulch was like
a desert, parched and dusty like it hadn't rained for centuries.
Duncan ran by and fell in the dirt screaming. I nearly killed
myself running down off the ridge to him, and he looked up at
me from the dirty ground and wiggled and laughed. Everyone's
a joker.

## 8 JULY 1915

Another note from Father, this in my morning oatmeal:

> What keeps the cow from merging inextricably into me?
> How can I look into that unfixed riot of colors and shapes
> that is out there, everywhere, and see what I see, the cow
> sitting placidly in a field of rye? Somehow things remain
> distinct, defined. I've made borders. I've expectations, maps
> made by memory, that outline arrangements I will see.
> There's a fine brown cow in that green field of rye. Out
> there, little fish.
>
> Europeans searching for Shangri-la are escorted by voice-
> less monks through the treacherous mountains of Tibet.
> The wise monks forbid maps. Visitors who attempt any sort
> of record are killed in terrible and strange ways. What do
> we forbid by forbidding maps? What do we make possible?
> Can you travel without maps? Really there is too much to
> see.

I do try to think about these things. This one is a bit more
baffling than the usual. Though I recall one when I was only just

ten or so that wasn't even grammatically sensible, at least it didn't seem so to me or Duncan, to whom I showed it, just in case I was being dense. How very brave of me that must have been.

Memory. Well, I've got some hunches there. We see what we see because memories make expectations? That's like things I've been thinking, how things have to fit somehow or they slip away. I like this inextricable merging too. I feel that with Duncan sometimes, that inextricable merging. And with the cold night air and water. Maps make no sense to me. What am I to make of *that?*

While we poked around in town waiting for the mail drop, a gaggle of kids ran past us through the grocery finding items from off a list, all flitty and flighty with excitement, so we asked them what was up.

"Mr. McKennan's hired out his launch for a moonlight ride. We'll be having a bonfire too, after."

Duncan, being bolder than I, asked, "May we come along? Three of us?" and after some confident calling back and forth across the store was answered "Yes, certainly, we'd all love for you to come." We were introduced to a boy about thirteen who said his name was Grover.

"Duncan," Duncan said, extending his hand.

"Max," I added. "Flora Profuso will be our third."

"Do I know you?" Grover asked, as two girls and another boy, all a bit older than he, crowded up behind.

"We're just here for the summer, along Bolinas Road at the end of the lagoon," I explained. "My father lives there."

The other three introduced themselves. "Tyrone," "Falillia," "Tiffany," they said in turn. Tyrone and Tiffany were twins and Grover was their little brother. Falillia and Tyrone held hands. We agreed to meet by the docks just after nine-thirty and Grover said we must bring something for roasting.

———

We bundled warm in sweaters and caps, our little bow ties sitting smartly on our collars. Flora wore a lovely dress and father's floppy hat, making her look like a cowboy who'd been through hell, lost his cowboy duds and been forced to wear a dress. I carried a sack of yams, for roasting.

The launch was long and low and we introduced Flora straight-away, chitchatting briskly about the stars and geography, the richness of the air and its comparison to the city. Flora impressed them with her bohemian tales, counseling Falillia and Tiffany on the importance of suffrage. Mr. McKennan sat by the wheel in silence sucking on his warm, smoky pipe. It was high tide and perfectly calm, the water sitting smooth as glass and black, reflecting a trailing glow of moon and individual stars if you looked very close into an especially still pool.

The wide empty air filled us full of silence soon, and we drifted, not speaking, lying back into the boat and gazing out at the black night, each with our private thoughts. Tyrone and Falillia were necking quietly nearby. I had thoughts but let them lie with a warm arm on Duncan's shoulders. Grover sat up close to Mr. McKennan and asked please could we go out over the bar, it being so calm and still tonight, and Mr. McKennan agreed.

As the boat approached the bar we all got up from our reveries and faced out into the brisk ocean. The breakers could be seen crashing ghost white far out into the night. The briny ocean-air smell came whipping in around us as the boat beat along into the waves, smashing into the rugged breakers head-on.

It was a wonderful white moon, and we rolled through the swells out beyond the bar, cruising almost to the clam patch and back again, everyone up and about and screaming to the rolling sea. We were back and docked very late, past eleven, and we thanked Mr. McKennan politely, wandering on through town, Grover rushing ahead to set flame to the previously built bonfire.

The yams were hot and sweet and delicious.

9 JULY 1915

Duncan woke me up today, I was so sleepy from our launch. He rolled me out of bed and we walked bleary-eyed and yawning out to the pond, stripping off our clothes there in the grass. And then we jumped in.

Duncan's worked the rib and beam skeleton onto the back of the boat now. It juts out forward, the ribs brushing back like the windblown branches of trees. I helped him seal the back end with pine pitch, brushing amber gobs across the old dry seams, fixing joints where the new boards meet. It's all so solid and strong.

10 JULY 1915

Flora made us dress up as dogs today. She'd fashioned dog hats by turning some old fur collars out and fixing furry dog ears on them. Just that and mittens she'd also fixed all furry and paw-padded, and big fluffy tails. She had us in our shorts, dressed up in this doggy wear, lying on our backs in the grass all stretched out and very undoglike. We lay there close with our arms around each other's shoulders and smiling. This was the latest photo. She took it.

I snapped her midair flight, just as she'd planned, her flying out into nothing, floating in the bright air. Flora says it will be just a blur but that she tried to keep her face still so you might see it was she.

But I don't trust photos. And I fear I'm beginning to lose faith in Cicero too. I could make a little list: photographs; frozen memories (as with Cicero); the Fair's fake monuments and flimsy plaster walls. All of them are brittle thin surfaces hovering over nothing. From a distance they seem so substantial. But if your head swings in too close, bumping recklessly against them, they shatter and vanish, leaving you swinging in empty air.

We tipped Squashtoe's cow for mischief tonight. They sleep standing up. Duncan and I sneaked up into their meadow, hiding in the oaks, and looked about for a victim. They're beautiful patchwork ghosts in the moonlight, swatches of black and white, floating there in the dark field. We watched and waited, confident the one we'd chosen was indeed asleep as it hadn't moved for many long minutes. We moved swiftly across the meadow, crouched low and quiet, coming up alongside. Then, two hands each on the starboard flank, *uumph* and over she went, letting out a terrible panicked little cry. We ran and ran away as fast and far as we could. That little noise was so innocent and helpless I felt bad the rest of the night. But there was nothing I could do to make amends, so I lived with it and made a little private promise before falling off to sleep.

———

## 11 JULY 1915

Under water almost two minutes today. Duncan timed me by his pulse. The longer I stay down the more scared he gets so the faster his pulse races. Good deal, huh?

Father's got zucchini squash that are nearly the size of baseball bats. He's got baskets full that are less grotesque, running the range from tiny frog's fingers to a good healthy forearm and every size between. But I fancied eating the biggest. We plucked it from its vine and carried it in at lunch, hung in a sling on the broomstick, like some wild game we'd bagged. We sliced it down its middle and baked it, basting its face in garlic butter. It smelled like heaven, as garlic butter does, but went down like snot-covered string, slimy and unmanageable. Thank God for the garlic butter, as that was all that saved it. The more manageable sizes, one must conclude, are ever more delicious and mouth-watering.

In town I saw Grover and he said, "Hi, pal," like we'd been pals a long time and just hadn't seen each other much. Maybe I'm becoming a sex maniac like the cases in Havelock Ellis because Grover didn't have a shirt on and I found myself looking down across his smooth belly and up onto his little muscular chest and getting all stirred up in my pants, sort of leaning into him and talking about whatever just to stay close by.

## 12 JULY 1915

Walking in Bourne's Gulch today, the sun burning sweetly among the cedar branches. Cicero prefers buildings (when choosing a memory matrix), but I think my landscape is the better choice. Everything here is in its proper place. Thick cool groves of redwood deep in the cut, growing near to the streams, then tall straight fir and cedar up the steep slopes, oak and grasses above that, all of it opening up onto yellow grasslands where the ridges round off. The land is organized by simple forces, reliable forces like the wind and weather and the seasons. It's not like buildings which answer to the ridiculous whims of architects. There is nothing arbitrary here.

And like my memory this place is changing in a slow and patterned way, spinning on a pivot, marking a path that retains every trace of its turning. An earthquake comes cracking through, and the land takes its full force, splitting open and spilling out on itself. The explosion's gone in a fraction of a second, but it stays here forever, torn out and tumbled across the gullies. The rain falls and makes its mark, rising back up in the green plants. Nothing here is ever lost or forgotten. And neither is it caught, held fixed and frozen in its moment, hard and brittle as the glass face of a photographic plate.

## 13 JULY 1915

Bright and sunny again, but now a brisk wind is blowing, full of salty freshness in off the sea. I'm dark as Duncan from my walks up into the woods, but when I'm naked my body wears little ghost shorts where I'm still pale. I like that. I like lying naked next to Duncan and looking down to where our middles meet.

Duncan's banged some boards on, up the middle of the boat. We sealed them tight with pitch, just at dusk down by the water.

## 14 JULY 1915

Flora says it is Bastille Day, French independence. I kept my dream a secret.

My mind is so muddled concerning Cicero. The thought of perfect powers of recollection is still seductive, yet the actuality seems like death to me. As if I'd ever known the actuality. Perhaps if I kiss Duncan often enough the entirety of things will begin to make clear sense. One never knows. All previous plans will be put on hold while I pursue this alternative.

Duncan wanted to tip cows again tonight but I said no and we swam in the moonlit pond instead. We took a blanket and lay there looking up into the night for a very long time.

———

## 15 JULY 1915

The lagoon really stinks at low tide. The water seems to be dragging out farther than before and all manner of disgusting goo and gunk lies steaming in the hot sun. It's not fit to walk in and makes me think twice about swimming there at all. I'm only going to help on the boat when the tide's in.

We rode the waves on our bellies in the roaring white water, it rushing into shore and us dumping hard into the sand all tossed and turned as the wave comes crashing down on itself. Grover showed us how.

I made dinner, *fruits de mer en chemise,* in the Parisian style. I found it in a little card file of recipes which Father claims bear no relation to him. Flora says it means "seafood in a shirt."

## 16 JULY 1915

This morning the covers were all kicked down around our feet and Duncan half-asleep tugged my boxers off and was going at me all over, reaching his long arms up and down the length of my body and pushing his mouth down over me, both of us making all sorts of odd noises. Flora was there, just across the porch, lying very calm and silent.

It made me feel very odd, knowing how rude we were being, and also very queer wondering what she must feel. She must have the patience of a saint to be putting up with us being so inconsiderate and still be so polite as she is.

There was a note on our bed tonight. "Please be more discreet," it said simply. We slept very chaste and sound.

The sunset tonight was a small, wonderful thing.

———

## 17 JULY 1915

Clouds came in overnight so the early morning was pearl gray and luminous. Father woke us before seven for a minus tide, passing through the porch with a steaming pot of coffee and and his usual buzz-lipped reveille. We were off to Duxbury Reef to collect mussels.

We walked up the windblown beach all wrapped in sweaters and scarves. The clouds came in thick, drifting down onto the headlands. We picked in pairs, each with a pail, looking for the fat healthy ones and tearing them from the rocks with little prying tools. Tidewater rippled in the wind, splashing about in tiny pools, their shallow rock bottoms aquiver with strange sea life, sturdy urchins and waving anemones. One fat fleshy sea cucumber jutted obscenely out from a barnacled crevice. We filled our pails and then some and walked back against the wind, heading home to a good hot chowder.

## 18 JULY 1915

I slept poorly. Duncan was fitful, dead to the world but tossing about and grabbing me, clutching my arm very tight and making whimpery noises. He said he hadn't dreamed anything, but ached and felt grumpy. I ached too, but was more sad than grumpy, feeling uncertain about the end of summer and silly about the particulars of Duncan. We don't talk about particulars.

I couldn't concentrate and went down to Duncan's boat. It stunk to high heaven, the tide being low, and Duncan felt a bit queasy so we walked back up in the woods over on the mesa and in along the Garzoli Ranch. We didn't talk, but Duncan walked close by me and we wrapped our arms round each other's backs and that seemed just right. At Pebble Beach we stripped and swam but the water was so icy cold we just shivered there on shore and couldn't really warm up until we'd climbed back up inland and sat to rest in amongst the lupine.

## 19 JULY 1915

We four ate a very long lunch. Flora and I regaled Father with our Rupert Brooke stories and Duncan told us his very earliest memory from when he lived in Persia.

He was on a caravan with his mother and father, him held up in his mother's lap high atop a dromedary hump. Really, this is true. The caravan included several dozen families. Duncan doesn't know why. He was never told, being just three, as he was. The caravan was making its way as close as it could to the next oasis, his dad told him so, before a terrible dust storm hit. He remembers seeing the enormous black swirling cloud of dust shutting off the horizon, growing and growing, spreading over nearly half the sky. Duncan had to go to the bathroom. He just had a terrible need right then and there to go. This next part I'm sure he made up because it makes no sense to me. His mother halted the whole caravan, fearing that they'd be separated from the rest and die, and dismounted from the ponderous height, carrying Duncan and a brilliant brass urn. This, Duncan says, was his potty and his mother insisted he always use his potty so as not to develop uncivilized habits. She is, you know, British. She set him up, facing into the endless open desert, the black dust swirling up into the sky, it raising a horrible high whistling sound and rumbling steadily toward them. There he sat on his brilliant brass urn, facing the bleak landscape, with some hundred camels and scores of grumpy people behind him just waiting.

Flora came with me to the pond for drawing. We'd been bickering about drawing and photos and she saw no reason to let my schedule interrupt that.

"Why not take a photo, Dogey?" she repeated, kicking a stone along the dusty road north. "You can trace from there and then paint it in colors, just as you remember it."

I turned to her. Some disgusting liquid came flying out my

nostril, whipping across the trajectory of my turn, and narrowly missed her sleeve. She politely ignored it.

"I'm not trying to draw a *photo,*" I insisted. "I'm drawing what I remember." The sun continued burning brightly down.

"But Dogey, the photo will help you get it just right. You're only a beginner, you know. This way the shapes will be right." She sounded like me talking to Mother. "Hills and water can't have changed that drastically in five years."

She wasn't getting it. I rolled my sleeves up like I'd seen Mr. Spengler do whenever he wanted to convince Flora of something.

"I didn't see it how it is. You see? I saw it differently." That seemed about right to me.

"What was different?" she asked, furrowing her brow quizzically and touching my arm with her soft fingers.

I pulled my little landscape out of its holder.

"See," I said. "That's what I saw." We stopped and gazed at the layered mess of lines. "More or less that." She looked and looked for a long while, then exhaled forcefully through her nose. "Don't you imagine we *all* see the same things differently?" I asked, hoping to preempt any further objections. "Like when you look out in the dark, everyone sees whatever frightens them?"

She'd tilted her head down low, bumping her crown up against mine, and begun nodding no, our heads so engaged that we both nodded no (though that's not what *I* meant).

"Cameras will put an end to all that," she concluded happily. And now I nodded no in earnest.

"No," I vocalized. "That's the awful trick of cameras. You *think* they've caught things just as they are but really it's just nothing. It's worse than nothing. It's nothing masquerading as something."

I was beginning to feel a bit heated up about it all. I took the little album she carried out from under her arm and opened it up at random. "Look at that," I said, pointing to the photo of me and my spear. "It's all very pretty, but it's not like a person seeing. It's just this paper turning all blotchy from chemicals." I had some sense my argument was getting messy, but I kept on. "It's nowhere, it's . . . it's like being fed through a tube or . . . or going to sea in a submarine." I paused to consider my point. "Does that make sense?"

Flora kept up her quizzical stare. "No," she said simply.

I thought some more, trying to think to the simple center of what I felt.

"No one *sees* the way a camera sees," I concluded, finally.

"No one sees the way you see either," Flora said bluntly.

"So?" I answered because that's precisely what I meant.

"So why are you badgering me about how horrible photos can be if your silly drawing is just as pointless?"

"I never said it was pointless."

"Deceitful then. You implied that photos were deceitful."

"Did I?" I stalled. Now I was worried my drawing was indeed pointless. "Why do you say my drawing's pointless?"

"Dogey! Don't get me all turned around." With that she shook me by my shoulders. "Your drawing's pointless only if you say a camera's view is pointless. Your view is no better than a camera's."

"Why not?" I objected. "I'm a person, and that makes it better." It seemed a sensible position.

"But someone's operating the camera, Dogey. That photo you complained about was taken by someone. Me."

"I complained because you said photos would make us all see the same because a camera sees better somehow."

"Deceit! That's your point about deceit, you implied photos claimed a superior view." She was clearly relieved we'd found this thread again.

"I guess I did," I allowed. "Don't they?"

"I guess you could say that, if people end up thinking it's wrong to see other than how a photo sees. Then people won't let themselves see differently. I don't know if you can really blame the photo for that, Dogey."

But I wasn't really listening now. I'd suddenly realized it was her photo I'd attacked.

"*Yours* aren't like that," I interrupted generously. "No one could ever think yours were real," and I smiled with praise.

"What do you mean?" She seemed annoyed by my interruption.

I thought carefully, looking for just the right way to put it, taking the album in hand and looking closely at the photos.

"I see them as so very, so," and then it came to me, "very individual." I pecked her on the cheek, knowing I'd seen just the quality she saw. I'd found a word on which we could agree.

"Yes," she agreed. "They're certainly that. Your drawing is too, you know," and she pecked me back on my cheek. I was glad we'd made up, as we always seemed to by the end of an argument.

Behind us the clouds had come back in, drifting in off the gray sea, all feathery and wet on the underside. We rushed for the pond, wanting to get in and out before the sun disappeared. We came running through the field and stripped under the oaks, diving into the clear blue pool without a pause. Our swim was quick and vigorous. Splashing and dolphin dives and furious laps but no horseplay on the rope swing, and we were out again, lying wet and clean and empty in the lovely green grass. We soaked in the bright warm sun for a good long time before the mists drifted in across the rest of the sky and shut the whole day down into clouds.

It began blowing strong before dusk, the sky progressively darker and Duncan deciding he'd best tie his boat down with ropes. By dinner it was almost dark as night and the frightful gusts were battering down through the trees, no rain yet, but that electrical smell of rain about to come in torrents. Father'd cooked a Welsh Cowle, lamb-bone stew with potatoes and leeks from the garden and ladles full of rich broth, which we sat down to eat, all chitter-chatter with excitement and talk to keep the scary night at bay. I was bump up against Duncan, all of us laughing at some thought of Father's, jostling and hoo-hawing, and Duncan kissed me on my cheek without a word or a thought and no one stopping to take any notice.

My discussion with Flora today touched again on that little disagreement with Cicero. Cicero or Ruskin (or Mother, for that matter) would have no patience for the sloppiness of my paints. Yet I've begun to enjoy it. It appears that I've left my painting in the realm of the nurselogs and landscapes, that lazy realm within which I can continue to embrace the painting's ever-changing face. I have no need for "accuracy."

But perhaps my enjoyment is a shelter of last resort, a position to which I am forced by the utter impossibility of my ever successfully using the paints with discipline and accuracy. If I *could* make my painting replicate exactly the original event, I wondered, wouldn't I delight in that power? Like Cicero, wouldn't I be intoxicated by the sheer certainty of it, the delightful precision and stability of exact reproduction? But paint defies me, and so, it seems, does memory. Even if I had a camera which made photos of the picture in my mind, that picture, the memory of Bolinas five years ago, would be vastly different than the Bolinas I am living in now. It is a blessing and curse for which I find myself feeling quite grateful.

## 20 JULY 1915

Flora saw lanterns flashing and heard voices through the noise of the wind and rain, down on the lagoon. She's gone to wake Father and find a lantern, blankets and rope.

I said we'd stay put till she got back, but Duncan said maybe we'd go down if things seemed desperate and Flora'd not yet returned. Of course Duncan saw things as desperate straightaway so we bundled up in sweaters and tied a length of rope around our waists, just in case. We wobbled down the muddy hill through the gusting wind and the rain blowing down in sheets.

Our meadow had become a raging pond, full up to its lip with water and rippling waves clear across its top from the wind blowing strong. We waded through it and scrambled up onto the muddy road. Rain smacked in fat drops against our faces, making it difficult to see properly. Ghost ridges of wind-whipped white tops floated pale and distant in the black night. It was hard to tell where the shore ended and the lagoon began. We kept stepping out into the cold water without noticing.

We made our way along the shore toward where Duncan's boat was supposed to be and there, indeed, it was. Duncan had lashed it tight with ropes up amongst last winter's driftwood, safe from the reach of even the worst summer storm.

"Where's Flora?" I thought to ask, feeling the need for a nice bright lantern. Duncan shrugged into the dark and pointed farther up the shore. The dim shadow of something crashed and wobbled out in the dark water, lunging and dipping dangerously. Sounds of creaking and collapse came clear to my ears. Duncan ran off, dragging me down into the water's edge because we'd both forgotten the rope.

"Sorry," he laughed at me, offering a hand. We ran in tandem up farther to get as close as we could.

The shore couldn't bring us close enough to see details. It was something big and built and mostly white, but dark all along its bottom. There were no lights burning and no answers to our calls. We looked all around and saw no lanterns in the distance, no footsteps in the mud, and no cryptic signs, driftwood arranged in an arrow or such as there are in adventure stories. The wreck kept crashing and crumbling out in the waves and we watched and listened so long I got to shivering and Duncan allowed that maybe there was nothing more we could do.

Flora still hasn't returned. Duncan's set a bright warm fire in the fireplace and we've dragged all our bedclothes out in front of it. We boiled up some water and washed what mud there was off each other's bodies with a hot soaped terrycloth. Now there's just the yellow and orange flicker of firelight making shapes and shadows, and the night so terribly dangerous out there. I feel so sheltered in here now, having been washed clean by the storm

and wrecked on the rocks with the ruined hull. Now it's all left
in my head. Like Father's cow, merged inextricably with me.

## 20 JULY 1915

For a long time I lay awake, looking down the hill, watching
the dim pale lines of the wreck out there in the blackness. Now
that we knew it was there, I had no trouble seeing it and hearing
a terrible orchestra of creaks and groans and cracking sounds
that, it was obvious to me, meant the wind and waves were
tearing the last pieces apart. It floated out there in the night,
going in and out of sight as I focused too close or lost it through
branches. I kept hearing voices out there, but they reminded
me of the calling voice of that man drowned at Land's End, so
I put them out of mind and curled in next to Duncan to try
to sleep.

I dreamed about Uncle Maury. I saw his legs blown off in
our pond, which was a bomb crater. I was trying to swim to
him, to get him away from the shell, but I couldn't swim fast
at all, like how you sometimes get bogged down in dreams just
when you need to go fast. Duncan says I was all fitful and grabby.

Flora and Father were down by the wreckage early in the
morning. We saw them, peering down the hill at first light. The
storm had passed and they stood in the various mists down by
the water, dawn light suffusing through it, all golden and orange
and purple and white. I have much more trouble locating colors
at dawn than at sunset. They seem to be everywhere and nowhere.

It was a launch not much bigger than Mr. McKennan's. This
one had a cabin built upon it and various hooks and hoists that
seemed to be related to fishing. It was a good fifty feet from
the shore, but could certainly be reached at low tide, as Duncan

pointed out enthusiastically. From up by the house it looked to be in good shape, save for the split across its middle.

Father says we're not to touch the wreck as the man whose boat it was came by and said someone'd sold him insurance on it. He's got to wait till this man can come look at the damage before he does anything and that won't be for some time, as the insurance man lives in Sacramento. So it rumbles and bobs out there on its little perch. Some big rock's stuck through its middle and even the highest tide doesn't raise enough to float it or sink it. Father warned Duncan about sharks that tend to congregate around lagoon wrecks.

The storm seems to have made quite a mess of the woods. In Bourne's Gulch one of the older cedars fell, taking down a whole line of younger trees with it, marking the woods with a sharp tear across the hillside so sunlight drifts in to places where it hadn't been before. It's hardly noticeable from up on the ridge, just a small line across the even trees, but it will change everything on that hillside, given time. The rain will run differently now, and some soil will go, eroded away from where it sat so safely. The sunlight on the forest floor and the changed run of the water will mean new plants in new places. Cedars will eventually grow again in the place cleared out by the fall, but that may be long after we're dead and gone.

We took the ropes off Duncan's boat, watching it steam in the hot sun. Two pelicans lifted off the wreck, circled up into the warm sky and dove straight down into the cold salt water. Sharp and clean.

## 21 JULY 1915

Flora stayed out again last night. She and Father must've gone to talking very late. It's made it so lovely with Duncan, not having to be polite.

The pond is full up to its lip. Much of the meadow's turned to mush, all because of the storm. No more lying in the grass for the next few days. Cows frequent the pond now, curling up to nap on a knoll back by the oak trees.

We washed smelt under a cold-water tap in town with Grover. Buckets of smelt all cut open down their bellies.

## 22 JULY 1915

Duncan nailed down the last boards today. We brushed a whole bucket of pitch up and down, inside and out, sealing every last seam shut and touching up each other's bellies. He says we won't sail until he's done painting his design.

Another note from Father. I found it in my shoe. "John the Baptist had a little fit, some variety of epileptic seizure. So very much (the totality of those numberless stimuli that we mediate through our thoughts with ease every day) flooded his simple mind at once it was as a white flash. An intensity. An infinity of presence. An absence of distinction. An immediacy. Imagine, the totality without mediation, no things to stand for other things."
    I'd best save it for later.

Duncan gave me flowers. A bouquet of wildflowers from the mesa, all rough and rumpled in his sweaty hand. I was sitting with my dumb book when he sneaked up from behind and held them close by my ear, and out of view. Oh their fragrance, sneaking around me. We made garlands and set them on Father's and Flora's heads.

## 23 JULY 1915

Ruskin tells me nothing about colors. How can they ever be right, all bound up in oily goo? Around me there is simply light.

We don't see Flora at all after dinners. It's me and Duncan and the dark.

## 24 JULY 1915

All day at the pond today, the meadow finally dry and the grass so thick and lovely green from water and sun. I did flips from the rope swing, showing off. Duncan did a double flip.

Duncan's done the whole boat in a base of silver gray. He says that's just the beginning.

## 25 JULY 1915

I've arrived at a small handful of modest conclusions. All of this mulling over memory may have actually moved me, forward, or somewhere.

(1)   My painting is glorious. The wet gobs of paint splotching unpredictably are glorious. The hundred different pictures it's been are blessed and divine. Its layers are wondrous, each and every one lying evident in the surface. That I may never actually finish it is staggering. It is a perfect picture of my memory.

(2)   Cicero is glorious. His high ideal of finding a way to hold fixed memories is inspiring, tragic and doomed to failure. His

confidence that hard work will succeed in making such a system work is alluring and stupid. I too *still* wish to be given that impossible blessing and curse, a perfect memory.

(3)   My memories form a glorious landscape. Weather washes over them all. Earthquakes burst through them from below. While always changing they are never gone. They shift and rearrange, rolling over and into each other like water that runs down the river to the sea and returns again in rain clouds. They emerge like trees growing from the rotting wood of fallen giants. It is a rhythm that doesn't end.

(4)   Duncan makes me delirious. He is an empty vessel. His body is miraculous, washed in the river of my attentions. When we're completely together we have both disappeared. Is there a word?

(5)   It's as if I've found Father's notes inside me. Scary.

## 26 JULY 1915

Flora took us punting on the pond. She'd cajoled a canoe from Mr. Squashtoe and brought a long thin staff. She sat in the back to punt, rather than standing as the Venetians do, and she pushed and poked us round the pond a half dozen times. Then I punted and then Duncan, the passengers lounging about on pillows in the middle of the boat, eating fresh fruits and sipping lemonade.

Rippling waves tickled up my ankles, shuddering cold in the brisk evening breeze. I'd dropped my feet into the water, sitting on a drift log, watching Duncan paint ice-blue fish scales up the flank of his boat.

## 27 JULY 1915

Duncan's prow is a perfect spiral spear. Thick at one end and tapering off to a point at the other. He's painted it pearl gray.

We burned a bonfire on the beach, starting late after dinner, the cold sky black and clear. We burned driftwood down by the lagoon, upwind of Duncan's boat. The wood crackled and spit, burning bright as torches and high into the night. Even the wreck, a good fifty feet distant, glowed all orange and warm, reflecting the flames.

Grover, Tyrone and Falillia came, having seen the flames from across the water. They brought corn for roasting and marsh-mallows too. Flora took a photo and we all held stock-still for the long seconds she felt were needed to expose a plate by firelight.

## 28 JULY 1915

Duncan got me going in the afternoon, laying me out all lovely in the grass by the pond, naked and wet and my muscles all tired and tingling from swimming fast laps. He had me stretched out full, me reaching out above me and stretching my toes to their farthest possible points, all that feeling rushing from end to end and about to burst out of my middle and come when he stood away and let me lie there, almost bursting, looking at me and waiting. I said nothing, just stayed all stretched out, my heart still racing, catching my breath and the sunlight dappling through oak branches and over my brown skin. Then he lay down again by me and started over, very slow and soft, just touching and then his mouth over me again, and the blood just aching in me until I was dizzy and almost dying and up he got again, just standing over and watching me. It went on and on till I was so tired and dizzy I thought I'd passed out there in the grass, blind to the day and my body just raw and tingling, drawing deep breaths inside me. His mouth came over me then and I could feel the full length of me in him and my warm push against the back of his throat, and him working me all up and down. The whole afternoon came rushing through my spine, bursting out my middle and into his throat, like that white flash, that intensity, that infinity of presence.

I was completely gone. I lay there breathing, and sank into the wet green grass. Duncan's arm lay near my mouth and I felt that feeling in my throat. It felt so lovely, the groan and growl of that unconscious song rattling inside me each time I exhaled, buzzing the soft underside of his arm where my lips lay against him. It was nothing more than a sound.

## 29 JULY 1915

We four went up in the hills picking berries. Father made us wear sun hats and we dipped them in water whenever we could find water. Blackberries warm up hot like hot syrup sitting in the sun. They hang heavy on their stickered vines, and so soft they burst if you touch them too hard. You've got to unch them off with gentle fingers placed flush against their collars, right around the stem. Best of all, unch them off into your mouth. Hot bursting berry juice, *boom!* across your tongue.

The Seals are in first place, Grover says. But there's still a month and a half left in the season.

## 30 JULY 1915

Duncan worked on the rudder today, sawing it with the jigsaw so it looks like a tailfin. I painted it, following his instructions, all silver gray and black, very detailed, so it looks scaly like a fish and matches the design he's made up the sides.

Flora's sewing the sail from a white canvas tent Father junked because it tore. Duncan asked if she could cut it kind of fancy, making it look like an enormous dorsal fin.

We played Capture the Flag at dusk on the beach at Bolinas.

## 31 JULY 1915

Mother sent a note reminding us to go to Berkeley, among other things. Matriculation exams are in two weeks. Flora's excused because Mr. Morton put her on approval from Lowell. Classes in three weeks.

Flora and I climbed the middle canyon with her camera and set up on its north ridge. She took a series of shots across the whole panorama so we can post them up all in a row and see it "just like it is" here. I'm glad her photos don't have colors.

After, we had the loveliest time gossiping, just like we used to at school, but now about the various kids in Bolinas. She feels Falillia is far too intelligent for Tyrone, whose only appeal is physical. I asked innocently if she found Grover attractive, and she just laughed at the very idea, adding, however, that his body would be beautiful like Tyrone's and very soon.

Duncan says the boat is ready.

## 1 AUGUST 1915

Flora brought the camera down for the launch. It was after lunch and a swim and Father came too. What with setting the camera and attaching all the boat's various parts, it was quite late into the afternoon before we actually put it in the water and christened it with a Coca-Cola. Duncan simply poured the beverage over the prow, not wanting to foul the lagoon with broken glass.

When assembled, the boat is a beautiful silver fish. Its front slopes up to a fine proud snout, thick fish lips pouting in an aristocratic frown. The spiraled spear attaches right in the center of the prow and helps explain the ship's name, *Narwhal*, which Duncan had painted in sky-blue script across the back.

We climbed aboard and got a good shove off from Father, wading in up to his thighs and pushing away. Flora stood on shore and fixed her second plate in place, ready for an action shot.

We drifted out toward the middle and Duncan hoisted the sail. The rope pulled clean and easy through its pulleys and held on tight where Duncan wrapped it round the irons. The wind came in, filling the sail, and we were off, gliding across the choppy water, not even a drop leaking in. Duncan worked the rudder. I lay back on the smooth wooden gunwale and looked up past the taut white sail, up into the blue sky, watching the tip of the mast bend back slightly with the pull of the rope.

We sailed up and down the lagoon, Duncan tacking skillfully to recover ground against the wind, till the sun had sunk almost to the shore and Father and Flora were long gone, the camera packed in its heavy case and hauled back up the hill. We were swift and clean across that lovely clear water, racing on toward Bolinas, then making slow strategic progress back up the lagoon. It was all so pretty a sail. Just wind and water and Duncan and me, and Winky and Blinky the dog, which I remember from when I was little.

Duncan let the sail down slack, the breeze blowing lightly now and warm, blowing over the hot inland hills. We lay low, back into the boat, watching the warm orange sun wash over clouds and shore and lagoon, turning the thin mast bronze and casting a long, pinpoint shadow across the water. It's another memory whose place I want to find, a moment I hope nestles in with all that matters to me, not slipping away. Duncan and I lying low in the evening, the soft wind washing over all of it and us, warm and close and touching, together in the same boat.

# Returning to
# the Fair

We came by boat, returning down the Marin coast and in at the Golden Gate. The sky was crisp blue, lightly marbled with thin wisps all combed out and curly, and the air was bright and clean. It wasn't Duncan's boat, alas. The *Narwhal* stayed in Bolinas, where it could succeed at navigating the small hazards and hardships so sheltered a place might pose. The open sea was a wholly different level of danger, one more fit for U-boats and dreadnoughts than little silver skiffs.

We rode a journeyman's steamer, all busy with ropes and hoists and hot oily motors spitting steam. A slight, graying engineer rambled roughly about the deck swearing a salty stream, jamming in wedges, wrenching pipes and yanking levers as if that was the activity by which the boat was propelled. Duncan and I were both dressed neatly, clean white shirts, collars and bow ties, our soft worn caps and twill shorts too. Flora stayed in Bolinas, due back in a week (or two, she said).

I watched the rough brown headlands, imagining them as Dover, and cultivated a nervous fear of U-boats and hidden mines. In a split second, I tried to convince myself, the rippling blue water could tear open in foam and flame blasting clear up to the wild heavens, ripping the steel plates from off our hull and sending us down in pieces to the mucky mysterious floor of the deep dark sea. I sat still on my satchel, gazing out over the gunwales, conjuring up this possible terror. Duncan was no help, chattering away about the Fair and Flora's motorcar, to which she'd given us the key.

"We'll drive to Hollywood," he proposed. "Your mother must know someone in movies."

I stayed mum, preferring my fantasies to his just then. I thought of Dunkirk, how the bombs came from nowhere, sailing invisible through the beautiful blue sky. Point Bonita jutted out into the sea just a half mile down the rocky, tumbling coast, one last weak push of land west before the sea came rushing in through the Golden Gate, flooding in to fill the wide flat bay. We sat on our luggage, out on the open deck, the wet salty breeze blowing over us.

A third passenger rode with us, sitting stiffly on her heavy leather portmanteau, trying to arrange her legs in a suitably feminine fashion and failing. She finally planted her feet firmly and let her elbows rest on her knees, as though taking a dump into her lovely brown luggage. A stiff straw hat was pinned fast to her neat gray hair. It featured paper flowers and a desperate stuffed canary, poised to leap off into the gloom. Its slight, feathered shoulders were back, wings lifting. Its chipped lacquer beak was wide open, waiting, I imagined, for its own queer song to emerge.

But other sounds came in from "out there," as Father calls it, interrupting my reverie.

"Are you involved with the cinema?" our companion asked, filling the long silence I'd let follow Duncan's whimsy. We'd come clear of Point Bonita and turned in. Rough shoulders of land plunged down suddenly on either side of the narrow channel. The choppy water was busy with boats and blue and beautiful. It ran right in, opening up on the sheltered bay. Alcatraz, a squat white rock of an island, cracking through the blue, sat smack in the middle, straight ahead now, as we pulled in past Land's End.

"We're college boys," I answered. "We'll be freshmen this year."

"If we're unsuccessful in Hollywood," Duncan added.

"You wish to be actors?" The eyeless canary dipped and bobbed inquisitively with each inquiring nod of this woman's head.

"Duncan," I gestured toward him, "wishes to be. I would like to direct."

"Hollywood is so full of deceptions," our companion mused, "or so I am led to believe."

The scene was suddenly busy, the air filled with noise. Boats crowded in close, ferrying about in all directions. Horns blasted and bells rang. There were fishermen and ferry boats and long, low, open-decked barges, loading and unloading. Far in front, proudly pushing east, two armored gray dreadnoughts cut across our view, black smoke rolling from their stacks, long and sharp as sabers, and solid and swift. The Presidio appeared, rising green and rugged away to our right. The boom of cannons could be heard marking the hour and puffs of smoke seen drifting from the trees. Whole columns of drab brown soldiers marched in military formation right across the crest of one field. Battalions of men on horses rode alongside. The Fair opened up below, rising like a fantastic dream of the Orient, all golden, pink, red, orange and blue. The domes looked more unimaginably grand than ever they'd seemed from land. Thin pillars and minarets, the Tower of Jewels, like liquid silver, washed in the sun— from the Presidio clear across to the marina, they rose, sparkling in the brisk salty air.

Our steamer rattled along, running parallel to the Fair. The oom-pah pounding of various brass bands sounded across the open waters, mixing with the hungry cry of sea birds and our boat horn. Its blasting announced our return to the city.

———

The business of landing and the confusion of the ducks had me in a dizzy spin. Bleats and blats and warnings and boys grabbing bags, jitneys roaring past. I hadn't been in a motorcar in almost two months, nor seen this many people at all, *total,* during our time in Bolinas.

Duncan seemed charged up, waving down this or that boy to see us through, buying hot Italian sausage and negotiating our steamer fare all at once (even getting sausage for our captain). I was numb from overstimulation, and could only stare dumbly at the spitting links, lying dead and bursting on a dirty black grill over coals. Duncan flagged a jitney down.

The mud-splattered jitney pulled away as I was still falling into the backseat, pulling the back door closed behind me. Duncan had already climbed in with our bags and I landed in his lap and nearly lost my hat. We tore through traffic, skidding about the crowded streets, blasting death calls on Gideon's horn and paying little mind to the unfortunate pedestrians dumb enough to walk these same streets. The buildings seemed so incredibly tall, rising up on either side of Post like sheer canyon walls.

We sped out of downtown on Bush, rolling over the long hills west to our house. The inhuman speed and noise of the motorcar rattled through me. It worked inside me so I wanted to either sleep or throw up, the two seeming equally viable and, somehow, quite similar. It was like that when I was a child.

(Vomiting Coke syrup, my little wet mouth sleepy with yawns. I've a dog in my bed, someone else's dog, and a funny rash all up and down my pale skin. I've never been up so late. What am I, five at the oldest? More likely four.)

———

Mother and Mr. Taqdir were home, still stocking the cupboards and folding linen. We'd sent word by mail, insisting they make no fuss and *certainly* not feel they had to meet us at the docks.

Mother had had her hair cut, scandalously short, barely reaching the bottom of her neck and bouncing with a slight bob. If that was not enough, Mr. Taqdir's thick mustache was gone, recently, it seemed, for a pale ghost of it sat all bluish with shaven beard just below his nose. I slumped in through the familiar door and collapsed on the divan.

"Lovey, pumpkin," Mother cried, smushing her face into mine. "You're a perfect wreck." I did feel a perfect wreck, rumpled and rattled by the confusion of the city, wanting more than anything just to go to sleep. Mr. Taqdir was squeezing Duncan lustily in the doorway, lifting him up off his feet like a bear mauling its prey.

"You're so thin," Mother said to me, though I wasn't thin at all.

"I'm fit," I explained.

"And so brown and handsome," she kept on, squeezing me more. "Your hair is a fright." She ran her fingers through my thick dark hair, all wild and wonderful. "We'll have it cut."

"No we won't, thank you very much." I loved my hair like this. I wanted only to wash it and, if it got much longer, tie it back in a ponytail.

"You must be starving for some nourishment." She was persistent, abandoning one motherly desire and picking up another. And I *was* starving.

"I am. Something warm and delightful, soup or bread. Let's not eat out." I nuzzled into her, smelling all the familiar smells—her lavender-and-soft-cotton-dress smell, the house all sweet wood and tinged with smoke and spices, nutmeg and coriander and pepper.

## 13 AUGUST 1915

From the whole summer's mail, just one letter from Maury.

Dear Robert,

What sorts of birds should one expect with spring here? I find myself wondering about the reality this place once was. I don't recognize it as land really. A few frightened starlings have arrived in the trenches, looking, I guess, for what scraps of bread or seed we might have left scattered.

Perhaps the war's a wound that will heal with the weather and the seasons. A golden thatch of wheat grows thick across the lip of a mine crater. The gray lifeless earth stretches away all around it, ripped by scars and crossed by dead wire and bones. Sheep and cattle who've made it through a year of war wander the middle ground, putting their noses to the dead or wounded. They stand in their beautiful animal stupidity and graze on the few tufts of grass that have sprung up. The winter was much more beautiful, and the smell was not so rich and terrible.

Cut the leg off an old friend of yours. Chapman, I believe. Mortar had ripped his calf silly. One of ours, it was. He sends his hello.

I had a lovely long bath this morning and we met Mother after breakfast, to shop for our college wardrobes. We've decided Hollywood isn't really an option.

Mother drove, which was a blessing. She drives slower than a horse. Usually it makes me crazy, but today it was bliss, turning the car into an oversized pram, rolling gently along the busy roads in no great hurry. She had a simple garland in her hair, about which a bee kept buzzing. Duncan and I squeezed in up front with her, me in the middle and Duncan suggesting routes.

Mother paid him no mind and kept rumbling along her round-about, taking whatever road looked widest and getting us to Market Street soon enough.

We parked down by Stockton, in the midst of the busiest jumble. Trolleys clanged past four abreast. Horses and carts and cars and bicyclists wiggled in amongst the mayhem. It seemed some disaster had struck, some terrible trembling from deep in the earth and this was the ensuing panic.

Ladies bustled into traffic, navigating boldly through the various conveyances, stopping to converse on thin islands of safety between lanes of traffic. One raised her little gloved hand and a jitney jammed its breaks and skidded to a stop nearby. Other cars swerved out behind into the trolley paths. I hesitated before following Duncan into the street.

I wanted to take my clothes off. They all felt so terribly heavy and constricting. I hadn't worn them in some time. Certainly my feet had grown. Coffee seemed like a good idea.

"Things don't seem quite right today," I suggested meekly, hoping Mother or Duncan might set the chaos back into order.

Mother put her hand to my forehead. "Perhaps, pumpkin, you're still feverish from your little boat ride." She gave an optimistic prognosis and promised coffee after we'd procured a few bare necessities.

She began with Cravanette pumps at Rosenthal's. I got tan Russian barefoot sandals, very airy and open and easy to slip off. I dumped my old shoes in the garbage when Mother wasn't looking. I am quite the peasant in them.

We swung past The Owl for a pack of Tiz. Duncan was poking his nose around the Spiro Powders, sniffing through the decorative bottles to try to determine the scent most suited to him. I believe I smell best when I've sweated. The air outside is so much more pleasant. Mother called the clerk a "paranoic loon" and Duncan bought some Beachnut and Sugar Fruit Tablets to appease the management and we left.

Hundreds of colorful shoes jumbled about in rows, filling the windows beside me from top to bottom. A disembodied hand reached in from behind them and pulled one away, leaving a gap, as in a boxer's bloody mouth. I'd never seen so many shoes.

"Things seem so much busier than I remember them," I observed.

"Maybe your memory's bad," Duncan suggested, peering into my ear to get a better look.

"No, no dear," Mother said to Duncan. "I believe Maxwell is right. Things have gotten much busier over the summer. It's all the visitors and the merchandising. The New Prosperity, the papers call it."

One advertisement fairly screamed, its loud letters leaping off the page of newsprint into my unfixed mind:

"Your hair is calling you." The lady in the picture was standing, letting her long hair tumble down her back. "Answer 'La Toska Bang,' and hear the ring of delight!" Her face was frozen, fixed in fear, apparently, searching for the telephone. I felt as though her hair were calling *me* and I couldn't find the phone to answer. I ducked into the nearest doorway to find some shelter from the noise. Mother pushed me in through the double doors, into the din of The Hub.

The Hub was packed and I was in no mood for suits, which Mother says all college boys must wear. If it's true I'd rather wear Father's baggy old suits than buy one of these trim-cut modern things.

"Max said we'd wear shorts and sandals and bundle in big sweaters," Duncan told Mother, revealing my college plans. It's true I'd said that, though I hadn't intended to tell Mother.

"He's mistaken, dear. College boys dress quite smartly, even here in the West." Mother picked through a rack of dark wool overcoats.

"I'll join the army," I threatened, as she pulled a horrible black funeral garment off the rack. "I can't stand suits."

Mother paused, then placed the suit back on the rack. "Don't be morbid, pumpkin," she said. "If you don't like a particular suit, just say so. No need for histrionics."

"I don't like that suit," I said simply. "Or any other. Father has suits and I'll wear them, should the need arise."

"I hate suits," Duncan echoed. "You said we wouldn't have

to dress like monkeys." He stood waiting for some sort of explanation. Mother had drifted on to dress shirts, evidently figuring she'd get us into those first and work us up to suits gradually.

"We won't," I insisted. "Mother's just being Mother. This is what she's here for. Otherwise she'd have just sent us out with the money. She's got to insist on suits, even though she knows we'll never do it."

"What if everyone else *is* in suits?"

"Then we won't make friends."

"We'll be lepers."

"Flora's going. She'll find friends and we'll be their friends."

"She'll find friends who don't wear suits."

"That's right, and who drive fast in their motorcars and dance naked in gardens."

"In the moonlight."

"Right. We'll live in the trees and attend class in loincloths."

"Pumpkin?" Mother interrupted, holding up a stiff white shirt. I nodded my head no.

"Let's think about suits later, Mummy. We should try Hale's for some active wear, something we can all agree on."

(I smelled a ghost smell from the ground. Light gas and fresh dirt and the smoking engine of a jitney. We were just nine and small as ponies. Duncan was knocked over flat by a crazy man with a plank and big tattoos. Right here, when we'd gone shopping for rope licorice.)

Next was the smell of chocolate wafting out of Borlini's as we ambled by. I needed it badly so we stopped and took a nice long rest, sipping cafe chocolatta at a little table by the window and planning the week's events.

"Tomorrow's your matriculation exam," Mother reminded us. "I do hope you'll dress nicely." I was pleased she'd not used the word "suit."

"Of course we will," I promised. "We'll wear our bow ties."
Even Duncan enjoyed the bow ties, especially with shorts, as
that made us look so queer.

"And registration," she added.

"And classes," Duncan added woefully.

"Not till Monday," I reminded him. "We'll find lodgings and
move before then."

We were all silent, thinking some about that ambiguous event.
I was excited to think of moving, our few things all bundled up
and gathered on the ferryboat, going across the bay. I imagined
we would find some third floor in a house or maybe an attic up
a few flights of narrow steep stairs. It was hard to imagine a nicer
house than the one we'd had all spring or, even harder, the one
we'd had all summer. No bed could be as beautiful and bouncy
as our mammoth feather bed in Bolinas. No fireplace could be
so warm and welcoming as ours in San Francisco. And I would
miss our mysterious neighbor, her work forever in progress,
perhaps until some terrible midnight fire, the little oil lamp
spilled across the drapes, the dog barking madly through the
flames, trying to wake his asphyxiated mistress . . .

"Can we bring some things from our house?" Duncan asked
Mother. "Carpets and lamps and things like that?"

"Of course, dear," she assured him. "You two may take
whatever you need to settle in. From either house. I don't
suppose you'll be needing a lot."

"I'm thinking of a few things," Duncan allowed. "Just things
I like to have with me."

I tried to imagine what Duncan felt about moving. He seemed
to me to have given up planning, allowing everything to happen
around him. I'd been the one making plans, Bolinas, Berkeley,
moving across the bay.

"What do you think about moving?" I asked him. "In general,
as something we're doing."

He looked at me, and Mother looked out the window, fiddling
with her spoon. I realized this was an important question I'd

never before thought to ask him. We three sat in silence for some time.

"We can't go to school there and live here," he offered. "That's for certain, anyway."

"No, we couldn't do that," I agreed. I pursed my lips and looked down into my coffee.

"And that's certainly the best school for us to go to," Duncan added. He stirred the chocolate up from the bottom of his coffee and drank it down, leaving a dark mustache on his upper lip. I felt his leg bumping up against mine under the table and looked up at him, his head tilted, his mouth soft with an ambiguous smile. He looked at me easily and directly with sort of sad eyes.

"We'll want to be getting to know a new place too," he added, "and learning how to live on our own." I just wanted to hold him, so he could stop talking and I could feel what he meant and not have to hear all those words. I looked at him dearly and nodded my head up and down yes yes yes I know how unsettling everything seems just now.

"Well said, dearie," Mother interjected briskly. "Those goals are admirable ones for this busy year. You're very lucky to have such an opportunity." She smiled curtly at both of us. "We mustn't waste the challenges that life offers us."

## 14 AUGUST 1915

We went to Berkeley for the exams today. We were told to see a Mr. Thwing in Admissions, who looked to be nothing more than an arrangement of sticks inhabiting a suit, with thin pasty hands and a melonlike head emerging from its various openings. He clattered up from his desk and leaned gingerly against the wide counter, pointing accusingly at the clock on the wall behind him.

"Examinations have *already* begun, boys," he spat, drumming his cadaverous fingers on the countertop.

"We've come from there," I explained cheerfully. "Miss Tartaine sent us to have our records checked."

He crouched down, the top half of his melon head rising like a harvest moon from behind the wide barrier. His two black eyes darted around like little fish. "Well, well," he began, staring at me and feeling around blindly under the counter. "Under what appellations might we find these 'records,' as you call them?"

"Kosegarten, Maxwell Field," I put in, using the order of the day.

"Taqdir, Duncan Peivand," Duncan added.

"One moment please, Mr. 'Kosegarten.' " Mr. Thwing flipped through a thick file of colorful papers, various greens and blues and pink, but mostly bright marigold. He pulled one out and held it up to the light, looking over at me, then back up at the sheet.

"Maxwell Field, was it?" he asked, leaning recklessly across the counter.

"Yes. Maxwell Field Kosegarten." I wondered what the bright blue little slip said.

"Very good. Next I believe is Mr. Taqdir, am I right?" And he put my slip into his vest pocket.

"Yes. Duncan Peivand," Duncan said, looking into the box.

Mr. Thwing drew it violently away from us, almost losing it off his side of the counter. "*Just* a moment, Mr. Taqdir." He fiddled about in the box for a few more moments and drew out another blue slip.

"Bingo," he burst, tearing my blue slip from out of his pocket and holding them both above his head, pinched between thumb and forefinger like some offensive soiled undergarment. "You *both* win!"

We stood in silence, waiting for Mr. Thwing to explain, but he remained motionless, frozen in his little pose.

"I don't understand," I said. "What do we win?"

Mr. Thwing drew his arm down carefully, as though it were a brittle limb, in danger of snapping. He slid the two blue slips onto the countertop and leaned out across them. "Why, university admission, of course. This *is* the Admissions Office, after all."

"Don't we have to take exams?" Duncan asked.

Mr. Thwing drew back from the question, looking physically wounded. "What do you suppose this *is,* young man, the Inquisition? We have no need to examine you." And here he plucked the slips from the counter and pushed them in our noses. "Mr. Morton at dear old Lowell High has approved you. He's given the A-OK. You're free to enter."

"Mr. Morton put us on the approval list?" I asked. "When?"

Mr. Thwing held the blue slips back up to the light.

"July 23, Mr. Maxwell F. Kosegarten. And the same for you, Mr. Taqdir."

"Don't we have to register?" Duncan asked.

"It would be my pleasure," Mr. Thwing answered, holding a box of pamphlets up to our noses. "One each, please."

I took one, expecting a course catalog.

"Orestes," it said. "Euripides."

"For class," Mr. Thwing explained. "Read it by Wednesday. I'll have you set in an instant," and he took our blue slips and disappeared behind a foggy glass door. The pulling and slamming of various drawers and the flipping of pages leaked out from the small enclosure.

This registration procedure seemed most unorthodox. Mr. Thwing had not even asked after our interests.

"How do you know which courses we're to take?" I called out loudly, throwing decorum to the wind. I heard all activity cease, and then a heavy silence.

"This is *not* high school, Mr. Field," our queer helper called back finally. "Believe me, I *know* which courses you'll need to take." And he continued with his mysterious fiddling.

The long silence passed slowly by, filled with thoughts of fiddlehead ferns and that strange immediacy of moments so distant flipping suddenly forward.

(Succulent green stems, sturdy and small; that little fist of leaves so sweet and tender, balled up snug and sporting a soft red fuzz. Father played the fiddle when I was young but injured his back, leaning romantically over a drunken woman while fiddling a little to-do. We'd not even had breakfast yet.)

"Don't ask questions," Mr. Thwing cautioned, offering up two pink index cards crowded with numbers and "Aldredge Thwing" in florid script at their bottoms. "Without my approval you'll be dropped down into useless surveys."

"Dropped down out of what?" Duncan asked, looking at the indecipherable cards.

"Out of the seminars I've placed you in," he explained, as though it were obvious. "I take a special interest in some of our more promising entrants." This flattery was not lost on me.

"How do you know which seminars we'd like to be in?" Duncan asked. He seemed uncertain if Mr. Thwing's kind interest was a blessing or a curse.

"We have information," Mr. Thwing assured us, menacingly. "Report to Miss Tartaine tomorrow. In the Grove. She'll be expecting you."

"When?" I asked.

"Very early. Impossibly early. Nine or ten. You give her the cards, she'll give you your schedules."

"What if we don't like them?" Duncan pressed on fearlessly.

Mr. Thwing kept mum, sliding his hands nervously along the smooth countertop, evidently gathering his energies to reply.

"If you don't like them?" he asked back.

"Right," Duncan said, nodding yes.

"If you don't like them?"

I feared his melon head might burst.

"Then *change* them!" he thundered, spitting wildly with every consonant.

———

## 15 AUGUST 1915

We were late reporting to Miss Tartaine. Very late.

We caught a trolley train to campus and wandered a bit helpless
and frazzled, everything going so terribly wrong as it was. There
were all sorts of signs and directions leading all new under-
graduates to a lovely grove near California Hall. There, spread
out on a field of tables and charts, was the registration labyrinth.

Miss Tartaine sat far off to the north, at a large oak table set
in amongst the eucalyptus, marked by a sign which said simply
"Miss Tartaine. Thwing."

"You're late," she said. "Very late."

"Should we get in line?" I asked, gesturing back behind us
at the long snaking rows of freshmen, all clamoring up to tables
in the bright sunny grove.

"Do you have cards from Mr. Thwing?" she asked simply.

"Yes."

"No need, then." She took our crumpled pink cards and
smiled pleasantly at the elegant script.

"Being late, of course, you've no appeal on this," and she
inscribed our class lists carefully on heavy white paper, fixing
our future with bold black lincs.

"Of course," I echoed, wondering why we were the only
ones in this dark dappled corner of the grove.

"Why have our schedules been set by Mr. Thwing?" Duncan
asked.

"You're curious why this privilege is yours?" Miss Tartaine
asked back, rephrasing.

"Yes."

She looked out into the sun and thought. "Your record in
secondary school, a recommendation, some kind word. . . . Evidently something has impressed Mr. Thwing. It's a service he
provides for a handful of bright young minds each year." She

finished up and handed us the two carefully scripted lists. "It is one of life's mysteries," she mused.

I looked eagerly at the form and noticed some important errors straightaway. Miss Tartaine saw me start stammering out my objections and simply raised a soft hand of warning, tapping her pen to the offending list.

"*That,*" she intoned, poking again at the paper, "is all ye know, and all ye need to know."

M-W-F, 8:00 a.m. Attic Tragedy, Assoc. Prof. Kurtz.
M-W-F, 10:00 a.m. Cicero and Pliny, Asst. Prof. Deutsch.
M-W, 11:00 a.m. Military Training, Mr. Dickie. [This was the first mistake.]
M-W-F, 1:00 p.m. Memory and the Process of Learning, Asst. Prof. Brown.
Tu-Th, 8:00 a.m. Principles of Hygiene and Sanitation, Prof. Legge. [This was the second mistake.]
Tu-Th, 1:00 p.m.–4:00 p.m. Advanced Free-Hand Drawing, Asst. Prof. Judson.
Various times, General Recreation, Mr. Wilson.

I must admit to being excited by "Memory," of course, and Kurtz, who taught Ruskin to the Upper Level.

I loosened the grip of my bow tie and let some air down my front, wiggling the baggy legs of my shorts too, for added ventilation. The hills rose up abruptly behind us, thick with lovely green trees and then topped by open grasslands. There were many houses clustered in amongst the trees, all along thin winding streets, wiggling up into the highlands. I fancied we'd find some suitable lodgings in one of them, owned by some kindly professor's family willing to let out the upstairs, it long ago vacated by their rebellious, fascinating children who'd run away to join some polar expedition.

———

Duncan took the piece of paper from my hands and held it up to his:

M-W-F, 10:00 a.m. Strength of Materials, Asst. Prof. Alvarez.
M-W, 11:00 a.m. Military Training, Mr. Dickie.
M-W-F, 2:00 p.m. History of Western Literature, Prof. Sanford.
Tu-Th, 9:00 a.m. Advanced Calculus, Prof. Noble.
Tu-Th, 11:00 a.m. Principles of Hygiene and Sanitation, Prof. Legge. [This, unfortunately, was not my section.]
Tu, 2:00 p.m. History of Architecture, Prof. Howard.
Various times, Track, Mr. Cole.
Various times, Swimming, unannounced.

I looked up from the schedules with a bad feeling in me.

"We don't have any classes together," Duncan said, confirming my suspicions, and sounding very mad like they'd done it to us on purpose. "Except Military Training."

I looked again at my list. "I'm not going to attend Military Training."

"It's required, Max. 'All able-bodied young men.'" He held the paper up to my face.

"I'm *not* going to Military Training. I'll cut my leg off and send it to them."

"You're so open-minded, Max." Duncan looked like he was about to burst. "I *hate* this place," and he dropped the two lists onto the dirty ground.

We walked downhill through the cool shade of a tall stand of eucalyptus. The trees crowded round a small creek that cut a gully through the middle of campus. Some of the buildings reminded me of the Fair, huge tan stone buildings, pillared and symmetrical, sporting doors and windows far beyond human scale. A collar of decorative ornamentation ran round their tops, thick with jutting gargoyles, Greek names and pithy sayings.

I thought about our situation, us shuffling along in silence, dragging our toes down the dirty hill as slow as could be, and tried to think what could make things better. Really I wanted to be back in Bolinas, even back five years ago in Bolinas.

"Let's go to a ballgame," I suggested, as a way of getting over this horrible morning. He looked out across the bay as we walked along, turning toward me as he thought.

"I don't know, Max," he started, as if apologizing. He stopped for a moment, keeping on with his own thoughts, evidently pursuing demons that even baseball could not dispel. "A ballgame doesn't sound right just now."

He cocked his head, hoping I'd understand.

I imagined, for a moment, that he was mad at me and that made me angry and a little panicky, like if he left right then I'd be so confused and nervous I'd curl up and cry. But that thought was far too complicated and I couldn't imagine ever finding words to get it right. So I just nodded yes, I understood, not wanting to risk speaking what I felt, and he nodded back.

"I kind of want to go running," he continued. "Just running by myself. It helps when I'm mad."

The sun sat still in the sky and the air was silent, the trees halted by the absence of wind, motionless. There really was *no* one around, no cars or trolleys. I could feel the wide green hills rising up behind me, looming large enough to make me feel a slight pressure on the back of my head and neck. I walked all the way to the ferry without really stopping to think, and rode across the open blue bay looking back at Berkeley, thinking I might see Duncan if I looked hard enough.

I imagined I could just think him back near me. Not that I could think so well he actually *would* appear, but just, I imagined, that I had so many and such particular thoughts about him that that would be enough to make me feel the same as if he *were* with me. I'd think them all as intently as I could, each tiny touch and tone of his presence. I'd remember so vividly, as I truly did, every possible feature of him being with me and then I'd feel the same as if he were with me.

If memory could hold him completely I'd not feel this sudden loneliness. But it couldn't and I did, and I could only lie there on the worn carpet of our little front room and cry over some elusive failure. Our failure to get classes together, or my failure to say "Don't leave me now," or his failure to understand that that is what I meant, though I couldn't find the words to say it.

## 16 AUGUST 1915

We made wonderful friends with an old Latvian woman and her daughter, and they've invited us for dinner this Wednesday. They live on Hillegass off Parker in a towering thin, three-story, some hybrid strain of row house with nothing else in its row. It must've been built by someone who fancies windmills, and needs only the blades to complete the picture.

Their rooms are full to bursting with Latvian doo-dahs: ornately carved little mushroom boxes, mammoth swaddling boards and wooden toy birds with articulating wings and dangerously sharp beaks. Mrs. Meekshtais, for that's her name, explained that these were intended for the Latvian exhibition at the Fair but then the plan was scuttled by the war and political squabbling among the Baltic states. Unt, her daughter (who'll be going to Berkeley as well), performed a quaint folk dance accompanied by the melodic howling of Mrs. Meekshtais, who also played the harmonium.

They offered us a tiny little room off the kitchen, as that was the only space available in the house. It really was far too small but we promised we'd take it if nothing bigger came up in the next two days and indeed we would have, had this other special place not been available.

This other place is nestled on the hill north of campus, set back amongst a grouping of young cedars. Its steep pitched roof rises to a crest above the trees. We found it by accident, calling at any house that appealed to us as we wandered around east of Euclid. The southern wall has a window stretching two stories high. It opens up on a vast living room with nothing but wooden beams and a rich wood ceiling overhead. There are two other wings, one running east, very squat, with stone walls and a fat thatch roof, and the other jutting out to the west.

We knocked on the heavy wooden door.

Mrs. Dunphy answered. It was dumb luck.

"Oh, dear," she said. "Oh, my, dearie. What a shock." Duncan wasn't sure what to make of this display of familiarity and looked to me for the introductions.

"Maxwell," I reminded her, "Maxwell Kosegarten. The Fair in late May?"

"Oh, yes, of course, Maxwell, of course. That awful night at the Fair. Your terrible dizzy spell." We both clucked with reminiscence:

> When you were a Tadpole and I was a Fish,
> In the Paleozoic time.
> And side by side on the ebbing tide,
> We sprawled through the ooze and slime,
> Or skittered with many a caudal flip
> Through the depths of the Cambrian fen—
> My heart was rife with the joy of life,
> For I loved you even then.

Mindless we lived, mindless we loved,
And mindless at last we died;
And deep in the rift of a Caradoc drift
We slumbered side by side.
The world turned on in the lathe of time,
The hot sands heaved amain,
Till we caught our breath from the womb of death,
And crept into life again.

We were Amphibians, scaled and tailed,
And drab as a dead man's hand.
We coiled at ease 'neath the dripping trees
Or trailed through the mud and sand,
Croaking and blind, with our three-clawed feet,
Writing a language dumb,
With never a spark in the empty dark
To hint at a life to come.

Yet happy we lived and happy we loved,
And happy we died once more.

Our forms were rolled in the clinging mold
Of a Neocomian shore.
The aeons came and the aeons fled,
And the sleep that wrapped us fast
Was riven away in a newer day,
And the night of death was past.

Then light and swift through the jungle trees
We swung in our airy flights,
Or breathed the balms of the fronded palms
In the hush of the moonless nights.
And oh, what beautiful years were these
When our hearts clung each to each;
When life was filled and our senses thrilled
In the first faint dawn of speech!

Thus life by life, and love by love,
We passed through the cycles strange,
And breath by breath, and death by death,
We followed the chain of change.
Till there came a time in the law of life
When over the nursing sod
The shadows broke, and the soul awoke
In a strange, dim dream of God.

I was thewed like an Aurocks bull
And tusked like the great Cave-Bear,
And you, my sweet, from head to feet,
Were gowned in your glorious hair.
Deep in the gloom of a fireless cave,
When the night fell o'er the plain,
And the moon hung red o'er the river bed,
We mumbled the bones of the slain.

I flaked a flint to a cutting edge,
And shaped it with brutish craft;
I broke a shank from the woodland dank,
And fitted it, head to haft.
Then I hid me close in the reedy tarn,
Where the Mammoth came to drink—

Through brawn and bone I drave the stone,
And slew him upon the brink.

Loud I howled through the moonlit wastes,
Loud answered our kith and kin;
From west and east to the crimson feast
The clan came trooping in.
O'er joint and gristle and padded hoof,
We fought and clawed and tore,
And cheek by jowl, with many a growl,
We talked the marvel o'er.

I carved that fight on a reindeer bone
With rude and hairy hand;
I pictured his fall on the cavern wall
That men might understand.
For we lived by blood and the right of might,
Ere human laws were drawn,
And the Age of Sin did not begin
Till our brutal tusks were gone.

And that was a million years ago,
In a time that no man knows;
Yet here to-night in the mellow light,
We sit at Delmonico's.
Your eyes are deep as the Devon springs,
Your hair is as dark as jet,
Your years are few, your life is new,
Your soul untried, and yet—

Our trail is on the Kimmeridge clay,
And the scarp of the Purbeck flags;
We have left our bones in the Bagshot stones,
And deep in the Coralline crags.
Our love is old, and our lives are old,
And death shall come amain.
Should it come to-day, what man may say
We shall not live again?

God wrought our souls from the Tremadoc beds
And furnished them wings to fly;

He sowed our spawn in the world's dim dawn,
And I know that it shall not die;
Though cities have sprung above the graves
Where the crook-boned men made war,
And the ox-wain creaks o'er the buried caves
Where the mummied mammoths are.

*Then, as we linger at luncheon here,*
*O'er many a dainty dish,*
*Let us drink anew to the time when you*
*Were a Tadpole and I was a Fish.*

I'd forgotten to introduce Duncan.

"Duncan," I announced, turning toward him. "Duncan Taqdir, my very best friend. This is Mrs. Dunphy," and he took her fishlike hand in his and shook it vigorously.

"I'm pleased," he said to her. "Pleased to meet you." The little poem drifted back into blurred unremembrance.

We stood at the threshold for some long moments, the aroma of curry drifting out across our noses. Mrs. Dunphy stood and stared, clucking thoughtfully and shaking her head in apparent disbelief. I smiled big and dumb.

"We'll both be attending the university this term," I tried.

Mrs. Dunphy snapped back into phase. "Oh, yes, certainly. *Do* come in, mustn't stand around on ceremony, come right in and have a seat in the kitchen." And we walked in through the cozy vestibule, all warm wood and carpets, and followed Mrs. Dunphy and the heady aroma into the kitchen, up and back of the enormous room we'd seen from the street.

"It's all coming back quite vividly, Maxwell," Mrs. Dunphy called over her shoulder, lifting pan tops to sprinkle spice and stir. "You'd been feeling ill that evening, am I right?"

"Oh, yes, quite ill. Rather dizzy really, and hungry."

"There was that nasty spell at the Fountain of the Ages," Mrs. Dunphy continued, sitting down by us with a little ladle of curry. "You disappeared off into the bushes, I believe. Curry?" And she held the lurid yellow ladle up to our noses.

"No thank you," Duncan answered. "We've just eaten."

Mrs. Dunphy smiled briskly and plopped the dripping treat back in the pan. "Did you meet Mr. Dunphy that evening?" she asked.

"No," I said. "He'd gone home. The Fair had 'tired him out,' you told me. In the Court of Mines? The pretty pink gravel?" I tried, prompting her memory. We sat again in silence, remembering.

Mr. Dunphy came knocking along the hallway (I presumed it was he) with his face in a book and an empty mug in hand.

"Dear." Mrs. Dunphy beckoned. "I'd like you to meet two young friends, Maxwell and Duncan." We rose from our chairs, me knocking mine over backward, and extended our two hands to Mr. Dunphy, whose two hands were both busy. He nodded politely and went to the stove.

"It's a pleasure, gentlemen. To what do we owe their visit, dearest? What brings them to our little kingdom?" He peeked into the empty teapot and put some water on to boil. Mrs. Dunphy turned to us, eyebrows upraised in wonder.

"Maxwell and I," Duncan started, "will be attending the university. We've come looking for lodgings, just a room and some sort of arrangement for use of the kitchen." He could be so cordial when he wanted.

"I thought we could let the upstairs to them," Mrs. Dunphy improvised, "up above the sewing room." We maintained our calm dispositions, taking this fiction as the fact Mrs. Dunphy intended it to be, and showed no surprise.

"Fine, fine, fine," her husband answered, putting his book down at last. "You're in charge here, dearest." He looked over at both of us, looking us up and down as if we were diseased trees. "They seem to be healthy young specimens, I'd say." And he snorted in conclusion, turning back to the stove to pour the whistling water, and trundled back from whence he came.

Our room has one wide window looking west through trees and across the water. The low walls slant in about four feet up from the floor and come to a white flat ceiling only eight feet high. The two beds tuck up into their own little window bays, facing out south with nothing but wild green branches to see. Mrs. Dunphy said we could drag a desk up from their basement and if we didn't mind would we keep the endless shelves of books right where they were in our room. There's no fireplace, but we'll adjust.

Tomorrow is the first day of classes.

## 17 AUGUST 1915

We stayed our first night at the Dunphys without going back to the city for fear we'd oversleep again. Mrs. Dunphy was being more than generous with linens and towels and that thick curry she let stew all day.

We slept together in one of the thin beds, which was fine and cozy for sleeping but proved comical and impractical for all else we might do in bed. Everything goes loose in sleep. Like that groan and growl I make in my throat if I've just come or am falling fast into sleep. Or the way thoughts which have been buried come drifting by, let loose from below. If I'm not yet sleeping and try to seize hold of the thought, it disappears. But if I let my mind loose, it all comes in again.

We might rearrange the furniture, pushing the two beds together in the wide western bay and making a little sitting area where the beds were.

## 18 AUGUST 1915

Professor Brown asked why *can't* you voice someone else's memories and I remembered what Father'd said about songs sung in our bones and spoke up. I thought, I said, it might be possible. He said try. It was so silent and dusty, with sunlight sliding in through trees, and our little gallery of desks fanned out in front of him. I knew no one there, though we'd all given our names. I felt bold and anonymous.

It was cheating really, because I didn't say whose memory I'd voice and the tale I gave was so general it must be that *everyone* remembers it from somewhere.

"It was a bright sunny morning," I began. Mr. Brown watched with interest, allowing me to let out enough rope to hang by, I presumed. "I had never slept so well, lying so relaxed and awake, or both asleep and awake, this particular perfect condition being something words can't describe, really. I felt eager and ready for the day ahead.

"I was very young. We were off to visit relatives, ones I feared because their house smelled so odd, all mothballs and camphor and such, and because their manner was so stiff and accusing. I often had nightmares about these particular relatives, especially, I remember, one in which I'm devoured. Today was a birthday and I was to bring a gift. Still the lovely morning had me feeling brave.

"Should I go on?"

"Whose memory is this?" Mr. Brown asked the class, looking to them for the answer. Some few of the thirty-odd students raised their hands.

"Mister," and he paused, looking to his list.

"Maxwell."

"Mr. Maxwell has begun a fable, or, potentially, a myth." Mr. Brown nodded to me appreciatively. I fairly burst with the pleasure of recognition. "A fine example of shared memory. In any group there is a common ground of experience, a history of trials and triumphs through which every individual must go and does go, somehow. *My* intention, however, was to establish quite the opposite point.

"My intention was to establish, by my little question, the *isolation* of individual memory. How will each of us remember Mr. Maxwell's story? Is there a correct memory of that event? Would the event have any existence without our memories of it? Given the inevitable differences in memory, what is the true nature of that past event? Is it Mr. Maxwell's memory of it? Is it only what we've remembered in common? The fact of Mr. Maxwell telling it, the fact of our being together here in this room? There is no question each individual collects those pieces of experience which somehow suit his needs, that memory is selective and idiosyncratic, and purposeful, though perhaps not consciously so.

"I hope we'll all begin this course with that as a given. Memory is an individual phenomenon, a struggle for persistence guided by the evolutionary forces at work in each man's psyche. What survives in your world may not survive in mine.

"As for Mr. Maxwell's welcome diversion, the myth or fable. Every culture has its fables." Here Mr. Brown paused to sigh, approaching what must've seemed an unwelcome can of worms (given it was just our first day). "Some set of stories that gives form and voice to their common experience. Especially as children we take these stories into our *own* experience, even enacting them as a set of struggles of our own making, practicing, perhaps, for our inevitable future struggles.

"As adults, however—and perhaps this point will help us synthesize the two views—as adults we manage a distinction between real memory and myth, experience and stories. It is typical—and this point is telling—typical of primitive cultures that they, just like children in our own culture, take the myth as real, regarding that which they've imagined as real experience.

"I can't stress enough the wisdom of that old rubric 'ontogeny recapitulates phylogeny.' Here, as always, it is true. Just as civilizations have advanced from that primitive infancy, in which what is myth and what is actual experience are so blended as to remain indistinct, just as they have advanced to a more mature separation of reality and fable, so we see individuals in our own lives grow from a childhood of wonder, of shared memories and stories enacted, felt as true, see them grow, I say, to an adulthood of wisdom, a clear sense of the separate experience of each individual. Myths may successfully abstract our individual experience, but they cannot be called equivalent.

"How many, I'd ask now, experienced precisely the experience Mr. Maxwell can voice to us? How many believe the actuality of their individual experience was precisely as he says? Certainly we must recognize the value in childhood of such wonderful tales, but also we must face the problematic fact of the individuality of memory, as wise adults."

I had no idea whether I agreed or disagreed, and, more important, whether I'd been praised or criticized. I'd only meant to try and guess what everyone might remember, but Mr. Brown took it far along some other path, pursuing some idea that must've been bugging him lately. It was like getting one of Father's notes, only I didn't have any clear written record of it to look at and contemplate.

I asked Mr. Brown, after, if he could recommend some reading, just to make things clear to me.

"Look, Mr. Maxwell, at the inscription on this building," he suggested cryptically. "That should be plenty for the first day."

It said "Social Sciences," chiseled in the stone. Deep, sharp letters cut in the rock by a metal blade banged hard with a craftsman's hammer. The bright white sunlight dappled through the tall crowd of eucalyptus that lurched and lapped over the stone façade, dancing across the even letters. "Social Sciences." The two words were falling apart in my head. The various pieces were so elusive, devoid of meanings, or rather too full of them. "Really, there's too much to see," Father had said. I felt I needed a map to navigate my way across their mysterious surface.

"Social Sciences." It was the fact of their existence in stone, I guess. Really I found the shapes, carved so neatly, had fixed my attention. How *could* a blade be made to curve so cleanly round as the one that carved "S"? Why was there no moss growing in these wonderful fissures? The "o," a perfect moat protecting nothing, a vertical moat in a climate where it seldom rained. I thought I'd best keep quiet in class until things became clearer.

19 AUGUST 1915

Dear Robert,

Many thanks for the poetry, etc. Darwin was a queer choice. I thoroughly enjoy his prose but I find his analysis particularly disturbing as I witness this slaughter.

My mind is far away, in music, or a fanciful memory of Primrose Hill or Cornwall, a soft evening in spring, the smell of narcissus. And on the table is another blood-soaked sheet of cloth with God knows what horror wrapped inside. Any word from Mother? I've not heard a peep in several weeks and find my mind ill at ease.

Jake brought this one in. We sing it loud enough for the Bosche to join in.

I want to go home I want to go home The whizz bangs and shrapnel they whistle and roar I don't want to go atop anymore Take me over the sea where the allemans can't catch me O my I don't want to die I want to go home

Mr. Dunphy gives me the creeps.

The wind chimes ring a strange, familiar song, but I still can't place it.

## 22 AUGUST 1915

I'd thought Saturdays would be lazy days, but Mr. Wilson scheduled General Recreation for Saturday mornings (and Duncan's swimming has been set for Saturday afternoons). So I spent yesterday trying my hand at basket ball, something for which I have a great deal of enthusiasm but very little facility. Today I slept in with Duncan for the first time since we moved.

We drove each other to delirium, it being so long since. I fancy I can make his body burst one of these times soon, and him mine too. We fell in and out of half sleep, dimly aware of a world that was fully awake and bathed in the day's sunshine. We weren't, and that was fine. I can say so much more to him when my mind is too tired to work. That buzzing, hummed growl comes crawling into my throat, replacing the confusing array of words that normally clutter our conversations. It's a song in my bones. It's like a dog's loving whine, simple and pure. My song has a tune, slippery and erratic, but a tune nonetheless. If I think and try to place it, the whole thing just disappears.

It reminds me of the problem of reading in the dark. You must keep looking to the side to see anything at all.

All my classes have begun and I find it quite exciting to be taught by actual professors and sit in lovely old lecture halls with students taking notes and none of the "flimsiness," as Flora puts it, of Lowell. Military Training is the only blemish on my schedule but I've just decided not to attend. I have no interest in learning the finer points of war or marching around a field with little wooden rifles trying to mind the diagonals. Duncan says it's great fun and I should think of it as a great elaborate game with a multitude of players and simple rules like he does. I don't understand its attraction.

There's that eerie chime again. I think it's a very old song. Like Latin, if ever it's sung.

## 26 AUGUST 1915

Mr. Dunphy is the chaplain from *The Cautionary Tales,* the one where George blows the house to bits with the cursed balloon. And Mr. Thwing looks rather like George, truth be told. Maybe this is why his face has bothered me, floating in my mind, obscurely wed to the awful chaplain whose death I'd imagined so many times when I was little. My first nightmares came from *The Cautionary Tales.* Evidently they'd lingered somewhere, contributing an unspecific bad taste whenever I saw Mr. Dunphy.

I didn't see Duncan until late in the afternoon (again), a little past five, when I came back from drawing—four hours every Tuesday and Thursday. He'd pushed the room around into our planned rearrangement, two lovely chairs and a small end table gathered in the double bays facing south. He looked up from a big picturebook of buildings and smiled big and bright as I've ever seen, bouncing up from the doubled-up beds and wrestling me back down onto them.

"You," he said. "Why've you been gone so long?"

I rundled my fingers round through his thick brown hair, scritching his scalp and squeezing the soft skin at the base of his neck.

"Drawing goes till five. Tuesday *and* Thursday. Where were you when I came back after Hygiene?"

"When?"

"Nine. I came back straightaway to have breakfast." I did. Mrs. Dunphy was puttering about in her housecoat, sniffing at old biscuits in the bread box.

"I have Calculus at nine."

I rolled over on top of him. "Hhmmph," I grunted. "I had breakfast with Mrs. Dunphy."

He licked me up my neck, and mimicked me. "Hhmmph. Was it a distinct pleasure?"

Professor Kurtz had mentioned "distinct pleasures" not more than a day ago, though without reference to Mrs. Dunphy. He'd put the emphasis on "distinct."

We'd begun with some sort of ancient ritual recitation, all of us muttering syllables from off the board. They were in Greek and I don't know Greek. Nor does most the class. The portly Kurtz (he'd chosen to wear black academic gowns that day) insisted we recite in unison our reading of these oddly squiggled words and so we did. There were twenty of us, using our voices uncertainly. The professor stood up front booming the correct pronunciations, waving his thickly draped arms like an over-weight bat attempting takeoff, and generally inspiring in us a reckless spirit of camaraderie. If an ancient Greek should have happened by I'm certain our "language" would've passed through his ears unrecognized.

"Utterly indistinct," Professor Kurtz whispered into the silence that followed our brief recitation. "Like a babbling brook to a deer." I gazed out the arched window imagining deer afoot in the forest, their soft ears stood up and stiff, listening to the distant babble of the brook.

"The sounds Greek men made in conversation, the melodious songs they sang onstage as drama. Through your mouths they are torn and mangled into noise, reduced to indistinct utterance." I sat in rapt attention now, as he'd brought the topic around to us, and I was beginning to fear his reproach. To my great relief it was not forthcoming.

"But you are not to blame for the ravages of time, the failure of man to preserve what has passed. The perfect song of Aeschylus, the lilting words of Euripides are to you nothing more than air. Loud empty air." I noticed the persistent scribbling of my more mature classmates, some of whom smoked pipes. They seemed to be making records of Kurtz's introductory comments. Eager to keep up, I opened my little pamphlet of "Orestes" and composed a few brief notes on the back flap.

"Greek air," I began. "Noise not song." It reminded me of those frustrating moments when words held nothing for me, as when Duncan ran away and I couldn't find words to say "stay." I know *I* failed, not the words. "Stay" is more than empty air. But it was not enough to say all I felt. This little daydream took me far away, sailing over the bay and above the ferry to watch myself looking back at the Berkeley shore, looking to see Duncan running. I didn't see him then, that day, but I could see him now, remembering, floating a few hundred feet above, in my head. I returned to class with the sharp slap of a yardstick across the tabletop.

"Clear distinction is the essence of a working language." Profesor Kurtz seemed to be addressing this elusive bit of wisdom to me. I scribbled it quickly onto my flap.

"Clear distinctions," I wrote.

"The pleasure distinctions give is communication. Words sit

separately from one another, holding and containing some meaningful portion of experience, carving out that simple part and capturing it in a clear sound."

"Distinct pleasures," I scribbled, summarizing a bit.

" 'Desk.' Said, heard. That simple thing held. 'Plate.' 'Cap.' 'Pipe.' Each sound said, heard. Each sound holding the simple thing inside."

"Hold my cap and pipe." Notes were really quite simple, once one got the drift of things. Others were nodding their heads judiciously, in time with Kurtz's steady, even syllables.

Do words hold things inside? I could easily think so. There is no better explanation for the mind's conjuring of exactly that right thing upon hearing the sound of the word. "Cat" is said, and what do I see? A cat, somewhere in my head. It reminds me of Cicero's memory matrices. They were meant to hold whole thoughts of things past. It is that same hope of holding something that is fluid and many-layered inside some frozen, fixed surface. "Cat." As thin and brittle a surface as you'll find anywhere, even at the Fair.

Or "Duncan." Some things words can't hold. They're too big or they never hold still. Somehow they keep exceeding the borders of the word or changing the shape of it. Like the word "fear" can never fully hold the actual experience it is supposed to hold. That's like holding hot molten lead in a thin gum bubble. The edge is indistinct and unfixed. There is no clear distinction.

Duncan and I lay there half-napping in the late evening in our room and didn't say any more. My mouth could not find reliable words to hold what I felt. Kissing him became the only fulfilling alternative. It was something my mouth could offer that was wide and wet enough to carry what I felt across to him.

———

## 29 AUGUST 1915

Flora's arrived in Berkeley and will begin classes tomorrow, only a week late. She'll be taking Professor Brown's course on memory, which I'm in, and Duncan's English course. The rest is a mystery to me, except she's got Ladies' Physical Education. She's asked if she may perform her little rite of spring with me and the five ladies.

She's taken that little room in Mrs. Meekshtais's house, on our recommendation. We bundled all her bags up, tying them by ropes to her motorcar, and she drove off round the bottom of the bay to move in today.

Duncan and I were in the city most of the morning, first with Flora and then at our house, packing up various things to bring back over to Berkeley. Mother dropped in to find out about classes and to gauge my general health and grooming.

We packed the magic lamp and a tiny metal vessel Duncan keeps by his bed, and two carpets, both quite small, one from by the fire and the other from the kitchen. I gathered up the books I'd been reading in the spring, the ones I'd never finished. Mother sat very primly in the window seat and prompted me with questions, gazing out into the street and brushing her short little bob as I packed.

"Does the art instructor use Ruskin?" she asked.

"No," I answered, "though he seemed interested when I told him I'd used Ruskin for the lines. He won't be giving me his own instruction until I'm through with this project." I reached around under my bed for any books I might've let slide there. "He believes one learns best by pursuing independent work."

"Is there any treatment of the history of art?"

*The Thousand and One Nights* came out, wrapped in a packing of dust.

"Not in a *studio* course, Mummy. Don't be daft. I'll take that in the history department, next term."

"Don't call me daft, pumpkin. Many great educators have worked wonders by combining studio time with historical investigation." She smiled a quick smile, drawing the brush down across her bangs. "I'm merely inquiring about those features I've come to expect from higher-quality universities."

"Well, truth be told, I've a feeling Berkeley isn't really so high quality a university." I shared this little confidence, letting her in on an opinion I'd originally thought to hide.

She brought the brush down to her lap.

"Really, pumpkin?" she asked with a tilt of her head. "Why is that?"

"They've required me to take Military Training," I began, inflaming her with what I knew would hit hardest. "And our schedules are so helter-skelter Duncan and I have no classes together and rarely see each other at *all* until the evening when we're long past pooped out and don't have the energy to beat a flea, let alone *do* anything together," I went on, getting to what really mattered most to me.

"Military Training?" Mother interrupted. "For you in particular?"

"For *everyone*, Mummy. Every 'able-bodied young man.'" I gave her the horrible truth straight out.

"Oh, pumpkin, tenderness. How *awful* for you." She came across to the bed where I was sitting with my little book. "Surely there must be some proviso for those who object to such folly."

I held my hands in my lap and looked up at her kind face.

"None." And I tilted my head just a touch. "I've not been attending. Because of my objections." I smartly left the nature of those objections vague (which, in point of fact, was an act of utter honesty; my objections *were* vague and purposefully unspecific). "I hope no trouble comes of it."

"And Duncan? What has Duncan done about this requirement?" She rubbed my slumping shoulders sympathetically.

"Duncan doesn't mind," I admitted, after considering a small lie. "He enjoys the exercise and the sheer numbers, as he puts it."

"Simply terrible," Mother muttered, still musing on my fate. "They're dragging you into the army by the back door."

"Not to mention my schedule," I added, returning to the real issue.

"Yes, of course," she agreed. "That awful schedule."

"All helter-skelter," I reminded her.

"Of course, dearest. Hardly a moment with your friends, as you were saying."

I was glad she remembered. "That's right. Do eastern schools operate in this same way?" I asked, knowing she was fond of eastern schools. "I mean, do they *require* military service and force you to split off from your friends?"

"Oh, of course not, pumpkin." She drew back at the very thought of it. "Oh, no, no. Harvard, Yale, Columbia. They're much more progressive in their attitudes toward military service, I'm certain of it. Mind you, their academic demands are strict and traditional. Only the finest minds flourish." And she smiled at the thought of it. "They're much smaller in size than Berkeley, so I'm sure you'd be with whatever chums you had there."

"I was only asking for instance, not to go there."

She brushed my hair back with her hand.

"Of course, dearest. One must give Berkeley a fair shake before thinking about other schools."

I patted her knee emphatically. "Mummy, we're *not* thinking about other schools. I don't know if Duncan would even *want* to go east."

"If he's happy with Berkeley, with their military training, I don't suppose he'd want to go anywhere." She drummed her fingers on *The Thousand and One Nights*.

"I didn't say he was happy here. He's as upset about the schedule as I am. That's the reason we'd want to change. Not just because of some military requirement."

"*I* find the military requirement *quite* troubling."

"Well, yes. It is troubling." I stopped to put my thoughts back together. Somehow they'd fallen apart in the wake of Mother's various enthusiasms. "I'm happy to give Berkeley its chance, despite the problems. But we need to think what would be best for us, and maybe it'll be someplace else. Who knows?"

Mother kept her lips smartly shut, pursed in a tight little line, and nodded her head judiciously. I took the book and put it in a pile I'd started by the door, blowing the dust bunnies back to oblivion and pawing through the few titles I'd rescued so far.

Dear Robert,

Have they located the soul, do you know? Is it in the pineal gland? It's got nothing to do with the legs or torso, I'm certain. A leg, by itself, even with spasms of movement, is entirely devoid of spirit. An arm less so. The face of course is imbued with personality even long after death has taken away any motility. A reaching hand, fingers grasping—even if completely severed—stirs nearly the same empathy as a face.

Didn't Father live in Abbeville? It's mentioned in the Ruskin you sent me, how the valley has been so terribly changed by the new architecture. I hope to visit on the Somme before returning, after all of this ends. I've been quite lucky.

What are the papers saying in the States? Did I once say I pitied you your neutrality? Forgive me.

## 31 AUGUST 1915

"Your body is a battlefield. As with any battle, one finds allied forces on both sides." I wrote it down in pencil. Bar-bar bar-bar. Mr. Legge droned on.

"I speak of microbes. We must pay homage to Semmelweis, for his was a martyr's life." I was quite unsure whether I was awake or still sleeping.

"Don't imagine, like the ignorant practitioners of just six decades past, that simple neatness will suffice to protect the temple that is your body. For it *is* a temple." I felt certain I'd read that somewhere before. Perhaps Mr. Legge has published, I thought. I found my lazy pen sketching out temples, ornate, fleshy temples, bedecked with prayer flags and thin pillars. My notes for Mr. Legge always went beyond simple words.

The classroom was filled with men. Women were not privy to the wisdom of Mr. Legge. An older fellow with a thick sweater sat near me. He seemed to be directing the note-taking activities of a boy my age and peering every now and then at my busy drawing. Whenever I'd catch him at it with a glance he'd smile and chuckle softly as a tolerant father might do. By the mysterious insignia on his colorful sweater I surmised he was a member of one of Berkeley's men's clubs.

As I penned in the name of the temple "Church of St. Legge," this one cuffed me on the arm and guffawed, impressed by my little witticism. His laugh was oafish, but the sweater and his age made me regard him as wise. He poked his young helper and bade him look at my sketch too. It was all quite brazen and disrespectful, I feared, but we were only three amongst more than a hundred and Mr. Legge rarely raised his eyes from the text he'd prepared. To my delight his drone ceased and class was ended. The sweater man cuffed me again, handed me an ornate card and winked. I was fumbling with my papers and didn't manage even a thanks before he'd disappeared out the door with his faithful charge.

The card was an invitation of some sort. It began with a motto embossed in the same style of script that I'd seen chiseled across the face of the Social Science Building: "Achievement. Distinction. Loyalty." A time and date and location were given across the card. It looked like a motto thought up by Kurtz. "Desk. Hat. Pipe." What was lurking there in that embossed surface? What qualities rushed and rumbled within those thin black lines? If I had a knife I'd cut them open and let their contents spill out. I brushed my fingertips across the face of the raised letters and tucked the card in with my notes.

"It's some sort of voodoo society," Duncan explained when I asked if he knew about this men's club. "It's like all these university things. Ritual and voodoo." We had walked together from the busy locker room out to the great pool. Its wet benign blueness lay there sloshing in the tile bed.

"Like registration?" I asked.

"Yes. And Health class."

And Military Training, I thought but didn't say. The iron lattice rose above us to a troubling height, holding the thick glass skylights, directing the steamy moist heat back down again. Duncan dove in and I sat down on the lip, dangling my feet in the warm water. Professor Kurtz's antics seemed like voodoo to me, it was true. His rambling lectures went round in mysterious circles, punctuated by sudden scribblings on the board and the occasional protracted silence. It was as though he were conjuring, carrying out some primitive dance meant to raise dead spirits. Duncan came bubbling along back to me and pulled himself up onto the lip all wet and panting like a dog.

"You don't *really* want to go?" he asked, meaning to the meeting of the secret club.

"To the voodoo club?"

"Yeah. It'll be so dull. They're just a bunch of stuffy old fat guys. I see them all the time."

"On your ritual march?" Words and calls and splashing rang out in endless diminishing echoes, filling the vast iron hall.

"In classes. They're in all those dumb classes."

"I met this one in Health."

"It's worse in English. They sit around puffing on pipes."

I watched his legs wiggle in the lapping water. The surface wobbled and warped like some living thing. Down into the depths the light danced, waving across the tiles. How often did water from the bottom come up to the top? I remember Father telling me about convection currents. But with water it was so hard to see. Duncan slid back in, turning to drape his arms across the lip, so he could look up to me and talk.

"Water never stays still," I said because that's what I was thinking.

"No, I guess it doesn't." Duncan looked at me from under his wet hair. It was a flat swirling mess of dark brown, dripping all down his face and neck.

"I mean the surface." It was a thought that rarely left me. It had begun in Bolinas and by now everything seemed to have a surface. Everything seemed to be either fixed or unfixed, thick or thin, honest or deceitful. For some reason it seemed suddenly very important that I tell him this. It was as if I'd had a small child or tumor growing inside me and I'd not yet told anyone, as if my new teeth had come in and no one had seen. I'd been waiting anxiously for this moment, this chance, and I'd never even realized it.

"The surface is always moving, you see. The hidden parts come up to the surface always. It's always turning over and showing itself, all of it."

"Not much is 'hidden' here, Max." Duncan laughed at me. "It's really quite transparent."

"But most things aren't."

"Aren't water?"

"Aren't transparent. You see, that's why it's important what water does, the way its surface changes and moves. Like if I remember something in a simple, frozen way. Just remember it one way as if that was the whole experience, and I *don't* let the surface of that memory shift and turn and reveal its undersides, then somehow that memory is wrong."

Duncan was staring at me with his eyebrow knit. Birds clattered about in the iron rafters, shifting in their uncomfortable nests. Really I'd covered a lot of ground in the last sentence or two. I shifted a bit on my butt, adjusting my weight so my bones wouldn't get too tired.

"I don't understand," Duncan informed me. "Is this something from class?" I looked at his wondering eyes and wondered why this need to explain it felt so strong, or even if I yet *had* the words that *would* explain it.

"No, it's something I thought about in Bolinas."

"The water part?"

"Partly that. Mostly about memory, and now sort of about everything." Duncan shifted closer to me and rested his chin on his arms. The way he bowed his head and pushed his lip out, I thought he must think I wasn't well and needed solicitations or comfort. But I know that's just his way of listening closely.

"What about everything?" he asked. I'd never heard it sound so enormous. The question echoed up into the steamy vastness and whispered through the leaden skylights. It wobbled inside my ears and worked its way around inside me. What about everything? It wasn't so big when I began. I'd simply wondered why photos made me feel so bad, but the thought I'd come to blossomed into this lush, engulfing thing.

"It's hard to get ahold of, really." Yes, it was. Words could help hold it. If there were words enough. "I'm suspicious of things that hold still. Things that are fixed and frozen and never change." Like words holding this thought. The more successfully they held, the worse I felt. "That's kind of it."

Duncan held still, resting his head on his forearms, looking at me as though I'd shown him an illness. "Ice always melts," he reminded me. "Nothing ever stays frozen."

I imagined him frozen, or embalmed, preserved somehow so he remained exactly as he was now. I thought of the unraveled mummies at the Fair. Their faces had collapsed, but their flesh remained, stretched like leather over their small Egyptian bones.

"But we *try* to freeze things forever, like with photographs. Or when people want to remember every detail exactly right." Duncan nodded sympathetically. "People want their memory to be like a camera."

"How else should it be?" he asked. "I mean, how could a memory be better than if it was exactly right?"

This was the thought that panicked me. How could a memory be better than if it was exactly right? Why did this feel like a tight sheet of rubber enclosing me? I wanted to rip its perfect, smooth face apart so I could breathe. "Doesn't it make you want to rip something into shreds?" I asked in all sincerity. "Maybe rip a huge photo apart so it blows away with the wind?"

"Excuse me?" Duncan pulled himself out of the pool and sat beside me. "Have I missed something?"

I watched his ribs move as he breathed and brushed my hand across his wet shoulder. I'd skipped a step or two in my argument and went back to try and express it more completely. There was us and there was the air all around us, and the iron shell with its thick glass. We sat together, bathed in the watery green light. I looked again at his fine brown skin, all glistening and wet with water. Would I ever want to rip that away?

"Each thing has a surface, you see." He nodded encouragement. "Even a thought or a memory. And if it's fixed and frozen, like a photo is, it makes me feel stuck or stifled, like I'm in a prison and the walls are straight and clean. Brittle, thin walls that cut across me so close. I can't move even a muscle."

Duncan kept plunging his foot into the water and wobbling it around to feel the resistance. He grunted thoughtfully and lay back onto the tiles. "So you'd prefer water? A watery thought?" He meant to be funny, but he was right.

"Watery words."

"An immense sloshing watery world?" He seemed delighted by the thought. Duncan wiggled his head back and forth in the small puddle he'd made, mumbling silly words as though this were a matter of play. I wondered what had happened to my exquisite panic. Delight was all well and good. Funny formulations and watery babbling might be healthy, etc., etc., but I seemed to have misplaced, somehow, my fear.

"Shut up," I said, and hit him in the stomach. "It's not so easy and fun as you make it out to be." He hit me back, still thinking it was all play, and started wrestling me toward the water. I started to explain but he smiled and wrapped his arm around my mouth, shoving us off the lip and into the sloshing blue pool.

The water closed around us, sealing shut as my mind finally found words for part of what I meant, but now I couldn't say. There was us, all tangled in each other, and our fine brown skin. Then there was the water wrapped around us and the sounds we made, muffled and bubbling. The air lay atop the wobbling waves, and the glass cage enclosed that, offering its other face to the open air, and that went on forever.

All the cautionary tales in my little book had such tragic endings. There was George, as you know, and Harry, who got beaten for playing in mud, and Alspeth, who was eaten by a lion, his head left severed and alone. He'd let go of his nurse's hand. Matilda, who'd yelled "fire" once too often, was left at home by her withered aunt (who went to see *The Second Mrs. Tanqueray* alone) and burned to a cinder in a horrible blaze.

(Mother asked me who would I like to have at my birthday and I told her, "Paolo and Rolph and George and Alspeth," because I really didn't much like Harry and Matilda was dead. Alspeth's head survived the lion's jaws, and his head would be enough for me.

"Tenderness," she cooed, "George and Alspeth are from a book. Wouldn't Skinny like to come as well?" I didn't like Skinny that day. He'd taken my place as digger in the Tunnel Through the Earth.

"I don't like Skinny," I said. She brushed my downy cheek with her soft hand.

"But dumpling, that leaves just two and I don't imagine two makes for much of a party." I knew it made four but I thought perhaps she'd start to talk nonsense if I asked more about George and Alspeth.

"Let's just *set* for four, can we?" I noodled, thinking she'd never guess.

"For George and Alspeth?"

It was uncanny. On top of everything else she could read minds. I blushed and nodded yes.

"Pumpkin," she exhaled my favorite name. "George and Alspeth can't come to a party. They're from a book."

"I don't mind," I tried explaining. "I could make cards asking them. I don't *have* to invite Skinny, do I?")

## 3 SEPTEMBER 1915

Mr. Brown says poetry began for memory, to give meter and rhyme so troubadours could remember more and more without it being written. They sang it out in every town. They sang whole songs of news, and all of it remembered in an instant. One reading and they were off on their sturdy horses, galloping over muddy fields, through thick forests full of druids and elves, and into the smoky thatched towns to sing the news.

## 5 SEPTEMBER 1915

*Pruinae perniciosior natura, quoniam lapsa persidit gelatque ac ne aura quidem ulla depellitur, quia non fit nisi inmoto aere et sereno. Proprium tamen siderationis est sub ortu canis siccitatum vapor, cum insita ac novellae arbores moriuntur.*

I run it through my head like a vacuum, sweeping things clean of meaning. It's an incantation. A musty psalm lifting the burdens from my mind.

*Sarmenta aut palearum acervos et evulsas herbas fruticesque per vineas camposque, cum timebis, incendito, fumus medebitur his.*

Frost high in the hills one night late, very late, while walking.

I hear a song at night in the wind chimes. Duncan sleeps heavy. He talks in his sleep, saying things *I've* said over and over in an odd voice not quite his and not mine. A night bird is singing to the chimes, calling a very soft warble into the black stars and I'm awake, listening to these voices, Duncan, the bird and the bell.

There's a density that frightens me, words carrying so many unwelcome thoughts dragging along with them. Or a single simple person, Duncan, becoming so many things, layers and layers of need or feeling or expectations that reside in his body for me. There is his body, simply his body, and so much is there when I'm looking. It drags out from my center like those awful fears I have of every surface dissolving. Or, equally, of every surface freezing shut. I become frightened by the stillness. Fear starts in me when the world is clear and fixed.

Dear Robert,

Wasn't it Abbeville? I'm quite certain of it, in fact. We'd made up that silly song while walking during a summer there. Father took us for a holiday. I'd a lad from Abbeville up on the table and he kept on and on about the river and the cathedral. It was some sort of delirium and he was out and dead before I could ask him about the "mousy plum" which I'm certain was the name of a small café (or our innocent reading of some French name). How long ago it all seems.

We've a pond back of the line much like Cooperstown. *I* was the better swimmer, wasn't I?

I was at the Albert Hall in a lovely clean suit just ten hours ago. Truly. I'd tickets for a Gilbert and Sullivan, a matinee shortly before my leave was up. I met a sweet young woman who kept on about a stomach ailment, hoping, I suspect, that I'd offer some professional advice. We sat in those plush velvet chairs, smelling of rosewater and soap, the whole building still standing. How could they ever understand this, this table of blood, this graveyard?

You stopped at the brow of the hill to put the drag on, and looked up to see where you were:—and there lay beneath you, far as the eye could reach on either side, this wonderful valley of the Somme—with line on line of tufted aspen and tall poplar, making the blue distances more exquisite in bloom by the gleam of their leaves; and in the midst of it, by the glittering of the divided streams of its river, layed the clustered mossy roofs of Abbeville, like a purple flake of cloud, with the precipitous mass of the Cathedral towers rising mountainous through them, and here and there, in the midst of them, spaces of garden close-set with pure green trees, bossy and perfect.

So you trotted down the hill between bright chalk banks, with a cottage or two nestled into their recesses, and little round children rolling about like apples before the doors, and at the bottom you came into a space of open park ground, divided by stately avenues of chestnut and acacia,—with long banks of outwork and massive walls of bastion seen beyond—then came the hollow thunder of the drawbridge and shadow of the gate—and in an instant, you were in the gay streets of a populous yet peaceful city—a fellowship of ancient houses set beside each other, with all the active companionship of business and sociableness of old friends, and yet each with the staid and self-possessed look of country houses surrounded by hereditary fields—or country cottages nested in forgotten glens,— each with its own character and fearlessly independent ways—its own steep gable, narrow or wide—its special little peaked windows set this way and that as the fancy took them,—its most particular odd corners, and outs and ins of wall to make the most of the ground and sunshine, —its own turret staircase, in the inner angle of the courtyard,—its own designs and fancies in carving of bracket and beam—its only bridge over the clear branchlet of the Somme that rippled at its garden gate.

All that's gone—and most of Abbeville is like most of London—rows of houses all alike, with an heap of brickbats at the end of it.

6 SEPTEMBER 1915

I watched the military drills from up on a little knoll above the field. Duncan's in charge of some sort of unit, getting to march all around them and yell this or that and run ahead and mind the diagonals and all that sort of thing that people in charge do with a flock of able-bodied young men. It made me sad to see him having such a time of it, like when I watched him running off into the rain that day up on the ridge in Bolinas.

Flora's dance will be next week, in the Grove, where we went through the mysteries of registration. I'll be carried about in my diaper as the infant Spring. I won't have to do all that hysterical spinning and leaping like we tried the first time.

## 12 SEPTEMBER 1915

Maybe from it being so warm and dusty, I was nearly sleeping, but very much present. It's that Latin, really, especially in Mr. Deutsch's steady even meter.

"*Fuere ab his et cognomina antiquis.*" From trees? I rather like the idea. It's best days like today when he turns the lights off and shows projections through the magic lantern.

"*Frondicio militi illi qui praeclara facinora Volturnum transnatans fronde inposita adversus Hannibalem edidit.*" I fancy Duncan's of the same stuff as Frondicio, the sort who'd think to use a screen of foliage and be ripe to jump in any river. The pictures show the ancients to be so handsome, all with their fine straight noses and beautiful bodies. Father says they liked boys, and even made sex a part of the program of education. The words are so solid and simple to me. I imagine their simplicity comes from my inadequate understanding. It is new to me, and so each word has clear meaning. It's a great relief.

"*Stolonum Liciniae genti,*" washing like water easy over me. Mr. Deutsch does love to read. "*Ita appellatur in ipsis arboribus fruticatio inutilis, unde et pampinatio inventa primo Stoloni dedit nomen.*"

And oh, the smooth hands running rough over me in that sylvan grove, there by where Miss Tartaine sealed our fates. We had quite the audience, as Flora's made more friends than the entire population of Lowell, it seems, upperclassmen with pipes and women who wore pants. I was so delightfully bare and given the simplest of parts, the violent beauty of Spring's grand assertion having been stricken from the program. "Work in Progress" it was entitled this time around.

And Duncan's hands rougher still, pushing and pulling me furiously about the bed, us sweating so slick we slide across each other's bare skin and stuck together at our mouths and legs entangled. I'm blind and possessed now each night with the desperate hunger of it all, and not a conscious thought in my head, the whole of me filled by the indistinct all of it rushing through our skins and the musty slobbery slick push of him into me. I can't think past the roar rolling out my body, of sinking our soaked soft bodies as completely into each other as time will allow, then empty. Still and empty. The window is open to the night air. That soft sound is in me, and sleep. I am so simple, and nodding. A loll and lull all in me, and so soft and small all warm in flannel, the lull of song. (Mother's voice soft in song. I'm so small and warm and nodding, wrapped in warm flannel. And tiny little fishermen sailed, she sang, all on a moonlit sea, sailed out inside a wooden shoe, she sang, Winky and Blinky the dog.)

15 SEPTEMBER 1915

I've felt better since saying those confusing things I said to Duncan a week ago. I have no idea why. I don't know what more to say to him. I will not, I imagine, find the words to make myself clear. I won't find words that satisfy me.

"I worry about this," for instance, is just wrong. "This worries me" gets closer. It suggests that I'm unable to stop the worrying. But it also looks to me like some "thing" hovering around me, kneading my flesh and soul like bread dough, with an evil grin on its amorphous face. "I'm worried with it" feels better because it doesn't assign blame. Because "it" and "I" are together there is "worry." It's like a meteorological condition. The wet ocean air made cold condenses into rain. Just as I have blown in among these thoughts and become worry. Worry. Worry. Now *that* ugly sound has begun to fall apart. Really, what *is* there that ought to be held inside that sound? Is "worry" a physical feeling somewhere inside the brain? Is it a fidgeting of the limbs? A slight trembling below the throat that rumbles intermittently, hardly noticed until some still, silent moment? It worries me, this endless train of thoughts. It's a thread I began to pull, and now it's all unraveling.

When it tugs at Duncan I start to fall apart. There are questions I cannot ask. It's like walking a mine field, fearing that the depths of this tender land will rip open and reveal something unfathomable. I stammer and stutter in the face of so many wrong things to say. I groan in my throat, that pure sound with my mouth pushed against his neck. I give *that* sound to him, fearing the dangerous words. I give him my tongue, often just to look at with my mouth open and empty, like I am speaking but no word could possibly fit. Maybe my throat rumbles like a baby's. I give him my tongue across his closed eyes and over his nose and lips. It says so much more by touch than by the words it could make.

I give him my body and only then do I feel a sense of clarity. It is our way of speaking, the only language that can carry whatever it is we're trying to say.

## 20 SEPTEMBER 1915

"Wax: grand hg teday!! Ten, two, fire. 55. D." This is a note Mr. Dunphy left me, right with my laundry so I know it's for me. He's afflicted with some disorder, Mrs. D. tells me.

Robert,

Today the aeroplanes came and dropped chocolates. We've stacked corpses up to make parapets, covered by thin mud. Hands fall out to wave or brush across one's face when the artillery shakes the dirt down. They shell the middle ground into nothing and launch the gas and we follow, endless waves of men stumbling into a stinking muddy grave.

A photo in the news. A bullet, many. Mortar ripping through a line of men. It will end as simply as it began, with a photo in the news.

I lost to Unt in tennis today, finishing up the match by launching the salty little felt ball over the fences and leaping the net for a victory hug. Unt has a general recreation course in the Ladies' Physical Education program, and Mr. Wilson generously allowed us to recreate together this week, setting us up with equipment and a brief review of the rules up on the courts in Strawberry Canyon.

The hills up back of the university are thrilling, particularly there by the canyon. Thick green groves rise up the steep hills and then the yellow brown grasslands lift out beyond the tree-tops. We played in the early morning so the mists still hung in the trees. The sun cut clean across everything, giving a wash of warm light to the air and the sturdy buildings, jumbled about on the low stretch of hills west of us.

I held the salty felt ball up to my nose and smelled its lovely smell.

(What was that soft song she sang? I held the salty felt ball close to my nose and it rolled around so deep inside me, calling at that song . . . a tiny little fisherman sailed on a moonlit sea . . . and that salty felt smell, feeling it near my nose, my wet little mouth open. Winky, I know, and Blinky the dog, and damp on my dingle and Mother's sweet song.)

## 29 SEPTEMBER 1915

## 12 OCTOBER 1915

I went to the city to get some of Father's suits, much to Mother's delight. I hadn't been at my old house since the spring and it made me feel queer. I walked along the ridge on Pacific up to Lyon, to where it all just drops off west to the Presidio and north to the Fair. The golden domes spread out like they've been there a thousand years.

There was Mother, the parlor windows open and her warbling out into the misty air. She's been attempting famous arias since she first started singing, sometime before history began. I banged in through the front door and felt even dizzier smelling the familiar smell.

"Pumpkin?" I heard her coming clip-clop on sharp-toed shoes across the hardwood floor.

"Hello, Mummy," I called back. And then there was a moment, a long familiar moment.

"You," she said, hugging me up to her bustle. "You're a perfect mess," and the moment passed. She rustled my wild, thick hair and looked me over.

"Thank you," I replied cordially. "I'm perfectly starving too."

"Oh, lovely," she went on, "what a fortunate coincidence. I'm a bit peaked as well." She looked to the kitchen thoughtfully. "Surely we can scrape up some small morsel from the larder," and she shuffled on through the dining room to find out.

I looked around the parlor to see what had changed and what was still the same. Nothing had changed. I wanted to curl up on the davenport and have tea. I wanted Father to read *Melmoth*.

"Fruit, tenderness?"

I peeked in over her shoulder to see what fruit it was.

"Yucko, nix on the melon." It looked fairly old and soggy, the little rind lips all curled in like an old man with his false teeth out.

" 'Yucko,' pumpkin?"

"Duncan says it, if he doesn't like something," I explained.

"He certainly didn't learn it from his father," Mother observed pointlessly.

"He didn't learn any English from his father," I said.

Mother just looked at me and curled her mouth into a disapproving frown.

"Cold roast beef?" she offered.

"Yummo. With horseradish, please, and may I have some red wine?"

"Are you perfectly serious about the wine, Maxwell? On a Tuesday afternoon?"

"A hearty red is perfect with cold beef," I tried, mimicking Mrs. Dunphy's sensible explanation from the previous afternoon.

"I'm sure it is, dearest, I was merely questioning the hour."

"Just one glass then. Surely one glass will do me no harm."

Mother got out the wine and beef and spooned a few hefty

scoops of horseradish into a dish. "Cress?" she offered, her head plunged deep into the ice box.

"Yes, thank you."

We picnicked on our little lawn and discussed school, which I said was not much better, emphasizing, in particular, Hygiene and the trial of Latin conjugations. Pliny I enjoyed well enough, as it was not the boring Younger and his limitless epistles, but rather the quirky Elder and his queer little bits about magical trees and frogs with feet growing out from their mouths. But Cicero, I assured Mother, was even more tedious in the original, clacking along like a judicious cow, all moo and maw and *anno domini* and such sounds as a broken Italian, stumbling along over his fragmented syllables, might make.

"The dead languages only come alive in the mouth of a true lover of the tongue," Mother explained obscenely, taking a wet lump of horseradish with just a sliver of beef. "Latin is as so much dust if one has no passion for the living culture it gave voice to. Perhaps your instructor has no feeling for Cicero."

I cleansed my mouth with a sprig of cress and a splash of cold soda. "Duncan says I should try Greek."

"Or learn Latin from someone who can give it spark."

"But Professor Deutsch teaches all the courses that interest me." I sniffed at the heady wine.

"Precisely, pumpkin." And then Mother paused, to great dramatic effect. "I've taken the liberty of sending for a few catalogs from schools back East."

This was both good and bad. I rather fancied going back East, but I'd not yet gotten up the nerve to discuss it with Duncan.

"Mother," I whined unconvincingly, leaving my precise feelings quite unclear.

"Professor Wilson is still at Harvard, you know." This remark was typical.

"Fine, Mother, Duncan and I will just go study with Professor

Wilson," I answered sarcastically. I was glad for her help, but it seemed she was pursuing her own little fantasies and not mine. "The point is to find a way we can be in the same program and not have to waste time with frivolities like Hygiene."

"Or Military Training," she added pointedly.

"Right."

"Your father is a Harvard alumnus, pumpkin, and that should help considerably."

"And what about Duncan?"

"I wasn't aware he was interested in Harvard, tenderness."

"He's *not*. That's the point. I can't just make him go there."

Mother gargled a bit of soda demurely and spit it into the grass.

"There's no need to *make* anyone do anything, pumpkin. I'm only suggesting you consider Harvard as a sensible alternative to a situation which you yourself have led me to believe is unsatisfactory. If Duncan finds that alternative inviting as well, then he'll have to think about arranging it. I presumed he hadn't thought about it because he saw no need to."

I pushed my finger deeper into the lawn, propping a bit of cress in the little hole I'd created by my nervous habit, filling it in with a bit of loose soil.

"The point, Mother, is that I'm not going to Harvard, or anywhere else for that matter, without Duncan."

She sat in silence for a moment, digesting this new thought.

"Isn't that rather unreasonable, Maxwell? I'd think it would be an awful burden on him."

"It *isn't*," I fairly yelled, barely getting out that crucial last syllable. "We *want* to be in the same program and that's what we'll arrange. Here or back East or whatever."

Our little conversation dwindled away into a palliative series of ifs and waits and maybes and sees, and we licked our plates clean and went back in to get the suits.

## 17 OCTOBER 1915

That Men's Club fellow took me aside and charmed me into saying yes I would come along for their little festival in the woods. Actually I stood my ground, insisting that Duncan be invited as well, though no club members had met him, and we shook hands to seal the agreement. I was uncertain it was the right thing. In fact, I was fairly certain it was not, but flattery is never lost on me and really we both like the woods well enough to enjoy ourselves even if it is with a bunch of fat, boring men, as Duncan had described them.

The way Fletcher described it (his name is Fletcher, though he allowed that I may call him "Fletch"), we were going on a picnic with delightful food and unspecified fun. He alluded to a game, a sort of treasure hunt, but withheld the details. We were to meet them at the corner of Euclid and Rose at five o'clock p.m.

The first thing they did was to blindfold us. Duncan had agreed to go because I was so insistent and I'd managed to make it sound like fun.

"You didn't mention blindfolds," he said to me as we bounced about in the bed of the truck they'd picked us up in.

"Fletcher didn't say anything about them," I answered. "He did say the game would be challenging. Maybe it's part of the game." We were sitting on the truck bed's dirty floor with seven or eight other boys our age and two or three of the elegantly sweatered men. All the boys wore blindfolds, I believe, and the men kept quiet. Duncan started talking to his neighbor, shouting over the roar of the engine and the noise of our bumpy ride up into the hills.

"Have you been in the club long?" he asked from behind his blindfold.

The one who answered had a voice I'd heard in Health class, though I couldn't remember the face that went with it. "I'm not in the club," he said. "I got a card once, but I never went." His face came back to me, a soft round face with blush on the cheeks and thin lips.

"Same here," Duncan said to him. "We got a card but it seemed dumb to go."

"Yeah," his neighbor agreed. "But this sounded okay. There's supposed to be food and a film."

"A film?" Duncan shouted back.

"Yeah. They've got a projector and the screen. That's why it has to be dusk and all. They're showing it in the woods."

"Max," Duncan called, turning toward me. "What about this film?"

I didn't know anything about a film. "What film?" It seemed an unlikely thing. Where would they find electricity?

"This guy says there's a film." It was all too confusing. I didn't want to bother Duncan with it.

"Yeah, the film," I improvised. "In the woods, right?"

"Right. Why didn't you mention it?"

"The film?"

"Yeah, the film."

"I didn't mention it?"

"Max."

But he gave up and we sat in the dusty truck bed, rumbling blindly along the winding road, on our way to the mysterious picnic.

When the truck finally stopped we were in a cool, shaded woods, east of Berkeley I surmised. The ride had been uncomfortable and dizzying, and I felt a great sense of relief when they finally told us to take our blindfolds off. It was indeed the woods that run by Wildcat Canyon. Duncan, just to be charming, at first refused to remove his blindfold. He stumbled around by the dusty shoulder of the road, bruising his shins on the truck fender and moaning as if he were an old man. It was just his way of telling them how stupid the whole thing seemed. Of course, his subtle critique was lost on them, and I finally convinced him to just take the damned thing off so we could get on with the fun part.

The sun was hanging low to the west, its light dappling through the green branches. The dust that had lifted off the road hung in the air, illuminated by shafts of sunlight. We sat in a small grassy meadow just a few yards off the road. "Fletch," as he now introduced himself, began to explain the treasure hunt while the other men in the club handed out small flags to each of the guests. The flags, in fact, had been our blindfolds only moments before.

"There is a treasure hidden in these woods. The picnic begins when it is found." I didn't much like the idea. Holding food for ransom is among the lowest forms of motivation. I harrumphed to myself and vowed to find the treasure pronto. "To find the treasure," Fletch continued, "you simply follow the markers in the woods." He stopped and smiled as if concluding his short lecture. But a few things had been left unclear.

"What do the markers look like?" the round-faced fellow asked, anticipating my very question. All of the sweatered men looked at one another and chuckled. This was some sort of secret joke.

"That," Fletch said, "is the hard part. You'll know them when you see them."

"Do we have to be blindfolded?" Duncan asked, holding up the little flags we all held.

"Those aren't blindfolds," the man who'd driven explained. "Those are flags."

"You've got to keep your flag to stay in the game," Fletch added. "If one of us takes your flag away you're out." The game was beginning to sound like fun. I still wondered how on earth anyone would find a marker in so big a woods with no idea what the marker was going to be. But the thought of being chased and eluding capture was really quite appealing. Duncan raised his brow at me, evidently delighted, too, by this new twist.

"Once we find this treasure, then we eat?" I wanted to make certain everything was laid out straight.

"*If* one of you finds it, you all eat."

The sun had sunk into the treetops, visible every now and then through the thick branches. The club men were sitting by the truck chatting, passing a little flask around. I'd started off into the woods, wandering in the meadow with Duncan and two other boys. The ground was firm and grassy but quickly became bare as we left the meadow for the trees. I could hear quail cooing and what I thought might be the distant buzz of an aeroplane. Looking up, though, I saw nothing mechanical in the sky, only a wisp of a cloud and the blue sky. The soft bird songs were suddenly shattered by loud screaming, as the men came rushing down off the road at full speed. The game, evidently, had begun.

———

I bolted straight down a small drop and into the cool woods, Duncan running a zigzag path to my right. The other guests had gone off in a different direction, unwisely I thought, for the chances of eluding the men near the road seemed slight. Already a small handful had been caught. I could hear the laughing and derisive yells of the club men rippling through the trees. I kept steady on, running and leaping by instinct, not really thinking out my course or direction. I caught a last glimpse of Duncan as he jumped up onto a rock outcropping with two or three following him. The air was cool and full with the smell of eucalyptus. My footfall crunched the long dry leaves and peels of bark with every step. I could hear nothing but that and my breathing and the wind whistling past my ears.

It was a thrill that ran through me like blood. The running and leaps and dodges, down farther and farther into these shadowed woods. It made me think kindly of Duncan's love of running, though I still couldn't fathom why he'd run on a track or a straight road. Careening through the wild woods. That's what thrilled me. Running like a cascading creek or like a deer. The blood was pounding in my ears. I could touch the trees as I flew past them, adjusting my direction in midstride and cutting back across to slip between two tall firs.

I wondered if Duncan might still be near and turned to take a quick look, but there was no one. No one at all. I looked quickly again and saw nothing and stopped. All around me the trees stood, bending slightly with the wind at their tops. It was empty. The wind sound rustled, as even as silence, and I gulped breaths of air, trying to catch my wind. Duncan must've gone far and fast, I thought, and maybe drawn my pursuers away.

Birds called, high up in the branches, near where the last sun was turning the woods golden. I shuffled my feet on the dry ground, rustling the peels of bark. I stood still and listened, but heard only silence. I wondered where, exactly, I was. I'd come downhill, mostly, and from the west. But where I stood now the uphill went north, not back west, and it didn't look like the woods I'd just run through. The woods west looked unfamiliar too. Above me the sunlight slipped up toward the tops of the trees, narrowing the small bright band until finally it was gone.

"Oooo-hooo," I called to the west. My little flag dangled from my belt where I'd tucked it. Nothing called back. A creek was rippling in a gully nearby, near enough to add its sound to the evening stillness. "Oooo-hooo."

I started walking north, up the steep hill, hoping to see something familiar from that vantage point. The woods were mostly eucalyptus and oak, the ground clear of cover and littered with old leaves and dried bark. In the gullies stands of fir grew, and the ground grew thick with brush and rhododendron. Fog had started drifting in from the west, slipping over the lip of the Berkeley hills and settling down into the trees. A quail burst out from a bush to my right, its round little body flung, but hardly flying. It came down like a bomb and landed squat, bobbing its tiny little tufted head.

"Oooo-hooo," I called again. The quail looked at me and waddled away into the woods, cooing and warbling as it went. The fog hung in the canopy, muffling the rustle of the trees. I didn't recognize any landmarks, so I decided to keep going west, knowing I'd hit the road eventually. I watched above me. The trees wobbled among the gray mists. Little animals and birds crashed in the branches, knocking dead leaves down to the ground. I was nervous in my legs, stepping forward tentatively, hoping the woods would open up ahead, or the sound of an auto or horse might be heard. It must've been near to half past six. Dusk had come with the fog. I dipped down through the rill, looking for footholds up the other side, when I saw a small pile of stones. It was only a few inches high, but it was clearly made, and made recently. A little stick extended out from it, pointing ahead.

It was a marker. I *had* recognized it when I saw it. Ahead of me the rill dumped down into a wider gully. No water ran there, but the stones were all washed clean as though it ran wet quite often. Someone had laid sticks down there to form another arrow, and so I followed. The cold air of evening was dropping down through the trees, trailing wisps of the thick fog with it. I felt a chill up my spine where my back was wet with sweat, and it turned into a shiver at my neck. The stones of the gully were easy to travel on. I leapt along at a slow run, easily seeing each marker now, though the light had grown dim.

At the head of the creek bed, where the gully had begun, a final arrow pointed in under a tangle of roots. I knelt down by it and reached my arm into the hiding place. The rich smell of dark, cool dirt wrapped around me as my searching knocked some of it loose. The stones settled some under my feet. There was a wooden box inside. I pulled it out to inspect it.

The heavy wooden box had a simple lid on two hinges with a small metal clasp to hold it shut. It was as big as a cigar box and sounded empty when I shook it. Inside there was only a card, another invitation to come to an initiation thing. This one was a bit fancier than the first and, I guess, more exclusive. It was hardly a treasure worth having. But I *had* found it, and it *did* mean we'd get to feast.

The woods were quite dark now. The brightest light came from the gray mists. It was all around me by now. The trees rose up into it, disappearing into the drifting fog about twenty feet above my head. I held my small treasure to my chest and climbed out of the gully, walking, I hoped, west again. I pulled my arms up into my shirt to keep warmer and held the treasure inside.

The forest floor was busy with scooting and scampering sounds. I saw squirrels, and heard much more. Something very big must have passed through the woods to my right because I felt its footfall through the dry tamped earth and heard it crashing through a fallen oak branch. Thankfully I never saw it. A chill drifted down from the fog like rain. I kept on with my even stride, making small sounds to myself to keep up courage. The crackling of bark and leaves kept on all around me and only finally frightened me most when it stopped. I heard it all go still. I stopped and held my breath, listening to the silence. There was nothing. I couldn't see well through the trees, but everywhere I tried I was certain I saw shadows. The leaves crackled again, under some heavy foot. I kept still but strained to see.

"Max?" a voice called. "Max? Is that you?" It was Duncan. I sprinted toward his voice and called his name back and there he was, looking dirty and disheveled but very glad, as I'm certain I looked to him. I knocked him over onto the ground and squeezed him so hard I thought I'd burst.

"I think we're lost," he said, not letting go of me even enough to get up off the ground.

"Yeah, we're lost," I agreed. "Did you get away?"

"No." He was all sweaty and smudged. "Did you?"

"Yeah," I said proudly, showing him my flag. "And we won, because I found the treasure." I put the little box into his hand and showed him the card. "It's a dumb treasure," I allowed as he looked inside the box, "but at least we'll get our feast." He put the card back and sat up, brushing dirt from off his clothes. He didn't seem very happy about my prize.

"There's not any food, Max, you know that." He stood up and offered me a hand.

"Yes there is. I've got the treasure." I stood up next to him and let him brush my back off.

"They've all gone, Max. They never brought any food. They left as soon as they'd caught us all."

"But they never caught me. I won." None of what he was saying made sense.

"They drove away."

"You let them just drive away?"

"They tied me to a tree. They tied a bunch of us to trees. They were laughing like it was a big joke."

I tried to imagine that they might have done that. I *knew* that they'd done that, feeling now like I'd been so stupid all along to ever think they *wouldn't* just do that. It made the pleasure

I'd felt about the little box so awful and embarrassing, knowing how pleased I'd been. Duncan tugged at my arm and we started walking, not saying any more, because there really wasn't any more to say.

The woods were dark by now and as full of frightening sounds as ever before that evening, but somehow I didn't hear them. My mind was too full of bewildered anger, and relief at finding Duncan, to focus on rustling leaves. We both walked on with an ease that belied our earlier worry. The cold air kept coming in over the hills and blew the fog away, opening up a clear black sky above us and letting moonlight down into the woods. The animal paths made for easy walking and our various preoccupations kept us from worrying over choices and direction. Within an hour or maybe more we'd found the road again and sat down to set a fire, breaking the stupid box into kindling to start the flames.

## 19 OCTOBER 1915

I got on Mr. Brown about stories again today.

"I always forget things if they don't fit somewhere, like when it's in a story," I offered boldly. "Don't you think every memory's part of some made-up story? How else could you remember it?"

Mr. Brown wasn't so fond of me as Mr. Spengler had been. The problem, I realized, was my failure to learn anything he was trying to teach, except for Guillio Cammilo, the sixteenth-century Mnemonist. I got an "A" for what I wrote about Guillio Cammilo. Everything else has been a bust.

"I believe, Mr. Kosegarten, we've covered at least a half dozen 'other ways' one might remember, other than creating fictions."

"I didn't mean strictly fictions, Mr. Brown, and I'm sorry if I missed something. I just meant any stories, any kind, true ones or whatever." I remembered something from last week. "Like Aristotle's all for making up stories, even if they're true or whatever they are. That's what I mean by stories." The Aristotle part seemed to perk him up a bit.

"Make a note of it, Mr. Kosegarten, work out your position on paper and bring it in," and he squinched his nose all quick like a wink, the way he did whenever he meant "Let's move on," and so we did.

Duncan and I went to the movies, sitting down in the lovely enveloping dark, racking up against the hardwood flip-front chairs in time for three of the four serials and a feature. Duncan kept his leg pushed in against mine and I mine against his and we watched the slow decay of innocent Blanche Sweet (performing as twins) under the evil spell of opium in *The Secret Sin*. Blanche played the good twin *and* the bad twin by some magic trick of the cinema, often appearing on screen in both roles at once. We stayed in to catch the serial we'd missed on the next time around, emerging into the gloam of evening all silent and sore from sitting so long.

> Dear Robert,
>     Thank you for the news clippings. For so long I'd thought the war was beyond our powers of understanding because of its insurmountable complexity. I realize now it is the utter simplicity of the war that makes it incomprehensible.
>     Tomorrow is Sunday and that is heaven for me.

## 26 OCTOBER 1915

I tried it out on him in the evening, while we did our work, during our hour or so together before bed. He was sitting in the bay where the beds had been, doing calculus and humming a bouncy Sousa tune. I'd thought very carefully about the best way of putting things, not wanting him to feel I was forcing it all upon him.

"Where do you imagine traveling to, in the U.S.A.?" I asked, to get him thinking on the right track.

"Just fantasy, you mean?" He poked his forehead with his lumpy eraser.

"No, actually, if you really were going to." I leaned up on my elbows, stretched out sideways across the bed on my stomach.

Duncan pushed the eraser all bent against his head and thought for a while.

"I'd go to the desert."

This wasn't the answer I wanted.

"I don't mean outdoors stuff or adventures. I meant like on a train trip or going to see the sights." I hoped this would clarify matters.

"But you said actually, what I'd actually do. That's what I'd actually do, go to the desert," he explained reasonably.

"Right, I know that. But I'm rephrasing it. What if it was a train trip somewhere and not for outdoors stuff, where would you go?" That seemed to narrow things enough.

"I don't know if I'd *actually* do that."

"Just imagining, then."

He brought his feet up on to the chair and squinched down into it, thinking still.

"I guess I'd go back East, go see the big cities."

"Like what? New York, or Boston?" I prompted.

"Yeah, and Philadelphia and Washington, D.C. My dad says we have relations in Washington, D.C." He looked back into his calculus book.

"I'd love to see Boston," I pushed on. "I'd love to see all the snow in the winter."

He looked up from his book again and stared out the window, imagining, I hoped, the lovely white drifts of snow, it falling thick from the sky and ivying up and down the rough-brick-walled buildings.

"What's the quadratic equation?" he asked.

It was the one thing I'd memorized in math: " 'X' equals 'negative b' plus or minus the square root of 'b squared,' minus 'four ac' all over 'two a,' " I told him as fast as I possibly could. "Now come on. What about the snow in Boston?"

He looked over at me and thought, pushing his eraser in under his upper lip now.

"Oh, yeah, the snow. That'd be something else. I'd love that."

"Yeah, me too," I agreed. "Can you imagine living there?"

He penciled some things onto his paper, then brought his eraser down, wiping it dry on his shirtsleeve first. I paused, hoping I wouldn't have to prompt him further.

"Well, living there? I don't know. I bet it gets so cold for so long. We'd probably die from freezing." And he looked up at me and shivered. "You thinking of moving?"

"What?" I said, wishing he hadn't asked.

"Are you thinking of moving there, to Boston?" He kept his gaze steady and even, looking at my eyes.

I turned over on my back and stared out the window at the stars in the dark sky.

"I wouldn't move there if you didn't," I said honestly. "I couldn't possibly." I felt his weight smushing onto the bed next to me.

"I *know* that," he said. "I asked if you were *thinking* of moving there, whether it was something you'd been thinking about." He poked at my back with his eraser.

"Well, Mother's been talking about eastern schools," I began. "She's sent for some catalogs."

"So *she's* thinking of going back East?" he asked, being a bit too persistent about all this.

"No, *she's* not thinking of going back East. She knows we're not perfectly happy with things here so she's just trying to help by finding out about other places." I turned over to look at him.

"And *are* you thinking about going?"

"I already said I wouldn't go if you didn't." We lay there for some moments in a confrontational silence, the small space between our bodies fairly alive with minute drawings toward and away.

"Well, good," he finally put in. "Because I'm not going anywhere back East."

I looked at him, me chewing at my lip and glancing all around his face, keeping clear of his eyes.

"And I'd appreciate your keeping me up to date on what you're thinking about doing," he finished, poking me a bit in the belly.

"That's what I was doing," I explained. "I was trying to tell you about the catalogs and the different possible things but you got all huffy about it."

He shook his head and rolled away from me onto his back.

"You did not try to tell me," he said up into the ceiling. "You started asking me if I wanted to travel anywhere and then you kept wheedling around to Boston is what you did."

I wished he wouldn't say that. I wished he'd just roll back and bury me in his arms and mouth and kiss me into oblivion. I felt sort of shaky lying there near him and knowing what he said was true. I couldn't think what to say in my defense. He got up off the bed and went back to his chair and his homework.

After our conversation we both worked a bit longer, me on my memory book and him on calculus, and we went to bed without so much as a word regarding anything but toothbrushes, lights and morning alarms.

Then we were at each other so fast it was scary. I guess we simply had a lot to say and knew somewhere inside us that talking more would only lead to trouble. I can feel it welling up like laughter inside me when I've got to get to him. And if I open my mouth the only sound that comes up is that buzzing growl of a song my throat makes when I let it loose. I push my mouth against his sweet skin and sing that song into his body.

When I do speak, my mouth reduces down around the smallest words to say. I need you. Love me. More words string out like fences, clamoring around in a dizzying jumble of dangerous meanings and slips and slides.

## 3 NOVEMBER 1915

As I speak less and less, and I do, losing my words to the fear I have of forever ruining the difficult, exquisite landscape Duncan and I roll around in together. As I speak less and less, my walking, waking time loses weight and floats free in air, never quite dropping down into me, never quite feeling solidly part of me until I see it written. Here, written. And I turn the page and it's shut down in and felt.

My painting gets thicker with each layer. They all stay present, lurking in the surface. These pages turn, flipping past. They layer in only on the surface I make by memory. Those dim shadows of hundreds of thousands of written words are left lurking in my mind, worked on by time and mysterious tides. I'll be sending notes to Father soon, if I keep on like this.

## 10 NOVEMBER 1915

Duncan baked two pies, one for us and one for the Dunphys, this morning while the rain beat in buckets against that high wide window and everywhere else too. They were plum pies with plums Mrs. Dunphy canned this summer and flaky crust like Mother showed Duncan how to make because of his loving pie so much. They had a light sprinkle of sharp Cheddar cheese melted on the top. I watched them coming out of the oven piping hot. Duncan and I had two hot slices and saved the rest for later. The Dunphys let theirs be, Mrs. Dunphy insisting she wanted to serve it to guests at the dinner they've planned for the evening.

## 17 NOVEMBER 1915

I'd just come from the musty Latin wing, out into the drizzly day, when I was tackled and knocked to the ground by Duncan. He goosed me all over and generally made a scene, right there in public view. No one did anything to rescue me, though he might have been a maniac for all they knew, molesting innocent freshmen as they emerged from the stupor of declensions.

It was almost eleven and so time for that dreaded marching in the open field. I was on my way to have coffee with Flora, as was my custom during the war exercises, so Duncan's friendly attack was a mixed blessing. I wasn't sure if it was a disguised form of conscription.

"Where's the pacifistics meeting today?" he asked cheerfully, beating leaves off my back with sweeps of his dirty hands.

"Oh, somewhere," I said vaguely.

"Yeah? Fomenting revolution?" he inquired.

"We'll be discussing the death of Rupert Brooke over coffee, in a secret anarchist's den somewhere underground." I thought it might sound attractive, more mysterious and romantic than banging about on the soggy turf. "Care to join us?"

"Yes," he answered straightaway and to my surprise. "I could use some coffee."

"And the army?" I asked. "Won't they fall into chaos and confusion?"

"Let them," he gave in, recklessly. "I've had enough of wet shoes for today. I take it Flora will be there."

"Yes, yes. Flora and possibly Unt if she finishes with her cello and makes it back home in time."

"Oh," he said in recognition. "*That* anarchist's den."

"*That* anarchist's den," I confirmed, meaning the home of Mrs. Meekshtais, avowed anarchist and alleged correspondent of Emma Goldman.

We walked down College to Parker, the blue breaking through in patches above us and the air blowing warm with a dry wind in from the south. Flora was home and Unt wasn't. Duncan told Flora he'd come as a counterrevolutionary and would make us march all the way to Devil's Island, but Flora had other plans.

"We're going on a picnic," she announced, getting the heavy basket from off the kitchen table and pointing me toward a pile of blankets and towels she'd stacked in the vestibule. "We'll drive to Lake Anza and spend the day."

"But I have my Memory class," I complained.

"Forget it," Flora recommended.

"And my English class," Duncan reminded her.

"We're ill," she said, setting him straight. "Sick in the head." She turned us both around and pushed forward toward the door, poking me a reminder to pick up the blankets as we passed through the vestibule and out into the brightening day.

The sky had cleared up in the hills and Lake Anza was empty, free of boats, swimmers or walkers, all discouraged, we figured, by the gray morning. Flora had packed some favorite foods and brought the bulky Rochester as well, its box all finely dusted with Bolinas and smelling of the warm sweet dirt that kicked up off the roads there. Flora, setting the tone, stripped promptly and ran headlong into the clear blue water, splashing about furiously and then simply floating on her back, her round breasts breaking the water and her thick hair spreading loose and dark around her peaceful face. I did the same, and Duncan too.

It was a long queer afternoon, too much like the past to feel entirely present. Our minds were in such entirely different places, so far as I could tell, that I felt the sad calm of being alone in the woods, though Flora and Duncan were stretched out there beside me. Flora, I imagined, was just as she always was, stable and entirely present. I was not, and Duncan slept. As in Bolinas, we didn't talk much. But now, I felt, there was so much *not* being said. Our picnic was filled with silence, not merely silent.

I finally fell asleep, waking up after a few hours with a chill shivering through me and Duncan rolled up against my side. Flora stood close by with the camera, recording it all for posterity. The lake was busy with birds. A small fleet of merganser cruised close to our shore and one belted kingfisher kept swinging out from the trees and down into the water. Walkers came through but we were smartly clothed, having toweled down and dressed after the initial plunge.

It was an odd displaced moment for me, that long silent afternoon, too high up in the hills to be Bolinas. Everything seemed strange down below, busy with buildings and foreign tongues and the carefully turned patterns of the marching drill, drumming on across the field. Our wheels were all turning in different directions, even while we slept together, there by the shore.

The weather had come blowing in again. Thick gray fog was rolling up the dusky hills now, and we packed our things in Flora's car and motored back down below.

Robert,

I've not been well. I'll be in hospital at Rouen for a rest. A few days, or a week. Maybe home. Gave it in and couldn't find the will, finally. Just curled up in a ball there on the table, whimpering as if I'd been a dog and beaten by my master. That last boy, so frail and cheerful, slurring through all that blood, foaming in bubbles past his pale lips, his skull laid clean to the bone and shattered, Robert. He asked me if I'd time to dress his elbow, feared he had a gash on his elbow. "Could you, Doc, after taking care of the others?" he said. "I'm in no hurry."

## 25 NOVEMBER 1915

Just a fever, and dreams I don't remember.

## 27 NOVEMBER 1915

## 30 NOVEMBER 1915

Mother says I'm very ill. I can only sleep.

## 2 DECEMBER 1915

I'm going on a train soon. Father will meet me.

## 4 DECEMBER 1915

I remember going then to the hollow, feeling so horribly weak. Mother says I've got to write this now. It's strange that it's possible, thinking it like a story. That's what I've been doing. I think of it like a story, to keep it all, because I'd lost it for a while.

Duncan and I returned to the Fair, so we could pass through and see it again before it ended. The crowds had not diminished. They were riding in tiny trains and walking in groups along the grand avenues, all wrapped up in thick winter cloaks on this cold gray day. I thought of our early visits. The brittle wooden frames had stretched up into the mists. The ground was a sea of mud. The iron tracks were littered with giant anomalous heads and feet, cast in fake marble. It was all put together in an instant, looking now like it was a part of the city if not an extension of the very land. I remembered this wasn't even land two years ago and felt the impossible thinness of the brittle domes stretch suddenly outward to encompass everything. What *was* here two years ago? What was here a thousand years ago? Every moment then and since was gone. I bumped up into Duncan and felt him all solid and flesh. His warm breath clouded, moist against my ear.

We went out the Presidio Gate and up into the trees. Our course was not strictly running. It included evasions and dodges and connivings, crawling under fences and leaping over hedges, scrambling down some steep hills through brush and winding fast and furious in amongst the trees.

"What we want's a nice even pace," Duncan said as we got set to start. "Never strolling, but nothing so maniac you lose control either."

I nodded in agreement, and wondered what was wrong with strolling.

I'd forgotten that this was war, that this was make-believe.

"You want to be capable of absolute silence at any moment," he continued. "So no running so fast you're gasping and choking for air."

"But you said no strolling," I objected.

"That's right. Otherwise you get picked off by snipers."

"Then you can't say no gasping."

"Try it, Max. That's why you should've stuck with training," he explained, as a matter of fact. "If you don't train you die."

"Oops."

"Yeah. Oops."

I was very good over the first third of our course, drawing on my Freight Train skills, dodging trees and leaping small chasms with the sureness and accuracy of a deer, hardly gasping because we hardly let up long enough to gasp, until Duncan put his hand up and stopped stock-still in amongst the long stand of fir.

I crouched down and heaved for air as subtly as I knew how, feeling a very deep pain inside my lungs, working my ribs and diaphragm to their full stretch. Duncan knelt beside me, breathing in steady silent breaths through his nose. Delicious dewy drops of sweat gathered across his flushed cheeks. I knocked him down onto the bare ground and kissed him all over his face, tasting the salty sweet taste of him, and sliding my hands up inside his shirt, running them across the warm wet skin of his belly and chest. I wanted to pull his pants down and take him warm and flexing into my mouth and fill me inside with him all bitter and delicious. But I didn't do that.

"Max," he objected, "we'll be shot by snipers." He pushed my hands back out of his shirt and bear-hugged me into staying still, laying us over low to hide from the eyes of the enemy.

"Shoot," I screamed, "shoot us now and end this terrible war." My voice echoed off into the misty woods, answered only by the long, throaty calling of sea birds lifting out of the trees. No bullets came singing through the still air.

"Jesus, Max," Duncan said, shaking his head. "I'm glad you're not going to war with me."

"We could die together," I said, pulling my shirt apart and baring my breast to him heroically. "Take me," I growled to him from deep in my throat.

He got up and looked out through the trees.

"Let's finish the rest of the way to the beach now, without any stops." He looked back to where I lay spread-eagled on the ground, my shirt undone, me looking up through the dark green tops of the trees. "You think you're up to it?" he asked.

I lay still for a long time, feeling the salty ocean mist slipping across my bare skin and breathing it deep and luscious through my nose and mouth. Duncan offered me a hand and I took it, standing up beside him and getting set for our run to the beach.

Through the thick woods along the western edge we found a good steady rhythm, me breathing nice and deep and relying on the quick step, slide, jump, push, step, slide, jump of our fast scrambling to keep me on track and rolling along with Duncan. It got dark and dense where we ran, and I started to feel the thrill Duncan felt, the dizzy tingle of my body pumping and the sense of the enemy, hidden behind every obstacle, ever-present and making our constant motion feel necessary, like blood.

We bounced and beat on through the brush, the high trees gone now, giving way to twisted, wind-bent hemlock and wild tangles, open areas thick with ice plant and the ocean smell rushing in now, fresh and full with fish and seaweed. Wet clouds of mist were rolling in off the swollen gray waters. I could feel it beading up on my sweat-drenched skin, swirling in around and rushing over us, like a lover running soft cool hands all over our bodies.

There was the beach, opened up down below, flat wet sand. We scrambled down the dirty path, cut all zigzag through thick low scrub, dumping off over one last ledge. A daring leap in stride and reckless, landing with a hard thud in the damp sand, our weak knees giving way to the force of the fall, my head dizzy from a lack of oxygen and my muscles tingling and sweet with exhaustion.

I lay there looking sideways across the sand, watching the gray-green waves tumble and roar, rising up high and rigid and collapsing into dirty foam and roiling, boiling runnels of ocean washed up hard onto the sand.

Duncan stripped down to his boxers and ran out headlong into the waves, leaping deliriously up against their dark faces, his body slapped cold by the sheer weight of them, and spun around and dunked. The ocean just stretched out forever, mixing gray into the gray-raining sky out on the invisible horizon. Black rocks thick with kelp broke off land, the waters raking across their rough edges, and there was Duncan, up and over the first waves and swimming now, his skin red from the salty slap of cold water, drawing his arms through the roaring waves and drifting fast away from me and out to the wide-open sea.

I watched from the shore, silent and motionless, standing in the wet sand, listening to that familiar sound I'd known, it seemed, forever—the steady rumble of the waves roaring near and far, the patient calling of birds, sweeping in close to land, diving suddenly down into the foamy sea. I watched Duncan disappear out into the gray, just his dark hair and the rough chopping stroke of his pink arms coming up now and again out in the swollen rolling sea. He was going in no clear direction, too tired to think clearly, it seemed, unable to find the shore, and too exhausted to cry out for help. He just kept moving farther and farther away, moving forward until I could not see him anymore.

That's all of it I can write, the story part. It's like all these stories, so I can remember. Parts come different in dreams. I can't write them how they come. But I remember the story part. I'll feel the other, maybe in different places, different places holding that other terrible feeling, where I can't have words.

## 6 DECEMBER 1915

Fair. The rains come in. In the fire, it burned three days. Now I remember, three days and heavy gray clouds hung over waiting, wet and thick. The whole city burned, burned out for three days and no water in the pumps. Today the clouds hang low, drag rain through the broken roofs, down onto the rubble and empty brittle domes. Now I remember the sky finally let loose only after the city had burned itself out, dumping sheets of gray, drenching rain into the ashes. Today they've dug up the walks and the mud washes like a wide sea. It all ripped, torn by trenches, and some buildings collapsed only one day after, them knocking them down in the driving rain. I'm feeling that other, that dumb, mute other.

Dear Robert,

I'll be in Serbia, after two weeks home. We'll be up the Vardar and into the quarantine. I've never been and find I can't even remember its location on the map. I've forgotten where I was stationed. The captain had me filling in forms and I wasn't able to find words to put in all those blanks. "Length of Service," "Field Status," "Assigned to (list, beginning with most recent)," "Casualty Clearing Station," "Nature of Injury." Nature of Injury. How could I possibly say?

# *The*
# *Train*

---

## 15 December 1915

The train leaves going east. I saw his body next to me, at night last night, just beautiful and warm. It was nothing, of course, except seeing it and then feeling. The window's dark still. I sleep some, but half not, seeing myself in the window. We're slow in the mountains now, I guess.

## 16 December 1915

Awake before dawn, then the light. Sharp-toothed silhouette all across the window and the light neither blue nor yellow. That impossible problem of light at dawn. I can sleep here, in a small bed by the window. This blanket smells of mothballs. Soft, thin blanket, dark green like mine at home.

I am eleven, riding a small wooden train north from Stinson Beach at night. It has no roof. Where the road drops down, just before Bolinas lagoon, the tracks cross through a rugged gap and descend down to a lake more beautiful than any ever, anywhere. There's no Bolinas and no lagoon. I realize I always knew that and the lake is what's been here all along.

My father emerges from a shack in overalls. He walks into the lake and pulls the train behind, floating it lightly on the water's surface, smiling to me and asking if I'm sleepy. The day is perfect and clean and clear.

The lake becomes blood, too thick to let us float toward the shore. Loons start from the trees, hit by the terrible stench. They fill the sky, sweeping down near the train for an instant, then off west over the trees, beyond the high hills, and to the sea. And I'm Duncan, and have always been, watching from the still train, knowing the loons are me, Max.

A friendly Negro face looks through my curtains sometimes when I'm awake. He says, "You gonna sleep all five days?" He gave me soup on a tray, and smells of Sen-Sen and good strong soap. It was bright daytime, the light white off tongues of snow slipping down from the sawtooth edge. There are rocks here big as houses.

That man left me Walt Whitman and a *Harper's*.

## 11

*I turn, but do not extricate myself,*
*Confused, a past-reading, another, but with darkness yet.*

*The beach is cut by the razory ice-wind——the wreck-guns sound,*
*The tempest lulls——the moon comes floundering through the*
    *drifts.*

*I look where the ship helplessly heads end on——I hear the burst*
    *as she strikes——I hear the howls of dismay——they grow*
    *fainter and fainter.*

*I cannot aid with my wringing fingers,*

> *I can but rush to the surf, and let it drench me and freeze upon*
> *me.*
>
> *I search with the crowd—not one of the company is wash'd to*
> *us alive;*
> *In the morning I help pick up the dead and lay them in rows in*
> *a barn.*

I'm to see a fellow in Chicago. Then to Boston, where Father is going to meet me. Mother gave instructions to the man who brought me soup.

The snow covers whole mountains. Now it's moonlight on the pale fields, stretching soft as sand, rising like monstrous dunes up into a sky more black than I've ever imagined. Ice-cold clear and black, stuck with stars, pinpoint perfect in the wide empty air.

## 17 DECEMBER 1915

We're riding across a flat sea of white. Father won't be in Boston. The man whose name is Teddy told me when I was awake. He had a little yellow paper from Western Union which Mother sent. Another man will meet me there.

It's colder now, I think, than even in the mountains. I tell by pressing my hand against the window and feeling until it hurts that dull ache of cold in the bones.

I am walking along high hills in China. The air is hazy with smoke and heavy and damp. There is no dawn or sunset or day or night in China, just this permanent condition. The valleys are busy with dirt roads and jitneys, crowds of people bearing burdens on their backs and yak-drawn carts loaded down heavy on their wooden wheels with enormous, rough roots like horse-radish. All these travelers keep moving, never stopping to load or unload, running slow and steady, like blood through the veins of this place.

The hills are bare dirt and terraced up their steep sides. Wild fields of wheat and rice grow together on these shelves of land. I walk the thin lip of each terrace. They crumble under with each step, dropping dirt down the long drop to the fields below and below and below. The City is built the same way. Clay shelters propped up by heavy sticks and stacked three or four high, all up and down the steep sides of the broad mountain, several miles distant at the head of this valley. The dim noise and acrid smell of the City drifts through the hot humid air and wood smoke. I'm going there.

Teddy brought poached eggs and two thick slices of smoky ham. I had such an appetite and a stirring in my legs, from lying down so long, I imagine. The sky's broken up deep blue with a high, wide ceiling of puffy clouds, bright white and light as popcorn. This is Kansas, Teddy tells me.

I found more books, pulling trousers out of my carrying case. *The Ad Herennium, The Picture of Dorian Gray* (which mother had been reading), the text from Mr. Brown's course and, inexplicably, a Baedeker for northern Germany. Mother packed my things.

I've been to the observation car now. I wobbled down the length of the rattling train, bumping up against things every few steps along the way. I passed Teddy and he smiled at me. A man brought tea on a cane tray with sugar lumps in a china bowl and cream slightly swaying with the train. I watched the wide flat fields rolling by the window and held Whitman in my lap. I felt frightened by him, the possibility of what I might find wherever I opened to. I'd rather stay with the bright white fields and the sun peeking through the ice-cold air out there.

---

Land like this must make things different than I've known. I've never seen it so solid and even as here. Weather comes in from a hundred miles away and you know it's coming. Look at it now, coming down out of the west, the blue blown clear of clouds in a straight line across the sky. And you can bet it's cold, dropped clean like a curtain down from that line of blue, a wall of cold coming in like thunder.

If I stood, say, back of that barn threshing corn and could feel the black earth stretching out from my feet, it laying its face out flat under this endless sky, and each and every season of weather coming in again like war, dumping down on the face of it. And I knew my father and his father and his father, buried here in the wide flat fields and where, exactly, marked by a broken cross and dogs that lived wild in the dry riverbeds come scratching at their dirt, starved to death in the next season of snows. If I knew like that, I'd not know what I know now, what I know from the wet sky coming down out west of these mountains and this sound I have of the salty gray sea.

They have tables set with linen and silver, each side of the thin aisle, down the length of an entire car. Teddy works there at dinnertime. I had beef with hollandaise sauce and green beans and a potato and seconds on soup because of Teddy. The moon came up as I had peach pie, all pale silver across the snows, showing off the knife-sharp sparkle of ice cut by wind, glazing the white fields as far as you could see in the night.

## 18 DECEMBER 1915

I'm on a war train through Belgium, leaving the front and going back into Germany. We've left Liège in the dead of night and crossed the frontier at Lüttich, bound for Köln with freight loads of dismembered soldiers and corpses. Their moaning is a song, long and low with harmony and counterpoint but no rhythm or meter I can hear. I understand precisely the meaning of their song. There are no words. It sweeps through me in waves of agreement or empathy and then distance. Closeness then distance, a drawing toward then away, being what meaning feels like without words.

Words have been blown out of me at the front, that is my injury. I haven't any words to speak with or hold thoughts in. I feel sounds directly, with nothing in between. I sit with my back up against the thin rattling wall of the freight car, the soldiers singing around me.

Duncan rises from among the dead soldiers and walks toward me, looking pale and frightened, and speaking, saying things to me that I can't understand. Words drop from his lips, falling off me like broken sticks. His face is moving closer. His voice is lost among the clattering of the rails. There's nothing. The heavy wooden door sliding open and shut with the lurching of the train. The moonlit snow stretching out away from the train into the blackness.

He pushes his mouth onto mine and I feel his voice come into me now. It fills my throat and hands, echoing up into my head. It's all inside me like laughter, signing in my bones, warm and wet like breath, rushing all over my body like his rough hands across my tender skin, holding my back in his strong grip, and I come, arching my back, pushing my naked body up against the rough wool blanket of my Pullman bed, and I wake up.

We get to Chicago today, Teddy says. I'm there just for an afternoon to see a doctor Mother knows. The train leaves again at night and gets to Boston the day after tomorrow. This other man who'll be in Boston is called Mr. Jobsby and will show me Harvard and arrange for me to talk to someone there.

The sun came up outside my window, rising orange and enormous. It slipped over the lip of the land flat straight east of us so slow you could see it moving. I had thick hot porridge with butter and sugar and cream, and two chewy sticks of salty bacon on a tray in my bed.

We kept on through flat fields, dipping down to follow a big river. The bare trees, all purple in the mists, had ice frozen fast to their lofty nets of naked limbs, bending the light and hovering over the banks of this wide slow water. The river ran, all scattered with ice and snow.

A man in a dark vest with his sleeves rolled up above his elbows played checkers with me in the observation car. I lost a number of games and he asked if I were a student and I said no, I was traveling. I thought about my dream some to myself. He filled the time with talk about his business and the opportunity the war had brought to those with initiative. I went to my Pullman and got my drawing kit and did some work by the odd purple light of the afternoon, thinking about Duncan and the dream with him in the train. His name now, here, makes me cry. My Duncan.

I saw Chicago from far away. It puffed steam into the cold winter sky. Huge stone skyscrapers rose at its center. The city spread out from there, pushing out into the farmlands, gathering along thin roads and rails. The dirty brick buildings tumbled in thicker and higher as we rumbled in. Tracks multiplied till we ran a road ten or fifteen rails wide, rusty metal fences clanking along its full length and the dirtiest streets busy with people, some bundled up in rags. Waves of them rolled into and out of a huge brick building with smokestacks pumping black dust miles up into the heavy clouds, the white snow coming down thick and furious.

I was to take a car to the address Mother wrote in my book. Dr. Berminderung would see me until dinner, which I could take at any nice restaurant near the station. Our train left again at nine o'clock p.m.

The car stopped by a big building facing the shore of the lake, which I'm certain is more than a lake, it having waves and no sign of land on the other horizon. I stood near to the water and watched the wind whipping blizzards of white in swirls across the lead-gray water and the snow blowing down against me as well. It piled in drifts higher than my boot tops, all up and down the broken, rocky shore. I thought it must be the worst storm of the new century but Miss Tollet, in the doctor's office, said it was just a light December snow.

The doctor had me lie down on a couch and I asked if I should strip to my drawers as well but he said no, he was a psychiatrist.

"Oh," I said, remembering the stories I'd read in *The Call*.

"I'm a psychoanalyst," he explained. "I'll just ask questions today and if we decide to continue, you'll come to talk for an hour or so every few days."

"I'm going to Boston at nine," I said. The couch was very uncomfortable, placed, as it was, in such a way that I had to twist my neck and stretch to see him.

"Yes, your mother mentioned that. I've a colleague there you could continue with." The afternoon was turning dark already, the snow coming clear now against the dusky background.

"How do you know Mother?" I asked.

"She knows of me through the university," he said quite plainly. "I offer a particular service she felt might be of value to you." He scooted slightly forward. "Do lie back. It's perfectly polite here to simply stare out the window."

I did as he suggested, wondering at the snow blowing up as often as down.

"Today I'd just like to get a sense of your mood and reactions to a number of things. I know a few facts your mother has told me, and I know the few things you've said since coming in just now. My goal is to help you make sense of the various parts of your own experience, help you look at the roots of things." He stopped for a moment, evidently to allow interruption.

"Are there specific things you'll help make sense of ?" I asked to fill up the silence and keep my end of the conversation.

"Are there things you'd like to make sense of?" he asked back.

My thousand thoughts came flooding in, and Duncan along with each and every one, things slipping away or fixed wrong and the fallen walls of the asylum grown over thick with foxfire and sage.

"Things generally, the way thoughts slip around so much," I began, trying to be as specific as I could. "Memory."

"What about memory?" he asked.

These were such big questions. My hand slipped off the couch and dropped to the floor, bumping up against the soft carpet.

"Excuse me," I began, still uncertain what was allowed. "I sometimes worry I've not remembered things right." I stopped and waited in silence, waiting for my mind to explain itself. "I think that things are just every moment *gone*."

I turned in my place to see if he understood, but he was busy scribbling so I turned back.

"Or I think there's a way past things stay which is different from how they were but isn't exactly 'gone' either, like when it rains and the ground gets all run down into gullies." I looked at the windows, dark as night now.

His pencil stopped tacking across the pad.

"Are there particular memories?"

I thought this must be the part Mother told him.

"You mean Duncan?" I asked.

"Duncan?" he asked back.

"Didn't Mother tell you about Duncan?"

"Perhaps you could tell me about him," he said evasively.

I wondered how I could tell about Duncan. Parts I don't

think of at all, except in moments like when I thought of my dream and tried drawing some more, or when I'm alone in my bed and I cry so much from thinking then. But not to tell about, I've not got words to tell some parts I feel. So I thought of the rest, the summer and last winter and spring. Mother and his father.

"He's my best friend since a long time. Since the fire when I was seven."

"The fire?"

"The earthquake and fire, when the city burned down."

"Why do you mention him?"

It seemed a stupid question and I laughed a little and unched around even though I could see him clear in the glass, knowing he couldn't mean for me to tell him since he obviously already knew or else why'd he think Mother'd send me to him anyway. He just raised his eyebrows in mock puzzlement and waited through the long silence.

"I guess because I figured that's what Mother would have told you about, so I thought it's what you'd want to hear from me," I put in finally.

"What would she have told me?" he pressed on.

"That he's dead," I said to him, wondering why he was playing with me this way.

"Is there more?" he went on.

"More what?"

"More about Duncan."

"What more?" I said impatiently. "What's more than dead?" I really couldn't understand what he was getting at.

"Why did he die?"

The question was so simple and impossible.

"Because of an accident," I began, "a stupid accident." It was my litany, as close as I'd come to an explanation. "He was so tired then, and cold." I stopped speaking and watched it all play back in my memory.

His slight, pink arm collapsing down into the rough waves.

Thick clouds tumbling lower and lower onto the sea, fat and swollen gray and dumping rain down on the face of everything. The flat sand, hard wet sand, slipping straight into the mouth of the ocean. I see it stretching out wide and forever, deep under the raging waters, caressed by the heavy bellies of ancient, hoary-spined fish, scattered with rocks, and pulling at Duncan, pulling him down into that deep water. His helpless, desperate panic is in my legs and the wide, flat sand I stand on. And the rocks and water and wild, gray sky rolling in off the ocean are all impossibly that empty, hollow desperation. It is the sound of this place, the unstoppable rumbling of the water on the shore, sea birds calling into the wind and mist, the absence of any panicked cry, Duncan's silence. And what of this is memory? What is present to mind now? We are standing at dusk in Bolinas lagoon, the thin surface of the water slipping away just below our bellies, our feet set soft on the muddy bottom. What of him remains with me?

I heard the door close and watched the doctor return with a box of tissues. He offered them to me and sat down again in his chair. Lights were going out in buildings all along the lake shore. The doctor shifted in his seat and took a tissue for himself.

"Can you tell me if the friendship was unusual, special in any way?"

"No."

"It wasn't unusual?"

"No, I can't tell you."

"Why can't you tell me?"

I began to wish he'd just shut up.

"I can't tell you if it was unusual. I don't know usual."

"Was it like other friendships you've had?"

"No."

He paused a long time, waiting for me to go on, but I paused longer. It must've been minutes, the snow drifting into the light of the window, the black night hanging out over the lake.

"Did you have a sexual relationship?"

"Yes," I said as I was getting ready to think about what answer to give. The short simple word surprised me more than all the others we'd said. I couldn't elaborate as the answer'd not really come from me yet, though now that it was out there, I started to think what words could be added to it. Some few words kept crowding around down in the base of my mind, pushing at the back of my throat, jumbling and jostling for place and position, and I let a small mouthful slip onto my tongue and out, wet with my spit and warm breath pushing past my lips.

"I loved him," I heard out loud and then a terrible long silence.

It's all I'd really wanted to say for such a long time, and I could just barely mumble it through my slobber and spit and tears. Dr. Berminderung stayed silent and still, waiting.

My crying was a way my body had of freeing me from the burden of speech.

Outside the black air stung me sharp on my bare face, blowing in off the lake colder than any cold I've known and almost too painful to breathe. Distant light looked different in this air, so sharp, and tinkling too, like candle flicker but bright like a show torch and brought tight into tiny brilliant points. I got into the rumbling car and curled in against the backseat, alone in this dark warm shelter, my breath still clouding up around me, my face flush and burning.

Teddy could tell straightaway. I kept a sad face knowing he'd see, and walked slowly to my Pullman, wishing he'd follow me to bed and I could curl in tight around his strong, warm body and feel his big arms around me. If he could just hold me through the cold night I'd not feel so alone. But that wasn't possible.

———

I lay in my warm bed, turned toward the window, hugging the pillow to my belly, holding my fingers near my mouth imagining they were Duncan's. Salty sweet fingers warm in my mouth, running my tongue down over them and closing my lips to pull from deep in my throat. The train shot steam, long and low, billowing up in clouds and we lurched forward an unch, two, and again, me sinking down into my bed with each chug and choof of slow motion forward, finally rolling steady along the rails, the rattling rumble wrapping around me, the bed warm and lonely. The train went out along the frozen lakes, out east into the cold black nighttime.

# Lullabye

1. Wyn - ken and Blyn - ken and Nod   one night Sailed   off   in a wood - en
2. Laughed the   old Moon, and   he   sung   a   song   As they rocked in   a wood - en

shoe, ........   Sailed on   a   riv - er   of   mist - - y   light
shoe, ........   The   wind   that sped them the   whole   night   long

In - to a sea of dew........ "Oh, where are you go - ing,
Ruff - led the waves of dew........ The lit - tle stars were the

What do you wish?" the old moon asked the three,........ We're
Her - ring fish that swam the dew - y sea........... "Now

go - ing to fish for the her - ring fish That live in this beau - ti - ful
cast your nets wher - ev - er you will," Cried the stars to the fish - er - men

sea, the sea, the sea........
three, the three, the three.......

Nets of sil - ver and gold have we For the fish who dwell in this
"Nev - er, nev - er a - feard are we!" So cried the stars to the

*marcato il movimento.*

*f*

beau - ti - ful sea," Said Wyn - ken, Blyn - ken and Nod, ...... Said
fish - er - men three, To Wyn - ken, Blyn - ken and Nod, ...... To

*p*  *rall.*  *a tempo.*

*rall.*

*f*

Wyn - ken and Blyn - ken and Nod. . . .
Wyn - ken and Blyn - ken and Nod. . . .

*f a tempo.*

*f*

3. All night long their nets they threw For the fish in the twink - ling
4. Wyn - ken and Blyn - ken are two lit-tle eyes, And Nod is a lit - tle

*mf*

foam,........ Then down from the sky came the wood - en shoe,
head,........ The wood - en shoe that sailed the skies

Bring - ing the fish - er - men home........ 'Twas all so pret - ty a
Is a wee trun - dle bed........ So shut your eyes while

sail it seemed As if it could not be,......... And
moth - er sings Of wond - rous sights that be,......... And

some folks thought 'twas a dream they'd dream'd Of sail - ing that beau - ti - ful
you shall see all the beau - ti - ful things As you rock on the mist - y

sea,      the sea,      the sea........
sea,      the sea,      the sea........

Shall I name you the fish - er-men three, That were sail - ing o - ver that
As you rock on the mist - y sea, Where the old shoe rocked all those

*marcato il movimento.*

beau - ti - ful sea? They're Wyn - ken, Blyn - ken and Nod,...... They're
fish - er-men three, Wyn - ken, Blyn - ken and Nod,......

Wyn - ken and Blyn - ken and Nod......
Wyn - ken and Blyn - ken and Nod......

*a tempo.*      *rall.*

# *Spring*

---

The hills are insane with green bursting velvet smooth and lush, not a blond spot to be seen. We live in fog-shrouded forests of rain and damp ferns. I roll here in mud made by my body beating in against the moss, a snuffle of air and snort of water run off waxy cedar fronds by my fingers soft and pink. Jack-in-the-pulpit. Amaranth and bracken fern. Storksbill, eucalyptus, gooseberry. Miner's lettuce and mountain grape. Wood sorrel and shepherd's purse. They are my friends. I listen to the loons, calling their long low song. I'm washed away into nothing, all possible distinction dissolved by that sound.

Down below the Fair is busted, blown up to high heaven with dynamite bombs rolling thunder across the hills. It's more than war or fire or the wild ripping fault come wrecking down the rill. Only Maybeck's ruin remains, saved by sentiment. Mother's married to the earth, I saw her toppled today.

How do you remember him?
   I don't, don't know this. I am innocent of this. What of him

remains? An outline, a footprint? The cut of rain on a muddy hillside? How can I remember? It's not that I remember him. It may not be him I remember. I am a living thing with roots planted in the ground. I'm a rotting tree.

Why did you love him?

I can't think of this. Everything I tell you will be a lie. I didn't know him. I knew him without ever thinking and that made me able to love him. That is, he wasn't disfigured by my thinking ideas of him until the end, when I loved him most, or loved what I thought was him, when I needed the words that would contain him, and he died then. I was desperate for him, for the words that would say it.

Why did he die?

Why? His body heavy as stone, the water raking across its bed. Flesh could not hold him inside, failed to resist the ocean dragging down his throat. His dull opened eyes, unseeing, turned toward the bottom. His body died, his shell.

Why does it matter, then, his dying?

Why must a body contain him? What is this experience of soft, warm flesh? Spirit? I don't know what it was I held in my mouth then. It was much more than simply him. What is it to be breathing the breath of another, to lie in sleep, our open mouths touching? Is that all gone simply because his body's gone? Yes.

Why do you remain here?

I returned because of the weather. It rains down on me. I'm knocked flat on the ground here into mud. Or else I'm no longer here. There are other places. They all bring me back here. I'm water caught in a storm.

Is this a resolution?

Is there a sound to tell us, a blessing, a cure?

Dear Robert,

We've started up through these barren hills, following the yellow torrent of the Vardar. We'll be the first back to

Gievgieli since Colonel Hunter withdrew, bringing, I pray, some hope that the typhus might be contained and beaten.

The Serbians seem to regard the epidemic with morbid pride, a badge of honor that is distinctive, not among the incomprehensible modern afflictions that now ravage the rest of Europe. A plague is the proper, traditional path to annihilation and the Serbians regard vaccination as a sign of cowardice, a breaking with the past.

In this valley the air is hot and moist. Irregular, white, red-roofed villages meander along dry rocky slopes where squat little oxen and black water buffalo drag their creaking carts. The train took us as far as the frontier.

The frontier marks the end of cultivation, acres of arable land, gone fallow or planted thick with graves, run the river's course, high into the mountains. Occasionally one sees a single, broken beast, dragging a wooden plow crudely fashioned from the dark twisted oak, led by an old woman in bright, colorful rags, a soldier guiding the plow. There are not enough men left in Serbia to work the land. Four wars in three years and now typhus. "All the men in Serbia are in the army or dead," we're told. "And all the oxen have been taken by the government."

Gievgieli is in quarantine, hundreds of hungry people pressing against the fences, looking out into the barren valley. Chloride of lime had been spilled up and down every post, marking every empty wall and tree trunk. Black flags hang thick down the narrow streets, the sign of a death within the house.

Those that saw me offered embraces, regarding me as one would a foreign priest, wanting a particular cure, a blessing, a kiss, to see them through their sickness. Everyone in this town will likely die during my few months here. Gaia Matitch asked if I would grow orchids. We passed the afternoon playing cards, the postmaster and Gaia Matitch and I in a wordless, laughing round of some three-card game with no rules and no winner, where one would draw a card and show it and we'd all laugh and the next would do the same until the heat was too much and we slept.